D0344807

ADVANCE PRAISE FOR
SEARCHERS IN WINTER

"Owen Pataki's second novel emerges from the rubble of the French Revolution into the legendary conquests of Napoleon. Readers will love the richly drawn characters and evocative settings in this story that pits the values of humanity against those lusting after power and greed."

— STEVEN PRESSFIELD, bestselling author of *Gates of Fire*

Praise for *Where the Light Falls*

"Compulsively readable...a compelling tale of love, betrayal, sacrifice, and bravery...a sweeping romantic novel that takes readers to the heart of Paris and to the center of all the action of the French Revolution."

— *Bustle*

"Succeeds in forcefully illustrating the lessons of the French Revolution for today's democratic movements."

— *Kirkus Reviews*

"Devotees of Alexandre Dumas and Victor Hugo will devour this tale of heroism, treachery, and adventure."

— *Library Journal*

"This is a story of the French Revolution that begins with your head in the slot watching how fast the blade of the guillotine is heading for your neck— and that's nothing compared to the pace and the drama of what follows."

— Tom Wolfe

"A beautiful novel that captures the spirit of the French Revolution and the timeless themes of love and truth."

— Steven Pressfield

"While not stinting on gorgeous detail, Allison and Owen Pataki know exactly how to write a gripping historical novel that concentrates on the intimate stories playing out against the epic background of the French Revolution."

— Melanie Benjamin, author of *The Swans of Fifth Avenue*

"For all those who didn't want *Les Misérables* to end...take us past the pristine archives to the blood and bones of the French Revolution, commanding our attention and winning our hearts."

— Sarah McCoy, author of *The Mapmaker's Children*

"Delivers everything a reader hopes for in a great book: passion, intrigue, insights, and, above all, a story you won't soon forget."

— Michelle Moran, author of *Nefertiti*

"This luminous tale of love and betrayal in a world gone mad is as imely as it is timeless."

— Juliet Grey, author of the Marie Antoinette trilogy

SEARCHERS
IN
WINTER

A Novel of Napoleon's Empire

OWEN PATAKI

PERMUTED
PRESS

A PERMUTED PRESS BOOK
ISBN: 978-1-68261-979-7
ISBN (eBook): 978-1-68261-980-3

PERMUTED
PRESS
Permuted Press, LLC
New York • Nashville
permutedpress.com

Published in the United States of America
1 2 3 4 5 6 7 8 9 10

Now the sneaking serpent walks
In mild humility,
And the just man rages in the wilds
Where lions roam.
—William Blake

"The surest way to remain poor is to be an honest man."
—Napoleon I, Emperor of the French

CONTENTS

To Mom and Dad, with gratitude and love.
Without your support this book would not have been written.

December 1804

Minister Fouché:

General Bonaparte is dead. He has gone, making way for Emperor Napoleon. The same citizens who cheered with glee at the beheading of their sovereign and shouted, "Death to kings," a mere eleven years prior now joyfully cry, "Vive l'Empereur!"

Within his ornately fashioned carriage, following a multitude of glittering cuirassiers and Mamelukes splashed with all manner of colors, rode our sovereign in royal splendor. The procession arrived at the Parvis de Notre-Dame around eleven this morning. Bonaparte, assisted by his brothers Louis and Joseph, took his time changing into ermine robes of purple, white, and red inside the bishop of Notre Dame's residence. Once outfitted he walked the short distance from the house to the cathedral between an impregnable phalanx of tall Imperial Guards, who fended off the thronging dregs of Saint-Antoine and Saint-Marcel with admirable aplomb.

Napoleon can now state with the conviction of legal surety that his blood, officially royal and blessed by the pope, is not made of mud.

The day before the ceremony, a suspected ring of conspirators was ferreted out of their hold in the Saint-Germain; their names have been passed to your office and any further developments will be offered to your person.

While the ceremony proceeded within, countless young ladies of dubious reputation mingled with soldiers and members of the Imperial Guard. Spotted with these harlots was the ever-present Madame B. of brothel no. 133 in the Palais-Royal, who surely found sufficient clientele among the soldiery of His Majesty.

Among the illustrious persons scattered among the crowd were four known Breton Chouans at Tavern Porte Verte across the Seine, who were found unarmed but nonetheless detained by my men until the proceedings were over; General Chabert's wife, who kept a watchful eye on the general's mistress standing nearby; and a "count from Königsberg" whose rented room was filled with English pounds sterling—needless to say this "count" remains in our custody at Le Temple and may need to be interrogated by one who speaks English.

With all of the business concluded without disturbance or undue violence, you may be sure that our offers of solicitation were hand-delivered, by myself, to the list of officials you requested: Novejean, Bounaix, Devaux, and St. Clair.

We await their reply.

— Carnassier

CHAPTER 1

Outside Görlitz, Germany (Prussia)

October 1806

The morning frost glistening across the fields was a sign that the growing season was over and winter would soon be approaching. The late warm days called "Altweibersommer" by the locals had passed, and a chill had begun to bite. Red and yellow leaves crunched as the soldiers marched over them in lines stretching far beyond the horizon. The Grande Armée was a vast force, a colossus that could be seen for miles, and its commander had no intention for it to remain hidden. Nor was it possible, at least in this region of the Prussian countryside, to hide from it.

Lieutenant-Colonel André Valiere, having no official command—or position—apart from his former commission as a major, liked to enjoy a moment's peace, when possible, by watering his horse alone in some secluded place before the day's orders were announced and the long hours of riding began. On this morning, as he walked a path that wound through a pleasant thicket of beech trees, he came to a small pond. Pausing, he stooped to splash water over his hands and face while his horse drank. He admired the beauty of this peaceful little forest, which seemed to have sprung from a verse in one of Goethe's folk poems. Satisfied with his wash, he mounted his horse and turned back toward camp, when he heard the sound of men's voices. His curiosity piqued, he pulled slightly on the reins, leading his horse away from the pond toward the muffled chatter. He rode slowly, without alarm or concern, for the army was far from any known hostile force.

Now, the sound of the leaves breaking beneath his horse's hooves seemed distinctly louder—the nearby voices had gone silent. André halted, listening; all he could hear was his horse chewing on the bit as it pawed the leafy ground. Assured that nothing was amiss, he exhaled deeply, his breath dissolving into the thin shroud of mist that enveloped the forest. Suddenly the trees shook, echoing with a sharp *crack*!

André flinched at the sound of two pistol shots being fired, the report of each shot within a second of the other, leading André to a quick conclusion. He'd stumbled upon that mortal contest played willingly between two men with an insoluble grievance—a duel to first blood, or to the death. Having no desire to look upon the aftermath, he made his way quickly back to camp.

Upon arriving at the bivouac, he joined the other cavalrymen in feeding and readying the horses for departure, saying nothing of the scene he had nearly come across. The army allowed duels in certain instances, but generally it was taken upon a man's honor that it was a matter for the two parties involved, their attendants, and no one else.

The day's march passed like the previous ones' had, with a few short halts for the horses to graze and the soldiers to chew on hard bread. That evening an aide summoned André to his brigade commander's tent, where he duly reported. Standing at attention outside the tent's opening, André could overhear the conversation the brigade's colonel was having with one of his subordinates. For the most part, it was standard talk of supplies and grumbling about poor roads, but André's interest stirred he heard the colonel remark on what had taken place that morning.

"Another one of my officers dead!" the commander said. "And a good one, too. Promoted only a few weeks prior, before that devil pounced upon him."

"He is a strange one; the killer, that is." André recognized the voice of Major Dupont, the brigade's executive officer. "I did not know Captain Dubois, but heard he was an excellent swordsman."

"An excellent swordsman whose only use now is feeding the worms."

André heard one of the men stand up and begin pacing. "This quarreling captain is a lunatic, a mad dog off his leash who'd be better off put down. Three men in four months! At this rate we'll have to start promoting corporals to lead our companies."

"There is something rather…*unsettling* about that man, on that I'm in agreement with you, sir. So, with these orders for you to promote the man to major, what do you intend to do with him now? Who in this corps can manage that hellhound?"

A tense silence followed. André leaned closer to the tent's opening, eager to hear the answer. The commander cleared his throat before continuing, "The new fellow, what's his name? Maliere?"

"Valiere, sir; a retired major plucked from his sleepy farm in Normandy. He joined the brigade at Leipzig last month."

"Whoever he is, I'd say it's time we made use of him. I've lost enough good officers to this brute that something needs to be done. We'll have no one left by the time we reach the front. Perhaps Valiere is made of sterner stuff than the others. If we reinstate him as a lieutenant-colonel then he will outrank this rogue, soon-to-be *major*. Perhaps if he's lucky he'll live long enough to see the bastard killed by the enemy!"

"If he manages to outlive his subordinate."

André felt a combination of curiosity and dread as he wondered what kind of man could so severely unnerve a colonel of Imperial cavalry.

With a prompt from the aide, André entered the tent and saluted.

"Welcome to Prussia, Monsieur Valiere." The older man gave André an appraising look before he leaned forward and offered his hand. "I am Colonel Menard, commander of the Ninth Regiment of Dragoons, and this is my executive officer, Major Dupont. We've heard good things about you and have been eagerly waiting to meet you. Any man who survived the expedition in Egypt deserves only the highest praise."

"Thank you, sir," André answered.

Colonel Menard gave André a final inspection. Finding everything to his liking, he offered a curt nod. "Please, be seated." He directed André to a stool facing the two officers.

"You've come highly recommended from our contacts in Paris," the colonel began. "The generals from Saint-Cloud tell me you've accumulated quite a record for yourself."

"I am sure they exaggerate, sir."

"Come now, major, no need to be modest. Look around you," the colonel said, directing his gaze outside the tent. "You're in the emperor's Grand

Armée. What use have we for modesty?" He laughed loudly, and his diligent subordinate followed his example.

André smiled respectfully. "I'll admit, sir, there were times during the Revolution when the front seemed a refuge compared to Paris." Colonel Menard and his subordinate nodded, feigning understanding. "But I should also confess that it's been some time since I've heard a shot fired in anger." *If you don't count this morning*, André thought to himself.

"Well, if it is battle you seek, major, you may not have much longer to wait. Our sector has been quiet, yes, but we all hope that doesn't last much longer."

André did not smile at this remark. "War is a soldier's duty, sir."

"Well said!" Colonel Menard tapped Dupont on the shoulder enthusiastically. "What did I tell you? We have a real soldier before us." His good mood restored by talk of battle, Menard walked back to his chair and sat.

"I'll not waste any more of your time. What we require of you is not quite what we require of other dragoon squadrons. You'll be scouting as our eyes and ears, yes, but as a man of experience you can help keep this army alive. By that, I mean, of course, the requisitioning of supplies, fodder for the beasts, and, above all else, our food. You'll be commanding the Seventeenth Squadron of Dragoons. Your sergeant-major is Paolo Mazzarello, a Corsican who's served in more campaigns than I care to count. Your executive officer will be joining us tomorrow."

With that Colonel Menard rose to his feet, prompting André and Major Dupont to do the same. "Welcome to the Grande Armée, *Lieutenant-Colonel* Valiere." Wearing a broad grin, he stepped forward to shake André's hand vigorously.

"Do not let me down."

The following morning as André walked past the rows of tents on his way to meet his executive officer, he felt his discomfort tempered with a feeling of reassurance. Discomfort that this officer had fought and won three duels in four months. Reassurance for the same reason; this was a man who was dangerous and would perhaps become a valuable addition if his violence could be constrained—and eventually unleashed toward the enemy.

"Are you looking for something, sir?" a voice called out behind him.

André turned and saw a well-built man about thirty years of age standing beside a barrel, shining his dragoon helmet with a horsehair brush. He met André's gaze—his features appeared sharp and intelligent, his eyes dark, unreadable pools—and a thin, scornful smirk belied his otherwise somber expression.

"You're Major Moreau?" André asked as he approached.

"I am," the younger man answered.

"I'm Lieutenant-Colonel Valiere, recently promoted, commanding the Seventeenth Dragoons Squadron. As I'm sure you've been made aware, you're to be my executive officer." Moreau responded with a blank look. Any hopes André had of a swift and easy rapport with his new subordinate were quickly dispelled. André extended his arm, and the two shared a firm, if brief, handshake. "I expect of you only that you perform your duty. I will allow you to conduct your business as you see fit, coordinating with our sergeant-major, Paolo Mazzarello, whom I have yet to meet. Together, we will ensure that we carry out our orders with efficiency and discipline."

André motioned for Moreau to follow him, and the two quickly paced across the bivouac toward their horses, the moist grass and mud squishing beneath their boots. André suddenly stopped in his tracks, almost crying out when he saw the apparition standing before him. He blinked to be sure that it was real. The man wore a red cahouk atop a white turban, a blue vest over a long green shirt, and puffy red trousers that sagged over the tops of his tan leather boots. At his waist he wore a sheathed scimitar, and André noticed a pistol sticking out from the man's vest while a dagger tucked inside a green sash hung from his waist. A Mameluke. As André stared at this figure from another world, a vision flashed in his mind's eye as clearly as if he stood there in the flesh: André saw the grimacing face of General Nikolai Murat, glaring at him with murderous rage as they fought each other to the death in sight of the timeless splendor of the Great Pyramid.

He was jarred from his waking vision by the sound of one of the Mameluke's comrades shouting in their foreign tongue. "Anyhow," he said, clearing his throat and turning to the man beside him, "once we've joined with Sergeant-major Mazzarello and the rest of the squadron we will continue toward Görlitz. Colonel Menard informs me we're not likely to encounter the enemy along the road. Nevertheless, this will be a good opportunity for us both to assess our men outside the comfort of camp."

"I've already taken a look at our troopers," Moreau replied as he fit a pair of riding gloves on each hand, spitting into one and rubbing them together. "They ride and drill to satisfaction, but I've not yet seen them in contact with the enemy. I'm sure that will change soon."

André nodded, fitting the saddle onto a dark, bay-colored gelding that whinnied loudly in greeting when Major Moreau led his gray mare forward. Both men mounted, Moreau waiting silently as André stroked his animal's neck, trying to calm its excitement.

"Not accustomed to horses, sir?" Moreau asked, with a barely perceptible grin. "I was told that you were originally from the infantry."

"You heard correctly," André replied flatly. "As a junior officer I was infantry, but since that time I've ridden my fair share. Now, when we clear that copse," he gestured east, "we'll ride double-file until we reach Görlitz. When we get there I'll find the burgher who will, I'm told, inform us where we can find the carts that Colonel Menard needs. Any questions?"

"No sir."

"Very good." André motioned to the squadron trumpeter to sound the call to arms.

Several minutes later the squadron rode out from camp, down a gentle-sloping hill onto the road east, which led to the lands where the people spoke Polish. For now, Lieutenant-Colonel Valiere and Major Moreau were only riding to the town of Görlitz to requisition several carts and wagons for the Grand Armée.

Or so they believed.

Riding in silence for over an hour the squadron passed through small hamlets and green thickets speckled with the first yellows and reds of autumn. Sergeant-major Mazzarello joined the squadron on the road, bringing with him the rest of the troopers falling under André's command. All told, they numbered just under three hundred men. The Coriscan veteran shook André's hand with a firm grip that attested to his broad shoulders and muscular neck.

Farmers reaping the harvest looked up from their fields at the passing horsemen, some no doubt wondering what the increasing number of French cavalry patrols might mean for the future of their land and safety of their families. Emperor Napoleon Bonaparte's march across the German states had been so rapid, many of the locals did not know whose side they were expected to support or oppose. Most were hardly concerned with the war as long as it did not disturb their peaceful existence. Sergeant-major Mazzarello ensured that no undue resentment was stirred up by rude words or gestures directed at the locals, and his troopers wisely chose not to tempt his Corsican temper by disobeying him.

The squadron entered the city some hours later as the bells of the Holy Sepulchre sounded the faithful to midafternoon prayer. Their horses' shoes sent sparks along the cobblestones as they rode beneath the large baroque buildings, the largest being the turret of the Reichenbach Tower that loomed imperiously over the city's narrow streets.

The meeting with the city's burghers lasted a little over an hour. They met privately with André in the town hall, where he delivered a fee allocated to him by Colonel Menard. Although less than they had hoped for, the occupants begrudgingly accepted the payment in exchange for twenty of their "most spirited" horses along with eight wagons, which was less than André had hoped for. All told it was not a bad morning of work, André mused, as he mounted his gelding in the city's square. Major Moreau and Sergeant-major Mazzarello sat on either side of him, ready to depart.

He glanced once more at the houses and spires on either side of the Untermarkt square, regretting being unable to explore more of the town. "The colonel is not likely to be pleased by a haul of only eight wagons," he said, tucking his boots into the stirrups and signaling the trumpeter to announce their departure. "But it's something. And the mounts will be a fine addition."

"Have they said anything about the enemy, sir?" Sergeant-major Mazzarello asked. "Some of the locals we spoke to heard talk of Prussian scouts being spotted across the Oder. Others said they'd seen French."

"That river you see there, sergeant-major, is the Neisse," André replied, motioning to the murky water reflecting the bright afternoon sun in wavy glimmers. "To your question—no, the gentlemen of this town did not seem preoccupied with Prussian scouts. And though I don't suspect today will be the day they pay us a visit, we will ride at the battle-ready."

"Sir, I would recommend sending an advance party before the squadron leaves the cover of the town," Moreau offered.

André shook his head. "We have no riders to spare."

Moreau lifted his chin. "It would only require a team of three or four men, sir, the risk of not—"

"The colonel wishes us back before nightfall, major," André cut in curtly. "Hitching our additional horses to the wagons and providing a guard for their protection will require thirty troopers. I will not risk the remainder becoming strung out or separated. We will stay together and move as quickly as we can."

Moreau looked at the sergeant-major, twisting the reins in his left hand. "Very well, sir," he replied at last, without turning his head.

Riding in silence, the squadron passed out of the town along a dirt track that led back into the wooded hills of the Saxon countryside. The orange and yellow leaves shone brilliantly in the afternoon autumn sun. A dog barked nearby, though none of the farmers they had passed that morning were to be seen. André gazed through the tree line, scanning for anything out of the ordinary, but only branches and vibrant foliage peered back at him. Satisfied that they would return to camp before the sun had set, he did not press the horses too strenuously; many were hauling the requisitioned wagons behind them. Seizing on a moment of quiet André turned his head toward Moreau, who followed several paces behind.

"Major, I would not mention this in front of the troopers, but there is a subject that I must have a frank discussion with you about when we return to camp."

Moreau met André's gaze with an impassive look. "If you wish, sir."

André looked back at the road before him. "I do wish. And I will be straightforward with you now. It concerns your dueling, a practice which I've been told you have turned into something of a habit." André paused, giving his subordinate time to consider the subject.

"I won't pretend to guess your reasons for fighting three men in four months, but for the sake of duty and your responsibility as an officer to the soldiers you now lead, the dueling must stop." André let the thought sink in. Hearing no reply, he turned to face his subordinate. "Have I made myself clear, major?"

After a long pause Moreau broke his silence. "If a man adheres to the principles of honor, sir, dueling is not only his right but his duty as a soldier and officer."

André tugged at the reins, firmly restraining his horse, which had begun to jerk its head. "I am not asking you to forfeit your honor—but in times of war, feuds between two men of the same uniform are necessarily subordinated before the needs of the army and the nation. When the current war is concluded, you may call out any officer of the same rank as you wish, but while on campaign you will refrain from risking your life unnecessarily or you will be reprimanded according to the laws of military justice..."

André's words trailed off as the two riders at the head of the formation stopped suddenly. In one movement they turned their horses around and started trotting back toward the main body of the squadron. André leaned forward in his saddle, straining his eyes to see what had caused the disturbance. Moreau scanned the woods on either side of the formation.

"The road is blocked, sir," one of the troopers called out, reining his horse to a halt in front of André and Moreau.

"What do you mean it's blocked?" Moreau asked.

"There's a tree right 'cross the middle of the road. Don't look like we can get anything through there, as is."

André spurred his horse forward. Several meters ahead, around a bend in the road, a large oak tree lay felled, blocking their way. Its leaves still held their full foliage, and no other trees lay nearby to indicate a storm had brought it down. André gritted his teeth, muttering under his breath.

The trooper beside him looked at the tree with undisguised dread. "Oh, no. This must be deliberate."

Major Moreau cocked his pistol. "Of course it's deliberate, you idiot." Without waiting for an order from André, he turned his horse and trotted past the troopers halted on either side of the road. "Well, what are you waiting for? Load your goddamn weapons!"

"Major Moreau," André called out in a steady voice, "take your place at the rear of the formation, see if you can find us an alternate path out of here." Moreau spurred his horse at a gallop back in the direction they had come.

"Sergeant-major," André continued, "make sure the carts are turned around in an orderly fashion. We may have to depart quickly—"

At that moment a shrill cry rose up from the forest. Unseen voices cried out in piercing calls on either side of the squadron. André felt the familiar swell in his chest, the sensation a soldier knows all too well, that seizes one's thoughts and threatens to grip the body in paralysis: primal fear. Unchecked, this fear seizes not only the individual it has taken hold of, but will emanate outward, touching every nearby man in turn.

As the cries grew louder André took a deep breath to steady his heart, which now raced in his chest. He moved his jaw to ease the slight twitch in his left cheek. For several seconds he was still, letting the fear wash over him until, without thought or intention, the long-dormant instinct within his breast began to swell outward. He gently urged his horse forward, passing his troopers as he rode behind them. At first he was unaware of the words he was speaking. His men held his gaze as he rode past, some nodding obediently, some even smiling as they too felt the elation of imminent battle surge through their veins. André's task as commander was not to set fire to their courage, but to restrain and direct it with discipline and effectiveness.

Unsheathing his sword from its scabbard, he halted behind two troopers scanning the tree line with their muskets. "Steady with your aim. Pick your targets, conserve your ammunition. Don't break formation until I tell you." He saw his sergeant-major shouting orders as the carts were being turned. In the worst case, André knew, they could abandon the carts and make a mad dash for the relative safety of Görlitz. But being unaware of the enemy's numbers and relative strength, he also knew they stood a better chance of fending off a larger force in a dense forest than in open country. They would just have to see what the enemy did first.

As he did his best to consider all these scenarios as quickly as possible, sharp musket reports echoed from the trees on their right. André searched the woods for movement or a muzzle flash, but all he could see were small puffs of smoke perhaps two hundred feet away. More shots rang out, and a tree several feet away took the smash of a musket ball. His horse reared back on its hind legs, and it took all his strength to stay in the saddle and get the beast on steady footing again.

He was pleased that none of his troopers had fired yet. Cool and disciplined, they were waiting for a proper target to reveal itself before expending precious ammunition.

All of a sudden, a slow rumble began to emerge from the direction of the smoke. André squinted, making out several figures on horseback charging through the trees. The soldier beside him raised his rifle, aimed, and fired. All around him a chorus of rifles discharged, and André urged his troopers on with firm reinforcement. The enemy horsemen came closer, and André switched his sword from his right hand to his left. Reaching into his belt he pulled out his pistol, cocked back the hammer, then aimed at a cluster of riders and pulled the trigger. A part of him felt like crying out in a wild frenzy, but he restrained himself, reholstering his pistol.

Behind the thick screen of smoke discharged from his troopers' muskets he could hardly see beyond the nearest cluster of trees, so he rode several meters along his flank to get a clearer view. To his astonishment, the horsemen had stopped their charge and were now riding in the reverse direction, perhaps fleeing, but more likely regrouping as they worked up the courage for a decisive charge. He heard voices shouting in a foreign tongue, perhaps German, and some of his men replied with insults of their own.

Seizing on this momentary lull, he galloped toward the center of the formation. A young lieutenant named Vitry was calling out orders in a hoarse voice. Seeing his commander, he turned his horse. "Sir, we've finished turning the wagon train around, and Major Moreau is preparing to lead a charge to see if we can break out into higher ground. What are your orders?"

"Dammit, lieutenant, I have not given him any such orders! Tell him to remain where he is and to protect the horses and wagons, but not to go anywhere until I've given the order. If we get separated, they'll cut us in two and destroy us one at a time. Hold your position!" André turned his horse back toward the front of the column when another growing din rose out of the woods. This time it came from the opposite side of the road.

André rode behind his troopers, who were frantically firing and reloading on either side of him. One man in front of him cried out as he dropped his weapon to the ground, grasping his left arm. André quickly dismounted, ran to where the weapon had fallen, picked it up, and handed it to the wounded soldier. "Keep firing!" he shouted at the dazed man, who could not have been older than twenty.

The enemy charged with a new ferocity now, shouting ever-louder as they got closer to André's line. André estimated their strength to be well over three hundred, judging by what he'd seen on both sides of the road. How many more remained hidden out of sight he could not guess. They were now advancing on foot from the opposite side of the road as the first attack, and André suddenly realized his advantage. Calling out to his trumpeter, whose horse was pacing near the squadron standard-bearer, he ordered an advance toward the enemy attacking their right flank. The trumpeter called out the signal for the charge, and André raised his sword aloft, driving his horse toward the enemy.

As the cavalrymen crashed through trees and over the underbrush they screamed at the top of their lungs, partly to intimidate the enemy but also to fortify their own nerves, which were now being tested as they advanced. André kicked his horse to a gallop, screaming as he rode headlong toward the enemy.

He did not let his men go very far. As they advanced, the enemy fired off a few shots and began running farther into the woods, where a slight hill sloped upwards above the tree line. Not wanting to ride into some unseen obstacle or new mass of enemy troops, André halted. He shouted out an order for his men to regroup and return to the road. With reluctant groans, his men turned their mounts and trotted back in the direction they'd ridden. When he'd surveyed the ground and made sure none of his men were lying dead or wounded, he returned to the road himself.

He was met by Major Moreau, who held his sword aloft, blood dripping from the blade. "They have us surrounded. Horsemen are blocking the road to the rear, and they have scouts and infantry on either side. I make their numbers at about two hundred. What are your orders?"

André looked to the front of the column and then back to the rear. They would have to abandon the wagons and any unnecessary baggage. The spare horses would most likely be lost in any attempt to escape, if they could manage to escape.

"We're surrounded. If we stay, we'll be bled to death. Our only option is to punch through the rear and hope we can manage to break the trap and outride them to our camp by another road."

"Sir, these are light cavalry, and they outnumber us at least two to one," Sergeant-major Mazzarello, who had ridden alongside the two officers, added. "They'll ride us down if they catch us in the open without infantry or artillery support."

"We can either stay here and die one by one until we're taken prisoner," André answered, "or we can try and make our escape and get some of us out."

Moreau spat. "If we had sent scouts ahead of us this would not have happened," he said to no one in particular.

André glared at his subordinate, willing himself to restrain his temper. Meanwhile the enemy had returned with renewed vigor and were firing on both flanks. "We leave the carts and the spare horses, and we make our escape before the sun has gone down."

ONE YEAR EARLIER

CHAPTER 2

Paris

1805

The dark-haired man standing outside the entrance gate fought back a frown, suddenly aware that he was one of the first guests to arrive at the soiree. "As I said a moment ago, I've come at the mayor's invitation and patronage. From the prefect of Marseille."

"You might well be the pope's emissary," the servant replied brusquely, "but if you're not on our register I cannot allow you inside the palace grounds."

The man was of average height, his black hair, speckled with hints of gray, pulled back in a ponytail. He bit his tongue, reminding himself that he had not traveled several hundred miles from home for this party, and he should not overestimate its importance. It had nothing to do with his mission. Still, he couldn't help but feel slightly embarrassed: he had clearly come to the Palais-Royal unfashionably early. He took a breath and spoke slowly: "I am a guest of Monsieur Bergasse, mayor of Marseille. If you could perhaps search for *his* name, you might find mine among those of his party."

Flipping slowly through his ledger the attendant ran a finger down the page, landing on a name that appeared to inconvenience him. He gave the visitor one last, thorough inspection, his features finally settling on an expression resembling disapproval.

"Very well, Monsieur St. Clair, it's all in order." He signed a ticket and handed it to Jean-Luc with a half-hearted smile. "Have a pleasant evening."

Jean-Luc snatched the ticket and walked through the gates and into the courtyard. He ordered himself a glass of champagne to calm his frustration and took a look around. Though the soiree had not yet begun in earnest, he saw small groups gathering on either side of the numerous arcades of the grand palais. Men in fine suits and large hats; beautiful and excited women in fine dresses and shimmering jewelry. In one corner a group of well-dressed men played cards and puffed on cigars.

Standing behind their stalls, vendors peddled tastefully to their wealthy patrons; wine and cider, fabrics, hats, jewelry, perfumes, porcelain, and luxury goods of all kind were available in great quantities. Jean-Luc found himself struck by the degree of wealth and opulence, the likes of which he had never seen in the dark and starving days of the Revolution. As he passed a stall selling toys and dolls, his thoughts turned to his children, and he decided to purchase them a gift. Reaching into his pocket, he suddenly noticed two women standing behind him, one blonde and one brunette. They looked charming in dresses of blue and white, and both waved fans in front of their faces. The shorter woman in the blue dress caught Jean-Luc's glance and smiled.

"Good evening, monsieur," she said in a soft voice, offering her hand.

Jean-Luc took her delicate hand in his, smiling with all the charm he could muster. "Good evening, madame."

"Oh, your accent is fine, just adorable!" she purred gaily through white teeth. "Are you Italian?"

Jean-Luc smiled. "Actually, I'm from Marse—"

"Oh, don't look so embarrassed, my dear," the other lady cut in. "There's no shame in it; our Napoleon himself is a Corsican. Why, you might even be a distant relative of his; from his tribe, perhaps?"

"From his *tribe*? Ha, you really are too much, Elaine," the shorter woman retorted with a cheeky smile. "What sort of barbarians do you think those people are?"

Jean-Luc smiled sheepishly. "Well I wouldn't claim to—"

"All I'm saying," the other woman exclaimed, "is that all of their crowd seem to be related; Bonapartes for every room in the palace. Perhaps the emperor will give this one a crown to wear and a kingdom to rule!"

"A kingdom to rule?" The other woman put a hand to her mouth, stifling a burst of laughter. "Ah! The duke of the washroom."

"The grand duchy of the billiard hall!"

"Why, he looks like he could be a cook—the order of the Roast Chicken Legion of Honor!"

Jean-Luc's face flashed red. "Yes, well, we all hope to make something of ourselves here, don't we?" he offered, instantly regretting the slip of his true intentions.

"My dear fellow, we're all here tonight for the very reason that we *have* made something of ourselves, otherwise we shouldn't have been invited."

"Oh, don't be rude to the poor man, Mathilde," the taller woman gently waved her fan while she surveyed Jean-Luc's appearance. "You can see he's only just arrived."

"Oh, do be quiet, you impudent little grisette," the woman called Mathilde playfully chided her friend. "Anyway, why are we standing here doing nothing when there are all these gorgeous soldiers about? Let's go *speak* to them, Elaine."

Grabbing her friend by the hand, Mathilde turned from Jean-Luc and directed their attention to a cluster of officers standing nearby. "Oh, look how tall that one is," Elaine said, fanning herself as if overheated. "He wouldn't fit under my roof."

"He'll fit under your duvet."

With a flurry of laughter, the two women were gone, and Jean-Luc stood alone, holding a half-empty glass of champagne.

After purchasing a few small gifts for his children, he drank one more glass of champagne and dined on a few bites of mutton. He took a short walk around the courtyard before deciding he'd had enough and made an early departure.

Later that evening as he strolled along the Quai du Louvre, his spirits sank. He felt a swelling bitterness toward Mayor Bergasse for talking him into this foolish journey. This famed capital, Paris, the City of Light, had changed so much since he'd once lived here, when every day had been a struggle to carve out a life for Marie and baby Mathieu; a struggle he believed worth waging if he could play some small part in helping his fellow citizens gain a better life. Standing here now he felt insignificant and alone, a drop in a great sea that rolled on with or without him. Had this new world passed him by?

The moon's light reflected off the Seine as it flowed gently beneath the Pont Notre-Dame. Like a whisper, something buried deep beneath the scaffold of his mind began to call out, faintly at first, but growing clearer with each passing second. He closed his eyes, and the memories returned with startling lucidity: primal screams of terror arising from prisons all over the city as priests and nobles were dragged from their cells and hacked to death by seething mobs. Wandering the streets the night after General Christophe Kellermann was condemned to the guillotine by the Revolutionary Tribunal; how the sting of a good and innocent man's death had weighed on his conscience as if he himself had passed the sentence. He remembered the night he had seen a young General Bonaparte riding across the Pont Neuf to the eager cries and shouts of the people, only to hear later of the horrible toll in blood and death exacted on the royalists in that uprising.

But he could recall happiness from that time, too; Marie's face when she told him of their second baby. The strength and resilience of Sophie de Vincennes even after her vengeful uncle had chased her into hiding. How happy she had been living under his roof, in the company of unexpected friends; her tears of joy upon hearing that her beloved André had survived a great battle in Egypt and was coming home.

Paris had seen so much pain and so much darkness, and yet, in this moment, that all seemed to be a world away. A young and powerful regime now held power in the Tuileries, and France's enemies had been expelled from her borders.

Jean-Luc reflected on his own contributions to his nation—how he had stood firm in his principles even when it meant danger and possible death. He had faced down the wrath of his fanatical enemy, Guillaume Lazare and his pack of Jacobin underlings, and emerged victorious. He recalled the words Mayor Bergasse had spoken before he had left: "You are capable of achieving great things. Whatever happened in your past, let it remain there. Your future has yet to be written."

Whether or not the new generation of "notables" had any room for him, he resolved that he would not slink away from Paris defeated. He had once plunged himself headlong into the maelstrom of revolution and war without flinching and had emerged from it stronger. No, he would not beg for the table scraps from a generation of rich latecomers eager to ride the nearest available coattail to power. He resolved that the following morning he would not play errand-boy and merely deliver his mayor's message to

Joseph Bonaparte, he would win the trust and confidence of Napoleon's older brother.

Years ago, in times of terror and revolution, he had made a name for himself in this city. Now he would reclaim it.

Jean-Luc rose early the next morning as the sun's first rays emerged over the eastern sky. Leaving a letter for his children with a clerk, he departed for the Tuileries before most of the city had awakened. He purchased a small piece of bread for breakfast and ate as he walked, making his way down Rue Richelieu with a renewed purpose in his step.

Although he had been in the palace before, the Tuileries seemed grander now than any other time Jean-Luc had traversed its corridors. Perhaps the awareness that a man of Napoleon's stature held the nation in so firm a grip lent itself to the awesome power that seemed to permeate the cavernous building. Jean-Luc forced himself to suppress a feeling of astonishment as he followed a secretary over plush carpets and past elegant furniture until he opened two vast wooden doors and ushered him inside, closing the doors behind him.

He stood in a room of ornate beauty. Posted on small stands along the walls were baroque candelabras, while above him hung glittering chandeliers of glass and crystal. The ceiling was decorated with elaborate images of eagles, cherubim, and mythical figures like a scene from the Sistine Chapel. His heels clicked loudly on the wooden floor as he crossed the room; he did his best to affect an air of nonchalance, but he could not deny the thrill of finding himself in such a place again. His excitement morphed into apprehension, however, as the minutes ticked by and he had to remind himself that one who had boldly challenged the will of the Revolutionary Tribunal of the Reign of Terror should not be overwhelmed delivering a message from one man to another, even if the recipient was the brother of Emperor Napoleon. Eventually, an antechamber door opened and a young man, evidently another secretary, announced in a voice that echoed down several corridors, "Come in. Monsieur Bonaparte is waiting."

Clearing his throat and reflexively straightening his coat, Jean-Luc entered the room. As he walked across the hardwood floor, he surveyed paintings adorning the walls that depicted famous personages from French history; conspicuously absent were any images of monarchs, however, and he wondered how long it would be until large portraits of the Bonaparte family filled the vacant spaces that had once displayed the scions of the Bourbon lineage.

He halted several paces in front of a desk where two men, one standing and speaking softly, the other seated, listening, pored over several parchments. Jean-Luc stood silently, unsure if either man realized a visitor stood before them. After a few more hushed words Jean-Luc heard the seated man say, "Yes, that is fine. Thank you, Meneval."

The standing man took the pieces of paper and folded them under his arm. Bowing slightly, he turned and left the room without acknowledging Jean-Luc.

The seated man, who Jean-Luc could only presume to be Joseph Bonaparte, finished scribbling some notes and set down his quill. He arranged the papers into a neat pile and looked up at his visitor.

"How may I be of service to you, monsieur?" he asked in a distinct Italian accent. His words, though cordial, were expressed more as a statement of command than a question.

The man's long nose, curly, dark hair, and round head reminded Jean-Luc of the paintings he'd seen of the Corsican's famous younger brother, though his curved brow gave him a somewhat sad appearance. Nevertheless, sitting in his large oak chair, adorned in a high-collared blue coat with gold piping down its front, he cut an impressive figure. Jean-Luc noted the large badge coated in white glaze on his left breast; shaped like a star with five double-points, the center bore the head of a man—the emperor?—wreathed with a laurel branch. The emperor's brother was apparently one of the first recipients of the Legion of Honor—though the award had not yet been publicly presented to the people.

Jean-Luc gathered his thoughts and answered in a sure voice, "Monsieur, my name is Jean-Luc St. Clair. I come on behalf of Pierre-Louis Bergasse, mayor of Marseille, to deliver an urgent message to the eldest brother of First Consul Bonaparte."

Joseph Bonaparte examined Jean-Luc for a moment before replying, "Very well. What is the message, then?"

Jean-Luc produced a small roll of parchment from his briefcase and handed it to Monsieur Bonaparte. Taking the paper and cutting the seal, Bonaparte asked, "And what does Monsieur Bergasse want?"

"I was not briefed on the contents of the correspondence, monsieur," Jean-Luc answered, "but I've been instructed to receive any questions or remarks upon your receipt of the dispatch."

Joseph Bonaparte took his time reading the letter, betraying no discernible reaction. After several minutes he set the parchment down, smiling humorlessly. He rapped his knuckles on the table twice and spoke in a quiet tone. "You've come from Marseille yourself, monsieur?"

"I have, sir," Jean-Luc replied.

"How was your journey?" Bonaparte asked.

"It was well enough as one could hope for, sir."

"I'm not asking you how comfortable your carriage ride was, monsieur. How was the journey *itself?* Were there any troubles along the way?"

"Troubles, sir?"

"Yes—troubles. Were you imperiled in any way—bandits, highwaymen, royalist coach-robbers?"

"Oh no, no troubles of that sort at all, monsieur. The road was generally quiet."

"Well, that is good. Poor Napoleon has had more than enough to deal with across our frontiers without having to fight off royalist bandits waylaying our own people on the highways. Now," he leaned back, picking up a quill, "I will provide a written reply to your mayor, and I would like you to deliver it with these words from me personally: 'When I have received *my* answer, Monsieur le Mayor, you shall receive yours.'"

"If I may be bold enough to ask, monsieur," Jean-Luc replied, tempering his insistence with a subtle bow of the head. "In order to ensure a better understanding and subsequent briefing upon my return…what is it that he desires of you?"

Joseph Bonaparte's eyebrows rose slightly. "Is that your business, monsieur?"

"The mayor's business is my business, sir."

"Well, without divulging to an unsolicited third party the finer details of our administration's policy," Bonaparte began with a good-humored scowl, "I can tell you that your mayor has his sights set on acquiring certain *favors* from my brother on his city's behalf regarding trade relations between itself and the kingdom of Naples. And he wishes for me to broach the matter with my brother."

Jean-Luc nodded thoughtfully. "What does he want?"

Joseph Bonaparte sat in silence for several moments, eventually puffing out his cheeks in amusement. "Aren't you an inquisitive little fellow? I see why that Bergasse sent you. Well, as it happens, he informs me that he has one or two carrots regarding his relations with the Neapolitans to offer my brother, should we wish to entertain his requests."

"And I presume, sir," Jean-Luc replied, "that his wishes of the emperor are to see the tariffs on sea-trade from Naples lowered so as to import larger quantities of certain desired goods—goods like, oh, say, timber from Dalmatia or Anatolia; which could then be purchased by the administration at a reduced price and put to good use in the growing production and development of our nation, our army, or, more specifically, our navy."

Joseph Bonaparte smiled slightly, quickly adjusting to the swift and discerning conclusions of Monsieur St. Clair. "Perhaps it is something like that." Though he did not say it, the elder Bonaparte felt a sudden desire to change the subject, aware of his obligation to keep valuable state secrets from this peculiar newcomer. "I'll confess that I find you rather curious for a mere *messenger*, Monsieur St. Clair."

Jean-Luc lowered his eyes for a moment. At length he cleared his throat. "Mayor Bergasse has entrusted me with a duty, Monsieur Bonaparte, one that I did not volunteer myself for. Nonetheless, when entrusted with a task, I see to it that I commit all my energies into its successful completion. At present, Mayor Bergasse is unsure of your intentions and simply wishes to gain every possible advantage in procuring your assistance. I have not spent much personal time with Monsieur le Mayor, but I believe his intentions are true, at least as true as a politician is capable of being. So, I find myself standing before you now, seeking only to turn an indifferent man into a potentially powerful ally; if that be your wish, sir."

Joseph Bonaparte held up his hands in an exasperated gesture of defense. "All right, St. Clair, all right." With a sigh he took a sip of water from a glass on his desk, looking down at his timepiece as he drank. When he had finished, he muttered to himself, "What hour is it? I feel like I'm back in Ajaccio being hounded by Paoli again."

Jean-Luc started at the comment. "Forgive me, sir; did you say Paoli?"

"Eh? Oh, yes—Paoli. Don't trouble yourself about it. Just remembering an old...*friend* from the days of the Revolution." His smile betrayed a genuine bitterness that Jean-Luc understood instantly.

"I apologize, monsieur. I did not mean to pry. I know—well I *knew* a man once, from the south, who had been in the confidence of Monsieur Pasquale Paoli."

Joseph Bonaparte had moved to stand; now he stopped short. "Is that so?"

Perhaps it was simple curiosity, or the catharsis that came when commiserating with another who'd endured the dark days of the Revolution, but Monsieur Bonaparte's curiosity got the better of him and he sat back in his chair. "And who was this man?"

Jean-Luc shuddered; he could not have hidden his emotions even if he'd wished to. As he looked across the table at the brother of Napoleon Bonaparte, his mind traveled through a scene of dark visions. The Revolutionary Tribunal staring down at him with blank faces, willing him to speak the words that would send another man to his freedom, or to the scaffold and its blade of impartial mortal justice. A room of pale and wordless figures enthralled by the dark charisma of a cold and hateful man determined to seize Jean-Luc's family from him, nearly tearing down his world before he fell—impaled on the sword of Saint Michael the Archangel, the patron saint of war, in a bloody twist of justice long overdue.

"His name was Guillaume Lazare," Jean-Luc spoke softly.

Joseph Bonaparte tilted his head forward. "You knew Guillaume Lazare?"

"Yes," Jean-Luc sighed wearily, "I knew him quite well, unfortunately. At one time he was even something of a benefactor to me. But after challenging him in the tribunal…well, he nearly took everything from me."

Monsieur Bonaparte nodded sympathetically, absorbed for a moment in his own memories before quickly pulling himself together. "Well, I won't trouble you with talk of that man, good riddance. But I admit I find myself continually surprised by you, monsieur. Lazare's agents took up where Paoli's left off when we fled Corsica and reached Marseille. It was his men who arrested Napoleon and me when Robespierre fell. That slippery old man played both sides, gleefully pouncing on us when the tide had turned. We were arrested on my wedding night. Thank god for Napoleon or I'm not sure what might have befallen us."

Jean-Luc eyed the elder Bonaparte with a look of understanding. "I do apologize, monsieur, I was unaware that you had ever been—it was not my place."

"Nonsense." Joseph quickly banished his hard memories behind the curtain of his good-natured smile. "It was not you who broached the subject. Let's bury it in the past where it belongs, hm?"

Jean-Luc nodded, though the trace of a shadow lingered on his face. "Agreed."

Joseph Bonaparte stood up, with resolve this time, offering his hand to Jean-Luc. "Now, you've stolen enough of my time, good man; take yourself away before I spend the whole afternoon reminiscing with you."

Jean-Luc stood, shaking the man's hand with the firmness of friendship. "I thank you for your time, monsieur, and know that my mayor conveys to you his warmest wishes."

"Oh, I'm sure that hulking rascal does, ha." Joseph Bonaparte ran a hand down his extravagant uniform and held the other out towards Jean-Luc. "And tell him, from me, that he ought to give me fair warning next time before sending one of his sharpest acolytes to treat with me."

With a bow, Jean-Luc turned and departed the room. After he had gone and the door had shut in a lingering echo, Joseph Bonaparte sat back in his chair, deep in thought. At last he snapped out of his reverie with a shake of his head. "Who was that man?"

CHAPTER 3

Outside Görlitz, Prussia

October 1806

Wiping the sweat from his brow, André surveyed the nearby ground in disbelief. A minute earlier he was readying himself to lead an all-out charge to escape with whatever men remained; but now he looked over his squadron, still overwhelmingly intact, and wondered what, or more accurately who, could have possibly delivered them from their grisly fate. Strewn across the meadow in front of their position were the bodies of half a dozen enemy. It was a miracle that they had fought off so many, killing at least six and wounding several more, for the small price of three of their own wounded. The answer to this miracle was now visible on the gentle rise across the open ground. Several horsemen gazed down at André and his squadron from atop the knoll.

"I wonder who they could be, sir?" one of André's men asked.

"It doesn't matter who they are," Major Moreau muttered as he rode up alongside André. "They're French, and they've just saved our skins."

André nodded as more horsemen, six or seven hussars, came out of the woods alongside their comrades. "Yes. They certainly did that." He arched his back, which had grown stiff in the lull after the action. "Now let's go and have a look at our deliverers and thank them."

"Hello there," André called out, as he, Mazzarello, and Moreau crested the slope. The hussar in the middle, presumably the leader, held his hand aloft in greeting. He sat straight in his saddle, which rested atop a large, leopard-skinned cloth. His brown coat was lined with four rows of shining buttons that angled down to touch at the waist, while over his left shoulder hung a brown pelisse over-jacket. The bulky fur cap atop his head denoted this particular unit as elite troops. The others were dressed similarly.

"You know, I'm quite surprised to see you men alive," he called out, his pelisse swaying as he lowered his hand and rested it on the pommel of his saddle. His hair was braided into two pigtails and, beneath his brown mustache—which thinned and curled slightly upwards—he wore a broad grin.

"We have you to thank for that," André replied. "Our gratitude cannot be overstated. I am Major André Valiere of the Seventeenth Dragoons. This here is my executive officer, Major Moreau, and Sergeant-major Mazzarello."

The hussar nodded at the two men in turn. "I am Major Carnassier, commanding the Seventh Hussars. This here is my second in command, Captain Alderic." The man beside him was tall and lean, perhaps in his mid-thirties, the left side of his face marked by a dreadful scar that ran from temple down to chin.

"And would you imagine, colonel, you've just had the good fortune of stumbling upon the vanguard of Prussia's elite cavalry! They're scouting these lands for Napoleon's Grand Armée." Major Carnassier held out his right hand, and a subordinate rode up alongside him. "And it seems they've found it." The hussar commander reached out and snatched a piece of tattered black and white cloth from his subordinate and tossed it to André. "Taken from the colors of one of the enemy's Guard Cavalry regiments," he explained. "They fought bravely to defend it—and paid with their lives."

"What happened to the rest of the standard?" Moreau asked.

"What happened?" Carnassier replied. "Why, with no marshal to receive our trophy, I cut it to pieces and distributed them equally among my men." This prompted a murmur of approval from the other hussars. "An enemy regiment who rides alongside a band of Cossacks deserves to be forgotten." His face took on a serious look. "In these parts you'll find business is conducted rather differently. The Poles, Russians, and Cossacks do not play by our rules, comrades. They are not the Austrian farm boys you've surely grown used to fighting. They take few prisoners—their women and children will smile, shake your hand, then slit your throat while you sleep. Remember that."

André noticed the sun slowly sinking between the autumn foliage and wondered if they would be able to return to camp before nightfall. "We will be sure to heed your words," he stated. "For your aid we thank you. Now, we must be returning to our bivouac. Have you any idea which roads might still be open to us?"

"Open roads? Surely, colonel, you may take any road you like from here to Berlin. But look well, for they are watched, all of them, by the enemy."

"Will we be attacked if we return by the westward Görlitz road?"

"Perhaps." Major Carnassier shrugged. "Perhaps not. But I can see that you and your men are weary, so I will save you. Come! You are with men who know these parts and who offer you the best chance to return to your camp safely."

Just then a commotion arose from across the open ground where André's squadron was waiting. He turned in his saddle, squinting. His men were waving their arms and pointing, and André finally saw what had caused such a stir. Perhaps a hundred paces from where they sat atop the knoll, a figure could be seen hobbling across the field toward the tree line. An enemy survivor. André turned his horse to pursue.

"No!" Major Carnassier rode alongside André. "Don't trouble yourself, sir. I'll take care of him." The hussar cocked back the hammer of his pistol and aimed at the fleeing enemy. A shot rang out, echoing across the open ground. Just as he reached the tree line, the enemy soldier stumbled several paces before falling facedown into the grass.

Moreau did not wait for the smoke from his musket to waft away before lowering it. He rested the weapon across his lap and spit onto the grass, certain his shot had found its mark.

André looked toward the fallen enemy, checking for signs of movement. Nothing. The hussars sat calmly as if nothing out of the ordinary had occurred. Some even nodded in admiration at Moreau's long shot. André gripped the reins of his horse. "Major, we will form our men into column and follow you to your encampment."

Carnassier nodded in reply, but did not remove his eyes from Moreau as the dragoons turned and rode back down the slope.

That evening André's squadron camped alongside the hussars in a thicket beside the Neisse River. They tended to their three wounded and were given food, ammunition, and a little wine by their comrades, who seemed unconcerned that the enemy might reappear in the dark of night.

Early the next morning, as his troopers ate a small breakfast of bread and whatever forage they could find, André noticed one of the hussars dressed in a uniform unlike the others; it was almost entirely black, tied with a sash at the waist with a thin, green stripe lining the pants, and a row of shiny copper buttons across the chest.

"I see you've noticed our Prussian friend," Carnassier said to André as he bit down on an apple. "Well," he said, between chews, "he's not actually Prussian. He's Silesian."

André examined the Silesian. It wasn't just his dress that set him apart from the French hussars and dragoons, but something else that he could not quite place. "Does he speak French?"

"He mutters about," the Hussar replied, wiping his hands on his leggings. "But I speak German. So, when I need to confer with him, I offer some words in his guttural tongue."

André found it curious that a man who spoke no French would be riding with a squadron of Napoleon's hussars. "What is his purpose with you?"

Carnassier patted André on the back as he walked toward his horse. "Knowledge is a dangerous weapon!"

The two squadrons departed together, fording the Neisse and ascending a slope that looked out over an open valley and offered a splendid view of the mountains on either side of the river. They were crossing into the lands of Silesia, where the locals had been ruled by a never-ending succession of nobles, kings, and duchies for over five hundred years. Now, they lived under the rule of the Prussians and thus could be considered the enemy, though in truth many felt more loyalty to the land itself than to any political dynasty.

The dragoons' encampment was west and yet they now rode east, taking them farther from the main army. André mentioned as much to Carnassier, inquiring as to the feasibility of sending out scouts to find a safe road back.

"The enemy we scattered rode north," the hussar major explained, "presumably in the direction of *their* main army. And two days ago we conversed with a troop from Marshal Murat's corps, who said the main enemy force was marching due west. So, given their unpredictability, it is best to wait for my scouts to return from their patrol north before we attempt to cross the open ground between us and the rest of your regiment."

"And besides that, sir," interjected one of Carnassier's subordinates, "*we are in command of the lands from here to Bunzlau.*"

The major cast a look at the man who'd spoken, who then lowered his head and had the good sense to remain silent. "What my talkative subordinate refers to is our familiarity with the locals, and their obedience to us—something which the conduct of war ever necessitates. Given our mandate, we have rather...*exceptional* autonomy to speak and act on behalf of the emperor. As though we were one of his marshals."

André wondered why he'd heard nothing of this squadron operating so far ahead of the main body of the army. "And your mandate? What would that be?" he asked.

Major Carnassier smiled wryly. "Suffice it to say there are old enmities in this hidden corner of Europe. Feuds that date back to the Dark Ages, divided loyalties, to say nothing of the endless variations in language among neighbors—a ridiculous circumstance that would hinder the unity of any civilized people. So, the emperor and his advisors have expressed a desire to make use of any *troublemakers* who have no love for their current masters—our enemies the Prussians and Russians—by sowing discord in their own kingdoms. So, we bring discord."

André did not wish to interfere in a mission ordered by the emperor himself, yet he had the lives of his men to consider. "Very well. But if we're to ride east away from our own encampment, I'd like to know where you are leading us."

"We rarely stay anywhere for more than a night. Our primary camp is in Czocha."

André nodded. Looking up ahead he saw a small brook flowing from the base of a long, sloping hill, its green face cleared for grazing. On top of the hill he saw two men, who he assumed were the farmers who owned the pastureland they were now crossing.

"Once we cross over these hills," the hussar continued, "the people speak Polish. One never knows if their uhlans are riding out to greet us or kill us. But one thing is certain, whether or not the Russians advance or retreat from the emperor, the Cossacks will be watching us."

As they crested the nearest rise, they came upon a sight of such natural beauty that some of the troopers gasped aloud. The vast landscape of the

Silesian countryside unfurled itself before them: rolling, green pastures and gently sloping mountains crowned with tall pine trees and crisscrossed by ancient goat trails and streams that meandered down into the valley below. Herds of sheep and cattle grazed in the meadows. The few deciduous trees—oak, birch, and maple—shone in brilliant shades of orange, red, and yellow. It came as no surprise to André that this fertile country had been fought over for centuries. "Some countryside indeed," he said.

"One that any man would fight for," Carnassier agreed. "And such as the world is, one finds its inhabitants hardly the equal of its natural splendor."

"You've had much contact with the local authorities?" called a voice from behind them.

Major Moreau had ridden to the front of the column, confident that any threat to their formation would be seen from a long way off.

"'Authorities' is not the word I would use," Carnassier answered without looking back. "From time to time the Polish counts wander from their wooden huts, which they call palaces, clad in animal skins to bleat about what Napoleon can offer them. Before we've located the enemy, they've made demands of us. That will change very soon, be sure of that."

"We still need their cooperation," André stated. "We cannot bring an army of hundreds of thousands this far east without support from the local population."

"They will be more supportive than they yet realize." With that, Carnassier set two fingers in his mouth and let out a shrill whistle. A moment later four hussars rode forward, among them the black-clad Silesian. Carnassier called out to his subordinate, "Alderic, ride forward and inform our hosts that we have returned. Tell them my requirements have not changed."

Without a word the hussar named Alderic, along with the Silesian and two others, galloped down the sloping ridge and out of sight into the valley below.

"That fellow with the scar," Moreau said, "he looks familiar to me. What other regiments has he served in?"

"Alderic?" Carnassier took a sip of water from his canteen. "Our Septembrist? Now that one, gentlemen, you would do well not to antagonize. During the Revolution he was a true blood drinker."

André felt a wave of unease sweep over him, and his cheek twitched slightly. The word "Septembrist" recalled to his mind the horror and bloodshed of Paris in September of 1792. Images of the blood-soaked guillotine that had claimed his own father's life flashed in his mind's eye. "The Revolution was a time many prefer to forget," he said, hoping the great swell of feeling within did not betray itself outwardly. Then he caught the cold, hard stare of Marcel Moreau, whose face betrayed no reaction or feeling.

"Revolutions make all men poor," Carnassier said, "equally poor—but poor just the same. War, however, makes the intrepid man rich." He spurred his horse forward and the rest of the formation followed him along the route the first four riders had taken to the bottom of the valley.

The pastures and orchards they passed were pristine. That changed, however, as the mounted troops of both squadrons picked up their pace and cantered through the trees along the valley floor. Plump pears and shining red apples dangled as if ready to drop from their stems as the thundering hooves shook the ground.

ONE YEAR EARLIER

CHAPTER 4

Marseille, France
Autumn 1805

Three weeks to the day after his meeting with Joseph Bonaparte at the Tuileries, Jean-Luc arrived back at his home on the Rue d'Aix. After he had unpacked and enjoyed a pleasant evening supper with his children, he settled into his study, finally admitting to himself that the trip had not been entirely unsuccessful. True, his treatment by some in Paris had been rude and dismissive; nonetheless, he had departed the city with a good feeling and a sense that he had completed his task. Furthermore, the encounter with Napoleon's brother, however brief, had stoked within him a subtle but unmistakable desire; a desire for more.

When he rejoined with Mayor Bergasse, after a lengthy retelling of the visit, minimizing the soiree and underscoring the remarkable vibrancy and vitality of Paris, he was greeted with congratulations on a job well done.

"Ha, what did I tell you?" Mayor Bergasse tapped Jean-Luc on the knee and poured out two glasses of wine to celebrate. "I knew you were the right man for this assignment, St. Clair. That Bonaparte wouldn't have forgotten how well we treated him when he was on the run from that fool Paoli. Neither has Napoleon, I presume; Corsicans rarely forget their friends, and they *never* forgive an insult."

Jean-Luc nodded and accepted the glass of wine, preferring not to mention his reminiscences of Guillaume Lazare and his role in hounding out the two Bonaparte brothers. He raised his glass. "Well, they've certainly come a long way. As you once told me, 'Whatever happened in your past, let it remain there. Your future, however, has yet to be written.'"

"Yes, yes, that is certainly true," replied the older man congenially, collapsing his large frame into his chair. "And indeed, those two rascals have come quite a long way. Which reminds me, did Monsieur Bonaparte have anything to say in response to my request?"

Jean-Luc recalled the face of the older Bonaparte brother, how rigid he seemed at the beginning of their conversation, and how congenial by the end. He smiled. "He mentioned no specifics, but he did tell me that he would speak with his brother about it and that they both held fond memories of their time here in our city."

Monsieur le Mayor held Jean-Luc's gaze, clearly expecting more.

Jean-Luc cleared his throat. "His official response, however, was *'When I have received my answer, Monsieur le Mayor, you shall receive yours.'*"

The mayor's disappointment was evident, but he smiled at the last remark. "Well, we'll just have to wait for Napoleon's response, then, won't we?" He stood up, walking Jean-Luc to the door. "But fear not, my dear St. Clair, I have a strong feeling that our work will soon pay off."

After that conversation, Jean-Luc did not hear from Mayor Bergasse's office for some time. While performing his daily tasks at his law firm, Dulard and Son, his excitement over the meeting at the Tuileries began to give way to a more pragmatic view of his circumstances. He had his home, his career, and two lovely children; what shame was there in an honest and decent life in Marseille as a comfortable widower?

One morning in early October as he sat eating breakfast with his children, Mathieu and Marie, he nearly spit out his coffee when he read the headline of the morning gazette: Emperor Napoleon Bonaparte Defeats Alliance of Austria and Russia – Occupies Vienna.

He put on his reading glasses and scanned through the report. He'd been aware of the emperor's recent victories at Ulm but had not expected him to seize the enemy's capital so quickly. What next caught his eye, however, was something quite different: the pronouncement that ten new senators were to be inducted into the Conservative Senate, and the gift for every man within that body a new "senatory." According to the article, these senatories were vast properties and domains, gifted by the emperor, to these men and their families to own for life as reward for faithful service to the newfound Empire.

Jean-Luc sat back in his chair and for a brief moment a vision came startlingly clear: a beautiful stone mansion on a hill with gardens and orchards sloping down into a scenic vineyard bordering a meandering river; his children strolling with him as he inspected his crops, a warm seat for him beside a fireplace in the chateau library, and a lovely wife sharing meals, walks, and a bed.

Setting the paper down with a sigh, he dismissed the vision as a flight of fancy. He snatched up his briefcase and kissed his children farewell, stepping out the door to head to work.

The pleasant days of October had shortened into the cooler days of November when at last he received a note from the office of the mayor:

> *My Dear St. Clair,*
>
> *I do apologize for my being so uncommunicative, but work on a number of subjects has preoccupied my time. I would like to reassure you that your errand to Paris has not been forgotten; in fact, it has been the chief focus of conversation in recent days between myself and deputies from the administration. To spare you the mundane I will say only this: Monsieur Joseph Bonaparte has been instrumental in petitioning his brother for favorable tax and tariff policies with regards to the Neapolitans, whom you know to be Bourbon royalists (hardly the people Napoleon wishes to unduly grant favors). There is something more involved in our current discussions, but I am not at liberty to divulge this through the post.*
>
> *My boy, the long and short of it is this: Joseph Bonaparte expressed to me a rather flattering first impression upon meeting you, and as much as you've stated that you wish to remain in domestic repose in Marseille—he has expressed a keen interest to recall you to Paris, to work for him for a time. If you've*

*already answered silently to yourself in the negative know this:
we are involved in affairs of state that go well beyond issues
of tariff policy, issues that few men in the administration are
privy to, and you would be involved from the outset! And if
that does not entice you, then I will tell you that Monsieur J.
Bonaparte has offered to open a rather generous line of credit
to Dulard and Son, on the condition that you agree to travel
once more to Paris, at a time of your choosing, no later than
the end of the year.*

*Think well on this, St. Clair; an offer from the brother of the
emperor is not likely to be given twice.*

*My sincerest affection,
Mayor L-P. B.*

In the end Jean-Luc's decision was made for him when he received a
note from Joseph Bonaparte himself inviting Jean-Luc to Paris to celebrate
Napoleon's victories—despite the fact that his enemies still had armies in
the field. Along with the invitation came a document marked with Joseph's
personal seal that validated a line of credit of up to five thousand francs from
the Banque de France for a period of eighteen months.

Mariette, aged six, had only begun a bit of instruction with a tutor, and
Mathieu, thirteen, had never fully engaged with his small class of students
at the Église Saint-Croix, so it was not difficult for Jean-Luc to convince
them to leave Marseille and join him in Paris. After all, he argued, it would
only be for a few months, and if they did not find it acceptable, they could
always return home.

In his conversation with Mayor Bergasse before departing, Jean-Luc
had been encouraged to put aside his characteristic "modesty of temperament" and embrace his new role in service to the emperor's brother. He
was now "engaged in affairs of true significance," so there was no sense in
assuming false modesty and pretending he was unworthy of a comfortable
life. Though these appeals amused him, Jean-Luc wondered if they were
truly necessary; had the mayor forgotten he'd once forged a career in that
city? True, his most recent visit had reminded him that Parisian high society
had become a world from which he felt estranged; even so, Jean-Luc still

knew the city: how quickly those with power and wealth could be venerated one moment and the very next seized, denounced, and torn apart with more savagery than the wildest jungle.

All these considerations notwithstanding, he was unable to chase away the thought of the new class of senators and their lavish senatories. If Joseph Bonaparte had indeed taken a liking to him, why should he not make one more strike at a life of success and abundance?

A day before Jean-Luc's departure a cryptic note arrived from Mayor Bergasse.

My Dear St. Clair,

I am overjoyed to learn that you have taken this extended hand from Monsieur Bonaparte and will seize this chance. I have no doubts that you will make a fine success of yourself, and I have passed my enthusiastic support up the channels accordingly.

Without wishing to cause undue alarm, however, I feel compelled to offer you appropriate warning of a man who has, in recent years, been given direct authority over my police commissioners, and who seems to exercise authority and influence in ways that may at times seem unsettling in their efficacy. Minister of Police Joseph Fouché is a man of extraordinary abilities and influence within the Empire. Should you have opportunity to meet him, be respectful, but never discuss or divulge anything of a personal nature, for intelligence is his game. If he learns too much about you, especially of a personal nature, you might find it difficult to remove yourself from his grip; believe me when I say that his is a web you do not wish to be ensnared in. Good Luck.

— Mayor L-P. B.

CHAPTER 5

Zaręba Village, Silesia

October 1806

The two squadrons rode beneath towering oaks and white willows for perhaps a quarter of an hour when the path widened and the larger trees receded from the road, leaving autumn foliage scattered along the underbrush. The horsemen emerged into a broad meadow divided by a network of split-rail fences and streaked with colorful beds of daisies and red poppies. A pleasant evening breeze blew over the open ground, shaking the stalks of the wildflowers, as if to announce the arrival of the soldiers. Somewhere further down the road a dog barked.

Major Carnassier slowed his horse to a trot and André and his troopers tightened their reins to ease alongside him. André was about to ask his host the reason for their slackened pace when he saw a cluster of houses up ahead. As they approached, he noticed most of the dwellings appeared to be simple cottages with thatched roofs, one or two made of timber or stone. In the center stood a tall, well-built church.

The hussars checked their horses near the church, circling and letting their nearly blown horses catch their breath or graze on any grass they could find. André rode over to Carnassier and dismounted.

"It appears you've found your destination, major," he said. "But where in God's name are we?"

The hussar major handed his reins to a subordinate. "We are not far from the Siekierka River. This small errand will not take long."

As their troopers dismounted, several riders approached from the other side of the village—the reconnaissance party that had left the main column earlier. Captain Alderic and the black-clad Silesian led the way, accompanied by an older man who ran to keep up with them.

"There's something in the wind," Major Moreau said in a low voice to Mazzarello. The sergeant-major nodded his agreement.

The scouts dismounted when they reached their commander. Carnassier took his subordinate by the shoulder and the two conversed quietly for a moment. André examined the villager who accompanied the hussars: he wore plain black pants and a rustic coat of light brown fur fastened with a thick leather belt across his chest. His weathered face and long gray beard gave the impression of someone of seniority, but the way he fidgeted with his hands indicated his uneasiness.

Small groups of villagers began to wander toward the cavalrymen in clusters of twos and threes, hushing their children if they made any noise. An uneasy silence hung over the village. André glanced at Moreau, who drummed his fingers on the butt of his musket with a look of cold indifference. By now André knew better than to expect any sign of solidarity from the man.

Carnassier walked over to the village elder with Alderic a few paces behind him. The hussar commander's eyes lingered on the old man for a moment before he turned, without hurry, and stood in a position where all the villagers could see him clearly.

"Less than a fortnight has passed," he called out in a clear voice, "since we first came to this village. We came, bearing no ill will, brandishing no arms against you, and making no demands of your people—save one. One. Simple. Request." He opened his arms wide in a gesture of easy confidence. Most of the villagers did not understand his words, but none doubted the tone or authority with which he spoke.

"Now my subordinate tells me that my message has either not been received," he turned his attention to the elder standing before him, "or been deliberately disobeyed."

"Major." André stepped forward. "If there is a dispute between your men and the people of this village, I would have you inform me before any further action is taken."

Major Carnassier nodded. "Of course. An officer's first duty is deference to the chain of command, and I will most assuredly keep you apprised of the situation." He nodded to André as if to say, *Thank you, now leave this to me.*

"It has come to my attention," he went on, raising his voice, "that someone in this village is guilty of a crime as unwarranted as it is treasonous."

At this, one of Captain Alderic's hussars made his way through the crowd of villagers. He was leading a young man who was blindfolded, hands tied behind his back. The trooper shouted in French for the people to make way.

"Now," Carnassier continued, "if what I am about to say proves in any way untrue, may God strike me dead on the very ground that I stand. Did I, or did I not, specifically declare that any person living west of the city of Wrocław found harboring the enemies of France—or providing them food, ammunition, or support—would be dealt with in the harshest possible terms?"

Carnassier waited, letting his words sink in. A few villagers translated his words in hushed voices, but none dared to respond.

"Well? Were my words unclear?"

The few who understood French let out a collective murmur: "No."

"Then I am having a difficult time understanding why this man—a man to all appearances in full possession of his mental and physical faculties—was found with two dozen muskets hidden in his cellar!" Carnassier turned his attention to the blindfolded man. "Surely no law-abiding man has a need for such armament. Certainly not when he has been promised protection by the emissaries of Emperor Napoleon."

Carnassier turned and faced his own men. His presence seemed to grow by the minute. The villagers looked too wary to avert their eyes and yet too frightened to make direct eye contact.

"Now, my good citizens of Zaręba, we come to the truly egregious crime." With a flick of his chin, another subordinate emerged from behind the crowd. He bore in his arms a wooden chest, gilded with brass hinges, and a gold finish on its lock. Its lid was decorated with a shining anchor motif; the words 'Rodzina Jarzyna' carved underneath.

The hussar set the chest on the ground at his commander's feet. "Found it in this man's cellar, sir." He indicated the elder.

"Open it."

Using the pommel of his saber, the hussar smashed the lock off the chest and flipped the lid open. Inside was a veritable fortune in gold and silver coins, jewels, gemstones, and other trinkets. The eyes of the nearby hussars lit up with undisguised longing; even André stared, transfixed.

"Well, look at this, count, look at this." Carnassier lifted a necklace with his sword high enough for all to see. "You've a hidden cache of *treasure* as well? Oh, count of Zaręba, I don't like this. Not at all. I'd considered us brothers-in-arms, ready to march out against our common enemies. And now, not only are you unwilling to fulfill your obligations, but you're hiding your resources from a man who offered you his trust and protection? That won't do."

Carnassier stared, seemingly waiting for an explanation that could redeem the man from his fate. The old man's shoulders slumped.

"That is wealth of village," he spoke in a thick Polish accent. "We pass down over hundred years. Put together for keep safe, in case that we are losing everything."

"Well, you see, count," Carnassier replied, swatting a fly from his face, "that cock won't fight. You notice my men there, yes? Men that have ridden miles—hard miles—to come to your eminent village, offering protection. They did not ride *all that way* to be told that they have the pick of only five horses and some potatoes—when you have a veritable fortune hidden in your cellar." He turned to Captain Alderic. "Does that sound fair to you?"

"Sounds like shit to me." Alderic was folding a rope in his hands.

"Major," André said, uneasy.

"And what about the weapons?" Carnassier asked, ignoring André. "Were you not strictly forbidden from caching arms without reporting them to us first?"

The man did not raise his eyes. Carnassier shook his head and gripped the old man by his shirt, leading him out in front of the huddled group, some of whom now cried out or pled for mercy. He pulled out his pistol, cocking back the hammer.

"Consider this my final warning. If you give me your full cooperation, we will treat you with fairness. If you lie and try to deceive me, you will pay the price."

He raised his arm and pointed to a tree several paces away. Captain Alderic gestured to two of the hussars and handed one of them the rope; they then threw it over a strong limb. With a few pulls they had lifted the noose to shoulder height. Alderic placed it around the old man's neck and nodded. With a strong heave, the hussars tugged the rope and the man was lifted several feet off the ground, his feet kicking and jerking. A collective wail emitted from the onlookers and several moved to help their compatriot, but Carnassier and Alderic leveled their pistols to check them.

André shouted at Carnassier to release the man, but, before he had taken two steps, a figure emerged from the crowd. An elderly woman, her head covered in a shawl, ran to the old man who now jerked in quick spasms, his face red and his eyes bulging in pain and terror.

"*Brat! Bracie, jestem tutaj!*" she cried out, her eyes wide with horror. "*Bracie!*" She let out a shrill, unnerving wail, and threw her full force at the first hussar she reached, smashing a fist into his face. Major Carnassier leveled his pistol and fired. The woman jerked and her body toppled sideways onto the grass. A dreadful silence hung in the air for several seconds, soon followed by a collective sound of bloodcurdling horror so unnerving that some of the horses bucked and stamped.

This violent sequence of events had occurred so quickly that all André could do was stare at the woman now lying still on the ground. He then looked up to the man dangling motionless from the rope, then turned his eyes to Carnassier, and finally onto the faces of the hussars mounted or standing behind their leader. Their calm and haughty indifference frightened him. They looked as if nothing out of the ordinary had occurred; only one or two seemed to notice the wailing that emanated from the villagers.

"What in God's name have you done?" he bellowed, taking several steps toward the hussar. "Who gave you leave to kill an unarmed civilian and an innocent woman?"

Holstering his pistol, Carnassier gave André a quick glance. "I am sorry if you are unnerved, colonel, but that *man* offered me and my men food and shelter. I have just learned that he provided the same for our enemy just a few days later. This is nothing new to you, sir—this is war. In war one must choose sides. He made his choice, and we have given him recompense."

"Major," André snarled, no longer able to restrain his fury, "do you know the penalty for murdering an unarmed noncombatant?"

"She may have been *unarmed*," the major replied in a cool voice, "but she struck one of my men. Every soldier here witnessed it. Your men witnessed it. I haven't the slightest doubt that any courts-martial would find me within my legal rights to defend my men from a foreign hostile."

André stepped forward, his face inches from Carnassier's. "Major, you will take no more action with regard to this village or its inhabitants. You are speaking to a colonel. I don't care about whatever mandate you think you've been given. You will obey the chain of command of the Grand Armée of the Empire of France. This company is leaving this town. You and your men have five minutes to assemble, and then we depart to return to the main army."

André turned on his heels, grabbing his horse's bridle and leading it away. Several of his soldiers followed. He turned to the two nearest hussars. "See to it that those two are given a proper burial. Now!"

He then called out to Major Moreau, who was nowhere to be seen.

"If you're looking for the executive officer, sir," Mazzarello said, jerking his chin towards the village center, "he went off that way."

André handed the reins of his mount to one of his troopers and walked off in the direction his sergeant-major had indicated. He passed by several houses with thatched roofs, and noticed a frightened woman leading half a dozen pigs lowered her face under a headscarf. She seemed unwilling to look André in the eye.

He found his subordinate leaning against the wall of the church in the center of the village. He had a ledger in his left hand and appeared to be writing.

"We're departing now, major."

Moreau nodded in silent acknowledgment.

"What are you writing?"

"I write nothing."

In the distance the trumpet sounded the unit's call to assembly. Moreau cleared his throat, snapping his ledger shut. "Shall we depart, sir?"

"Do you have something you wish to say, major, while we may speak privately?"

Moreau shrugged, returning André's hard stare with a look of indifference. "Why would you think I have something to say, sir?"

"Major, I don't have time to play about. If you wish to speak, do so now."

Moreau took a step closer, picking up his musket and resting it on his shoulder. "You're right, sir. We should be going. Our superiors should be informed of the able soldiering we have done here." He walked past André, brushing his shoulder as he passed. "I'm sure congratulations are in order for our squadron and its brave leader."

Too stunned to speak, André stood motionless for several seconds. He took a deep breath and looked up at the spire of the church as he exhaled.

The building was tall, taller than he had originally observed. Its spire was painted green, and its conical shape reminded him of a church in Rouen. His brief thought of home was interrupted, however, by a strange feeling—as though he were not alone.

He turned quickly on his heels. A few paces away, a woman stood looking at him. Her bright blonde hair was partially concealed beneath an orange headscarf. She was perhaps twenty years of age and, in spite of his dour mood, André found her rather striking.

"Can I help you, mademoiselle?"

"What did that soldier just tell you?" she asked, in an accented but clear voice.

"He—" André paused, gathering his thoughts. At last he shook his head, renewed in his purpose. "He told me nothing."

The woman took two slow steps toward André.

"Mademoiselle, I'm sorry for what has happened today. I did not—"

"No monsieur," replied the woman, in French. "My anger is not for you. It was he—" she nodded in the direction Moreau had departed, "I believe he might have saved me."

"What do you mean?"

The woman wiped a tear from her cheek. "He saw me. After that…*beast* killed Eliasz, I went to my house, right over there," she indicated a small house behind the church. "I went to my house to cry, but instead I found myself holding a carving knife, and I was going to kill that devil. I—I don't know what came over me."

André eyed the woman in silence.

"That soldier, the one you just spoke to…he restrained me as I was walking toward that man, meaning to kill him. He told me—"

Just then Captain Alderic rode up, and she went silent. André exchanged a word with the hussar, and the order was given to depart. When he turned back, the young woman was gone.

The sun fell behind the horizon as the two squadrons rode through a dense forest of pines en route to Major Carnassier's transitory fortress redoubt, a stronghold secluded enough for them to pass the night in relative safety.

Czocha Castle overlooked the Kwisa River, the ancient border between the Polish-speaking duchy of Silesia to the east and the German-speaking Upper Lusatia to the west. Appearing as little more than a large brook, the river had nevertheless marked the divide between two kingdoms locked in an endless struggle for political power. The French cavalrymen riding through were simply the latest chapter in the contentious history of this land.

André and Moreau had passed the ride from the village of Zaręba to Czocha in a tense silence, neither willing to look directly at the other. André did not pretend to understand the mind of his brooding subordinate, nor did he care very much for the man's thoughts; he had spent the ride preoccupied by Carnassier's conduct in the village. As he considered the untroubled demeanor of the hussar commander, he began to wonder how the man had come into a position of such power; perhaps he really had been granted extraordinary methods of securing loyalty, however brutal they might seem to outsiders. After all, in the course of a campaign that could cost the lives of tens of thousands of soldiers, tragedy invariably occurred. Still, André could not bring himself to dismiss the cold brutality of executing an unarmed woman pleading for an old man's life. There had been no military justification.

Carnassier had promised André he would see his men safely back to the location where the two squadrons had first met. From there, they could attempt to regain their lines. In the meantime, both squadrons would pass the night in safety within the walls of Czocha Castle, where the horses could recover and the men could rest. There would be plenty of food for hungry mouths and more than enough wine and ale to restore the vigor of weary soldiers.

A light rain started to drizzle as the horsemen splashed their way over the Kwisa and made their way through the small village, eventually crossing a long, narrow stone bridge that led to the castle keep. The locals scattered as they passed, peering out from doorways and windows, curious about the green-coated dragoons with their bronze helmets and horsehair crests waving behind them as they rode. For their part, the dragoons eyed their temporary new quarters with relief: a roof over their heads to block out the rain, which fell heavier as they led their horses into the castle courtyard.

Once his troopers had found shelter and fodder for their horses, André penned a combat report before joining his men in the castle's great hall. He was relieved to find a warm glow from the fireplace and an atmosphere of pleasant revelry within. His dragoons sat on benches and around wooden tables drinking, playing cards, and mingling with their hussar hosts, who drank and sang as if they were in a salon in Paris. Mazzarello and Moreau were seated with two hussars in a far corner playing cards. He walked across the room to join them, noticing several women, likely residents of the town, serving mugs of ale and wine. To his relief, none of them seemed to be receiving any unwanted attention—though he knew that could change quickly.

André approached the table and pulled up a chair. "Mind if I join you?"

"Please, sir." Mazzarello indicated an open space. Moreau, looking up from a deck of cards, nodded curtly. He dealt a hand to the other men at the table. André noted the ranks of the two hussars beside him, a sergeant and a lieutenant. Sipping from large wooden mugs, they kept silent as they eyed their cards.

"If either of them cheats," André said, nudging the lieutenant to his right, "tell me and I'll see that they're flogged."

The hussar smiled dutifully at the quip. "We rarely lose, colonel."

Major Moreau, still dealing, gestured across the room. "Do you wish to offer our host a seat, sir?"

André turned; Major Carnassier had entered the great hall, his brown pelisse swinging from his left shoulder and his sword clanking on his thigh as he walked. He cut a swaggering figure as he crossed the room. Opening his arms wide as he approached the card players, he flashed a congenial grin.

"So, what am I interrupting, Quadrille or Piquet?"

"You're not interrupting anything, major," Moreau said. "Are we not sitting in a fortress that belongs to you now?"

"Come now, let's not be absurd. I would not be so immodest to pretend such a splendid abode belongs to me." He motioned to one of the women for a drink. "Though this castle is magnificent, is it not? For a people as backwards as these, their history is quite fascinating. And now, our emperor is on the verge of bestowing to them, worthy or not, the gifts of our Revolutionary freedoms! Liberty *here*, can you imagine? 'A people dwelling in darkness have seen a great light.'"

After a hand was played the two hussars cursed under their breath, setting their cards face down on the table. Moreau collected the small pile of coins and set it in front of him. After a quick count to make sure he wasn't cheated, he began reshuffling the deck.

"One would be quite fortunate indeed," Carnassier went on, as he packed tobacco into a pipe, "to make a home of such a citadel. For those of us who fashion ourselves as children of the Revolution, we ought to consider ourselves lucky just to glimpse the inside of so splendid a structure!"

André set his mug on the table. His two comrades looked at him, both aware, as surely as the other soldiers of his squadron, of his noble birth.

"I come from a house of nobility," he said. "From the department of Rouen."

Carnassier eyed him with a look of surprise before smacking his lips and breaking into a high-pitched laugh. "A Norman prince? Who would have believed? Ha!" He tapped André on the shoulder and took a swig of ale.

"I often recall the days of revolution as if they occurred yesterday," André said quietly. "Through circumstance of birth, not choice, I found myself tossed through that blood-soaked mill. When I emerged on the other side, I suppose I was a better man for it. Some found hatred. I was blessed to find the love of my life."

"Of course," Carnassier replied, waving a hand in exaggerated apology. "With all due deference, colonel, I simply marvel at the twists of fate that spring eternal from our Revolution. A man of noble birth survives the terror and now finds himself in the company of low-born thieves and cutthroats. Not least of which, that rogue you met earlier, Alderic, the bloodiest of Septembrists! Ha."

André raised his eyes from the table to find Moreau staring at him as if his eyes could cut through stone. Moreau held his gaze several seconds before turning his attention to Carnassier.

"You say Captain Alderic was a Septembrist?"

Carnassier let out an exaggerated sigh. "He was not *a* Septembrist—he was *the* Septembrist. If I told you *half* the stories, I believe you'd piss your breeches. He was just a lad when he stabbed a priest on the steps of the Hôtel de Ville in front of half the Constituent Assembly. I tell you, he is a blood-drinker, that one."

"You sound rather approving of that fact, major," André said flatly.

"Oh, come now," Carnassier said, setting down his pipe. "You are still haunted by memories of that cruel time? Life goes on, yes? We have an emperor now. Family feuds are moot. We serve Napoleon, and where Father Violet orders me, I go!"

The two other hussars at the table rapped their knuckles firmly on the wood.

"Corsica is a small island," Mazzarello added, "but we've bred the greatest giant living."

"Hear, hear!" Carnassier stood, raised his mug and shouted, "*Vive l'Empereur!*"

"*VIVE L'EMPEREUR!*" roared the men in the room, hussars and dragoons alike. Satisfied with their gusto, Carnassier bowed and returned to his seat. "Colonel, as much as I hate to interrupt these reminiscences and break apart your holy trinity here, there is something I would like to speak with you about." He leaned in closer, his voice hushed. "In private."

"Private?" Moreau cut in. "Surely your notorious blood-drinker will be privy to the conversation, no?"

Carnassier returned Moreau's stare before returning his attention to André. "Colonel Valiere, what say we continue our conversation without the presence of lackeys?"

"The last man who called me lackey had his entrails spilled onto the grass."

An uncomfortable silence ensued, until Carnassier leaned forward and spoke in a cold voice, "What a *frightening* thought." André and his sergeant-major exchanged an uneasy look. The tension was broken when the hussar commander leaned back in his chair and let out a bellowing laugh.

"Now, colonel," Carnassier said, still chuckling, "before your man makes any more ungentlemanly remarks, may I beg leave of a word?"

André stood up. "Keep an eye on our troopers. Nothing out of order happens tonight," he said to his sergeant-major. "The sentence for rape is a firing squad. Remind them before they get too drunk."

He followed Carnassier up a flight of stairs and down a corridor before entering what appeared to be a dimly lit study or library. Large bookshelves lined the walls and a circular chandelier with long, thick candles provided an orange pool of light. A stack of scrolls and leather-bound books piled on a solid oak desk in front of the room's only window caught a soft glare of moonlight.

"I'll speak plainly." Carnassier turned and faced André. "I've no interest in playing games with your attack dog. I have before me a more important matter, one that I believe you might find quite interesting." At that moment the door opened, and into the candlelight stepped the mysterious man clad in black and green—the Silesian. He closed the door without a sound and leaned against a bookshelf. "I've not been entirely forthright with you," Carnassier continued. "Our Silesian gentleman is in fact a good deal more than a simple intelligence officer."

Striking steel against flint and catching the flame with a char cloth, Carnassier lit his pipe and took several puffs, exhaling a plume of smoke that filled the room with its aroma.

"What I am about to tell you is unknown to anyone outside of the emperor and his closest advisors, so I need not warn you to keep all this information with the utmost discretion."

"You need not tell me anything at all, major," André replied. "You invited me into this room to hear what you've offered to tell me."

"Very well." Carnassier took another puff of his pipe and jerked his chin at the Silesian. He joined them at the table and unfurled a long parchment. He looked at André with pale blue eyes and a mask of stolidity.

"Does this gentleman have a name?" asked André. "Or is he to remain a mystery for this entire conversation?"

"I wouldn't trouble with his name. But, if you wish, you may call him Conrad. We'll come to him in a moment. Now, as you see spread before you," Carnassier lowered his eyes to the parchment, placing an inkwell on one corner, "we have a map of the Prussian territories." He ran a finger along a blue line. "Right now, the emperor is marching somewhere in the vicinity of Erfurt and Jena, where he hopes to fight a decisive battle against Friedrich Wilhelm and knock Prussia out of the war."

André nodded. "This is no secret."

Carnassier continued. "What Father Violet has planned, however, is to confiscate the property and lands of the governor of Hesse-Cassel. Or in the words of his own edict, 'to remove the house of Hesse-Cassel from rulership and to strike it out of the list of powers.' The governor has only recently been made aware of this."

André looked up from the table. "I'm still unsure what this information has to do with me."

"We're coming to it. Less than a fortnight past, our good gentleman here intercepted a message from Wilhelm IX, Landgrave of Hesse-Cassel, to his faithful administrator, a Monsieur Mayer Amschel Rothschild. A Jew from a family of modest means, yet, through diligent service in recent years, he has been elevated to the role of advisor in Wilhelm's household. One of his most trusted, if rumors are to be believed."

André looked at the Silesian, to confirm the truth of this statement. "I take it this note was of importance?"

Carnassier grinned. "This Rothschild has been invested with the entirety of Wilhelm's estate, and perhaps the estates of the neighboring governors, who stand to lose everything if—rather—*when* Napoleon wins." He looked to the Silesian and back to André, leaning in for emphasis. "He's been entrusted to smuggle out in excess of 400 million in English pounds sterling."

André stood, dumbfounded, staring at the map. *Four hundred million pounds?* He looked at the Silesian, then back to Carnassier. "How did you intercept this message?"

Carnassier smiled. "Precisely how we chanced upon this piece of information is not what's important. What matters is what we do with the knowledge. Our emperor expects—no, demands—our success."

"How can you be sure this information is not a false flag, a morsel of fiction to mislead the emperor on the eve of his conquest of Prussia?"

Carnassier turned to the Silesian; the man spoke a few quick words in German, nodding as Carnassier asked him several short questions.

"Our comrade here has proof considered beyond reproach." Carnassier tapped his pipe against the Silesian's chest. "He has seen it."

"You've seen this treasure?" André asked, astonished.

"Frankfurt, *Herr*," the Silesian replied in a low voice.

"Alderic accompanied him to verify it," Carnassier cut in. "I was as incredulous as you when I first heard these claims; I dispatched these two to Frankfurt to glean the truth of it all. In the cellars of several noble houses one will find a hundred wine casks filled with notes, coins, and jewels."

André's skepticism was yielding to a budding curiosity. "Have you sent word to the emperor?"

A clock on the mantel ticked noisily. "He will be made aware in due time. He is the emperor. But I'm sure you understand—the man who delivers this hidden horde of riches will receive a reward utterly unprecedented. Lands, castles, honors of nobility, a marshal's baton. We both know how generous our emperor is to his faithful subordinates."

André would not have chosen the word *faithful* to describe the man standing before him. And yet, in his mind's eye, he could see a vast cellar with endless rows of large wooden casks filled to the brim with notes and riches beyond count. The image faded, and his thoughts turned to the corpse swaying lifelessly from the rope earlier that day. That was replaced with the seething, desperate look of the woman who'd accosted him about Moreau, her body shaking with anger and fear. He shuddered involuntarily.

"So, will you aid us? Will you aid your emperor?"

"Major, tomorrow at sunrise you will have my answer." With that, André bid the two men a good evening and departed the room.

He returned to the smoke-filled chamber in a brooding mood, at first impervious to the atmosphere of drunken chaos. Two of the hussars lay drunk on the floor, while one of his troopers had a local woman on his lap; she was slapping his greedy hands away. His attention eventually came back to the scene around him, and he made his way back to the table where he had been sitting earlier. A dozen soldiers were milling about, observing with amused expressions whatever was transpiring.

André felt his stomach tighten when he noticed his executive officer sitting across from Carnassier's "blood-drinker," Captain Alderic. Both men appeared somewhat inebriated. In Moreau's palm sat a small whiskey glass, in the other a small knife, which he now lifted, holding the blade at eye level. A hush fell over the assembled troopers. Closing one eye, Marcel inhaled and dropped the knife. With a sharp clang the knifepoint dropped into the glass and both tumbled onto the table. A loud cheer erupted from the crowd. "*Vive le major!*"

Moreau sat back in his chair as several dragoons tapped his shoulder. He nodded toward the hussar captain. "Your turn, Septembrist."

Smiling wolfishly, Captain Alderic took a shot and placed the glass on his outstretched palm. "I'm still not sure what your squadron is doing out here, major, away from the protection of the main army. This part of the world is no place for gentle soldiers and milksops who wander into ambushes."

Moreau nodded to André. "There's our commander; why don't you ask him yourself?"

André gave his executive officer a frosty look. He then turned toward the hussar captain. "Are you stalling, captain? I believe it's your turn."

Alderic smiled at André, raising the knife aloft. "If you say so, colonel."

Without looking down, he dropped the knife. Time seemed suspended for the half second it took for the knife to fall, dropping with a clang into the glass and toppling onto the table. Another cheer, louder than before, rose up from the hussars gathered around their captain. With alarming speed, Alderic picked up the knife and proceeded to spike the blade between his outstretched fingers several times before stabbing the blade into the table and raising a fist in the air. "Major Carnassier and the Seventh Hussars! *Vive Carnassier!*"

"*Vive Carnassier!*" the hussars echoed.

"Loved by every wife, hated by every husband!" another shouted, clinking his cup with a comrade's.

André had seen enough; soldiers with enough to drink and no enemy in sight would inevitably find a reason to fight their own. He nodded at Sergeant-major Mazzarello, indicating for him to begin collecting the more inebriated dragoons.

Alderic wiped his mouth with his sleeve. "You lot should follow your colonel and return to your corps; this castle is home to real soldiers." With that, he placed his palm on the table, facing up. He raised the knife to eye level, smiling at Moreau. "*Vive l'Empereur.*" He dropped the knife, its point sticking itself firmly into the flesh of his palm. He showed no response—simply took a mug from one of his soldiers and drank. A shocked silence hung over the room.

"We live in a world where strong men make their own laws. I'm a soldier. I do what I like, because I'm strong enough to do so. If that bothers you, go back home to Paris and sell bread."

Moreau stared at the captain for several seconds. Concerned he might do something rash, André took a step toward the major; to his surprise, Moreau smiled. It was the first time he had seen the man do so. Moreau then placed his palm flat on the table and picked up his own knife.

"You're not a soldier," he said calmly. "You terrorize those weaker than you, who are afraid of you. Who fear death. Look into my eyes; you'll see no such fear."

Moreau dropped the knife, its point piercing into his hand with a thud. He did not move or flinch.

CHAPTER 6

Carcourt, Normandy
Autumn 1806

Sophie Valiere held up her hand for quiet. After scribbling down some notes, she looked up—half a dozen farmers sat across from her, among them Monsieur Burnouf, one of the more trustworthy landowners on her estate of Carcourt, and Guy Le Bon, her steward and bookkeeper. Intentionally or not, the two groups had arranged themselves along disagreeing sides, angled so that they were facing each other in a sort of miniature parliament.

"We will not solve all your grievances today," she said at last, "but can we at least agree that by sitting here together we are providing ourselves with an opportunity to address and, God willing, *resolve* this problem? Monsieur Abadain," Sophie said, turning to the farmer seated to her left, "you say that the supply of wheat and potatoes you've recently brought to market in Rouen is inadequate?"

"To say the least," Abadain answered, setting his pipe on his lap. "For the second consecutive year."

"This accords with what I've been told—"

"And that's not the worst of it," he interrupted, leveling his eyes at the men seated across from him. "The drought hurt our crops to be sure, but nearly all *my* hands have moved up to the northern fields. I've no one to take my produce to market. Lured and snatched up by these gentlemen, they were!"

"Gobshite," Monsieur Talbot, one of the farmers seated to Sophie's right, barked in response. "You lie, Abadain and you know it. I never took a single worker from you—they left of their own will. It was *you* who took on a score of outlander hands, who speak a foreign tongue and offered their workshite labor for next to nothing. You pay them less than half what our own lads are accustomed to making, so your boys haven't seen their wages rise like the other domains in the province; they pack up and volunteer their services to me. And if you recall, Pierre, last June I asked *you* what I should tell your lads, and what did you say to me then? 'Devil take them all, I could give a fig where the ungrateful bastards go.' You see, madame? That is what has monsieur out of sorts. He can't hold on to his help, and I shoulder the blame."

Pierre Abadain was seething; his face covered with sweat.

Sophie stood quickly and occupied the small space between them. She knew the time had come to settle the matter with fists, and she was unwilling to accept this result. "Before anymore insults or calumnies are exchanged," she said in an imperious tone, "I will offer you gentlemen a proposal that I hope you both find suitable: it might seem somewhat unorthodox, but perhaps it will help us in finding peaceful resolutions to our differences. I propose the creation of a landowner's council."

The terms she laid out in detail were met with skepticism but ultimately agreed upon, albeit reluctantly. The council was to meet every fortnight, composed of property-holding farmers and their wives. Two leaders were to be elected every six months, their responsibilities to hear the petitions and grievances of the families and work with Sophie—and André, when he returned—to find an agreement. They would bring to a vote any major changes the estate might effect to improve the lives of the farmers. Additionally, Monsieur Talbot was to send Monsieur Abadain's farmhands back to him. Abadain would raise their wages. The outlander workers would be given the right to work wherever they pleased, as long as they did not threaten the labor or wages of the native-born. The meeting ended with a civil handshake. With one or two men grumbling their displeasure over the state of the current crop, they all rose to their feet and shuffled out of the barn without further rancor.

"Amusing, isn't it?" asked Guy Le Bon, when the last of the farmers had gone. "Two years of diminished crop is enough to undo seven years of peace and harmony."

Sophie collected the papers in front of her. "It's more than a failed crop, Guy. You know that."

The two stepped out into the fading autumn light, and Monsieur Le Bon clasped his hands together behind his back. "We shall do everything in our power to maintain Carcourt while Lieutenant-Colonel Valiere is gone."

"Maintain," Sophie responded absently. She pulled a shawl over her head and together they walked up the sloping hill that led to the main house. "Why not make it better?"

Monsieur Le Bon responded with a curt smile. His nimble steps belied the old age evident in his posture and features.

"Anyhow, before I begin supper, is there anything else I need worry about?"

"I regret to answer in the affirmative, madame."

Sophie nodded in resignation. "All right, what is it?"

"Two days ago," Le Bon began as he accompanied her to the front of the house, "a man rode onto the estate. He told me he came at the behest of his master, a count."

Sophie shrugged. Undeterred, Monsieur Le Bon continued. "This man relayed a message of greeting from his master, who wondered whether it might be possible to arrange a visit to his estate near Le Havre, or, perhaps, visit with you here."

"What sort of man was this—"

"He called himself Sylvain, madame," Le Bon replied. "And, if it pleases you, you may meet him yourself. He is waiting just here in the front driveway."

"Good evening, monsieur," Sophie said as she walked over and offered her hand. "I don't believe we have had the privilege of being acquainted. I am Sophie Valiere."

The man was dressed in a fashionable yellow coat, its tails reaching down to his boots, which were made of fine leather and extended up to his knees. His plump features loosened into a smile at Sophie's approach. He held her eye as he kissed her extended hand. "I am called Sylvain Lavalle." Although a magnificent carriage waited in the driveway, indicating whoever employed Sylvain Lavalle to be a man of wealth, he nonetheless carried a riding crop tucked under his arm. Offering her a low, courteous bow, he added, "And I serve as the chamberlain of the Count de Montfort's household."

"Chamberlain?" Le Bon murmured, standing beside Sophie. "Are we to expect a visit from the queen of England?"

"Thank you, Guy," Sophie said, tactfully. "I'll manage from here."

Le Bon offered a slight bow and turned away, crossing the grass and entering the house.

"Guy Le Bon," Sophie explained to her guest. "He is something of a steward to my husband and me. His manner can be…disagreeable at times. Nevertheless, he is very important to the functioning of our estate. How may I be of service, Monsieur Lavalle?"

Lavalle, who had been discreetly sizing up the property, now turned his full attention to Sophie. "Well, madame, I come at the behest of my employer, as previously stated, with a message of greetings to you and your household. Count Jean-Claude Etienne-Marie Devereux, Count de Montfort, is newly returned to this comely province from exile in England."

Sophie tucked the notebook she'd been carrying into her apron. "Please reply with our family's warm greetings to the count. If he had reason to flee, then perhaps our families have experienced similar troubles."

Monsieur Lavalle raised his chin slightly. "Yes. Well, you see, the count has no living relatives. At least not here in Normandy—"

"I'm so sorry. If he is a widower, then I should not—"

"Think nothing of it. The count has never married, and in truth I do not think he laments the passing of his father and mother, who were rather late in years. I believe it is the count's intention to acquaint himself with the leading family of this province in hopes of learning the way of things, and, perhaps, striking up new friendships. He has instructed me to extend an open invitation to you and your husband to visit him at his estate, which is situated some miles to the east of Le Havre."

Sophie nodded, lost in thought for a moment. "As it so happens, Monsieur Lavalle, the 'way of things' is currently in flux. The crop yield for the past two seasons has been short of expectations, the war has forced many families to consider the likelihood of conscription, and, presently, our farmers are at each other's throats, to say nothing of the arrival of—"

She was interrupted by Le Bon, calling her from inside the house. Sophie turned to see his tall, thin frame in the doorway.

"Yes?" she asked, irritation in her voice.

"Madame, it's your two boys," Le Bon replied. "It seems they've had something of a disturbance."

Two boys appeared from behind Le Bon. "Mama," the older one cried, thrusting an arm out to stop his little brother from passing him as they both ran to her. "It's his fault!"

"Christophe, Remy, go inside. I'll be with you in a minute." Sophie cast an apologetic look at her visitor.

"Mama, she didn't do it; it's all right now."

"*Who* didn't do *what*, Remy?" Sophie demanded.

The two boys exchanged glances. Chistophe stood tall and straight; Remy had cast his head down. Christophe nudged his brother. Remy cleared his throat. "Mama, the girl from the village stole my tadpole. It was *my* tadpole."

"*Our* tadpole," Christophe corrected him.

"Well, she wouldn't give it back," Remy bravely continued, "so I played a trick on her."

Sophie placed a hand on her hips, no longer aware of the well-dressed visitor standing only a few paces away. "What trick?'

Remy looked up at his brother for assistance. Receiving none, he let out a giggle, causing his brother to turn his head to the side as well. A smile arose onto the younger boy's features. "I told her if she ate three sous then…"

Sophie glared down at him in anticipation.

"If she ate three ten sous pieces," Remy repeated, "then she'd poop out thirty sous tomorrow." Christophe dropped his face into his hands, mortified.

A sharp smack broke the silence. With a look of shock, Remy rubbed his cheek where he'd been hit. His older brother looked straight ahead, fearing he was next. Sophie pointed at both her boys. "Christophe, Remy, you have both done something horrible."

"But she didn't *do* it!" Remy squealed, face still red from the slap.

"I don't care," Sophie snapped. "You are both expected to be kind to the other children, and this disgusting trick reflects poorly on you both, as sons of a lieutenant-colonel, and on me. I raised you to be better than that."

She took a moment to collect herself and turned back to her visitor, who was waiting patiently twenty paces away. He wore a bemused expression tinged with a hint of revulsion. Her frown disappeared and her features lit up in a smile. "As you can see, Monsieur Lavalle, we have quite a busy life here at Carcourt. It is with deep regret that I must decline, at least for now, the offer for us to visit the count on his estate. I'm sure you understand."

Sylvain Lavalle forced a smile and bowed courteously. "Madame, I assure you, I understand. I will relate to the count—"

"Please give the count my apologies," Sophie interjected. "Tell him that he is welcome to visit us here at any time. With their father gone, these boys might profit from instruction in refined manners."

Sylvain nodded, bowing once more. "It has been my honor and privilege to make the acquaintance of the lady of Carcourt."

Sophie bowed as well. "Thank you, monsieur. Good evening, and pleasant journey home."

CHAPTER 7

Czocha Castle, Poland (Silesia)

October 1806

The sleepy castle town rose with the sun, and the crowing of the roosters was drowned out by the sound of seven clangs of the church bell. André joined Major Carnassier in the study for a breakfast of coffee and buttered bread, informing him that the dragoon squadron must make the attempt to return to camp today. They would not be joining or assisting any attempts to find a horde of hidden treasure. Carnassier relented with a nonchalant shrug: "Nevertheless, we will accompany you on the initial part of your journey."

In the courtyard, the hussars and dragoons dutifully readied their horses for departure. One trooper held his horse's reins while he vomited in the mud.

Sergeant-major Mazzarello barked out a slew of profanities attempting to rouse the tempo of the troopers' movements, if not their spirits. The men responded by singing a song about Napoleon in low voices; a song saved for when their Corsican superior was in a foul mood:

> A little man from Corsica,
> a lion of his time
> a little man named Bonaparte,
> his livery so fine.

The little man was blown away
his love he'll see no more
the little man who went away,
he ne'er returned from war.

Moreau walked his horse out from the stables, his left hand covered in a white bandage. His grim expression encouraged the troopers to give him a wide berth as he passed, none daring to look him in the eye. It was unspoken, but the dragoons seemed to have altered their view of their morose executive officer. Wary ambivalence had turned into a subtle wonder. He mounted his horse and rode over to where André was sitting.

The damp mist lingering over the surging river would be gone within the hour, André wagered, leaving little natural concealment for the squadron as they moved. A handful of Carnassier's scouts had returned after a routine patrol, reporting no sign of the enemy. If they rode northwest for perhaps two days, they would reach Görlitz, and from there they should find the Grand Armée with little difficulty.

André looked at his subordinate. "Everything all right?"

"My hand fucking hurts," Moreau answered.

André laughed. "I imagine it does. As soon as our hosts arrive, we will go."

"I'm ready when you are."

On cue, Carnassier and his subordinate rode out across the bridge leading to the castle. Captain Alderic and Major Moreau avoided looking at each other as the former rode out ahead of the main body troopers, joined by the black-clad Silesian. The assembled hussars and their commander looked formidable with their large bearskin hats, curved sabers, and brown shoulder pelisses swaying as they rode forward.

"Before we depart, colonel," Carnassier said in a low tone, "are you sure I cannot say anything to make you reconsider my offer?"

André looked back at his squadron, all his men saddled and eager to rejoin their comrades. He kicked his horse into a trot, signaling the entire column into motion. "Just lead us out of here, major."

He rode forward, and the column followed him in a noisy stampede through the town and into the wide countryside beyond.

After a morning of hard riding, the squadron halted on a small hill that provided another stunning view of the Silesian countryside. They had travelled perhaps thirty miles and would need to continue at a fast pace if they wished to reach friendly lines before the next day's sunset. The harvest had officially begun and, in the fields before them, stems of wheat glistened like gold in the autumn sunlight. Perhaps a hundred yards away a farmer looked up from his reaping, the blades of his scythe reflecting the sun with a glossy sheen. The presence of several hundred cavalrymen did not seem to disturb his business.

Carnassier reigned in and dismounted beside André. "Major, I regret to inform you that this is where I leave you."

Although inwardly relieved by their imminent separation, André offered him sincere thanks for the protection of his men, and for aiding them during the ambush.

"Colonel, I must reiterate, at the crossroads that you will come to in two or three miles, it is *imperative* that you do not take the right road. Right goes east, and in that direction, you will find only Polish huts and Cossacks." André nodded and Carnassier shook his hand. "It's a shame I could not sway you to join me in my pursuit, Valiere. There are untold riches to be had, my friend. The men who find it—God only knows how they shall be rewarded! Think of it, a marshal's baton in your hand." He hopped nimbly onto his horse, signaling to his men that it was time to go. The bugler signaled the departure, and the hussars led their horses away. "Farewell, lieutenant-colonel! I doubt we will meet again, but if we do it may be under quite different circumstances. *Bonne chance!*"

André returned the major's salute and watched the squadron of hussars disappear over the far side of the ridge. When they were out of view, he took out his spyglass and surveyed the valley before them. He felt an undeniable apprehension. He considered the advice of his colleague: "…it is *imperative* that you do not take the right road."

"Shall we depart, sir?" Moreau called out.

"What kind of marshal do you think Carnassier would make, major?"

"*That* man a marshal?" Moreau eyed André with visible impatience. "I think there's a greater chance of me being crowned king of England, sir."

André nodded. "Send me three of your best scouts, major."

A few moments later, three troopers cantered alongside André and Moreau. One of the dragoons saluted, addressing André. "Corporal Laporte reporting, sir."

André spoke to the corporal for several minutes, pointing at specific landmarks visible in the valley below. Moreau drummed the leather of his saddle impatiently with his uninjured hand, watching as the corporal nodded in agreement. Satisfied that his instructions were understood, André sent the corporal and his comrades ahead. They cantered down the hill and out of sight into the tree line.

Mazzarello joined André on the knoll. He itched at the lining of his pants, remarking on his hopes for the chance to bathe and wash their uniforms when the squadron returned to camp.

André surveyed the landscape with suspicion.

"Where have you sent Laporte, sir?" the sergeant-major asked.

"Either I've lost whatever soldiering instincts I may have once possessed…or we're being led into a trap."

The dark-haired Corsican nodded. "Sir, in these parts, we know firsthand that that is always possible."

"Colonel," Moreau spoke, "with your permission I'd like to join the reconnaissance."

"No." André shut his spyglass emphatically. "Sergeant-major, ready the rear of the formation to move. Major Moreau, go with him."

"Sir, if the enemy are in those woods—"

"Major, you've been given an order." André's nostrils widened. The strain of the previous few days and his impatience at Moreau's constant challenges had pushed him to the edge of losing his temper. "Now go and carry it out."

"Let me understand, sir. We stumbled into an ambush that was clear as day, but you, our commander, hadn't the foresight to anticipate it. Now, when we *know* the enemy lies in wait, we are bound by temerity to hesitation?"

André turned and the two men locked eyes, neither willing to yield.

For a moment André felt he would be overcome by his anger—when suddenly his vision flashed with a bright light, and he felt a sense of clarity that he had not experienced in years. It was as if a thick fog had lifted, and his mind was calm. "Marcel, I admire your readiness to face danger, but now you must go carry out your orders."

Moreau's horse pawed the ground and bucked in agitation. He grimaced, baring his teeth. A few seconds passed until he shook his head with frustration; turning his horse, he rode off to the rear of the formation.

A minute later the three riders emerged from the trees into the fields below. André, relieved to see them alive, rode forward to meet them.

"Sir." Corporal Laporte reined in before André; both horse and rider were out of breath. "We've just spotted fifty to a hundred men, in coats of gray and black, waiting on either side of the road, set in an ambush formation."

André's vindication was curtailed by the cold realization that the squadron was in danger. They had been betrayed by their hussar comrades. He looked into the tree line. "How far were they?"

"It weren't far at all, sir," the corporal replied. "Maybe a mile?"

"Were you seen?"

"To tell truthful, sir, I don't know. We left without hearing any disturbance from them."

"All right, well done. You have saved lives today."

The corporal beamed, but the surge of pride was short-lived. Out of the forest came a blood-curdling call. A loud cheer followed, and the din of hundreds of hoofbeats shook the trees. André turned his horse, motioning for the troopers to follow. "It's time to go!"

As he galloped back up the hill, André stole a look back and his heart sank. Emerging from the forest in great numbers, the enemy swarmed like bees from a hive, moving with individual autonomy as part of a greater whole. The Prussians they thought defeated had returned. He spurred his horse on faster.

"That son of a whore betrayed us!" Moreau shouted as André rode past.

"I know! We have to get out of here. We can deal with him after!"

André led them back down the road they had traveled with the hussars. Moreau and Mazzarello brought up the rear of the formation, glancing back from time to time to make sure they were out of range of the enemy, who now swarmed over the hilltop. As the squadron descended into a small hollow and splashed across a stream, André considered the possibility of Carnassier and his hussars lying in wait for them as they fled back to the castle stronghold. It seemed unlikely, but he did not want to chance being caught between two groups of hostile cavalry—they'd be trapped and destroyed in minutes.

When the squadron emerged from the hollow and had reached level terrain, André wrenched his horse sharply to the right, through a wooded thicket and toward the hills and open ground beyond. If they were to be forced into a fight, occupying the high ground would give them a better chance of survival. The horses snorted in exhaustion; André knew they would not be able to evade their enemy indefinitely.

The vantage point from the hill gave a clear view of the surrounding countryside. André looked through his spyglass toward the road but did not see anything. Mazzarello rode up beside him. They both knew the trouble they were in. The troopers looked at the two men expectantly. "What are you waiting for, a fucking invitation?" the sergeant-major bellowed at them, agitated, his Italian accent surfacing. "Dismount and get ready to kill the devils!"

A tense minute passed in silence as the troopers dismounted and prepared to fight on foot. André strained his ears for the sound of hoofbeats, imagining that he heard the sound of fifes. There was no sign of the enemy, but nor were his ears deceiving him. Those *were* fifes.

One of his men called out, "Look! Sir, behind you!"

Moving slowly along the hill opposite their own was a massive body of cavalry, infantry, and what appeared to be a large baggage train of supplies. André nearly cried out in astonishment. He scanned for several moments, looking for a familiar tricolor or regimental standard. He thought he recognized one flag—a red crown resting atop an opened red banner, two angels holding a coat of arms showing two white eagles on either corner. It was the Godło, the coat of arms of Poland. André laughed aloud, then crossed himself.

Signaling for Major Moreau to follow him, he rode to meet a group of horsemen who were now heading in their direction. They must have seen the squadron's standard, for they did not appear alarmed or wary as they approached. Four riders reined their steeds a few feet from André and Moreau, the leader holding his palm in a gesture of peace. The three others held long lances.

"*Francuski?*" the unarmed rider asked in a deep voice.

"Yes, French," André replied. "Napoleon Bonaparte," he added, uttering the two most well-known words on the continent.

"*Niech Bóg błogosławił* Bonaparte!" the man replied. His three lancers echoed his words. "Napoleon is good friend." He jerked his thumb toward the main body of troops. "You come."

André turned to Moreau, who looked equally astonished.

"We're safe for the time being. I will gather some information from whoever commands this group. Look after the men. I won't be gone long."

Moreau nodded, eyeing the Polish lancers as they rode back to their legion. André followed the four men, riding past hundreds of marching infantrymen who eyed him with curiosity. The escort halted among a group of a dozen mounted officers arranged in a semicircle, one of them looking out over the valley with a spyglass.

The officer who had escorted André spoke to a man he assumed to be the leader. "*Masz rację Generale, są francuskie.*"

The man turned, lowering his spyglass and closing it slowly. "Welcome, soldier." He urged his horse forward. "Who are you?"

"I am Lieutenant-Colonel André Valiere, commanding the Seventeenth Dragoons of the Grand Armée of France."

"It is privilege to make acquaintance, monsieur. I am General Dabrowski, in command of legion you see here." He motioned at the soldiers marching on either side of the small assembly. "I hope you come to my country as friend."

"General, we have not come as foes, I assure you. My squadron has found itself cut off from our army corps, and we are trying to make our way back."

"How long you been away from your army?"

"For four days, general."

General Dabrowski burst out in a deep belly laugh. "I think Emperor Napoleon come to our country to help *us*, and now *we* saving *you*!" André grinned respectfully while the entire group laughed at their general's translation.

"Please, Monsieur Lieutenant-Colonel, do not feel insult. We find exchange of fortunes humorous. I'm surprised you been out here, alone, four days and do not have your throats cut by Cossacks." Another round of laughter. André nodded in humble appreciation at the truth of the general's statement; he, too, was surprised.

André informed Dabrowski of the presence of Prussian cavalry in the region, and that they had nearly been ambushed just minutes prior.

"Colonel, in Poland we surprised when we *don't* have enemy riding through our lands. As we get closer to Napoleon, we expect more. Do not fear, our uhlans are worthy of trust your emperor has given."

André had read in a journal that Foreign Minister Talleyrand claimed Poland to be a nation "unworthy of the life of a single French soldier." Even so, he was relieved by the man's confidence.

General Dabrowski invited André and his men to join their formation while they marched north toward Poznan; the squadron could reunite with the main body of Napoleon's army when they found them. Unlike the unease he felt while with the hussars, André felt only relief to be back with friendly troops, even if they were foreign and spoke a language that sounded unbelievably strange.

That evening, after attending the commander's council—translated from Polish to French by Captain Falkowski, the man who had first greeted him—André slept soundly for the first time in several days.

Citizen Jothan,

On his previous visit to Paris, Monsieur SC passed into the halls of the palace. A word from the secretary informed me that he paid a visit to Monsieur J. What was discussed you will no doubt learn in due course, though I advise you to keep a more watchful eye on your man, as I should not be learning of this from my secretary. Any movement in public is your care; do not fail to follow him into a place of such public importance again. I am sending you a ticket to the opera that will come courtesy of Monsieur J. See that it is delivered to monsieur's offices and that he has a pleasant evening.

—Cardinal

TEN MONTHS EARLIER

CHAPTER 8

Paris, France

December 1805

The St. Clair family passed the final hours of their bumpy journey from Marseille with yawns and naps. When Jean-Luc woke, he felt the carriage laboring its way up a hill. As it reached the crest, he peered out and, despite his grogginess, felt an unmistakable stirring in his chest, for over the horizon was the great cityscape of Paris. Clearly discernible were the grand domes of Les Invalides and the Panthéon looming over their respective quarters like islands in an urban sea. Standing proudly over the Seine were the famous towers of Notre-Dame, having survived the ransacking of the Revolution, unlike many less fortunate cathedrals and houses of worship. Despite a surge of conflicting emotions, Jean-Luc could not help but smile. He was returning to Paris.

The finest houses for new officials and friends of the administration were located in the western quarters of the city. Using the credit given to his office from Monsieur Joseph Bonaparte, Jean-Luc had secured a modest yet charming residence on Rue de Grenelle, on the left bank in the Faubourg Saint-Germain.

His new office would be on the Rue Sainte-Anne, a stone's throw from the Tuileries. As a former public advocate of some reputation, at least among those who had survived the Revolution, he was informed that his day-to-day tasks would be to consult with the administration's legal teams, fine-tuning and implementing the new civil code; laws that many simply referred to as the Napoleonic code.

His first few weeks were uneventful. There was little work, and his busiest hours seemed to be spent across the street at a tavern drinking wine with his new colleagues. He did not wish for this pace to last indefinitely; his mind needed work like a horse needed to run. Still, he had ample time to furnish his new house and arrange for the hiring of two domestics for part-time cooking, cleaning, and care for his children. The end of his first month brought an unexpected surprise: an invitation to join Joseph Bonaparte's retinue at the opera in the Boulevard Montmartre.

After a surprisingly arduous walk uphill from Saint-Germain, Jean-Luc arrived at the Théâtre des Variétés alongside a swelling crowd. Presenting his benefactor's pass, Jean-Luc was privileged to skirt the crowd and walk directly inside. Recalling his discourteous treatment months prior at the Palais-Royal, this was especially satisfying.

The crowded lobby smelled of tobacco smoke and sweat, as the male-only crowd engaged each other in a competition of who could speak the loudest. Jean-Luc peered around the assembly but did not recognize any faces, and he felt the familiar sensation of being a stranger in a room of men who seemed to be lifelong friends.

When he reached the mezzanine three flights up from the lobby, an unexpected sight greeted him: a crowd of nearly all women dressed in beautiful and rather revealing dresses and skirts. It did not take him long to understand what he was seeing; these were the courtesans of the sponsors and patrons of this theater sent to mingle and find wealthy new clientele. He noticed the curious gaze of a dozen or so of these tall and immaculately made-up Parisian beauties, causing him to blush and smile politely as he moved on toward his suite.

At the box, his colleagues were already seated. They politely acknowledged his arrival and resumed their conversations. Jean-Luc surveyed the hall below; though he had attended theater in Marseille once or twice, the gallery of that city's auditorium was not nearly so grand. Yet, in spite of the magnificence of the setting, Jean-Luc's attention quickly wandered from the performance. He found little amusement in Italian opera; even his colleagues seemed to have eyes only for the wives and mistresses reclining in the adjacent suites. After sitting, discomfited, for over an hour, he admitted to himself that he felt a tinge of disappointment at not having seen Joseph Bonaparte. He checked his timepiece—would he not be better served by returning home for a restful night's sleep? Fighting back a yawn, he decided to remain in his seat, hoping that something might happen to make this evening worth his while.

As the performance's final act approached its long-awaited crescendo, the door to the suite opened. Two figures sat down behind him. He heard the whispered voices of two women and chided himself for foolishly hoping that it might have been Monsieur Bonaparte. *Harlots*, he thought, dismissively. Straightening his coat, he moved to leave when one of the women whispered loudly, "Will this infernal racket never end?"

Jean-Luc smiled in grim amusement. "My thoughts exactly."

The women who had spoken wore a bizarre, gold decoration on her head. "It's called a turban, monsieur," she said, in answer to his stare. "And I wore it on a lark."

The lady's companion clasped a hand to her cheek. "Oh, Pierre, you devil. I knew I'd find you here." Rushing up from her seat she crossed the small suite to join one of Jean-Luc's colleagues.

"Well, there *she* goes," the seated woman said. Beneath her turban she wore a black dress with a low neckline of plaited gold that matched the color of her headdress. A long and slender nose extended under a pair of dark brown eyes. "Would you care to keep a lady company?"

Perhaps it was her charming smile or the unfamiliar but welcome offer of companionship. He took the vacated seat beside her. Taking her offered hand with no pretext of charm he said, "How do you do, madame?"

"I'm better now that you've joined me, monsieur," she replied. "Watching the conclusion of this spectacle by myself was an unpleasant prospect."

"I could hardly agree more, madame." His companion returned his smile. "Pardon my manners; my name is St. Clair."

"It is a pleasure to meet you, St. Clair. We seem to agree on the disagreeableness of Italian opera."

Jean-Luc laughed a little too loudly. His colleagues in front turned their heads in disapproval. "I am grateful to have been invited," he said, whispering. "But I do believe that the joys of the theatre are lost on me."

Glancing briefly down at the stage, she returned her attention to him. "You don't appear to be a soldier, and yet you bear yourself well. You're certainly dressed better than these sycophantic dandies," she said without muffling her voice in the slightest. "So, what do you do?"

"At present," Jean-Luc said, flattered by her compliment, "I am doing consulting work for the administration, implementing its legal code."

"Important work. Though I am not sure how interested those Bonapartes are in consulting with anyone. Tell me, are you occupied this weekend?" she asked, leaning in. "Say, Saturday?"

At this close proximity Jean-Luc noticed her perfume and rouged lips. His eyes stole a quick glance at her ample bosom. She was not conventionally beautiful, but she had an indefinable quality that struck him as rather unusual, exotic even.

"I had thought of bringing my son and daughter to Tivoli, or Jardin des Plantes in the afternoon."

He observed her slight hesitation upon hearing of his children; though this was not entirely unexpected. Most unmarried women met this news with some variation of surprise or disappointment.

"I do love children, I should admit," she said, and quickly dispelled his doubts. "How long have you been married?"

He breathed a sigh of relief. "I married many years ago. But she is gone." He held up his wedding ring. "I wear this to honor her memory. She was more dear to me than I care to forget. Now my children are what I live for."

The woman placed one hand on his and another to her chest. "I must apologize monsieur, what a foolish question to have asked. It is no business of mine, forgive me."

"No, madame, please." Jean-Luc waved a hand. "There is nothing to apologize for."

Mercifully, she turned her attention to the stage, allowing Jean-Luc's painful thoughts to pass. After a moment he turned back to her. "I don't believe I've gotten your name, madame."

She looked at him with a smile. "My name is Isabella. Isabella Maduro."

CHAPTER 9

Oder River, Prussia
October 1806

T he third night of their march north with the Poles was cold and clear. An almost full moon lit the camp with an ethereal glow. The dragoons groomed their horses and set up their bivouac. Word had spread from the Poles that they were no more than a day's ride from one of the corps of Napoleon's Grand Armée. Excitement passed from campfire to campfire at the prospect of glimpsing the emperor, and young Polish soldiers sought out the French dragoons, asking for language lessons and inquiring as to whether French women traveled with the army.

André found Moreau sitting beside a fire with Sergeant-major Mazzarello and Captain Falkowski. He looked unusually lighthearted this evening, saying something that made the Polish captain laugh out loud. André interrupted their chat with a request to speak privately, then led Moreau to a spot of open ground where they were out of earshot of anyone else.

"Major Moreau, I regret to say what I am about to say, but your conduct while serving as executive officer of this squadron has left me no choice." Moreau's jaw clenched, and he stared at André with obvious displeasure. "Your occasions of ill-discipline, challenges to my authority, and overall lack of soldierly bearing make it so that we are unable to function with full efficiency." André was unsurprised that the taciturn major had nothing to say. "I readily admit that I have made mistakes while in command, and I take ownership of them. But I will not tolerate insubordination from an individual who puts his own despondency before the consideration of those he must lead. I'm sorry, major, I cannot help you if you are unwilling to help yourself."

After a lengthy silence, Moreau cleared his throat. "May I speak freely?" André nodded.

"Truly, sir, I don't give a goddamn what you think of me. You recognize in me all the qualities of a villain, and I admit you may be right. But blundering into an ambush was not my doing. It was not I who failed *your* troopers." It was André's turn to be silent. "Lieutenant-Colonel Valiere," Moreau continued, his lips pursed in a sneer, "by trusting Carnassier it was *you* who put our men in danger. If you possessed any qualities of an officer, you would have done what needed to be done and gotten us out of there. You have not failed *me* sir, you've failed…"

"Major," André cut him off, "in the best interests of this squadron, and for your own benefit, I have decided to initiate your transfer to another squadron."

Moreau scoffed. "Do what you wish, sir. I am here to complete the only true errand left to me. I've avenged myself with nine successful duels." He tapped the sword at his belt. "Three remain. *Then* I will be done with this war and the life of a soldier forever."

André looked at his subordinate, struggling to comprehend his words. "You've killed *nine* men?"

"Only those that offered the first offense; a few may have survived their wounds. Whatever the case, only three remain."

"What could possibly drive a man to do such a thing?"

"That is none of your damned business."

"For God's sake," André muttered, "you're worse than I thought."

Moreau turned to walk away. "A reprimand from you is hardly a stain on my honor."

André gripped Moreau's coat, jerking him backwards. "Don't think you can insult me and walk away, major."

Moreau shoved André with all his might, nearly dropping him to the ground. Recovering, André grabbed Moreau's collar and pulled him closer, so they were face to face; a fist thumped into his gut, and his breath left him. André staggered, nearly keeling over. Moreau's look of disgust faded as André rounded on him, faster than Moreau expected, and smashed a fist into the left side of his face. The force of the blow was so severe that the major toppled to the ground. André stood over him, crimson with a brutal rage. Then, recovering his senses, he touched the man with his boot, checking for movement.

"Marcel." He knelt down next to him. "Marcel, are you all right?"

With startling quickness, Moreau sprang from the ground, knocking André off balance and onto the grass. Seizing the element of surprise, he landed several blows onto André's chest, knocking the wind out of him again. With great effort, André swung his legs around and toppled Moreau so that they both lay on the grass. He blocked a punch with his forearm and landed two or three strong punches until Moreau again went limp.

This time André was too exhausted to examine his opponent, and he lay still on the ground. Moreau did not stir. After another a minute or so, André lifted himself to his feet, groaning with the effort. He took another glance at his subordinate, who remained motionless.

Limping like a wounded animal, André walked several paces to regain his breath. He returned to find Moreau sitting upright, his back resting on the wheel of a wagon from the baggage train. His nose and mouth were caked in blood. He looked at André but did not speak.

Groaning again, André sat on the grass several feet away. As he glanced at his subordinate, he saw something that reminded him of his two sons; the eyes of a frightened boy. The image forming in his mind's eye of his children and wife disappeared when Moreau's voice wrenched him back to the present.

"The first day I saw the sea was the first day I killed a man."

Crouching down in front of Marcel, André held a cup of water to his lips, allowing the man to take a few slow sips. Moreau nodded, and André took the cup away.

"We had been marching for nearly two weeks," Moreau continued, sounding raspy. "We were tired and hungry. That's when the rebels fell upon us."

"In the Vendée?" André asked, his breath slowly returning to him.

Moreau nodded, his bloodied face and large eyes reflecting the bright sheen of the full moon. "Perhaps ten miles from Nantes. I was walking in a field less than a hundred yards from my battalion, looking for berries to forage. The hedgerow to my right erupted in smoke and flame. I fell to the ground, thinking it was the end of the world, or at least of my life. I had just turned nineteen, and I had never been in combat before. I saw the right flank of my battalion drop like wheat before a scythe. Ten or twenty men dead—instantly. I didn't know how I was still alive, but I was. From the smoking hedge came a dozen men in gray coats. Some were armed with farmers' tools; axes, pitchforks, maybe a musket. Others were not armed at all. They were twenty yards away, and I knew I was dead. I did the only thing I could think to do: I rose to my knees, aimed my musket, and fired at the man closest to me. Through the smoke I saw him drop into the grass, and his startled comrades fled back into the hedgerows."

A soldier leading a horse walked past several feet away, unaware of the two battered officers sitting in the grass nearby.

Moreau cleared his throat. "My shock at this first engagement was so strong that I did not feel anything—no pride, no guilt, just an immense gratitude to be alive. Once we had evacuated our wounded, we finished our march and bivouacked on a hill overlooking the sea. I sat there, watching the sun go over the horizon…glimpsing into the endless void for the second time that day."

André cleared his own throat. "I was twenty-two when I first killed a man. At Valmy. I've never forgotten the feeling."

Moreau eyed his commander for several moments. "Did you kill him with your fists?" He touched his nose and winced. "Christ, sir."

André laughed aloud, then grimaced as he rubbed his bruised ribs.

Moreau exhaled slowly. "It's not a feeling one easily forgets. But that day was a skirmish, it wasn't battle. The next month was a nightmare from hell. Something that I've never spoken of to anyone outside my company. Those few that survived." He shuddered involuntarily, before continuing. "The orders came to our battalion to put an end to the royalists remaining in our sector. We had long since chased the armed rebels out of our operational area, and there were few men left to fight. So, the orders came down from our generals: we were to remove anything and anyone that could offer even a remote threat of further uprisings, including those General Carrier referred to as 'brigands-to-be.'"

Moreau lifted his knees to his chest and gripped them, shivering as if from the cold. "After we executed several hundred rebels, we then went to a church, where two hundred of the city's children sat in pews, awaiting their release. They did not know what was to happen next. Some of them held hands as we marched them a mile to the river, others sang songs to cheer up their younger siblings. They were afraid but hopeful that they would be reunited with their parents, who had been shot in a field across from the church. We took them on a path round, avoiding the sight of the slain. When we reached the banks of the river, we set them on four or five large barges. They were packed in tightly, and the older ones, sensing what was happening, began to—they began to scream. Their fear started a panic in the younger children, who cried out for their parents. As they cried, we released the boats out into the river—and sank them. Their hands were bound, so most sank almost instantly. The ones who could swim struggled to stay afloat. Our more merciful generals, in their disgust, ordered us to put them out of their misery. I fired above their heads. I was unable to shoot a screaming child. I simply watched them drown." Moreau's bloody cheeks were streaked with tears, and he dropped his head between his knees. He remained still for several minutes. "The bodies floated down the Loire to neighboring towns, where another regiment recovered them. Some of the soldiers, out of pity, buried the children. Crosses were not allowed over their graves, by order of General Carrier."

A cold chill passed over André. His mouth hung open, but he was too stunned to speak.

"Perhaps worse than the killings," Moreau continued, "and the circling buzzards ready to feed on their remains, were the cries of gratitude from our admirers—reveling in the slaughter of their neighbors, of children with innocent souls. The congratulations from our political leaders, nodding their approval as we marched past. Mounted on his horse sat General Carrier, like some chieftain watching over his demonic host. If God exists, he abandoned us in that hour."

Overwhelmed, André stared at Moreau. "Christ in heaven." He stood, removed his coat, and placed it around the shoulders of his bloodied executive officer. Moreau wrapped the coat tightly around his shoulders. André sat alongside him, his eyes lost in the distance. There were no words left to be spoken.

NINE MONTHS EARLIER

CHAPTER 10

Paris, France

January 1806

Two days after the opera, a courier dropped a dispatch from the Tuileries on Jean-Luc's desk. It was the type of assignment he'd been waiting for. The briefing was assigned to a colleague on regular retainer, but the man had been called to the provinces, so it fell to Jean-Luc instead.

During the short walk across the Seine to the law courts of the Palais de Justice, he felt his heart beat with an anticipatory thrill that he had not felt in some time. He and another lawyer from the bureau entered the building and took their seats before the judge in the role of prosecutors for the state. Once again, Jean-Luc St. Clair found himself in a courtroom, albeit one less crowded than the days of the Revolution.

Seated across the aisle, the defendant, Monsieur Cruchet, eyed Jean-Luc and his partner with a combination of curiosity and disdain.

Monsieur Cruchet, from Montmartre, owned a number of taverns and *guinguettes*—shops outside the city barriers where wine was taxed and sold at much lower rates than within. Cruchet was the supposed leader of a smuggling ring and had allegedly used his legal establishments as cover to traffic wine barrels into the city to be sold discreetly at untaxed rates, using an elaborate network of tunnels and corrupt guards. Through the opening statement of his defense counsel, Cruchet claimed that his businesses had been crippled by the administration's taxes and that only by selling his product at vastly reduced rates could he compete with other, larger purveyors of Paris's red lifeblood.

Privately, Jean-Luc empathized with the man's situation; nevertheless, when given his turn to speak, he pressed on the extravagant process Cruchet had developed to evade the emperor's laws.

"Monsieur," the defendant responded, "my trade is to sell my product in as fair and honest a way as your laws will allow. It doesn't much matter to me personally who pays me—or for that matter who governs the land—as long as they are just in their treatment of us common folk. But these taxes are so high that an honest merchant is better off not selling his product in Paris at all, if he wishes to see any profit. Those of us small folk who wish to sell it within the barrier have to get 'round the tariffs. None of us wants any trouble—our time of Revolution is past—but at present I'm surely not the only man chapped with the administration's bloody taxes."

Jean-Luc listened attentively. After a thoughtful silence he held his hands up. "I admire your candor and your principles, monsieur, but you've circumvented the law in the execution of your trade."

"As I've said, Monsie—"

"Furthermore, you've done so to sell wine at illegally low prices."

"If you call them prices your Napoleon sets *legal*," Cruchet retorted.

"At *illegally* low prices," Jean-Luc persisted, his voice growing impatient, "to drunkards who destroy not only themselves, but their means of employment, their families, and all manner of relationships. Do you deny any of this?"

"A man must make a living," the defendant answered unflinchingly. "And I know plenty that make theirs in worse ways."

"Indeed," Jean-Luc replied. "But in a society of laws one's living must adhere to certain principles, ethical and moral, elsewise it will inevitably result in professional and personal ruin."

"So then, you would lock me in jail, leaving my family and children with no means of survival?"

"I would see you obey the laws of our land that exist to—"

"Damn your laws," Cruchet fired back. "They don't exist to serve the people; they simply help the rich fatten their already-bulging pockets. Tell me, *lawyer*, how many days of toil and labor have you ever given yourself to? Or is that just the lot of society's humblest and most wretched members? Don't lecture to me of your laws and morals when you've never spent a day struggling to live in dark streets. Men with silver tongues talk of society's troubles while men with blistered and bloodied hands work to keep that society living."

Jean-Luc was taken aback by the force of Cruchet's words. There was little he could say in reply as he found himself in silent agreement with the man's sentiments. He quickly regained his footing, however, and adjusted his focus so that he could keep one eye on the judge.

"I respect your sentiment," he conceded, "but the fact remains we are not here today to debate the *merits* of the law, nor am I here to answer your questions. You will answer mine. And before I ask my final question, I would remind the persons assembled here and our honored judge who presides, that *you*, monsieur, find yourself here because you are accused of coordinating a ring of conspirators out of Faubourg Saint-Denis who are smuggling wine, spirits, and other taxable consumer products into this city. The evidence presented by the administration has been submitted to our judge, so I have but one question to ask you, and I sincerely beg you to consider the consequences of your answer, for none of my superiors within this administration wish to mete out punishments that are unduly severe. Monsieur, do you plead guilty or not guilty to these accusations?"

The man offered a defiant sneer. "You know I plead guilty."

"Very well." Jean-Luc felt a quiet relief. "Allow me to confer with my associate briefly, and we will offer our recommendation for sentence."

Jean-Luc leaned down to his associate, Thiery, who declared that his instructions in the event of a guilty plea were to offer a midlevel sentence appropriate to the crime. Jean-Luc nodded in agreement, but, as he looked over at Cruchet, he observed his defense attorney lean forward and sneer at Jean-Luc, a row of yellow teeth and flushed cheeks revealing malevolent scorn. It was a barely perceptible expression, yet it made Cruchet's words echo in Jean-Luc's ears, and he found himself unable to preserve his sympathy for the man. *Tell me, lawyer, how many days of toil and labor have you ever given yourself to?* With a pat on Thiery's shoulder, Jean-Luc approached the judge, who asked, "What is your proposed sentence then?"

"Your Honor, I propose the maximum sentence for trafficking of contraband into the city. Those who circumvent the emperor's laws to enrich themselves do not deserve our leniency; I propose a fine of five hundred francs and a prison sentence of no less than five years."

After a brief moment of stunned silence, a loud clamor rose across the room. Jean-Luc ignored the angry stare of Monsieur Cruchet.

"What are you *doing*?" Thiery whispered.

"That's enough." The judge rang a bell for silence, which succeeded in quieting the small but vocal crowd. He made a few notes on a scroll of paper and sighed before putting a hand up as Cruchet's counsel stood to speak and motioned for both lawyers of the prosecution to come closer. When they both stood before him, the judge cleared his throat. "No."

"Your Honor?" said Jean-Luc.

"No," the judge repeated. "I will not sentence this man, who is plainly guilty, to five years in prison. I have seen four cases of this kind within the last six months and do not wish to see any more, but I find five years and a fine of five hundred francs excessive. I will hear your amended offer for punishment now."

"Your Honor," Thiery answered, "forgive my partner for his brief lapse of judgment; he is new to Paris and is only now learning how we manage our affairs. The state is prepared to offer the punishment of three months in prison with a probationary period of restricted liquor sales of one year, with bail for immediate release set at one hundred francs."

The judge wrote the new offer into his ledger and looked to the defense counsel. "Does the defense accept the terms offered?"

"Your Honor, the defense accepts."

Jean-Luc dropped his eyes with a vague sense of embarrassment.

"Very well, do I have anyone present at this time to offer bail for the accused?" the judge asked. "Bail set at one thousand. You gentlemen make your way to the clerk of court's office to arrange the imbursement." The judge rose. "This court is closed. Bail set and paid at one thousand francs."

Jean-Luc descended the steps of the Palais de Justice alongside Thiery, who walked at a brisk pace. He glanced at Jean-luc with a disappointed frown. "You were doing so well, St. Clair, and then you nearly scuttled us with that ridiculous proposal!"

Jean-Luc smiled sheepishly. "Good thing you were there to save the day."

"I don't know what you were thinking." He shook his head and scrutinized Jean-Luc, who no longer wore the scowl with which he had departed the courthouse. "Wait a moment," he said, squinting as he gazed at Jean-Luc. "That was done on purpose—wasn't it?"

Jean-Luc returned his gaze with a wry smile. "Perhaps."

Thiery exhaled. "What, so you decided to pick a fight? What for, and with whom?"

Jean-Luc looked back at the courthouse. "That remains to be seen."

Thiery shook his head, clearly still puzzled. "Anyway, I'm going for a glass of wine and then back to work, care to join me?"

Jean-Luc declined, claiming a desire to walk off the morning's events on his own.

Thiery sighed. "You know the others at the office are asking why you never join us for drinks or cards. Some of them mutter that you consider them beneath you."

Jean-Luc shrugged, remembering how they had largely ignored him when he'd first arrived, and only took a liking to him when it became known he was an associate of Joseph Bonaparte. "Let them think what they like, I have work to do."

With a rueful grin, Thiery bid him farewell and departed through the courtyard's elaborate gate.

When his colleague was out of sight, Jean-Luc glanced back at the courthouse and noticed someone scurrying down the steps to catch up with him. The approaching man, although short, walked with his chest slightly puffed out, his gaunt shoulders swaying from side to side. He clutched a bundle of papers in his left hand and held a black riding hat in the other. His thinning hair was pulled back into a short ponytail, and he tilted his chin back slightly as he halted before Jean-Luc.

"Well, monsieur, you made a fine attempt at destroying my client's future," he exclaimed, getting straight to his point. "Allow me to introduce myself; I am Pierre-Yves Gagnon."

"How do you do?" Jean-Luc shook his hand, recognizing the yellow teeth and red face. "I am Jean-Luc St Clair. I presume that you are Monsieur Cruchet's counsel."

"You presume mistakenly," the shorter man corrected him. "I am what you might call his…patron. Monsieur Cruchet does not work for me directly, though I own eight boarding houses and taverns in the Faubourg Saint-Denis alone. As a former member of the Council of Five Hundred, I often find myself in a position to defend the livelihoods of those who, by way of petty mistakes, find themselves run afoul of the current administration."

"Petty mistakes like orchestrating smuggling rings across the city and bribing gendarmes for their cooperation?" Jean-Luc asked.

"Smuggling is one of the many unfortunate aftereffects of the administration's heavy-handed fiscal policies."

"Perhaps so," Jean-Luc responded. "But if that is the case, I suggest you take up your concerns with one of the emperor's representatives, monsieur, instead of using criminal proxies to needle his government."

Gagnon fidgeted with the hat held beneath his right arm. "You work for the administration, St. Clair, so clearly you're not stupid. And you seem to regard yourself as someone of *importance*, so I won't waste your time listing all the reasons our petitions have gone unanswered by a man recently crowned emperor by his holiness the pope, a man victorious across the battlefields of Europe and the Near East and who is currently drawing up plans for an invasion of England. But if we're to be frank, then I must tell you I find your *eagerness* to enforce unjust policies in the name of 'obstructing crime' to be rather distasteful."

Jean-Luc held out his arms. "I do not set the administration's policy, monsieur. I merely carry out the assignments I've been given."

Gagnon nodded slowly. "Well, St. Clair, I'll be seeing more of you, I'm sure."

Offering a curt smile, he turned on his heels and departed, quickly disappearing out of view across the Pont au Change.

"That did not take very long," Jean-Luc said to himself with a sly smile. He then walked through the gate, turned onto the Rue de la Barillerie and left the Palais.

CHAPTER 11

Paris, France
January 1806

The following morning was a bright and beautiful Saturday, and Jean-Luc decided he would take his children for a walk in the Jardin des Plantes, across the river from the ruins of the Bastille. When they arrived at the park that afternoon, Mathieu and Marie quickly hurried off to explore the grounds while Jean-Luc bought a cup of hot wine and sat on a bench. He recalled the events of the past few days, and how a note had arrived earlier from Joseph Bonaparte; it conveyed a congratulatory message for his day in court. Though he'd said nothing of it to his colleagues, Jean-Luc felt great relief to have escaped his first court appearance unscathed and without censure from his boss.

Several minutes passed, Jean-Luc lost in his thoughts, until he noticed the arrival of a lovely woman. She approached with a shorter man leading her by the arm—or was she leading him? He walked with a pronounced limp, leaning his weight on his right side, like an invalid. It was the woman from the opera.

"What a joy to see you again, Monsieur St. Clair." She smiled charmingly at Jean-Luc as he stood to greet her.

"It is certainly my pleasure to see you as well, Mademoiselle Maduro."

"Please, call me Isabella," she chided him, extending her hand. He gallantly kissed it. Then, noticing her companion's stare, Jean-Luc smiled, offering his own hand. "And how do you do, sir? My name is Jean-Luc—"

"This is my brother, Camille. If he could manage, I'm sure he would tell you how charmed he is. Isn't that right, Camille?"

The young man twisted his left leg slightly and lowered a shoulder to give the impression of a bow, which Jean-Luc took to be a sign of greeting. He nodded in return.

"Isn't this a pleasant surprise indeed? You've found us in the middle of a family excursion." Jean-Luc turned in the direction his two children had run off and saw they had both climbed a tree. Mathieu was holding his sister by one arm as he dangled precariously from one of the higher branches.

"Mathieu!" Jean-Luc called out, excusing himself momentarily. "Let your sister down and come away from there." He moved to help his son climb down but was preempted when Mathieu set his sister on a branch, lifted his feet over his head and spun over in a somersault, landing both feet on the ground. Although momentarily stunned at his son's agility, Jean-Luc quietly scolded him for endangering his sister. He ushered the two of them over to Isabella and her brother and made the introductions.

"How lovely," Isabella stated, leaning down to shake both of their hands. "You are quite nimble, Mathieu!" Turning back to Jean-Luc she said, "Camille and I have been invited to Rosny-sous-Bois for a demonstration of the new semaphore telegraph line that has been installed there. A short carriage ride outside of the city." She put on a pair of white gloves she'd been carrying. "It would be lovely if you were to join us; it could be a lovely little picnic!"

Jean-Luc looked down at his children. "It sounds quite interesting, but I think perhaps—"

"Come, a bit of fresh country air is always a good thing for us city folk. Mathieu, Marie, what do you think?"

"Yes!" Mathieu cried. "Papa, please can we go? We might get to see soldiers!"

Jean-Luc shrugged, smiling at Isabella in agreement. "Oh, all right." He motioned for her to lead the way.

The carriage veered from Rue Saint-Antoine onto Rue de Montreuil and soon passed through the Barrière du Trône. From there it left the city and passed into a pleasant expanse of farms and rolling hills. Traffic on the road was light, and Jean-Luc felt his mood buoyed by the tranquility of the countryside.

He turned to his companion. "So, madame, tell me about you; Maduro? Is that Spanish or Portuguese?"

"Monsieur, you've found us out," Isabella replied with mock defensiveness. "I do, in fact, originally come from Spain. Catalonia, just outside of Girona."

"A Catalan!" Jean-Luc smiled with genuine enthusiasm. "I've never been, but I've heard it is beautiful, especially Barcelona."

Isabella shrugged. "My family never liked it. As secularists we were not especially admired in our homeland. And when your little Revolution burst into life, we were fairly ostracized by the court."

"By the court?" Jean-Luc did not hide his surprise. "So you come from a family of reputation."

"We came from wealthy bourgeois merchant stock, though not ennobled. The higher families of Catalonia respected my grandfather, but my father was a stubborn fool, who saw the king as a pious and pompous impostor. I was loyal and devoted to him, but because my older brother and sister shared his political inclinations, he left the bulk of his estate to them."

She brought her thumb and index finger together, sniffing a small clump of tobacco into her nose. Jean-Luc had never taken the habit of snuff, though he had to admit it seemed less invasive than the great clouds of smoke that lingered in common taverns and inns. He politely declined Isabella's offer of a pinch.

A quarter of an hour later the carriage rolled to a halt at the top of a small hill. To their right was the small village of Rosny-sous-Bois, and beyond that, as far as they could see, were fields, pastures, and verdant copses of oak and birch.

The machine they had come to see was situated on top of a small lookout tower overlooking the surrounding countryside. It consisted of a system of wheels and pulleys attached to a long, flat beam with two alternating arms, which could be twisted to form various shapes. Each of these shapes indicated a letter, and this preset "alphabet" could then be relayed as messages passed from generals in the field to the government in Paris, or vice versa. Each message could be seen by spyglass up to twenty miles away, enabling a message to be passed hundreds of miles in a matter of hours.

Milling about at the foot of the tower were several dozen members of Parisian high society. Women in long, colorful dresses and hats and silk shawls sipped limonade and punch while men wearing fine coats, silk neckties, and long riding boots escorted them around the grounds. Above all, one wished to see and be seen.

Jean-Luc had read of the semaphore lines in the papers; now he held up a hand to shield his eyes as he studied the strange contraption. It looked to him like an insect one might see in a scientist's jar. His attention turned to a man positioned at the front of the assembly, who spoke loudly to the crowd.

"It is my honor and privilege to introduce to all of you our distinguished guest." Behind him stood a taller, thinner man with a receding hairline dressed in a blue coat and tight-fitting breeches. "*Mesdames et messieurs*, from the department of Lot-et-Garonne, the honorable Senator Bernard-Germain de Lacépède."

Senator de Lacépède took a step forward, bowing to acknowledge the applause. "I wish to welcome all of you," he declared, "to our newly renovated semaphore tower. This simple instrument behind me is but one of several hundred that comprise a signal chain that reaches from the English Channel all the way to the Mediterranean Sea. Each one of these towers is used to convey vital military dispatches at speeds unheard of in the history of warfare. This system provides us with a distinct advantage over our enemies, and they would no doubt benefit greatly by breaking our codes and learning our secrets. So, you'll forgive me for not translating *directly* what the most recent incoming message conveyed, but I *can* tell you the exciting news that the north-east winds from Boulogne toward d'Outreau have subsided." The audience laughed at the senator's quip. "I can also tell you that this device reduced the length of time to send that message from roughly two days' journey by horseback, to just under three hours." The audience gasped. The senator continued speaking until a man inside the tower began arranging the arms of the semaphore to create a mock message; V-I-V-E-L-E-M-P-E-R-E-U-R was spelled out to rapturous applause.

As the machine contorted its mechanical arms, Jean-Luc turned and looked out beyond the roads, fields, and meadows, feeling as though he were standing on the precipice of a great and miraculous future. The clumsy-looking instrument carried within it limitless potential, a new era of unending possibilities. For now, this "telegraph" would be used to transport messages of war and conquest; but someday a faster, more streamlined machine might traverse great distances conveying more harmonious ideas, shipping goods, perhaps even transporting people themselves. After all, weren't men now rising into the skies in large flying balloons? What else had the human mind in store for the future? He felt a swell of hope, sensing that a new era would someday come when mankind held ever more meaningful and advanced ideas first in its mind, and then later in its hands, changing the story of human civilization.

Jean-Luc's thoughts were interrupted when he noticed one man standing slightly apart from the crowd. He wore a brown coat and black riding hat and seemed to be the only spectator uninterested in the moving arms of the semaphore. When he saw Jean-Luc watching him, the two held each other's eyes a moment too long for comfort.

"Are you all right, Monsieur St. Clair?" Isabella gently touched his arm.

Jean-Luc released his gaze from the man. "Yes, perfectly fine."

"The senator is greeting guests now," Isabella said, pointing to the base of the stone tower. "I would hate for us to miss our celebrated host."

Jean-Luc nodded. Looking back, he saw the man had gone.

They made their way over to Senator de Lacépède, who was chatting with a small group. "Senator, how do you do?" Jean-Luc greeted the man, offering his hand. "My name is St. Clair. I have so many questions. Could I ask you about the effect of weather conditions—"

"Ladies and gentlemen, we do apologize," Senator Lacépède's aide interrupted, "but the Senator has been called to the Tuileries and must be going now. Thank you all very much for attending! Let us send our most fervent hopes and well wishes to our brave soldiers as they prepare to embark to victory!"

With that the two men were ushered into a waiting carriage and sped away, leaving a trail of onlookers.

On the ride home, several miles from the barrier, the carriage came to a sudden halt.

"What have you stopped for, Michel?" Isabella called out to the driver.

"Riders up ahead, madame," the driver replied, pulling the carriage to the side of the road. He hopped down and, a few seconds later, the man's dust-stained face popped into view outside the open window of the carriage.

"Monsieur, madame, there's no cause for alarm, but coming along this way is a sight your young ones might want to see."

"Oh?" Isabella asked. "What might that be?"

"Come on out and see for yourself." The driver opened the door opposite the road. As they made their way to the front of the carriage, they saw a tremendous cloud of dust billowing in their direction. "Thought the little lad might want to see some of the emperor's finest horsemen up close. Think I saw one of the Eagles held up there as well."

Jean-Luc squinted into the setting evening sun. Emerging from the billowing dust was a cluster of riders with bright coats and glittering helmets. As the cavalrymen rode closer, Jean-Luc watched his son climb up to the driver's perch, and from there the boy looked out over a large body of approaching horsemen. The cuirassiers, distinguishable by their polished and shining breastplates, passed the carriage at a slow and deliberate pace; the drumming of hooves and clinking of weapons and equipment against the breastplates caused a low cacophony. Some of the helmeted men turned and looked down at the family, each offering a gleaming smile, especially to the lovely Isabella, who smiled back at the sight of so many tall men on tall horses.

Michel held his arm up and pointed. A few seconds later Jean-Luc noticed what had caught the man's attention. Looming over the lumbering mass of horses, soldiers and armor passed one of the hallowed symbols of the Grand Armée: the Imperial Eagle.

Based on the Roman *Aquila*, the Eagles symbolized and glorified the various regions of the French Empire. Napoleon encouraged his soldiers to defend them in battle at all costs. As the bright golden bird of prey with its wings outstretched passed, Jean-Luc could not deny that he felt a swell of pride in his chest. He looked up at Mathieu. His son's eyes were transfixed, his arm reaching out as if to touch the symbol. Beneath his patriotic pride Jean-Luc felt a chill run down his spine; his boy was absolutely entranced by the sight of the horsemen.

A few minutes later the cuirassiers were swallowed up in a cloud of dust, riding away on the road north to undertake whatever daring exploits their emperor required of them.

CHAPTER 12

Carcourt, Normandy
Autumn 1806

"Now this is a fine piece, Sancho," the visitor said, bending down to get a closer look at the marble statue of Isis displayed beside the drawing room entrance. "Much better work than the mock-up bronze in our front hall."

His companion nodded. "What is it?" he asked.

"If I'm not mistaken," the taller man replied, "this is Eset. Known to most as Isis, the ancient Egyptian deity. Revered as a goddess. *The* goddess. You see in her hand a cymbal which, when struck, is meant to give off a keynote of natural beauty. And here you see the grapes next to the sheaf of wheat? These are the nourishments that generate and regenerate life. But, alas, as the story goes, she is famed for her stoic fortitude after the tragic death of her king and husband, Osiris."

The shorter man inspected the statue, reaching a hand out to touch it when he saw someone standing in the hall observing them. With a hurried movement the taller one tapped his companion on the arm, forcing him to look in her direction.

"I hope I'm not interrupting anything," Sophie Valiere said. She stepped farther into the front hall, smiling at her two visitors. She wore a dress of blue and white, her only other adornment a necklace of small white pearls. "Monsieur Lavalle, it is a pleasure to see you again."

Sylvain offered a courteous bow. Sophie turned to the second man. Around his shoulders he wore a gray cloak, its collar lined with red fur, beneath which was a light-blue vest covering a fine white shirt with lace trim. His polished riding boots reached up to his knees. His attire gave the unmistakable impression of refined, elegant taste; his face, though somewhat fleshy, bore the dignity of ancient nobility. His eyes were dark brown. After offering her a low bow, he took several steps closer and clasped Sophie's hand in his, gently kissing it.

For her part Sophie recognized this well-dressed stranger and smiled, glad to finally have met the Count de Montfort. When she said as much, the count laughed.

"By my faith, the pleasure is all mine, madame," he said, at last releasing her hand. "Monsieur Sylvain told me he had made an introduction of sorts, but his relating of your beauty failed to do you justice."

Sophie, accustomed to such compliments, smiled in response, though the count's lingering gaze caused her to turn her head. "If you gentlemen have traveled all the way from Le Havre you must be tired." She motioned for them to follow her into the drawing room. "Please, come sit and rest a bit."

The men sat on a sofa across from Sophie, who occupied a long chaise. A tray of coffee, tea, and biscuits was brought out. The men drank sparingly of the tea, declining any biscuits.

"Monsieur Lavalle tells me you have established yourself on a new estate since your return from England?" Sophie asked, after they had all been served.

"Ah, well," Count de Montfort said, slapping a hand on his companion's knee. "Please, Madame Valiere, I understand that this fellow may have introduced himself as Monsieur Lavalle, but such formality is hardly appropriate, especially once you've gotten to know the rascal. I prefer to call him Sancho. As in Sancho Panza." Lavalle smiled at Sophie and bowed slightly. "Monsieur Sancho has accompanied me on many travels and shared in all of my adventures."

"Oh?" Sophie said. Not since André had left for the war had she enjoyed the company of someone with so similar an upbringing and background, and she relished any occasion to hear of the comings and goings in the world outside Carcourt. "I'm curious to hear more."

"England was a fair enough country," the count replied, waving away Sancho's attempt to pour milk into his glass of tea. "To be sure, the noble classes were rather refined and well-bred but, ultimately, I found it to be a dull place. The countryside is nothing compared to that of France—to say nothing of the meals one might consume. And the cities are rife with disease; cold, damp, and hardly fit for society." He took a long, slow sip of tea. "But we managed, didn't we, Sancho?"

Sylvain nodded. "My lady," he began, "the count is being quite modest. Perhaps the weather was dreary and the food significantly worse than what one might be accustomed to in this country. Nevertheless, Monsieur le Count made quite a name for himself in the lands of Oxfordshire. Hunting, dancing, and instructing the locals in our beautiful tongue."

"The man boasts," Count de Montfort cut in with a smile, "but I hardly think it is necessary. It is true, we made our way in society—*eventually*—but our first few years were fraught with anguish for our countrymen. Those unfortunates, born to high station, targeted with a senseless cruelty more suited to a vengeful crusade or some other scene of medieval butchery. I shall never forget those first few months on the coast before we escaped."

Sophie nodded, her thoughts drifting to an epoch of her life that she felt she had never truly escaped. "Yes," she said, staring out the window. "I remember the days of the Revolution all too well."

A silent moment passed before Sylvain cleared his throat. "Assuredly he'll scold me for telling you this, my lady, but you sit in the presence of one of the most celebrated smugglers of nobles on the Normandy coast."

"It is hardly a tale worth telling, Sylvain," de Montfort said, casting a sharp look at his companion. "And you can see that she has her own memories to contend with. We will leave her in peace."

"No, it is all right," Sophie said warmly, setting down her glass, hoping they would not see her hands shaking. "Those were days of trial and misfortune for so many, but it is all behind us now. More tea, messieurs?"

"Ah, I am expected back at home for supper, so I must decline any more refreshment, but I would not be so rude as to cut short such a lovely visit. Would it be impertinent of me to ask to see the grounds?" the count asked, gracefully changing the subject.

"Not at all. Come, I'll show you the gardens."

They stepped outside into the autumn sun, the freshly cut grass and lilies and roses in the garden creating an intoxicating aroma.

"You know," she offered as they crossed the field behind the house to stroll among the flowerbeds, "it has been some time since anyone has brought news of the wider world. Though my husband sends word as often as he can, I think it might benefit my two boys were they to have an educated and well-mannered man to learn from. To be sure, the assistance Messieurs Le Bon and Burnouf offer is invaluable, but there is more to life than the managing of farmland. I want them to grow to be more than planters. I wish for them to take an interest in language, culture, even travel should they share their parents' enjoyment of it."

"My dear Sophie," Count de Montfort replied, his voice easy, "you need say nothing more. I understand what it means to be born to a noble house, and the subsequent desire to raise a boy into a young gentleman." He kicked a dandelion weed. "The Revolution cut down many of our number, but it did not, *cannot*, extract the centuries of breeding and refinement that is our very birthright."

It was old habit, borne out of the dark years of fear and disquiet, but in her heart, Sophie had never allowed herself to return to the life of a true noblewoman. She did not say it, as she did not wish to insult her guest, but a part of her always carried the sight of the cruelty one of such birthright could mete out to those born lower; she did not want to return to that life—nor raise her boys to be those kind of men.

"Monsieur le Count," she said as they rounded the corner of the cha-teau, "in your travels did you ever find yourself at odds with our Revolution? Were you ever forced to take up arms against your countrymen in one of the Armies of the Émigrés? Perhaps you and my husband once stood in opposition on the field?"

Count de Montfort had been taking in the front grounds. Now, he turned and faced Sophie. "Several months after my arrival in England I spent some time with a battalion of the exiled noble army, under the Duc de Chateaubriand. But they were sent to Mannheim, and I considered my place to be with my people—friends, relations, you see. After mustering for weeks and seeing it come to nothing, to say nothing of the pay (which was less than meager), I found that the life of a field officer wasn't suited to my tastes, and I subsequently departed for diplomatic missions to Sweden and Denmark."

"That sounds quite adventurous," Sophie replied. "Perhaps you may share your tales with my boys, who I'm afraid find more amusement playing with frogs and climbing tress than they do in learning history, geography, poetry, and, well…really, any area of study."

"Of course, Madame Sophie," the count remarked. "Any assistance I may bid you would be nothing short of a privilege. In fact," the count continued, offering her his arm, "that is one of the primary reasons for my visit."

"Oh?"

"I have learned from my good friend Sancho that you have been experiencing some difficulties of late, owing to circumstances outside of any of our control; some minor trifles, others concerning the entire province."

"Well yes—"

"I wish to offer you any service I might provide. Of course, you are welcome to come and visit us on our estate any time you might wish. It is less grand, but if you should ever find yourself desiring the company of one who would take on your troubles as if they were his own, you need only call upon us and we will see to your every need."

"That is too kind of you, monsieur."

The count waved a hand. "It is the very least I could do. Now, to come to the other matter; Lavalle has informed me of the plight of these outlanders, how they have wandered into this province, content to stay indefinitely. I'm not sure what is to be done about this on the whole, but we would have little trouble accommodating two dozen or so of these newcomers on our estate. Temporarily, mind you, but the state of disrepair that I've found my new estate in will require more hands than we currently possess. If this were to be agreeable to you and your steward, Monsieur Le Bon, then we would oversee the collection of these men's duties, as well as offer any assistance in conducting this monotonous duty of tax collection on your own estate. I see your skepticism, and I do not ask for an answer today—I only wish to introduce the idea to you in hopes that you might think on it for a while. Your estate is overpopulated, and, if Sancho's report to me is to be believed, the farmers are in a state of rivalry that grows by the day. When all is considered, our estates might profit from mutual friendship and cooperation."

Sophie considered his points. True, they had an abundance of laborers, especially when counting the new arrivals from the neighboring provinces. But was she ready to make such an important decision without consulting André first?

"I will think on it," she said resolutely. "Your offer is an act of kindness I could not have expected, or even asked for, but I thank you all the same."

"Do not thank me, my dear Sophie," de Montfort replied. "I will be happy to receive your wish, any wish, and I will take it on as if it were my command." He offered a charming smile. "I almost forgot—how foolish of me! I have recently come into a business endeavor with an acquaintance in the city of Rouen: the journal—the *Norman Gazette*, to be precise. It is nothing really, more of a habit of amusement I picked up during my sojourn in England. They have some of the sharpest, most biting periodicals you will ever read. And their take on Napoleon is nothing short of fantastic. They skewer the poor little man almost daily."

Sophie smiled politely but bit her lip, aware of the power and reach of her husband's commander.

"Anyhow, I've purchased the paper for a modest fee, and while I expect little to come of it, I suppose no harm can come from the proliferation of a bit of positive news. It is also my hope to share something of the lessons learned in England, be they political, philosophical, musical, or otherwise, with the provincial inhabitants of these lands. If, should you desire, I would be delighted to submit any editorials or features to promote your own enterprise here. Why, I'd be curious to read the pen of Madame Valiere herself, were she to have such an interest."

"That is truly a kind offer, monsieur."

"My dear Sophie," de Montfort bowed slightly, "from now on refer to me as Jean-Claude. Formality between friends is little more than a barrier that hinders the affection that should be given freely."

Sophie offered a slight curtsy in return. "Very well then, Jean-Claude. I find myself at a loss for words given so many generous propositions. I will take your offer for mutual assistance between our lands and present it to the landowner's council. It was recently institutionalized here, for the free exchange of opinions, and I hope it will help dispel the tensions you've heard about."

It was the count's turn to nod politely. "A landowner's council—that has quite a ring to it. No doubt a fine republican sentiment. I offer you my congratulations on so inspired an initiative. I hope it carries the express hopes and wishes of the lady of the estate?"

"Yes. I preside over the council along with my stewards. It may be come to nothing, but we must all act according to the times we live in. Anyhow, as to your second proposal, the *Norman Gazette*, I think it is a splendid idea."

"You do?" The count's eyebrows raised in relief. "I thought it might have been a foolish notion."

"Yes," Sophie hesitated, "I will wait for its first publication eagerly."

They had made their way to the count's carriage. He retrieved a small black box from inside. "For your boys," he said.

The box held two polished flintlock pistols. Sophie's mouth twisted and she gasped.

"They're not real," the count reassured her. "But, from what I hear, your boys take after their father. It would be foolish to deny your two brave young soldiers the right to defend their own home."

With a bow he kissed Sophie's hand and climbed into the wagon. He rapped the top of the carriage, and it drove away in a cloud of dust.

CHAPTER 13

Tuileries Palace, Paris

January 1806

Jean-Luc found himself once again waiting outside the door of Joseph Bonaparte. As he stood in the long gallery, his eyes fell on a large painting, notable for its contrast of bright colors and ominous shadows, *The Lictors Bring to Brutus the Bodies of His Sons* by Jacques-Louis David. Jean-Luc had heard of Monsieur David's celebrity during the early days of the Revolution. The artist, who now held great personal favor with Napoleon, had built a reputation as one capable of instilling the fashionable and Revolutionary virtues of duty, personal austerity, and loyalty to the state into his pieces. As he examined the painting, Jean-Luc found the subject matter ironic. Considered a celebration of civic virtues triumphing over family ties in times of crisis, it depicted the bodies of Brutus's sons being carried into his home after he had condemned them to death for treason. Jean-Luc was about to meet the brother of the emperor, and he wondered where these two brothers' loyalties would fall if they were ever forced to choose between family and nation?

The door opened and a young man, closer to a boy, ushered him into the adjoining room. He walked across the polished wood floor and presented himself before the eldest Bonaparte, who was staring at a piece of parchment. After the better part of a minute, Joseph Bonaparte lifted his eyes and appeared surprised to see Jean-Luc standing in front of him. After the slightest hesitation, recognition dawned, and he rose to embrace Jean-Luc warmly.

"Pardon me the delay, St. Clair," Joseph Bonaparte said kindly. He looked exhausted. "Preparations for my brother's next campaign." He poured glasses of wine for himself and Jean-Luc. "Let us not waste precious time; I'll come straight to business. My people tell me you've made the acquaintance of Monsieur Pierre-Yves Gagnon." He sat down with a heavy sigh. "You knew the sentence you recommended for Cruchet would be rejected." He looked at Jean-Luc, the trace of a smile on his features. "And that, I presume, was why you felt free to offer it?"

"I thought it unlikely, yes sir," Jean-Luc replied, sitting at Bonaparte's prompt to do so. "In my preparations, I also learned that Monsieur Gagnon has great reputation and influence in his community and does not take kindly to outsiders interfering in what he believes to be *local* matters."

"So you decided to ruffle his feathers?" Joseph asked, setting his glass on the large oak desk.

"It is my understanding that you and your brother have enemies abroad, but also closer to home. As men of stature and widespread influence you cannot afford to be seen taking sides in petty local disputes; it is below the dignity of your positions. So I decided I might take it upon myself and fire the opening salvo."

"That you did, St. Clair," Joseph replied. "And you shall receive a returning volley soon enough."

Jean-Luc nodded. "In a nation of laws there are always those who wish to use the discontent of others as a firm footing to pursue their own ambitions. While I don't enjoy ruining the livelihoods or reputations of others, if it is in the best interests of the nation, I will do what needs be done."

As Jean-Luc had been speaking, the door was opened, and someone could be heard approaching from across the room. Noticing his superior's attention had turned, Jean-Luc looked to see who had entered. When his glance settled on the man behind him his heart skipped a beat and he sprang to his feet. Napoleon Bonaparte stood in a relaxed posture, wearing an untucked, long, white undershirt, and a pair of tight-fitting white breeches. In either arm he held a coat, one red and the other a light blue.

"I'd like to speak to you of something gravely important if you can spare me a moment, Joseph," he said, lifting the coats in either arm. Before his brother responded, Napoleon turned his attention to Jean-Luc, who had startled the emperor with his quick snap-to. "Who is this?"

Jean-Luc bowed his head. "I am Jean-Luc St. Clair, sire."

"He is the one I have dealing with that rascal Gagnon," Joseph added.

Napoleon nodded, examining Jean-Luc up and down to determine if he had ever met the man or should recognize him. "You may stand at ease, monsieur, we're not on the parade ground."

Jean-Luc complied, horribly embarrassed at being caught so off-guard.

"Well, Joseph, I came here to ask your opinion. It appears I have interrupted important work with this gentleman. I will not detain you." He turned to leave but paused. "If Joseph trusts you to deal with Gagnon, you must know this city quite well. Tell me, monsieur…"

Jean-Luc felt another strong rush of nerves.

"Do you frequent the theatre?" Napoleon asked with a serious look.

"I have only been once or twice, sire," Jean-Luc admitted.

"Well, then," Napoleon held up the two coats slung over either arm, "tell me which one you would wear. The red or the blue?"

After taking a closer look at both coats, Jean-Luc managed: "I like the red, sire."

Napoleon examined the two jackets as though they were an enemy army corps. "I was going to wear the blue."

Jean-Luc stole a look at Joseph, who betrayed no surprise at the odd exchange.

"But red it is. Now, before I go," Napoleon continued, stepping closer to Jean-Luc. "You're here to deal with that pest Gagnon, and rarely does Joseph dispatch weak men to accomplish important tasks. So tell me, monsieur, what has truly brought you here?"

Jean-Luc felt a wave of uncertainty wash over him. "Your Majesty." He exhaled deeply to master himself. "I have found myself, whether by chance or the work of providence, arrived into the service of your brother, Monsieur Joseph. And thus far it has been a privilege to offer any modest skills I have to assist your government."

Napoleon moved to speak, but Jean-Luc continued. "In truth, however, I admit that my heart's desire is to rise and attain the rank of senator; that is, if I prove myself worthy in the eyes of your family and your administration, sire."

Joseph's surprise was written plainly on his features, but Napoleon simply stared at Jean-Luc for several seconds; a silence that felt almost unbearable.

He blinked twice, turning to his brother. "There, you see? That is boldness that makes one into a general. If Villeneuve and his admirals had that kind of nerve, I'd be in London already." He pointed a finger at Jean-Luc, keeping his eyes on Joseph. "You would do well to keep this one around—perhaps he would get things moving again." He turned his attention back to Jean-Luc, straightening his posture. "So that is it, you wish to be a senator? Well, show my brother your worth and, if he endorses it, perhaps one day your wish shall be granted. And Joseph, do not allow me to be late again. Josephine will chide me, and I'm in no mood for it tonight." With that the emperor bade the two men good evening and turned to leave. "Meneval," he shouted as he opened the heavy door, "we're wearing the red!"

When the emperor's looming presence had dissipated, Joseph urged Jean-Luc to be seated. "My brother, to put it mildly, has a strong will." He took a sip of wine and set the glass down with a sigh. "I spent six months negotiating with Lord Whitworth, only to have Napoleon storm in and ruthlessly harangue the man in front of a crowd of perhaps a hundred senators and nobles. Needless to say, that closed negotiations."

Jean-Luc nodded. He'd known of Napoleon's famous rebuke of the English diplomat, ending the peace of Amiens. He was astonished to hear it recounted firsthand.

Joseph resumed, "Now that we've managed to solve my brother's wardrobe conundrum, we can get down to business. His efforts to reorganize this city and put an end to the disorder and unsanitary conditions that have plagued it since—well, forever—are beginning to bear fruit. We've begun work on a new canal that will carry fresh water from the Ourcq River to the La Valette basin—point in fact, that is why I've brought you here this evening. Because that rascal Gagnon has interfered, as he does with everything we try to do for the people of Paris. Now he's at his old tricks, disrupting the construction of this canal. Specifically, in the commune of Pantin, outside the city barriers."

"Where he uses his connections most effectively," Jean-Luc concluded. "On the periphery."

"Exactly." Joseph smiled ruefully. "He's a clever little fellow, I'll concede that. He knows that the mayors of the *arrondissements* would never openly defy my brother, so he gins up popular support in rural communes where top-down political control has less practical influence. Wherever construction is slow going he always manages to have a street closed down or some accident or demonstration occur, slowing the building to a halt. And, of course, he is never to be found during one of these mishaps, so we cannot prove it is him stalling the work."

"Why does he wish to stop the canal?" Jean-Luc asked.

"The canal is funded almost entirely on the new taxes." Joseph replied. "Taxes on wine. Gagnon is not a difficult man to understand. He was a middling young merchant just starting out when the Revolution began. In this he saw his opportunity to rise; and time and time again he was either overlooked, ignored, or rejected outright. Not radical enough for the Jacobins, not theoretical or erudite enough for the Girondists, and not loyal enough for the moderates. With his political prospects in shambles, he turned to more *underhanded* means to make his fortune. He speculated and managed to make a few small deals here and there selling leather, wine, and liquor to the army, but when the Revolution ended the Directory threw him in jail. Barras would not tolerate competition to his own lucrative army contracts from a little runt like Gagnon; so, they clamped him in chains, galvanizing the little hothead even more."

Jean-Luc nodded, knowing all too well how the Revolution lifted some to astonishing heights while smashing others to pieces. "I suppose he's lucky to have made it through—with his life, at least. If he'd been successful, he might've lost his head."

"That is true. And despite his many shortcomings, he has always had one card to play—he enjoys a tremendous popularity among the people, especially the smugglers and brothel owners on the periphery of the city. They see him as one of them, indeed as their voice pushing back against an 'overly virtuous administration.' Mark my words, he will not stop attempting to thwart this canal until he has won—or is removed from the issue entirely."

Jean-Luc took all this in. "What is it you wish me to do, sir?"

"My brother has left me to figure this out and present my plan to him. But he *has* allocated me one extremely formidable instrument."

"What would that be?"

"Not what…who," Joseph replied, his words a whisper. "The only man who compels more obedience in this city than Napoleon: Minister Fouché. Some whisper that he's the only man alive that Napoleon fears."

Jean-Luc swallowed hard when he realized Joseph had just named the man Mayor Bergasse had warned him of, the minister of police, whose network of agents and informants stretched across the entirety of France and beyond.

Resuming his normal voice, Joseph continued, "Rumors are spreading in certain quarters that Monsieur Gagnon is just the latest scapegoat of my brother's heavy-handedness. First the arrest of the Jacobins, then the assassination of the Bourbon Duc d'Enghien, and now Gagnon. From what I can see," Joseph concluded, "the wine merchant is more than pleased to lay claim to being the emperor's latest martyr."

Jean-Luc grinned. "The way I see it, a little less wine and a little more fresh water might help this city. But why bother with health and sanitation when you can sell wine to poor wretches who drink themselves blind to run away from their troubles?"

"Quite well said," Joseph said with a sigh. "Now, I'll see to it that Minister Fouché offers you some measure of assistance, but St. Clair, what I am about to tell you is of utmost importance—do I have your word you will abide by what I am about to tell you?"

"Of course, monsieur."

Joseph's eyebrows remained raised for several seconds before he relaxed his features. "All right. If you do in fact meet with Minister Fouché, it is *imperative* that you inform me before you act on any of his counsels. The man is a renowned intriguer; if he offers you something, anything, you can be sure a price will be exacted sooner or later; whether on your terms or his."

Disconcerted, Jean-Luc shifted in his seat. "Very well, monsieur, I will keep you informed should I have any correspondences with the man."

Joseph leaned back in his seat, satisfied that his point had been made. "For as you might surmise, with men like Fouché or Talleyrand, you're swimming in deep waters."

"I thank you for the warning, monsieur." Jean-Luc swept a hand through his black hair. "Though I should say that I learned how to swim long ago, your excellency."

Joseph returned Jean-Luc's weary expression with an icy stare. "Not with a man like Fouché you haven't."

CHAPTER 14

Oder River, Prussia

October/November 1806

The day after Moreau's grisly confession to André, the dragoons reunited with the advance corps of the main French army. Colonel Menard had given the squadron up for dead; nevertheless, André's return and accounting of their experiences behind enemy lines did not seem to impress him. André was forgiven for the loss of the wagons and ordered to fall into formation alongside the other squadrons on the road north.

For the next three days they marched roughly one hundred miles, enduring the cold winds gusting down from the Baltic Sea, which seemed to grow stronger each mile they advanced. On the morning of the fourth day forward patrols of the Imperial Guard reached the Brandenburg Gate in Berlin; a day later Napoleon arrived in the city to a conquering hero's welcome.

André reported to the palace at Charlottenburg for an audience with his corps commander, General Margaron. Although he was sorely tempted, he did not share what he had learned about the wealth of Hesse-Cassel from Carnassier—but he did report the extrajudicial executions of the burgher and his sister in Zaręba. General Margaron assured him that he would recall Carnassier to headquarters as soon as possible.

Though André had hoped they would be given adequate time to rest in Berlin, he was informed that his squadron was to lead the vanguard of the army corps to the gates of Posen, where a body of Imperial senators would be joining the emperor and holding an audience with representatives from Warsaw; the issue of granting nationhood to the citizens of Poland as recompense for their sacrifices on behalf of the former French Republic—and now Empire—was a hotly debated issue among Napoleon's inner circle.

André's men spent two days in the city. Clothed only in tattered boots and weathered uniforms meant for summer campaigning, they took every opportunity to warm themselves with shirts and scarves "borrowed" from the citizens of Berlin. The veterans among them knew it was best to be prepared; their marches would not cease due to the onset of winter. On the third morning they resumed their march east toward the Oder River and the Polish frontier beyond.

A few days later, the squadron halted in a village twenty miles east of the Oder. Königswalde's inhabitants were a mixture of Polish and German speakers, and judging by the closed doors and shuttered windows, they did not appear enthusiastic about their French visitors. After posting sentries on the roads, the squadron made their way to the town's inn. While they sat in the dining hall, dipping stiff bread into cabbage and carrot soup, the doors swung open and several soldiers wrapped in heavy blue greatcoats entered and surveyed the room.

"Where is your commander?" one of them demanded.

"I am commanding," André answered. "Who are you?"

The soldier replied, loud but respectful. "A battalion of infantry and a squadron of cavalry are marching here, and their arrival is imminent. I have come to find them quarters. Are there rooms available?"

André indicated the crowded room. "You may share any available rooms if you can find space. Here or across the road. And you are welcome to any remaining stables for your horses."

"The buildings across the road are cowsheds and stables—"

"And we're sure you'll find them comfortable," Moreau cut him off.

With a grunt the soldier departed with his men. A few minutes later the sound of hooves could be heard pounding the freezing ground.

"The fool should learn some respect," one of André's troopers said.

"He was a hussar," Moreau replied. "They think mustaches and braided hair mark them as a superior breed. They're nothing but jumped-up dandies in fancy coats."

"And who is this man," demanded a familiar voice behind Moreau, "who heaps scorn upon his own comrades?"

Moreau and André turned in their seats: behind them stood Major Carnassier and Captain Alderic. Both were wrapped in thick coats and, from their windswept faces, appeared to have ridden a great distance in a hurry.

"Ah yes, look here," said Carnassier. "It's Achilles and his loyal protégé, Patroclus."

André's left cheek twitched.

"May we sit with you two gentlemen and share in a tale of your triumphs and glory?" The two men approached André's table. "Or is this country so inhospitable that you won't offer us a seat? Should we settle ourselves in the stables with the horses, lieutenant-colonel?"

"The last time we saw you and your men," answered André, "we rode into an ambush. Rather, an *attempted* ambush that nearly destroyed our squadron."

"At least now you find yourselves on the proper side of enemy lines, eh colonel?" Carnassier sat and bit down on a piece of bread, chewing in long, exaggerated bites. "It's quite a country, Poland, is it not? One minute you're under the protection of those familiar with the terrain—and the principles of mounted warfare—the next, you find yourself surrounded by marauding Prussian cavalry! The emperor must see something here that we cannot."

Moreau fixed his eyes on Alderic, who returned the look with a glare of his own.

"Anyhow, we are quite tired from our ride east," Carnassier said, changing the subject. "And we've only just begun our journey. It is still several hundred miles from here to Warsaw, so I suppose one ought to be content to have any sort of roof over our heads."

André whispered for Moreau to stay with the men before sliding his chair back and rising from the table. "Major, before you retire for the night, I would like a word with you outside. In private." André motioned for Carnassier to follow him and left the room. After taking a few more bites of bread and swallowing some ale, the Major rose and followed.

Outside in the darkness they immediately felt the bite of an eastern wind nipping their faces. Carnassier cupped his hands and blew on them for warmth. Muffled voices of soldiers laughing and singing could be heard from the surrounding buildings.

"What a charming village, I wonder if—"

"Shut up, major," André interrupted. "I have something which I must inform you, then you are dismissed. I reported nothing of your plans for acquiring the wealth of Hesse-Cassel to General Margaron. So whatever you have in mind in that regard remains between us. However, your extra-judicial executions of the burgher and his sister in Zaręba village cannot be overlooked. While in Berlin I informed the general of your deed. He will recall you to his headquarters—"

"I saved you and your hapless squadron when you blundered into an enemy ambush, and you repay me with this?" The major's levity was gone; his face full of contempt. "An officer from noble stock should place the honor of fellow officers and countrymen above a few miserable Polish peasants." He spat onto the frozen ground.

"You speak of honor among officers? You sent us into that trap!" André leaned closer. "Deny it if you will, but your betrayal is as clear as day. You used the enemy to have us killed. You will answer for your crimes. I will see you in chains, or otherwise, before this campaign is over."

"Do what you will, colonel." Carnassier's voice betrayed no concern. "My Silesian agent is riding ahead to Frankfurt as we speak—to secure the Hesse-Cassel riches. When he takes it, Napoleon will come into possession of resources equivalent to a small nation. Such a gift! I doubt he will reward me with anything short of a marshal's baton."

André's face twitched slightly.

"Once I have that baton, and a dukedom, I will rule in the east, molding these backwards inhabitants in the image of France, for the propagation of an ordered, prosperous, and peaceful continent. Meanwhile, you and your wretched lapdog are being marched into the teeth of the Russian army—who have wisely waited for bitter cold and great distances between our supply lines to string us out. I need not mention the Cossacks, who are raised from birth to hunt their enemy in winter. In one year's time I will be toasted in Paris as the hero who enriched Napoleon's empire. You? You and your men's bones will be food for the wolves."

André's face twitched again, and his jaw clenched.

"We shall see, major."

Cardinal,

Your summons has been delivered.

— Jothan

CHAPTER 15

Paris, France

February 1806

J ean-Luc opened his morning paper, one of the few journals that still dared to criticize the Bonapartes, to an amusing illustration. It depicted an undersized Napoleon at table, stabbing a caricature of Gagnon with a long, skinny fork. The caption on the utensil read: "St. Clair who?"

A few days after his meeting with Joseph Bonaparte, it was agreed that the administration would take Gagnon to trial on the charge of illegal obstruction of the emperor's canal. Jean-Luc had less than two weeks to build a case against the man. Immediately, he began interviewing potential witnesses from Pantin, the suburb through which the canal was to run. No sooner had he started than a note appeared under his door bearing the Imperial seal. It was a summons for a meeting at the Tuileries, yet did not say from whom it had originated; it simply requested an audience at 1300 hours the following afternoon.

At the appointed hour, Jean-Luc showed his credentials to the guards and mounted the grand staircase of the Tuileries Palace. The clerk, who by now had received him more than once, grinned. "Another routine visit with the notables, eh monsieur?"

"In truth, I have no idea who has summoned me today," Jean-Luc admitted.

The clerk's face assumed a serious expression. "This comes from the minister of police."

Jean-Luc felt his stomach turn as he recalled Mayor Bergasse's warning: *Joseph Fouché is a man of extraordinary abilities and influence within the Empire. Should you ever have opportunity to meet him, be respectful, but never discuss or divulge anything of a personal nature.*

After following the clerk through a corridor of ornately decorated drawing rooms, Jean-Luc finally entered an office similar to that of Joseph Bonaparte. The man seated behind the neatly ordered desk set down his quill and folded his hands together.

Joseph Fouché was not an attractive man. His auburn sideburns and small eyes, held in a perpetual squint, distinguished him among his peers. During the Revolution he'd been repeatedly chastised for his brutality by Maximilien Robespierre, the man who had orchestrated the Reign of Terror. He had rightfully earned the nickname "shooter of Lyon" for his practice of tying enemies together en masse and having them shot to pieces by cannons firing grapeshot. Thousands had died by his decree until the Committee of Public Safety eventually recalled him. Not only did he escape prosecution, he succeeded in instilling enough fear in his colleagues to convince them to rise against Robespierre and remove his head.

Jean-Luc recalled his first meeting with Guillaume Lazare many years earlier, and, as he glanced out a large window, he felt grateful that this meeting was being held in the light of day.

Minister Fouché sat motionless as he peered at Jean-Luc with his narrow eyes. "So it is you who will be presenting the charges against Gagnon in court."

"The task has fallen to me, yes, monsieur."

The minister nodded, motioning for Jean-Luc to be seated.

"My name is Jean-Luc St. Clair." *Be respectful. Never discuss or divulge anything of a personal nature,* he reminded himself.

"I know who you are." Fouché shuffled a stack of papers and placed them in a drawer within the desk. "That Gagnon is an interesting fellow," he said, coming straight to the point. "Exploited by the nobility, slighted by his peers, and overlooked by his enemies; a man with a gambler's instincts, and nothing to lose. You would do well to arrive at the trial well-prepared."

"Well, we have certainly done our due diligence, and we will continue to do so; though, admittedly, we've had difficulties in penetrating his support network, especially anyone or anything outside of the brothels, taverns, and gambling houses of Saint-Denis and Montmartre."

Fouché stared at him for a moment before replying. "You may try speaking with your neighbors; the Faubourg Saint-Germain is a known refuge of royalist spies and intriguers. If you dig a little deeper into Gagnon's past, you'll learn who his real friends and benefactors were, and why Barras and the republicans were loath to admit him to their circle."

"You're saying he holds quiet sympathies for the royalists?" This information seemed too good to be true. "Is that why he would wish to be a thorn in the emperor's side?"

"What I've said I've said. It is up to the state's prosecutor to draw his own conclusions."

"I have done all I can up to this point," Jean-Luc replied. "But, as the trial takes place tomorrow, I must admit that I cannot be certain I have enough to put the man away." *And if I fail, I may lose the opportunity I've been given to advance my prospects.*

Fouché squinted. "I am sure you have learned that I deal in the game of acquiring information."

"Yes, monsieur, I have heard as much."

"If I am to offer you assistance, then it would hardly be enough for me to simply acquaint you with the petty business practices of a dubious merchant nibbling at the scraps of society's feast. To put the man away for good, you require more substantial information."

"More substantial information?"

"You wish to gather the full picture?" Fouché asked, crossing his legs. "Well, then, you must take control of events tomorrow and not blindly follow the instructions of your superiors. It is no use to be a puppet on a string, wasting your efforts to carry out the will of a larger man. Or, perhaps, that is your aim."

"No effort is wasted if it is taken up with true intentions and executed with faithful industry," Jean-Luc replied, hearing the hollowness that both men knew rang in his words.

"Please don't waste my time, monsieur. If you seek more information on your man, more *useful* information, you might try going to Monsieur Julien-Henri de Landreville, formerly Monsieur le Marquis. He returned from exile abroad around a year ago. His residence is on the Rue de Verneuil in the Saint-Germain. If you tell him I directed you there he might scoff, but you will be admitted. But let us come to the real point now, the reason I called you into my office." Fouché uncrossed his legs and laid his hands flat on the oak desk. "Napoleon would not be much of an emperor if he allowed Gagnon to pose a legitimate threat to any of his plans. This whole charade is not about Gagnon."

"Who else might it concern?"

Fouché looked down at his hands. "Monsieur St. Clair, don't be a fool." He raised his eyes. "I am referring to your benefactor, of course."

"Joseph Bonaparte?"

Fouché's lips curled in a sardonic smile. "Monsieur Joseph has a generous heart," he replied, reclining in his large chair, "of a tolerant disposition by temperament. And yet, he is among those chiefly responsible for destroying the domestic enemies of his emperor and enacting his iron will; the very man who happens to be his closest relation. Napoleon wishes to blood his gentle brother on easy prey, as one would a docile hound. Joseph, and for that matter you yourself, may find it distasteful work; but in a choice between principles and obedience to the source of all your wealth and power, where would your loyalties lie?" Jean-Luc sat silently with his thoughts. Minister Fouché mirrored him for several seconds before continuing: "To be sure, one must repay confidence with fidelity, of that there is no question. But if one wishes to hitch their horse to the Imperial carriage one would be wise to know the price of his proximity to such power—the misery of the defeated, and the enemies made as a result."

"This lesson you learned all too well; nearly at the cost of your own life?" Jean-Luc asked with unfeigned curiosity.

"Veritably so."

"Why are you telling me this?"

"You had occasion to first meet Monsieur Joseph sometime last year, yes?"

"Last October."

"And you met to discuss what?"

"I came to Paris to deliver a message from Mayor Bergasse of Marseille."

"What if I told you that letter was not what you believed it to be, that included in those correspondences was something else entirely?"

Jean-Luc furrowed his brow. "What do you mean? I was in the room with Joseph. I watched him read it myself."

"Your generous benefactor is brother to a man with many enemies, and as such, one must occasionally resort to *furtive* means of conveying information. The letter you delivered may have concerned tariffs and trade rights to be sure, but after applying a few drops of sodium carbonate to the parchment it revealed quite a different message."

Jean-Luc's confusion betrayed itself in a brief burst of laughter. "Monsieur, I'm sure that I have no idea—"

"Are you familiar with invisible ink?"

"I have heard of its use, yes."

Fouché gazed at Jean-Luc like a patient teacher might appraise a slow student. "Whether you accept my word or not, I will tell you that the letter's true purpose was to reveal a list of names; names the Bonapartes acquired from your mayor in exchange for guarantees of future shipping contracts and trade rights." Fouché folded his hands together, interlocking his fingers. "The city of Naples is ruled by the Bourbon king, Ferdinand IV; this you may already know. Over a year ago, this king signed a treaty with our Napoleon in which we agreed to evacuate all French troops from Apulia in exchange for Ferdinand expelling all foreign troops from his army, as well as barring any English ships from landing on their territory. Through my own channels I have come to learn that Queen Maria Carolina, the good king's wife, had no intention of honoring this treaty, virtuous monarch as she is. We've lately been informed that they plan to summon an expeditionary force of English—and possibly Russian—troops to assist them in a preemptive maneuver to attack our forces on the Italian Peninsula. In the letter that you delivered to Monsieur Bonaparte, hidden in invisible ink, was a list of one hundred and thirty-eight Neapolitans of some reputation; members of the clergy, discontented merchants, political prisoners, and so forth. What they all share is a severe hatred for King Ferdinand and his lovely queen. Whether Republicans, Bonapartists, or angry nursemaids, it doesn't matter; we seek to employ them all in fomenting an uprising against Ferdinand—an uprising that will, in due course, receive the assistance of our own army."

Jean-Luc's incredulity gave way to a dawning sense that the minister was telling him the truth.

"Originally," Fouché continued, "these named individuals were to be nothing more than informants; eyes inside the city, to ensure the terms we'd agreed to were upheld. Since I've come to learn of the king and queen's duplicitous intentions…well, now the emperor and his brother have decided to utilize them for slightly more *active* purposes."

Suddenly remembering with whom he was speaking, Jean-Luc attempted to appear unaffected by this information. Nonetheless his chest swelled with a feeling of betrayal and wounded pride. *Was Joseph going to inform me of any of this?*

Fouché did not allow Jean-Luc to wallow in his disbelief for long. "Disillusionment is a common reaction to learning one has been deceived, but it is a useless sentiment. I will share with you the unseen contents if you wish, under one condition."

These last words caught Jean-Luc's ear like a pistol shot.

"The plain fact is this, there is little Monsieur Joseph Bonaparte can do without his brother's blessing, but in many respects I am the emperor's blessing. With no pretense to false modesty, I will tell you straight that I am in a position to offer you advantages you may not achieve with the friendship of the Bonapartes alone."

"What advantages?"

The police minister cast a quick look down at his cabinet. "Perspectives you have not hitherto seen—nor likely even knew existed."

Jean-Luc smirked. "I would prefer to have the rest of this conversation spoken plainly."

"If we come to an agreement," Fouché replied, "the terms I offer are this: you will be under no obligation to serve me or my office, but I would like to call upon you for information when needed. In exchange, you will be offered information necessary for the execution of your daily duties, as well as advanced warning of any movements by the emperor, members of his administration, or any personal rivals you might have—or acquire—in coming days."

"Monsieur," Jean-Luc sighed, "as yet I have no need for *warning* of the emperor's movements or protection against any rivals or enemies. I am but a servant of the State."

Fouché offered no response, and in the silence that followed Jean-Luc sat uncomfortably, fighting back the urge to speak.

After several long moments the police minister spoke again. "You are a man incapable of deceit then. Just as well, the game of empire is quite a dirty business."

"A man without deceit is as common as a fish without bones."

Fouché's lips curled with a malevolent smile. "I see plainly that you are an educated man. Though I would caution you not to be haphazard with your cleverness, St. Clair. Fools will mistake it for arrogance and despise you for it; powerful men will see it as a challenge."

"If I am hated then at least I have stood for something."

"A man may be hated or loved," replied the minister. "It makes no difference. But one who finds himself alone and adrift in dangerous waters would be wise to mind the crags and shoals ahead, else he find himself dashed upon the rocks, like so many other brave sailors."

Jean-Luc leaned forward. "Circumstances, as I see them, can be stated thusly: the Bonapartes are a wild tempest. And you are the rock that foolish challengers are broken against, to be destroyed and sunk to the bottom of the sea. Well, monsieur, I heed your warning clearly enough, though I bring no challenge to your or your master. If rough waters should appear—you may find me a cut above the ordinary sailor."

Fouché's eyes held an unsettling calmness. "Even the finest captains must be vigilant of their crew, if they are to avoid mutiny."

After another uncomfortable silence, Minister Fouché rose slowly, indicating that the session was over. He offered a cold hand to Jean-Luc, who shook it and bowed respectfully.

"I thank you for your visit, monsieur. I am sure we shall meet again."

Jothan,

A lawyer is coming to the Saint-Germain; potentially of great importance in the coming days. Make him welcome and answer any questions he might have.

—Cardinal

CHAPTER 16

Paris

February 1806

Turning off Rue du Bac toward Les Invalides, Jean-Luc arrived at his destination: a large building of five floors. After announcing himself to a servant, he was ushered past a gate and through a charming courtyard to the private residence of Monsieur de Landreville.

The residence was on the top floor, and Jean-Luc reached it with labored breath, stunned that the old aristocrat would choose to spend his time traveling up and down so many stairs. After walking through a plush apartment adorned with exotic plants, marble busts, and dozens of oil paintings, Jean-Luc found himself in the drawing room of Monsieur Julien-Henri de Landreville, formerly le marquis. A warm fire glowed beneath a stately marble mantelpiece.

After formal introductions were made, the elder gentleman, dressed in the fashion of the Ancien Régime with a matching dark green coat and waistcoat, a shirt of plain fabric ruffles, and white satin breeches, bade Jean-Luc take a seat. They engaged in several minutes of small talk before Monsieur de Landreville came to the point, asking how he could be of service. Jean-Luc answered guardedly, revealing only that he had questions regarding Monsieur Pierre-Yves Gagnon's past.

"Ah," Monsieur de Landreville said, stabbing a log on the fire with a poker. "You come from Fouché, eh?" He set the poker down. "And how is the old jackal? Still gnawing at the carcasses of better and more honest men?" Before Jean-Luc could reply, he asked, "And what was it he wanted from you, then?"

"How do you know he wanted something from me?"

The elderly man waved a hand. "Men like Fouché see only two kinds of people: those whom they must serve, and those who can be made to serve them. You needn't worry, in fact it's his *superiors* who have the most to fear; the man is unequalled at finding one's weak spot and twisting it—with threats of public exposure of some scandal or the risk of loved ones learning a dark secret—until one can no longer distinguish who is subordinate to whom. At any rate, if he offered you an audience it was not out of the gentleness of his heart."

"Minister Fouché asked me to provide information in exchange for knowledge beneficial to me; I refused his offer."

"You did well to refuse. In my experience it is often the fools who argue with the most vehemence; it is the quiet man who one must be wary of." The old man stared out the window for several moments. "Does anyone else know you had a meeting with the man?"

"Monsieur Joseph Bonaparte is aware," Jean-Luc lied. The sting of his benefactor's deceit still lingered, and he had decided against informing him of his visit to the police minister. He wondered what else the elder Bonaparte might be concealing.

"At any rate," de Landreville continued, "you've come here to gather *unsolicited* information, so I will not hold you longer than necessary. I should begin by telling you what a wise man once told me: if you wish to solve any problem, you must first ask the proper question. Now, I presume your task is to take down Monsieur Gagnon, in some manner or another?"

"That is essentially the task."

"And it involves him and some sort of conflict with Napoleon and his people?"

"Yes."

"So, then, we must now ask the real question." The older man took another small sip from his saucer. "What drives a man like Gagnon? I'm not referring to greed or financial gain, for that is only ever means to an end. No. What is it within the man's heart that feels the need to thwart the most powerful man on the continent?"

"If I could answer that question, monsieur, I would not be sitting in your drawing room."

The old man smiled. "In this little man's soul, a great engine is turning. It is not one of ambition per se, or even of revenge. It is of validation; and a man like that, a mouse in a city with its share of lions, has only one way of asserting his power and thus validating himself. Provoking the ire and subsequent wrath of men infinitely more powerful than he; his provocations and spoiling of these 'great' men's ambitions are the only ways he believes he can gain their attention, and after a lifetime of rejection and exclusion, attention is what he craves above all."

Jean-Luc mulled over the idea. "So what was it that caused this man, who, despite his flagrant corruption, is not completely inept, to be so rejected by his contemporaries? Especially in a time of revolution and upheaval."

"Gagnon's problem was not an unwillingness to pledge his loyalty; he simply chose his friends poorly."

"Oh?"

"Jean-François de La Motte," the old man continued, "Count de Sanois."

"I'm not familiar with the man."

"Then you are not from Paris, I presume. All who lived here in the years prior to the Revolution remember the ill-fated Count de Sanois. Despite inheriting a tremendous fortune, he mismanaged his family's finances and fled from his estate in Pantin to the mountains of Switzerland. His unhappy wife, whom he'd left behind, was under the mistaken impression that he had fled with the remains of the family's fortune. Furious, she summoned the lieutenant-general of police and compelled him to sign a *lettres de cachet* authorizing the arrest and seizure of her husband, who was thrown into an asylum for his actions. In the end the count was freed and Madame de Sanois was permitted to keep the couple's possessions as long as she agreed to pay an annual income to her husband and admit that her charges against him were unfounded."

Jean-Luc, though intrigued by the tale, found his thoughts turning to the mountain of work he had yet to finish for the upcoming trial.

"I suppose I should come to the conclusion?" said his host, sensing Jean-Luc's distraction. "I had known the Count de Sanois many years prior when we both served in the army, at Fontenoy; so I offered to assist him in any way possible. Once he had been released and begun to get his house in order, he informed me of his many debts, one of which was a line of credit for twenty-thousand livres to an ambitious young merchant, Pierre-Yves Gagnon. But as his fortune was now in his wife's possession, he could not pay the man. Mind you, this was all happening as the Revolution was turning extreme; but before I fled to Mayence I paid Gagnon half of what the Count de Sanois had promised him. By this time Gagnon was in direct competition with another *intriguer extraordinaire*, Joseph Fouché, for the most lucrative army contracts. As fate would have it, using the funds I'd paid him on the count's behalf, Gagnon bought up several contracts under Fouché's nose. The future minister of police did not appreciate this, and had Gagnon thrown in prison for nearly three years. As this occurred during the height of the Terror, no one took particular notice. Fouché had simply rid himself of a personal foe. After the Terror ended and Gagnon was released, Fouché went into hiding for his own political reasons, but the damage to Gagnon's future business and political prospects had been done. Furthermore, that same year saw the meteoric rise of an unknown twenty-five-year old officer from Corsica—"

"Bonaparte."

"Who is responsible for fetching Fouché out of obscurity and ushering him back into the halls of power. So, perhaps it is becoming clear why your man Gagnon holds so hostile a stance against anyone connected to the Imperial regime."

De Landreville turned his attention toward the doorway, rising slowly to his feet with the assistance of a cane. "Ah, Mademoiselle Lucille Laurent! Monsieur, may I introduce my most trusted marshal."

Jean-Luc turned in his seat and saw a woman, perhaps thirty years of age. She wore a simple gray dress and held a tea tray at her hip. Her expression was difficult to interpret.

"Good evening, monsieur," she said, bowing slightly.

"Good evening, mademoiselle," Jean-Luc replied.

"I've been regaling our guest with the story of Count de Sanois. Our visitor comes from the Tuileries, on behalf of Monsieur Fouché, to put away Monsieur Gagnon."

"I see," Lucille replied. "So you've come to bury the Imperial fasces in the back of a man too poor to buy his patronage with the new administration?"

"I'm afraid it is more complicated than that, mademoiselle," Jean-Luc said, amused by her blunt assessment. "It is not so much a matter of *wealth* as it is corruption on behalf—"

"If Minister Fouché calls it corruption," Lucille interrupted, "then surely it must be so."

"You'll have to forgive mademoiselle, Monsieur St. Clair," de Landreville intervened. "She is the fiery warmth in this cold house."

Jean-Luc nodded, attempting to ignore the young woman's stare. "It is a fine house, monsieur. Frankly remarkable, as I am sure you lost much in the Revolution."

"Only a sister and two brothers," the old man answered with a labored sigh. He clutched his cane close to his chest and peered out the window. "He is a wise man who does not grieve for things he lacks but rejoices for those which he has."

"Epictetus," Jean-Luc said, smiling sadly. "For all that I object of hereditary privilege, your breed were certainly an educated lot. I'm glad some of you outlived the Terror."

The old nobleman smiled, shaking Jean-Luc's outstretched hand. Pulling him close, he whispered, "And now, we will outlive Napoleon."

Jean-Luc left work early that evening. He had spent nearly every waking hour for the past two weeks in preparation, researching and poring through the past dealings and contracts of Pierre-Yves Gagnon. He felt a sudden desire to clear his head and decided to pay a call on Isabella Maduro. To his delight, she accepted his invitation to dinner at a coffee house in a quiet corner of the Marais.

They passed several leisurely hours together dining on grilled fish, fresh vegetables, raw meats, and even polished off two bottles of wine. "Marie is adjusting well," Jean-Luc said over a piece of chocolate cake. "She's made new friends. Mathieu, on the other hand—his schoolmaster informs me weekly of his disappointing performance." He pushed the rest of the cake away. "I'm not sure what to make of it. In Marseille he was doing well. He's always been a bit headstrong like his mother, but he never misbehaved."

"Well, I can't speak to his familial temperament," Isabella said, scooping up the last piece of cake, "as I never knew his mother. But I can tell you this—he had stars in his eyes when he watched that band of horsemen ride past, after we saw the telegraph. How splendid they looked as they rode off to battle and glory."

Jean-Luc had felt unnerved by the zeal in his son's eye watching the cuirassiers that day. He had swept the memory from his mind, until now. "Perhaps we could allow him to take riding lessons?"

She took a sip of wine. "I find myself fascinated by your flights of fancy. He is *your* son; it's not something that *we* should decide, is it?"

"Forgive me." Jean-Luc felt foolish. "I—just, sometimes I find myself quite lost as a father."

The waiter hovered nearby offering more wine; Jean-Luc waved him off.

"When I am at work, I find myself able to achieve some manner of control. I feel equipped to handle the most daunting challenges. But ever since her loss, I've felt utterly out of my depth. I wish to be a good father; I try, but it seems that I'm grasping. My wife always seemed to know what to do."

Isabella rested her hand on top of his. "If I can be of help, I hope you know that I am here." She reached into her snuff box and offered him a pinch; this time he accepted.

"I don't mean to be rude. Enough about my troubles. Tell me about your family. Camille seems like a wonderful lad; what are his interests?"

Isabella pursed her lips. "He enjoys items of simple machinery; he cannot grasp complex tasks. He was happiest when he worked for a wainwright; wheels fascinate him. He would still spend hours drawing carriages, after he was released from the hospital."

"What happened to him—his injury, that is?" Jean-Luc asked, genuinely curious.

"He was born with his ailments: a misshapen leg and a mind that never truly developed beyond childhood." After a long silence she smiled at Jean-Luc. "He is content. Now he spends his days in the salons of older ladies and gentlemen with whom I have made acquaintance. They treat him kindly, and he is happy to be given small chores assisting their domestics, but it is machinery that truly draws his attention. If not for his condition, he would have made a fine carpenter or cartwright. Possibly even a clockmaker." A look of regret passed over her face. "Anyhow, it is growing late, and you have quite a day tomorrow."

Jean-Luc placed his hand on hers. "I am in no rush for this evening to end."

They were among the last patrons to leave the coffeehouse. As they put on their coats, Jean-Luc spotted a man standing across the street, staring at them. The man wore the same brown coat and black riding hat he had seen on the day he and Isabella visited the telegraph. He seemed to know he had been spotted, as when they stepped out into the street he was gone. Jean-Luc was relieved that Isabella had not noticed.

They left the Marais and took a leisurely walk along the newly paved Rue de Rivoli, crossing the Seine at the Tuileries. Jean-Luc took Isabella's hand as they passed into the narrower streets of Saint-Germain. It had grown late, and apart from one or two slow-rolling carriages and small groups of revelers, the streets echoed their footsteps in a hushed, shadowy murmur. They arrived at Jean-Luc's house, which showed one light still on in Mathieu and Marie's room. Jean-Luc turned and faced Isabella.

"I've had a wonderful time this evening."

"As have I, monsieur," she replied softly.

Jean-Luc hesitated before asking, "Would you like to come inside?"

Isabella held his gaze for a tantalizing few seconds. She nodded her head, and he led her inside. Before either had said a word, his lips were on hers. Initially surprised, she returned his kiss; softly at first, but soon her hands caressed the back of his head and his hands were on her hips.

A masked figure leapt out of the shadows, and Isabella screamed.

Raising a fist Jean-Luc prepared for the man's onslaught: he quickly noticed the diminutive size of their assailant. Reaching for the mask he tore it off to see the face of his son. "*Goddammit,* Mathieu!" he thundered in a voice so filled with long-stifled emotion that it startled everyone, including himself. His breath was short and his embarrassment plain. He threw the mask to the floor. "Apologize immediately to our guest," he demanded, "whom you've so rudely frightened half to death."

His was glaring so intently at his son that he missed the eager smile growing on his companion's face.

Later, after Mathieu had gone to bed, Isabella set down the glass of wine they shared and took Jean-Luc in her arms. She kissed him with even more vigor than she had before. He returned her passion with his own, feeling her lower back and reaching down for her hips, slowly pulling them down together on the sofa. He removed his shoes while she did the same, she then removed his pants, and they made love until they fell asleep in each other's arms.

CHAPTER 17

Carcourt, Normandy

Autumn 1806

Sophie had not requested the fine china be brought out since André's departure for the war. Plates of porcelain, silver-plated serving trays, painted vases, and two large punch bowls sat arrayed across the long table in the dining room, while each individual setting was flanked with lace napkins and shining silverware. Even when André had been at home, such items were rarely used except for the most special of occasions. Tonight, the reason for such ceremony came in the person of their visitor, Jean-Claude Devereux, Count de Montfort, who had ridden with his chamberlain Sylvain and half a dozen of his household domestics to assist with the banquet.

Sophie turned to her guest of honor as the bowls of soup were removed. "Monsieur Burnouf thinks we will have a better crop than previous years."

Count de Montfort, seated to Sophie's right, took a sip from his wine glass. The next course was set in front of them, a plate of meadow-salted lamb with a side of mushrooms, creamed potatoes, peas, and sliced apple. To the count's right sat Monsieur Abadain; across from him was Guy Le Bon. The other end of the table was occupied by Pierre Burnouf, Monsieur Abadain's wife—who was being enthusiastically engaged by Sylvain Lavalle—and the two Valiere boys.

"And our council of landowners," she continued, "held our inaugural meeting this week. I'm happy to report there was much discussion, one or two disagreements, but no hostility; so that is progress."

"Indeed," the count replied, cutting into the lamb. "Though you'll forgive my impertinence if I venture an opinion, my lady?"

Sophie nodded, taking a sip of wine.

"In my travels across the English countryside I had occasion to see many of the old manor homes of the English nobility. Our Revolution was a topic of much interest to these landowning squires. Some held a quiet sympathy for the revolutionary crowd. But, as I come to the point, I nevertheless beheld a certain *firmness* that was possessed by all of the competent holders of ancient privilege. And dull though the elite of English society may seem to us, I nevertheless came to the conclusion that these landowners seem to grasp that men of low means and rustic manners do not abide the language of weakness."

Sophie's eyebrows rose in an inquisitive expression. The count had not noticed, so she pressed him on the point. "You think our efforts at representative leadership to be mistaken then?"

"Madame Valiere, I do not believe you to be mistaken; rather, I caution against too much, too soon. I do, however, think it slightly misguided to cede too much influence to those unprepared for its burden, however magnanimous the intent."

A lengthy silence followed. "Monsieur le Count," said Guy Le Bon. "If you'll pardon *my* impertinence, as well intentioned as your words may be, I believe your proclivity to autocratic management betrays your separation from the people of *this* land. England is not France, monsieur. As you doubtless are aware, those born to this soil have lived through years of unparalleled social upheaval and, as such, their inclinations toward, what was the word you used, ah yes—*misguided*—notions of self-government are by now firmly entrenched. To go back on this would spell disaster."

Count de Montfort smiled. "Well said, monsieur, but are these not rather lofty ideals to be thrown about by a steward? I believe these are decisions best left for Madame Valiere. Not you."

Sophie spread her napkin across her lap. "Well," she said, reassuming her hostess smile. "If you two messieurs will forgive *my* impertinence, I have made my decision. We will now present the Teurgoule pudding, flavored with cinnamon, and a delicious port to accompany it."

Sophie's guests returned her smile, and Sancho took the change of subject to remark at the excellent manners of her boys. "Thank you, Sylvain," Sophie said.

"By my faith," the count interrupted, "please, my dear Sophie, call this fellow by his preferred name—Sancho."

"Sancho, Sancho!" Christophe and Remy called out, smiling at the man sat beside them. His look indicated that he felt little enthusiasm for his Quixotean alter ego.

"Very well," Sophie replied. "Sancho, thank you for the compliment, but these boys have been in a good bit of trouble lately."

"Trouble?" Sylvain replied. He cast a look of mock horror at the boys. "Why, whatever have they done?"

"I'll save you from the long version, but not only were these two caught tormenting a poor farmer's daughter, but just today I've learned of them fighting with one of the boys on the grounds."

"It was Lucas's fault," Remy said, scooping a handful of pudding from his plate.

"It's true," Christophe added, his face red from embarrassment. "The boy attacked Lucas, and then Lucas asked us to help get him back. We were trying to help our friend."

"How many times," Sophie asked in a sharp voice that caused everyone in the room to straighten in their seats, "have I told you that boy is a little terror? That you are *not* to play with him?"

She paused, taking a deep breath. "Monsieur le Count, Sylvain, I apologize. My outburst was not polite. I can't hide my disappointment. My boys were harassing the son of one of the outlanders. They were caught chasing the lad up a tree, calling him 'smelly outlander ninny' while they threw rocks at him. Don't *speak*, Remy—I don't care who goaded you into it. In this family we never, ever behave like that, do you hear me?"

Both boys lowered their heads. A tense silence hung over the table; it was interrupted by an incongruous sound. Laughter.

"Eh, *mon dieu*," Count de Montfort said, wiping his mouth with a serviette. "I'm sorry, I am, I do not mean to make light. You boys," he said, pointing a finger at Christophe and Remy, "your mother has enough to deal with. She is to be obeyed and respected. I tell you, in some families you would receive a switch to your back for such behavior. Though 'smelly outlander ninny!' That is a fiendish little slur! I wish I had thought of it."

"Now really, Jean-Claude," Sophie exclaimed.

The count sat up straight and assumed a look of solemnity. Beside him Guy Le Bon stared ahead with a look of wry amusement, and Messieurs Burnouf and Abadain exchanged an uncomfortable look.

De Montfort, his face still red from laughing, looked down at his plate and realized he had not yet removed the covering tray from his pudding. With a long sigh he reached down and removed it. He opened his mouth to resume speaking—when his eyes bulged, and his face contorted in a look of sheer horror. "Ahhh!" he cried out, lifting his hands protectively. Every head in the room jerked toward him, and Sophie, thinking something terrible had happened, rushed instinctively from her seat. Le Bon turned his head slowly toward their guest, and a rare smile formed on his usually glum features.

With a few loud "ribbits" and a quick swelling of its cheeks, a large bullfrog hopped from his plate and across the table, leaping in a bound past Madame Abadain and out into the front hall where a gaggle of servers scrambled to grab hold of it. Remy and Christophe leapt from their chairs, fleeing the room in a fit of laughter. Sophie stared at their empty chairs with a look of exasperation.

"I must apologize again, Jean-Claude," Sophie said, placing a hand on her forehead. "I have no words for how mortified I feel." She sighed, lost in thought for a moment. The boys, after a lengthy chiding, had apologized to the count and been put to bed. The other guests had used the incident to offer a quick farewell and return to their homes. Left alone, Sophie had invited the count to join her for a glass of cognac and a stroll through the ground floor.

"Sophie, my dear," the count replied, placing a gentle hand on hers, "it is nothing. It is less than nothing. Two boys doing what boys do."

They stood together in the library in front of a painting that depicted a scene from the wars of the Italian Renaissance.

"Now," he said, nodding at the painting, "this work is rather brutal. The choice was your husband's, I presume?"

"This is one of André's favorites. He's always taken an interest in European history."

"Lieutenant-Colonel André Valiere, commander of His Majesty Napoleon's legion of gallant horsemen." De Montfort slashed an arm through the air in a display of mock swordplay.

Sophie's eyes remained on the painting, her smile fading.

"Oh, come now," he said, placing on arm on her lower back. "I do not mean to unsettle you; I just find your husband's martial reputation so formidable...as to be almost intimidating."

Sophie reflected on the comment for a moment before chuckling. "No," she said, her smile returning. "André is indeed a fine soldier. But he is hardly intimidating, once you've come to know him. He's a gentle man."

"To his family," the count said, looking back at the painting. "To his enemies on the field I have no doubt that he is a Norman conqueror."

Sophie nodded. "I know him to be quite brave."

"Doubtless."

Sophie called the count's attention to a second painting.

"Goodness," he remarked as he looked up at the next piece. "Another depiction of our brave fellows at war. Your husband can't seem to hide his affinity for it."

Sophie stared at the painting for a moment. "I think André hates war," she declared. "In fact, I *know* he does. But it always seems he is drawn back to it. It was not his wish to return, you know. To war. At least, he never expressed such a wish to me." Sophie smiled to herself, lost in thought. "Ever the gallant officer, Andre offered himself to spare others; from conscription, that is."

De Montfort gazed at her with his eyebrows raised.

She cleared her throat, her eyes returning to the count. "The emperor's conscription law required that every male on our estate, upon reaching the age of twenty, make himself eligible for service in the army. Two years ago the emperor called on those *men* to serve. Our population here at Carcourt required us to send ten men as soldiers. Or, one man as an officer, along with a payment of substitution. We all knew the toll this would take on the farmers' livelihoods, losing their best laborers. So Andre—unwilling to force the youth of his estate to leave their families, when he had his own rank and experience to be drawn upon—offered himself. He resumed his commision, and offered the remaining substitution payment so that none of the farmers would lose their sons."

A heavy silence hung in the air. Then, abruptly changing the subject, she said, "I'm sorry, I don't know if it's because of that incident with the frog or something else, but I seem to have drunk more than my fair share tonight. Perhaps even more than you, monsieur."

"My dear Sophie," The count replied, turning his full glass in his hand. "It would be ungracious for a visitor to become drunk in the house of a woman such as you."

Sophie smiled at the compliment. "A woman like me. But monsieur, I hardly know anything about you. What brings you here, truly—or if you prefer, what has brought you home after so many years away?"

De Montfort focused on the painting. " I spent the early days of the Revolution in a state of denial. I helped many noblemen and their families escape, charging for safe passage to southern England. Some called me a hero, but in truth I did not expect the Revolution to turn into what it did." He glanced at Sophie before continuing. "But—the time came when I found the noose tightening around my own neck and like any other with a desire to survive, I fled. When one has looked into the face of death, other considerations seem to melt away. Since the day I left this country, chased out by an angry mob of *sans-culottes*, I had but one true desire: to return home."

Sophie nodded, her expression one of genuine empathy. She offered him another smile, which he returned.

"But upon my return, the families I had saved from losing their heads have acted as if they do not recognize me, ignoring my offers of friendship and petitions for mutual enterprise. I came home to find my estate a heap of ruins, my wine cellar empty, and my bed occupied by a half-deaf refractory priest who'd moved into the house during the Terror and never left. I suppose that is the way of things in this mad world; one does right by another only to see the act repaid with scorn and exclusion.

"I suppose it must be quite difficult," the count continued after a long silence, "for a man such as your husband to return from the front lines, to return to a tranquil life; to close away that part of himself that required violence to survive." Sensing that he'd made Sophie uncomfortable, the count clarified. "I would never doubt your husband's bravery, though I wonder if he did not make a selfish decision to rush back to war. With two young boys—"

"I am grateful for your concern, monsieur," Sophie interrupted. "But I assure you, I am capable of taking care of myself and my family in my husband's absence."

"Madame Valiere." The count held out his hands in apology. "You need *never* doubt my faith in your abilities. Of all those I've met since my return, no one has made quite such an impression on me as you."

"That is kind of you to say—"

"Sophie, my child," the count said, gently placing her hand in his. "Your attentiveness toward your sons is surpassed only by your love, which they are blessed to receive. I only raise this matter because I wish to help. I worry that in the absence of their father, an absence that he doubtless considers an act of duty, they seem to lack a firm hand."

Sophie lowered her head. "My husband's absence these past months has been felt by all in this household."

"Everyone can see how hard you try," de Montfort said. "But managing an estate so large, with so many divergent interests, things can go wrong; invariably, they do go wrong. Take me into your confidence, Sophie. Everything I have will be at your disposal. Your man Le Bon and my Sancho could share tax collection duties. You have more workers than you need; I would be happy to accept the transfer of a hundred of your outlanders to my estate. If you do not close me out, I will make your success my success." De Montfort gently squeezed her hand. "Do not break the heart of a lonely man so long removed from the land and people he loves."

Sophie took a sip from her glass, emptying it. "So, the dinner made such an impression on you that you now feel that you must help me?"

"You have the world here," he whispered. "I wish you would accept the help of one who wishes the best for you."

He leaned in and his eyes closed. Sophie, thinking perhaps he was lost in thought or becoming sick, did not notice until his lips nearly touched hers. She jerked her head back and held out a hand. "Jean-Claude," she said, her voice unsteady, "monsieur, what are you doing?"

"I wish for nothing more than to see your happiness, Madame Valiere."

"And I thank you for such a wish," she replied, her tone now more serious. "But if you think I desire you, you are mistaken, sir, as my husband provides me with all of the happiness I could ever need or want."

De Montfort released her hand with an understanding nod. A moment passed, and the count took a sip of cognac, his eyes never leaving hers. "If your husband survives this war, will the same man return to you?"

What?" Sophie asked.

"If such a man were to return from battle *changed*, well, any action might be justified by such experiences—I know this is an unpleasant thought, but was André ever…violent to you?"

Sophie's eyes narrowed. "Monsieur. Not only has André never struck me, but in my time of desperation he offered his life so that I might escape with mine. It is quite bold of you to insinuate he could ever treat me with violence."

"Perhaps you're right," he rejoined, gazing into her eyes. "Violence is not always committed with brute force. I've seen men come back from war changed—something, some light had gone out of them. They returned to their families almost vacant."

Sophie averted her eyes, turning her body slightly away from him. For a moment they stood in silence. At last the count sighed. "We're never hurt so much by our enemies' threats or slanders as we are by the silence of those we love."

Without a reply Sophie walked into the next room and stood beside the door. "Monsieur," she said, "until a minute ago, I have had a pleasant evening in your company, and I thank you for your visit. But I believe it is now time for you to leave."

De Montfort strode slowly across the room, the old wooden floor creaking loudly under his boots. He paused as he approached Sophie, his expression serious. "I hate to see you unhappy and alone, my dear."

"I thank you for your kind words. Have a pleasant return home."

"Know that you will always have a dear friend in me." he said before he turned and departed.

CHAPTER 18

Oder River, Prussia

November 1806

André was jolted out of a fitful sleep by an urgent voice. "Wake up, sir! Wake up now!"

He looked up in a daze, momentarily unsure of where he was. Standing over him was Major Mazzarello, shaking him by the shoulders. The typically stoic sergeant-major was in a state of panic. "It's Moreau. Come quick, sir; he's in trouble!"

"Calm down, man; I can hear you." André threw on his pants and wrapped himself in his green coat. "What has happened?"

Mazzarello had already exited the room and shouted back, "He's been wounded sir! It doesn't look good."

André leapt down the stairs of the inn in long bounds. Storming past the soldiers sleeping on the floor of the dining room, the two men ran out the front door. The sun had not yet risen above the rooftops, and a dense fog lingered. André blew on his hands, which were already aching from the cold morning air.

They rounded a large building and the sergeant-major came to an abrupt halt. André pulled up beside him and saw two of his dragoons crouched on the ground. One held a canteen in his hand and, as André and Mazzarello approached, he leaned back, revealing the figure of Marcel Moreau. He was propped upright, resting against the wall of the building. His eyes were closed, and he did not move or speak as André crouched down in front of him.

"Marcel?" he asked in a quiet voice.

The two dragoons dabbed his chest with bandages dipped in hot water. Beneath his open coat multiple slash wounds to his chest and arms were visible. His lips were purple and his skin pale, but André was relieved to see his chest rising and falling, albeit slowly.

"When did you find him?"

"Weren't more than a few minutes, sir," one of the dragoons replied. "We was changing our pickets and seen the major lying on the ground. He weren't moving, so we propped 'im against the wall and sent for the sergeant-major."

"You did well." André took a breath to steady his nerves. "Now go find the surgeon. He should be quartered at the inn."

The trooper took off at a dead sprint, and André surveyed the nearby buildings, which were becoming more distinguishable with the lifting fog. An eerie quiet hung over the town. André turned to the remaining dragoon, who was cleaning Moreau's chest wounds. "Did you see anything else, Paquet?"

"I've not seen what 'appened sir, but there ain't a need, really. We all know who done this." Paquet dabbed the bandage with gentle care. "Them 'ussars is all gone. Their 'orses and kit is gone. It was them who fuckin' done it, sir."

André took a look inside the stables where the hussars had billeted their horses. A pitchfork lay propped against a wall next to half a dozen other farm tools, and clumps of hay were strewn across the floor. No horses remained; he closed the door, swearing to himself.

"Will he live?" Sergeant-major Mazzarello demanded. He stood alongside André in the hall outside the room where Moreau was resting.

"His wounds have been cleaned," the surgeon, still wearing his nightcap, replied. "All seven have been dressed and sewn up to the extent possible. Loss of blood is considerable, but no major arteries were severed, and your troopers found him in time. So, for now, it is impossible to say. Only time will tell."

The three men stared vacantly, nodding in silent reply. André had sent out riders to check the roads for signs of Carnassier and his men, but without witnesses or word from Moreau he could not prove the hussar was responsible for this violence.

"When can he speak?" André asked the surgeon.

"He's barely breathing. He may remain unconscious for hours, even days."

To give his executive officer time to recover, André was able to delay his squadron's departure for two days. Their brigade commander, despite misgivings, was more preoccupied with reaching the warmth of Posen than arguing with one of his subordinates. However, before departing with the rest of the regiment, Colonel Menard offered André a clear warning. "If you push your luck any further, lieutenant-colonel, you might just fall over the edge."

Two days later, André was dressing in his small room at the inn. As he inspected his uniform in the mirror, he contemplated how worn and tattered his green frock coat looked; his pants were frayed and streaked with cuts, while his boots were worn almost to where his toes showed through. The campaign had been one disaster after another, and every decision he made seemed to come back to haunt him. Had he gotten himself into something that was beyond him? The days when he was a young captain, hurling himself toward the enemy at Valmy, shouting his defiance along with General Kellermann and his brother Remy, seemed a lifetime ago. Had he lost his soldiering instincts?

He was shaken from his despondency when Mazzarello came to inform him that the squadron was assembled for departure.

"Major Moreau has a place with the baggage train?" He hoped his voice did not betray his mood.

"Has a cart to himself. He'll be riding like a king, sir."

André wrapped his belt and sword around his waist and picked up his helmet. His sergeant-major was hovering sheepishly by the door, as if he had more to say.

"Is everything all right?"

"Sir, the troopers who offered to personally escort Major Moreau's cart in the rear of the column—or to stay behind should he be unable to move—are mounted outside, waiting for your blessing."

André felt a surge of pride at this act of solidarity. "Very well. Let's be on our way."

The two men descended the stairs. André handed the innkeeper several coins for his hospitality; compulsory and free of charge though it might have been, he wished to express his gratitude for the food and shelter. In the days ahead, they would not be living so comfortably.

Once outside, André was astonished by the site before him—his entire squadron sat mounted and in parade formation in the road. A feeling of intense admiration swelled in his chest. Given their recent trials, he decided it was time to offer a few words.

"Troopers of the Seventeenth Squadron," he began, ignoring the lump in his throat. "You do yourselves and your officers great honor by presenting yourselves in support of your executive officer, Major Moreau."

Drums and fifes echoed in the distance as other regiments marched out of the town. The dragoons kept their eyes on André.

"Although the major cannot respond to your gesture of solidarity at the moment, I am sure that were he able, he would offer you all heartfelt gratitude—with his customary warmth and cheerfulness."

A hearty laugh swept through the squadron, and André indulged them this moment of cheerfulness.

"He will accompany us to Posen, where we will rejoin the rest of the corps. After that, we will stand ready to carry out any further orders."

André gave the signal to the trumpeter and standard-bearer for departure and mounted his horse. Putting on his helmet, he turned back to his squadron. "I have not forgotten about the men who did this to Major Moreau. When we find them, they will answer for their crimes and regret the day they decided to challenge the Seventeenth Dragoons. *Vive l'Empereur!*"

"*Vive l'Empereur!*"

CHAPTER 19

Palais de Justice, Paris

Spring 1806

J ean-Luc arrived at the Palais de Justice before any of his colleagues or lawyers of the opposition team. He spent the next three hours refining his opening and closing statements until he was satisfied he had done all he could possibly do to prepare. A short while later the judge entered the chamber and took his chair, announcing the opening of the Administration's trial against Monsieur Pierre-Yves Gagnon.

Gagnon's counselor, Monsieur Bounaix, delivered his opening statement by proclaiming the defendant nothing more than a slandered and vilified merchant, whose biggest crime was falling afoul of the emperor's current political mood.

Jean-Luc's opening statement was brief. His strategy: wait until the opposition showed their full hand and all witnesses had been cross-examined before revealing the information Monsieur de Landreville had given him. He would wait until his closing statement to land the masterstroke.

In the meantime, the defense mounted a stirring case on their client's behalf. It came not in the form of proclaiming Gagnon's innocence, but rather taking aim at the prosecution's legitimacy. They assaulted Jean-Luc's credibility at every possible opportunity. This was not unexpected, but after several mocking references to his office's inability to uncover instances of bribery or intimidation in connection with the construction of the Ourcq Canal, Monsieur Bounaix unsettled Jean-Luc with a surprise of his own.

"So we deliberate here today," the counselor declared, "relying on the word of a lawyer who was born, raised, and educated in a city nearly four hundred miles away, but who presumably understands this city and its long-suffering inhabitants more than a man who has lived and conducted business here his entire life."

"Most men I know," Jean-Luc retorted, "don't conduct their business by facilitating local crime rings."

The judge ordered the prosecution to wait their turn and motioned for the defense to continue.

"Your Honor, I only mention the prosecution's origins because, on the few occasions he *has* practiced law in our city, his record has been nothing short of abysmal. His most high-profile case involved General François Christophe Kellermann—a man disgraced by his crimes against the state, for which he was executed."

Jean-Luc, visibly agitated, rose to his feet. "Christophe Kellermann was a man of honor with an impeccable army record. His only crime was eliciting the envy of cowards like Nikolai Murat and Guillaume Lazare. If you wish for your word to hold an *ounce* of weight in this courtroom, you will stop this needless slander of a national hero."

The counselor smirked, allowing Jean-Luc to stew in his frustration a moment before continuing. "As you can see, mesdames and messieurs, old defeats leave dreadful scars. Notwithstanding Monsieur St. Clair's personal affections for the man, he nevertheless *failed* to convince our Revolutionary Tribunal of the man's innocence; he was exec—"

"We know what happened to General Kellermann," Jean-Luc interjected, his tone icy. "Every man and woman in this city knows the Revolutionary Tribunal was no more than an antechamber of the guillotine."

"Be that as it may," his opponent replied, "the prosecution's dubious record cannot be overlooked if we are to arrive at a fair and just conclusion for my client. *Perhaps* Monsieur Kellermann was a brave man, perhaps he was innocent of any crime; we will never know. But it would be unwise for us to suppose that the failed defense of a man almost *certainly* involved in a conspiracy against the State—"

"What conspiracy?" Jean-Luc asked, turning to the judge. "Your Honor, what relevance does this slander have in determining the guilt of Monsieur Pierre-Yves Gagnon?"

After a brief reproach and a pause to restore calm, the judge asked the defense what conspiracy he referred to regarding General Kellermann.

"Why the charade of Valmy, Your Honor," the counselor stated matter of factly. "Are we not familiar with this? Allow me to give a brief summary."

"*Brief* it will be, counselor," the judge declared.

"Very well, Your Honor. It was September of 1792, and the Prussians were marching across eastern France, our armies fleeing disgracefully before them. Thankfully, our National Convention took matters in hand, sending an emissary to the camp of Prince Frederick in an attempt to draw him away from his allies and into a separate peace with our deputies. General Dumouriez, meeting secretly with the prince, was joined by Georges Danton, who attended this secret meeting in possession of the crown jewels of the house of Bourbon, which had been stolen from the Tuileries on the fifteenth of September and not seen since. Danton and Dumouriez offered the prince said jewels in exchange for a charade of a battle in which Frederick would advance and subsequently retire after minimal losses."

"Your Honor," Jean-Luc said, rising to his feet. "Thus far I have received the insults leveled at me in stride, knowing them to be the slings and arrows, albeit underhanded, that any public advocate must endure. However, in all my years of practicing law, amongst even the most bloodthirsty radicals, I have *never* seen a trial veer so far into the gutter of scandal and conspiracy. This lawyer is making a mockery of your court, and I dare presume he does so at the behest of the man whom he represents."

Jean-Luc turned on his heels with surprising agility. "Your Honor, I was going to wait until the defense offered all their evidence before introducing the following piece of information." He took several strides in the direction of Gagnon. "This fact will, perhaps, change the course of these proceedings, which up until now have taken on a shambolic and ridiculous character. It has come to my attention that Monsieur Gagnon's sordid past has more relevance than we have yet to appreciate, a series of unfortunate blunders have led to the current circum—"

The doors at the back of the chamber opened with a loud crash, and the entire room, including Jean-Luc, turned to the man now standing in the entryway. Dressed in a plain black coat and breeches, he made his way to the front. Behind him waited half a dozen soldiers of the gendarmerie, their presence indicating something out of the ordinary was about to take place. After exchanging a few quiet words with the judge, the man in the black coat turned to face the courtroom. "By order of His Majesty Napoleon I, Emperor of the French, this trial has been annulled and is no longer in session."

The man signaled to Gagnon, whereupon the waiting gendarmes trudged into the room and forced the man to his feet.

"Monsieur Pierre-Yves Gagnon," the man declared, "has been declared an outlaw of the French Empire and is hereby sentenced to prison for an indefinite period. His property, holdings, and businesses are to be confiscated and turned over to the State, by order of the emperor."

Jean-Luc was dumbfounded. The judge sat in stunned silence, the scowl on his face betraying a deep disapproval; but even he would not dare challenge the will of Emperor Napoleon.

After Gagnon had been clasped in manacles and escorted out, the magistrate turned to those still in the courtroom. "You may all depart."

CHAPTER 20

Paris, France

Spring, 1806

The crowd outside the Palais-Royal observed Jean-Luc and Isabella's entrance with eager fascination. Despite the cold, it seemed as if the entire city was in the streets, as crowds of onlookers jostled each other to catch a glimpse at the latest couple among the Parisian "notables" to have gained the Bonapartes' favor. Wrapped in a white silk necktie beneath an expensive new Italian overcoat, Jean-Luc waved with a smile, soaking in the curious gazes and enthusiastic murmuring of the crowd. At his side stood Isabella, who dazzled in a pleated white mousseline dress beneath a blue cashmere shell that matched her pearl earrings.

Once inside the Palais, the finely dressed duo presented themselves to the ladies and gentlemen from the circles of notables, who had gathered tonight for the celebration of Napoleon's victory at Austerlitz. Their invitation had come at the behest of Joseph Bonaparte as congratulations for Jean-Luc's success against Gagnon in court; an experience that still held the unmistakable feel of an unfulfilling sideshow.

Their gallery overlooking the *cour d'honneur*, though secluded and offering a fine view of the Palais courtyard, did not prevent the occasional interruption of their dinner by the felicitations and well wishes of strangers. To Jean-Luc this was a slight surprise, though not an unwelcome one. Isabella, for her part, seemed poised and graceful, as if already accustomed to such attention. As they dined on several cheeses, legumes, and roast duck, Jean-Luc suddenly thought of his children, at home and already in bed. He had hardly seen them prior to the trial and now felt guilty not to be sharing this moment with them.

"On Mathieu's fourth birthday," he confided in Isabella, "I did not have enough money to buy him any gifts or special food, nothing as elegant as this. Marie carved a spoon into a toy soldier, and he was happy. But I've never forgotten the feeling of failing to provide for my wife and child. I will not live that life again, and lately I feel that I have not seen enough of them—"

"No father in this city cares for his children more than you, my dear."

Jean-Luc sighed. "These days it's as though he cares for nothing; not his schoolwork, not his father. His tutors tell me he hardly applies himself and clashes with his schoolmates more and more."

"Well, you and I both know what is troubling him." She leaned in close. "He wants to be *more* than just another schoolboy." Her eyes revealed an eagerness that Jean-Luc found both enticing and unsettling. "He's grow-ing into a young *man*, for goodness sake. He wants to show the world his courage and fire. In this city, the heart of the empire, surrounded by soldiers winning honors and decorations, can you really blame him?"

Jean-Luc stared at his plate, his appetite not what it had been when they had arrived. Isabella cast a look around the room, noticing more than one pair of eyes on them. "Smile, my dear," she admonished him. "It is quite unseemly for a man of your growing stature to blemish your public appear-ances with inexplicable displays of fretfulness."

A commotion arose in the hall below. A crowd of finely dressed men and women were making their way up the carpeted staircase; at the cen-ter was Joseph Bonaparte, distinguished by his senator's uniform. He was talking with two men. When their conversation concluded, Joseph made his way over to Jean-Luc and Isabella. "I can't imagine why Monsieur St. Clair never mentioned his stunning wife." Joseph took Isabella's hand and kissed it. "My name is Joseph, madame."

"I know who you are, your majesty," Isabella said, demurely. "Though Monsieur St. Clair and I are not yet betrothed, I must tell you that I feel blessed indeed to be with a man who seems to lead a charmed life; two lovely young children and the honor of serving the emperor and his eldest brother, the finest royal dynasty Europe has seen in centuries. Or so Jean-Luc tells me."

"You're too generous, madame." Joseph smiled. He then turned to Jean-Luc and tapped him on the shoulder. "I am loath to part you from the company of so fine a woman, but I must steal a minute of your time. If that is all right with you, my lady?"

Isabella smiled and bit her lip. Jean-Luc was momentarily tongue-tied, the words "not yet betrothed" ringing in his ears. In the pause that followed, Isabella bowed, graciously taking a step back. Joseph took Jean-Luc by the arm and led him out of earshot across the mezzanine, stopping at an unoccupied spot on the balcony overlooking the crowded halls below. In a hushed tone, he said, "You should be smiling, my friend. Tonight is a happy occasion."

"Yes, sir."

"Oh come now, what troubles you on a night of gaiety?"

"Nothing, Your Majesty. It is a very happy occasion."

Joseph smiled and waved to the crowd below; Jean-Luc mirrored his movement. A sight in the throng caught Jean-Luc's eye, and he nearly laughed aloud: Thiery and several of his colleagues stood chatting with a group of women in fine mousseline dresses and silk shawls. As he peered down at them, their group turned their gazes up toward the mezzanine. One of the ladies motioned at the two men standing on the balcony, and Jean-Luc was suddenly aware that Joseph's royal presence had captured the attention of half the banquet. To his surprise, and no small satisfaction, his colleagues all wore frowns, except for Thiery, who smiled up at him. Jean-Luc ignored him and turned to Joseph, who offered a final wave before pulling Jean-Luc back from the balcony.

"Don't tell me it is that fool Gagnon." Joseph accepted two glasses of wine from an aide, passing one to Jean-Luc. "Or his lawyer, Bounaix. I heard about his ill-mannered assaults upon you last week. He was simply doing as he was instructed," Joseph said. "Trying to goad you, hoping you would become overwhelmed and appear unsure of yourself. You know those attacks come because agitators don't wish to waste their time going after small fish. Such men are highly efficient at what they do, and they target talented men such as yourself. That is one of the reasons you were chosen; we know of whom you have dealt with in the past."

Jean-Luc did not rush to dispel the compliments, suddenly feeling a keen satisfaction at being seen by so many in the close company of the emperor's brother. "I understand, sir," he replied before taking a long sip of wine. "But that is not what preoccupies my thoughts."

"Oh?" Joseph asked, once again waving again to the onlookers below.

"No, monsieur. In truth, it is more a matter of trust and honesty; and as much as I regret to say it, I have had my trust shaken in recent days."

"And who is it that has shaken your trust thus?"

Jean-Luc exhaled. "You, sir."

Joseph let out a hearty laugh. "Me? Why, however so?"

"Your Majesty, the correspondence I was entrusted to relay between Mayor Bergasse and yourself was not at all what I understood it to be. I thought it to be a correspondence concerning trade and other legal matters. But in truth—" Jean-Luc turned to ensure no one stood nearby, "it bore a list of names. *Concealed* names."

Joseph Bonaparte's face went somber, and for a moment his dark Corsican eyes took on a severity that resembled that of his younger, more powerful brother. "And how did you come by this information, monsieur?"

Jean-Luc did not flinch. "The minister of police."

Joseph turned his attention back down below. "And you never thought of informing me of this?" After offering another wave and polite smile, he indicated for Jean-Luc to follow him as he left the balustrade.

"The minister of police offered it voluntarily, monsieur," Jean-Luc explained. He nevertheless felt a pang of guilt. Joseph eyed him for a moment, finally nodding his understanding.

"Never mind that now." Joseph leaned in closer. "St. Clair, what I am about to tell you is a State secret. Not even the emperor's marshals know of what I am about to tell you. Do I have your word that you will keep our discretion?"

"Yes, your Majesty," Jean-Luc answered, thrown by the sudden admission.

"First allow me to offer you an apology for this little game; we never meant to keep you in the dark for so long. This correspondence you mention, it is part of an ongoing maneuver. Napoleon has been so preoccupied in Austria that he has been unable to trust *anyone* outside of our family with Naples. That is why we were not permitted to tell you. Events were fluid on the Austrian front; even a minor slip could have resulted in disaster. But now that he has crushed the allies, he has realigned his sights to the south. He will not let the Neapolitans, English, and Russians make common cause on our doorstep." Joseph grasped Jean-Luc by the shoulders. "If all goes well, St. Clair, you may be granted your wish."

"My wish?"

Joseph shook Jean-Luc's shoulders. "Senator St. Clair."

Jean-Luc nearly gasped aloud before Joseph hushed him. "Yes, yes. It has been discussed. But in order to merit it there is something that we both ask of you." He threw back his shoulders, assuming the posture of a dignified statesman; the twinkle in his eye remained. "The emperor is calling upon you to journey to Naples and enact his will; the details, as such, will be given very soon. Can we count on you, my friend?"

Jean-Luc's head spun, and as he looked around the room his eyes landed on the pretty face of Isabella, who met his smile with her own.

On their way home, Jean-Luc broke his silence as they crossed over the Seine along the Pont des Tuileries leading toward Saint-Germain. "It is extraordinary, I know. But, you remember what I told you earlier this evening? The memory of those days of struggle and hardship have never left. I feel more determined than ever not to live that life again."

Isabella, her arm slipped about his, laughed. "My dear, you've just been told you are on your way to being made a senator, and yet you fret about the past. My dear St. Clair, you've done it…you've arrived!"

"Perhaps," he said, as they passed over the bridge. Its stone pillars still bore the scars of the violence of the Revolution. He looked back across the river at the Pavillon de Flore of the Tuileries. Sconces that had once held the statues of kings were now empty, black burn marks where torches and muskets had been brandished had yet to be washed from the stone, and blemishes where pikes had scraped against the doors all reminded one of how close the city had come to losing one of its oldest and most treasured structures.

"But now that we've come so far," Jean-Luc resumed, bringing his thoughts back to the present, "we must fight so that we do not lose it all." His mind conjured all the new possibilities of his soon-to-be position. He could see the grand *maison* of his senatory, perched atop a grassy hill overlooking a quiet countryside below. And yet, in spite of the unmistakable joy of the evening's news, he felt a strange shiver pass over his body.

"We *must* not lose it all."

CHAPTER 21

Posen, Poland
November 1806

The ride east to Posen would take several days due to the number of soldiers and horses clogging the roads. André maintained an easy pace that ensured the squadron's baggage, including the wounded Major Moreau, kept up with the rest of the squadron.

On the third day church spires could be seen above the trees in the distance. André halted the squadron a mile from the city gates to allow the horses to feed on what grass remained after the trampling of an army numbering in the tens of thousands; it looked to him as if his entire country had marched to this very place. Spanning from the gates to the opposite horizon was a mass of men, horses and appendages of war that brought his mind back to the great battle before the pyramids of Giza.

As the dragoons rode into the city and past the town hall, André was surprised to see many of the town's inhabitants lined on either side of the streets. Some threw lilies and red poppies in front of the horses' hooves, while others waved the flag of Poland and the French tricolor. Shouts of *"Niech żyje Dabrowski!"* and *"Vive Napoleon!"* echoed throughout the jubilant crowd.

Once the men were quartered, André and Sergeant-major Mazzarello sought out the regimental surgeon to check on Moreau. They found the makeshift hospital established in the St. Stanislaus Parish Church, an imposing structure of Roman baroque inspiration. The walls of the interior were lined with various paintings and sculptures from Polish history, some dating back to the eleventh century, though these relics were obscured by the presence of hundreds of sick and wounded French and Polish soldiers who lay on the ground or in the pews. Moreau's cot was tucked in the transept next to a small altar. To their surprise and relief his eyes were open and, though pale and gaunt in the face, he appeared in decent form.

"You're back with us, eh?" Mazzarello tapped his shoulder. "How are you feeling?"

Moreau adjusted himself on his cot. "I feel like horse shit."

"He's back, sir," Mazzarello said to André, and they both indulged in a bit of much needed laughter.

"I think you're right. Welcome back, major."

"How long have I been unconscious?"

"Too long," Mazzarello answered. "We'll have you fit and back in the saddle in no time."

André took his eyes from the ornate images on the stained-glass windows above the choir. "You lost a lot of blood. But the sergeant-major is right; we need you to get well, back to your cheerful self."

Moreau expelled several raspy coughs, and André knew it would be some time before he was fit to fight—both physically and mentally. The sergeant-major took his leave to check on the men, and Moreau indicated for André to come closer, asking if he could have a word with him on a personal matter. André nodded in the affirmative.

"After Carnassier killed the two villagers," Moreau began, "you came into contact with a woman."

"Yes," André replied. That day felt as if it had taken place years ago. "She'd worked herself into a bit of a frenzy; she was brandishing a knife."

Moreau cleared his throat, hacking up phlegm and spitting it into a basket beside his bed. "She was the granddaughter of the old man who was killed. When I had got her calmed down, I asked her name: Alicja Jarzyna. She said that she did not trust me or my countrymen, that we were murdering devils. I took a liking to her immediately."

André grinned, but Moreau's features remained serious, pained.

"I thought—rather I knew," he continued, "that our business with the hussars was not finished. My desire to tear that fucker Carnassier limb from limb was matched only by a feeling of guilt for what we had done. Murder. It was foolish of me, but that night I wrote a note to the girl promising that I would avenge her grandfather's killing. I signed it in my own blood. I gave it to a villager early the next morning, telling him to find someone who could deliver it to the granddaughter of the slain burgher—and a beauty at that. He told me he would do it, or at least that was my impression. I gave my billeting post where her response might find me. I did not expect to receive any word from her. It was a stupid idea."

Moreau coughed again, and he leaned forward, reaching beneath his cot. He pulled out a small ironbound chest of varnished wood and opened it. André glimpsed two flintlock dueling pistols polished to a bright sheen. Reaching beneath the weapons, Moreau pulled out a small parchment and unfolded it. "To my surprise, she did respond. This arrived a week ago. I told her that we were marching to Posen to provide security for a group of our senators. The news must have roused in her some national pride, I don't know…" His voice trailed off, and he gently placed the paper back in the wooden box and slid it underneath his cot. "I'm not sure why I'm telling you this, sir, but I wished to inform you that she will be in the city. I'll have a nursemaid, so you and Mazzarello can stop fussing and get back to your duty while I'm absent."

"God in heaven, Marcel." André laughed aloud, unable to hold back his relief. "When you took out that chest, I thought you might have hidden a trophy of Alderic's ears or Carnassier's tongue beside your pistols."

Moreau looked at André with a curious expression.

"Poor attempt at humor." André laughed again. "At any rate, I'm relieved. This is good news."

Moreau nodded, the trace of a grin showing on his hardened features.

A week passed, and André took turns with his sergeant-major visiting Moreau at the hospital. He seemed to be improving, due in part, André believed, to the presence of an attractive blonde woman with green eyes and an unmistakable frankness of personality. Alicja Jarzyna had arrived as Moreau said she would, and she divided her time between tending to him and visiting, whenever possible, the ambassadorial assemblies in the town hall, pretending to be a housekeeper to gain admittance. She attended the meetings with a quiet reserve at first, but her personal experience with Carnassier's hussars had left her with so vivid and painful an impression of the French that on the third morning of her attendance she interjected herself into an exchange between General Dabrowski and one of the French generals. She reminded them that the French Grand Armée was on Polish soil and asserted that the native inhabitants possessed an equal right to judge the French emperor's intentions as he did their worthiness as a people. General Dabrowski had laughed heartily, unwilling to either agree or disagree with her statement on record, but he admitted that although the French army had won the loyalty of Poland's soldiers, they still had work to do if they were to win the hearts and minds of its women.

One morning as André departed his brigade commander's briefing, he heard a commotion coming from down the hallway. The corridor in the town hall was largely empty, but as he peered ahead, he saw a familiar face. Standing between two servants, who seemed to be struggling in their efforts to restrain her, was Alicja. When she saw André, she broke free and rushed toward him.

"Quick! You must come quick!"

André held out his hands. "I'm here. Tell me what has happened—"

"You must come *now!*"

André noticed a growing number of people milling about behind him, whispering their disdain rather loudly. "All right. Show me the way." Alicja grabbed André's hand and practically pulled him out the front door. "Calm yourself, woman. What can be so urgent to cause these hysterics?"

"Hysterics?" She stared at André as if he had pulled a pistol on her. "Colonel, Major Moreau is *dying.*"

With a groan she released André's hand and ran across the large square in the direction of the church. André stood in stunned silence. "Dying?" Shaking his head, he pulled himself out of his dark thoughts and hurried after Alicja across the square toward St. Stanislaus Cathedral.

André found Moreau lying unconscious in his cot, the regimental surgeon kneeling beside him, dabbing a wet cloth on his forehead. "His pulse is normal, but his breaths are shallow and faint."

André shifted uneasily. "What happened?"

The surgeon stood and removed his glasses. "To tell you truthfully, lieu-tenant-colonel, I haven't the faintest idea. His body has recovered remark-ably well, but sometimes there are wounds deeper than flesh and bone, injuries that our medicaments are powerless to repair. Time will determine his fate." The man picked up his satchel. "I will return tomorrow at first light. Continue applying the wet cloth, but do not remove the bandages. Good night."

An eerie silence settled inside the basilica, disturbed only by an occa-sional cough echoing through the cavernous hall. Alicja sat down on the pew across from Moreau. Apart from the slight rise and fall of his chest, there was little to indicate life.

"Alicja, get some rest," said André. He knew that if the squadron were to be ordered out to the field, this time Moreau would be left behind. "There's nothing we can do for him right now."

Alicja applied the cloth to Moreau's face with gentle dabs.

"Alicja, did you hear me—"

"Yes, I heard you!" she snapped, tears welling in her eyes. "If this is how easily you French give up, how could you ever believe you could free my country?" André said nothing. After a few minutes Alicja set the wet cloth down with a sigh. "There *is* something we could do," she whispered. "Your people think you have the world figured out with your reason and your philosophy; but sometimes things happen—beyond reason—events that philosophy cannot explain. If your doctors cannot save him, then there is something else that can. *Someone* else."

André's eyes narrowed. "Speak plainly."

"In this country there are those who still practice ancient arts, who know the ancient secrets, with answers to questions you have never thought to ask."

CHAPTER 22

Carcourt, Normandy

Autumn 1806

"**I** choose not to ride sidesaddle," Sophie said, patting her horse, "because when I was young, I was thrown from my horse, quite forcibly, riding that way. So I choose dexterity over fashion or, as some might prefer, morals."

Count de Montfort held her gaze for an instant before turning his eyes back to the landscape ahead of them. "It is your land, madame; the rules are your prerogative. But I know some who would find the sight…unsettling."

Sophie smiled sardonically. "Like you, monsieur?"

"Perhaps," the count replied airily, "once. Though I'll concede your propensities for shooting and eschewing a bareback saddle would fairly stun those of fashionable society across the channel, they find such pursuits… unwomanly." He shifted in his saddle, trying to mitigate the discomfort in his backside. "But, you must know, I say all this in jest, for they are a dull and rigid lot. Forsooth, my dear, I've come to accept change as an inevitable circumstance of life, so I suppose I ought to be open to any and all changes."

"Good." She took another look out over the gentle slopes of the apple orchard to the south. "Fashionable society has been rendered rather unfashionable in these parts."

"True," De Montfort conceded with a smile. "We're a long way from Paris."

In the distance, a handful of farmers were picking apples and tossing them into baskets, singing as they worked in the fading autumn sun.

"I've often dreamt of Paris." The count flicked a piece of dirt from his saddle and straightened his torso. "For several years I saw the city when I slept. Its ringing bells and the shimmering waters of the Seine; and, as if on cue, I would hear screams, shouts, and the sound of guns. Mind you, I never saw Paris in the days of revolution, thank God, but for some reason, whenever I slept, my mind would conjure the twin towers of Notre-Dame looming over the burning city. It seemed to call out, as if it were beckoning me, and I'll admit a part of me felt some strange compulsion to go there, to see what had happened in those streets. To see the great city at the center of the world as it devoured itself. I could see the guillotine fall…and then I would wake up."

A long silence fell, and both riders stared out over the picturesque valley when a flock of wood pigeons flew out in front of them, causing the count's horse to buck nervously.

"Monsieur…" Sophie began, pausing as she searched for the right words. "I would like to apologize for the curtness that ended our previous meeting. We had both drunk our fill and, while I do not regret preventing you from kissing me, perhaps I was overly harsh in my reaction."

Count de Montfort readjusted the riding crop in his hand, resting it on the pommel of his horse. "Sophie, my child, a rebuke from you is more reward than all the romances one might find in Paris. It is nothing."

"It is gracious of you to accept my apology—but I must tell you the real reason I've invited you here."

"Ah," De Montfort replied with a sigh. "I was wrong to presume I'd been invited for an afternoon ride with a lovely woman under no pretense other than that she desired my company?"

"I've been considering your proposal," she said, her expression turning serious. "Our capabilities have been stretched almost to the breaking point. Your proposition for Guy Le Bon and Sancho to share tax collection duties on my land while transferring a hundred of the outlanders to your estate is not only suitable, but indeed quite helpful. I accept."

"Sophie, my child," the count replied, "you are a pearl of great price."

"Often I feel out of my depth, monsieur." She continued, "I come to the *other* topic of discussion I wished to broach with you, Jean-Claude. The other night you offered a suggestion after we'd finished dinner and well…I've implemented it. We've converted the rundown mill on the Saint-

Paër stream into a brasserie, to offer the farmers reasonable refreshment after a long day's work."

"I'm quite glad to hear—"

"No," Sophie snapped. "You will *not* be glad to hear that three days ago an almighty brawl erupted between my farmers and a group of outlanders. One of my gentlemen had his head cracked open; he's going to be fine, but, Jean-Claude, this was a disaster that could have been avoided. And I feel foolish meddling in the private affairs of farmers I know little about. And now I must go and meet with them and try to manage the situation."

The count lifted his head back and shook the hair from his face. In a deep voice he cried out, "Enlarge the man committed yesterday, that railed against our person; we consider it was excess of wine that set him on, and on his more advice we pardon him."

Sophie looked at him in total confusion.

"Oh, my dear Sophie," De Montfort sighed. "In England the people spoke of how under Napoleon our country had at least rediscovered its fondness for culture. We've truly diminished if we do not honor the great bard—Willem Shakespeare. Oh, my poor Sophie! Farmers and uprooted outlanders were bound for something of a scrape sooner or later. Deep down most men are hardly more than brutes who will seize on any perceived weakness of those below—or above—their station. Now they have vented their spleen—and they may be happier for it."

"Perhaps you're right, but I still question whether it was wise to mingle the two crowds with drink involved."

The count tilted his head. "As acting owner of this estate, you are right to ask such questions; after all, it is *your* estate. If they step too far out of line, simply burn their houses to the ground." He looked at her with a grim expression for several seconds before bursting into laughter. "Sophie, my child, it was only in jest! Do not trouble yourself over the drunken behavior of a few foolish men. It is in their nature."

"Nature or not," Sophie challenged, "it has caused an even greater rift among the people of this estate than that which already existed. And this is hardly a time for jesting."

The count held up his hands. "Try as we might, sometimes events simply unfold contrary to our plans and wishes. It will pass, my dear child."

"I do wish you would stop calling me *child*," she interrupted him, meeting his eyes with a hard expression. "I am a woman, an adult, and as *acting* landowner of the estate of Carcourt-sur-Seine I would request such out-dated labels not be used when on my land."

"As you wish, my lady," he replied, a smile reappearing on his face. "My intention is not to discourage you with bleak words—"

"It is not your words that perturb me. It is the condescension of your manners, however genteel and chivalrous they seem to you, that I find quite irritating."

"Understood." He reached into his breast pocket with a sigh and removed a piece of paper. "Now that we are to be partners, or at least *colleagues*, I will share with you my newest venture. This," he tapped the paper on his thigh, "is how one leaves their mark. And I believe it will help you, help us, manage unfavorable incidents and turn them to our favor. Our first article concerns a subject near to my heart." He offered the paper to her. She took it with an outstretched hand, unfolded the first page and began reading. "*The Norman Gazette.*

> *Carcourt is an estate owned by war hero Lieutenant-Colonel André Valiere and his wife, Sophie, formerly Sophie de Vincennes, a woman of both unsurpassed beauty and wits, who has thus far proven herself more than equal to the task of managing so large an estate in her husband's absence. Furthermore, her grace and equanimity of temperament has had such a happy effect on her peers and employees alike that it is hardly an exaggeration to say that half the men from Rouen to Honfleur have fallen in love with the beauty of Carcourt-sur-Seine.*"

She lowered the paper. "Thank you, Jean-Claude," she said, her voice catching. "I can hardly put to words what it means to, at last, have a supportive friend. But really, 'half the men from Rouen to Honfleur have fallen in love with the beauty of Carcourt?' That is quite an exaggeration. On my own estate, I've hardly managed to win the—"

"Madame Sophie," he cut in, "your beauty speaks without need of exaggeration."

She forced a smile. "Thank you."

As they urged their horses forward, she whispered under her breath, "Their love maybe—their respect is another matter."

CHAPTER 23

Paris, France

Spring 1806

Several weeks after the conversation with Joseph Bonaparte on the mezzanine at the Palais-Royal, Jean-Luc and Isabella hosted a small but elegant party at his house. Dressed in a blue coat gilded with gold and tied with a red sash stretching from his right shoulder to the opposite side of his waist, Jean-Luc smiled warmly at the men standing on either side of him, who also wore the official uniform of the senate. The senators had come to celebrate his nomination to that illustrious body, while the men facing him were his former law colleagues who had come to bid him farewell, for this would be his final night in Paris before departing for Naples.

Emperor Napoleon, though recently departed on a new campaign in the German States, had sent a letter that was read aloud to the assembled guests by the Senator Nicolas-Louis François de Neufchâteau, acting president, who officially welcomed Jean-Luc into the elite group. Napoleon's words of welcome were followed by the proclamation of his recent senatorial decree, which granted Jean-Luc his much sought-after senatory. The new estate, called Rose-Épineuse, encompassed one hundred and forty hectares of grazing land just outside Sainte-Maure, some ninety miles southeast of Paris. Already populated with a dozen servants and laborers, as well as forty heads of cattle, two bulls, and thirty sheep (among other farm animals), the senatorial estate encompassed woodlands and rolling fields, as well as streams and ponds stocked with carp, catfish, and trout. Renovations to the chateau were currently underway, though Jean-Luc was told he could visit the grounds at his earliest convenience—which would have to be after his return from Naples.

The warm well-wishes of friends and colleagues that evening moved Jean-Luc deeply. To his surprise, even Monsieur de Landreville made an appearance, the old aristocrat offering the crowd a gracious toast, wishing Jean-Luc all the best on his Italian adventure. De Landreville was accompanied by Mademoiselle Laurent, the woman Jean-Luc had met during his visit to the elder man's house. Despite her evident discomfort among so many Bonapartists, Lucille Laurent chatted amicably with Jean-Luc and his two children. After the guests had all been served champagne, Jean-Luc ushered Isabella over to meet her, and the two kissed on both cheeks.

"Welcome to our home, mademoiselle," Isabella said after she had embraced the younger woman. "We are delighted to have the friendship of so illustrious a family as the Landrevilles."

"You are too kind, Madame St. Clair," Lucille answered, bowing her head politely. "It is we who should be thanking you for extending your friendship to my master."

Isabella laughed aloud. "Oh, no, my dear," she said. "Jean-Luc and I are not married."

Lucille's face flushed, and her eyes dropped to the floor. "My apologies. I heard 'our home' and assumed…"

"Think nothing of it, Mademoiselle Laurent," Isabella intervened. "Jean-Luc and I agreed that his Imperial duty should come before any other considerations. Though we have agreed to discuss the matter when he returns. In private."

"In the meantime," Jean-Luc turned to Isabella, hardly able to conceal his happiness, "I *have* entrusted her with the important tasks of helping care for my children and looking after the property in my absence."

Isabella took his hand and returned his smile. "If that brute Gagnon and his ruffians think they can harm my Jean-Luc's interests in his absence, I will be here to teach them a lesson."

At the mention of Gagnon, the conversation transitioned to the recently concluded trial. Several of the guests standing nearby offered their congratulations to Jean-Luc. Lucille, however, raised several eyebrows when she asserted that Gagnon's trial had been a charade.

"Though no fault of yours, monsieur," she reassured Jean-Luc. "Nevertheless, to all with open eyes, it was a sham. There wasn't even the pretense of a guilty verdict. The trial was merely terminated with the arbitrary imprisonment of Monsieur Gagnon for an indefinite period of time."

Jean-Luc took her declaration in stride. "I am just happy the issue was finally resolved."

Isabella, who had been silently observing the exchange, finished her champagne and cleared her throat. "Darling," she addressed Lucille, "your service to wealthy aristocrats has clearly not softened your Revolutionary edges. The emperor found the little man guilty of unlawful obstruction, and that's that. I hardly find it appropriate to criticize the work of my Jean-Luc, the only man willing to collect evidence, while other, more wealthy men who knew more, remained silent."

"I have not laid any fault at the feet of Monsieur St. Clair," Lucille responded. "But, madame, if you're implying that my master knew the facts of the case and was not prepared to offer them, then you are mistaken. His words are not welcome—"

"This is Jean-Luc's happy celebration," Isabella interrupted, casting Lucille a cold look. "It would be quite rude for one to spoil the mood with conjecture and slanderous insinuations."

"No one has been slandered, my dear," Jean-Luc intervened, placing a hand on Isabella's arm. She removed it and took a sip of champagne, smiling toward Lucille.

"Personally, I find it a shame that the people of this long-suffering nation cannot come together," said Isabella. "The vitriol with which some slander Napoleon and his administration smacks of envy, and there's really no need for it. Resentment toward the generals, toward the new notables, and the new administration, which are achieving so much for the people of this city and this nation."

Lucille looked at Isabella with a barbed grin. "Some of us just lament that a revolution which began with such promise and hope could so quickly revert to an all-powerful monarchy that abuses the rights of the weak, *privileges* that some of us thought we'd left to the pages of history."

Jean-Luc cleared his throat and stepped between the two women. "All right, ladies, that's enough spirited debate for one night. As for me," he said, turning toward the other guests who were watching this exchange with amused expressions, "I am afraid that I must save my oratorical ammunition for my impending journey."

Several of the onlookers laughed, and Isabella took a breath and smiled warmly at them. "Of course, my love." She cast a final glare at Lucille before turning to Jean-Luc. "I shall leave the talk of politics to the pretty philosophe here. Though I do think it a bit rude to get carried away with all that when tonight is meant to be your celebration. Now," she opened her arms to the others, "who would like to see the guest rooms upstairs? We've just finished the furnishing and would be delighted for you all to see what we've done."

With a murmur of amusement, some of the guests began shuffling toward the stairwell. As she passed Jean-Luc she whispered loud enough for those nearby to hear, "Please, darling, make sure she doesn't drink too much. I would hate to be embarrassed with all these eminent people about." She turned back to her guests with a smile. "Upstairs we go!"

Jean-Luc sighed ruefully, and a moment later noticed Lucille hovering behind the Marquis de Landreville as he chatted with two senators. She stood with her hands folded in front of her and her shoulders slumped. She looked up at him, and, as their eyes met, Jean-Luc, despite knowing her fiery disposition, couldn't help but feel a pang of sympathy for her. He moved his mouth silently to utter, "I'm sorry," and flushed red as she mouthed the same thing right back to him. In spite of his formal attire and efforts to comport himself with the dignity befitting a newly minted senator, he found himself laughing like a child. Lucille, noticing his lightened mood, returned his laughter with a smile.

With a shrug he finished his drink and moved to sit down on the sofa when he was startled by an unexpected voice. "Hello, Papa."

He looked behind him and saw the bashful smile of his daughter. "Mariette, my darling!" With a joyful cry he scooped her up in his arms and kissed her cheeks, aware that he had hardly seen her since early that morning. She was now nearly eight years old and allowed to stay up past her bedtime for special occasions. Setting his glass of wine on a table, he sat down with her on a sofa, showing her the heavy silver badge of the *Légion d'honneur* hanging from a red ribbon.

"They've just made me a senator. I have to wear it any time I dress fancy. They also gave me a big hat with lots of feathers."

"It's very pretty, Papa."

"Yes, it's quite beautiful." Jean-Luc placed it in her palm and laid his hands under hers, turning the ribbon around. The badge spun and the silver flashed in the candlelight. "But not as beautiful as you."

Mariette tried to stifle a yawn. "I wish you didn't have to go, Papa."

Jean-Luc was taken aback. He set his daughter down. "You stay right here." Shaking a few hands and accepting the congratulations from several guests, he slipped into his study. A minute later he returned and sat back down with his daughter.

"Now, Mariette," he said in a hushed voice, "I want this to be our little secret, all right?"

"What secret, Papa?"

"Well, the hat I have to wear, official business and such. But this…" Jean-Luc pulled a hand from behind his back and produced a large, white feather. Taking an exaggerated peek around the room, he handed it to her. "…This is for you, love. If you ever miss your papa, just hold this feather and remember that he will never be far away." He kissed her on the forehead. "And he will always love you."

CHAPTER 24

Posen, Poland

November 1806

"Could you repeat that, sir?" Sergeant-major Mazzarello asked, incredulous.

André fastened the final button on his green coat. "I understand it sounds strange, Paolo. And I don't like it any more than you do, but Moreau's condition has taken a turn for the worse, and our regimental surgeon has done all that he can. I've no other ideas."

"How long do you think you'll be gone?"

"No more than a week." André motioned for him to follow, and they headed down the narrow staircase. The family that had been quartering André since the Grand Armée arrived often reminded him they had nearly had their house burned down twice; drunk and careless soldiers were taking their toll on the city, even if they were welcomed as allies. André did not think he would be missed. The two men walked out into the street, which bustled with its routine procession of local inhabitants mingled with marching soldiers and mounted cavalrymen. André put on his helmet and turned toward his subordinate. "I cannot just watch him die. I don't know this woman well, but I do trust that she wants to help."

"Sir, you told me her grandfather was killed by our own men while she looked on. Are you sure she's not luring you into a trap?"

"It wasn't *our* men she rode all this way to avenge herself on. Carnassier and his hussars are the ones she's after. Besides, it was Moreau who stopped her from attacking the hussars and getting killed herself."

Mazzarello nodded reluctantly. "If you're set on this course, sir, I won't be the one to stop you."

André returned Mazzarello's salute. "Captain Vitry can manage as executive officer, and I trust you to manage the quarters here. Maintain camp discipline if you're sent out of the city; if that happens, I'll find you as soon as I can."

André took two troopers with him on the road heading southeast. Major Moreau, wrapped in warm clothes, rode propped in the saddle in front of the smaller of the two. Alicja, barely visible beneath a large fur coat and bayka hat, served as their guide and translator. At that morning's regimental briefing they'd learned Marshal Lannes had seized Warsaw, so they anticipated the roads east would be clear of hostile forces. Acutely aware of the risk presented by his absence, André drove them as fast as the horses could manage.

Over the next few days they stopped only briefly to feed and water the horses, passing short nights at whatever inn, house, or stable they could find. Moreau's condition continued to deteriorate, and by the evening of the fourth day, as they neared their destination, he appeared paler and sicklier than they'd yet seen him.

When night had fallen and their horses' heads drooped in exhaustion, André halted the party. He chose for their camp a hill overlooking a pristine lake, beyond which was a clear view of the Tatras Mountains, whose jagged peaks silhouetted the cloudless autumn sky. After setting Moreau up against a tree beside their fire, André pulled Alicja to where they were out of earshot of the two troopers.

"He is fading fast. I've taken a serious risk coming here; there are now hundreds of miles separating me and my men—the least you can do is tell me exactly what we should expect tomorrow."

Alicja gazed at the fire for several seconds and then back at André. "If he makes it through the night, we will not have far to go. It is perhaps a mile or two, walking in that direction." She pointed toward the mountains looming in front of them. "The entrance to the Szeptucha's cavern is on the western slope. Once inside, I will recognize about as much as you."

Looking at the steep slope, André felt a sinking feeling in his chest. His legs and back were exhausted from four days of hard riding, and he had not slept or eaten nearly enough in that time. What if this journey was all for nothing? What did he expect to find in these hills? A witch demanding a steep price for a few words of babble? He stalked off to find a place to sleep, kicking a rock and listening as it echoed down the slope. He sat down with his back against a tree, utterly dispirited. Not long after, an image appeared in his mind, clear as day: Major Carnassier in his hussar uniform, only he was not the man André had met; in this vision he appeared as the very icon of Imperial power and splendor. Like a conquering consul of ancient Rome, he rode underneath a great triumphal arch into the heart of Paris, thousands of horsemen following behind. The city's population screamed deafening ovations as he passed, which he received gleefully. He brought his horse to a halt and dismounted in front of the waiting emperor, who stood with his marshals outside the gates of the Tuileries Palace. Napoleon took the crown from his own head, held it aloft for all to see, and set it down upon Carnassier. Turning to face the roaring crowd, Carnassier held up his arms, drinking in the worship. A tall woman with blonde hair and a distinguished bearing walked slowly forward to meet him. She bowed to Carnassier and turned to face the crowd. To André's sudden horror, he saw the face of his wife, Sophie. Beside her was a tall man with long black hair. André tried to glimpse his face but could not distinguish who he was. André ran to meet her, but his legs were growing heavy. He felt a shove from behind, and with a shout he tumbled end over end and plunged into the brackish water of the Seine.

With a violent shake, André opened his eyes, his heart thumping in his chest. He ran a hand over his face, feeling beads of sweat on his brow, suddenly aware of how cold he felt. Rising to his feet, he muttered, "I might have frozen to death out here."

"You might still, if you don't put on your cloak." A woman's voice in the darkness.

"Alicja, is that you?"

"Who else would it be?"

André rummaged through his saddlebags to find his cloak. He draped it around himself, relieved to feel the warmth, even if his body still shook from the winter cold. "What are you doing awake?" he asked. "It must be well after midnight."

He heard no response; only the howling of the wind as it shook the branches around him. Settling himself back against the tree, he closed his eyes.

When André woke again, his heart beat at a normal pace, and he noticed a faint glow to his left. Dawn was approaching. He was grateful for his cloak, as it provided just enough shelter from the biting wind that gusted over the hills. After taking care of his morning toilet and swallowing a few bites of cold bread, he joined his soldiers, who had rekindled the dying fire and brewed a small pot of coffee. Alicja stood beside them, rubbing warmth into her hands. André was about to thank her for waking him in the night when she preempted him.

"We should go now, major; he does not have much time left."

Moreau was propped up on the two troopers' saddles and wrapped in two thick cloaks. André recalled his dream. To stop a man like Carnassier, it would undoubtedly help to have a man of Moreau's resilience on his side. He took a fortifying swig of coffee and then gave the two troopers instructions to watch the horses and signal with two shots if any danger approached. He would be back by midafternoon; if he had not returned by nightfall, they were to begin the journey back to Posen. With a hearty effort he swung the major onto his back, letting the younger man's arms droop over his shoulders for balance. Moreau felt lighter than he had expected.

"Have I died? Is this hell?" moaned a raspy, slurred voice.

"By the gods, he's alive! Does that mean you can manage to move yourself, eh major?" André exclaimed. "And no, you're not in hell just yet, but at Mademoiselle Alicja's request, we're about to enter some unknown and mysterious place."

Alicja smiled at Moreau as he tossed about on André's shoulders. If he was pleased to see her, it did not show on his features.

"If I have to be dragged by you, Valiere, I think I'd prefer death."

"Keep your thoughts to yourself, major," she replied in a firm but soothing voice. "You will need every ounce of your strength for what you are about to face up on the mountain."

The ground ahead of them rose steadily, a winding trail carved out in merciful switchbacks for the first mile or so. André breathed heavily under his burden, but his legs held true. As they ascended, the footing became rockier, and more precarious. Alicja traversed the rocks with ease, like a nimble mountain goat, pausing to allow André to keep up pace. Far overhead a white-tailed eagle cried out in successive calls, alerting its mate to the presence of unwelcome visitors.

As they climbed ever higher, André's eyes watered as the wind bit at his face. He was about to ask how much farther when Alicja turned to face him and a notion flashed across his mind: this would be the perfect place to kill them, out of earshot and miles away from any witnesses. As he wrestled with this thought, he noticed that they had come to a patch of flat, stony ground marked with clumps of rock and steam rising from little ponds. Hot vapors billowed up and drifted over the precipice.

"It's a hot spring," Alicja said. "This mountain is full of them. Do not step into the water, unless you wish to lose your boots...and maybe your foot."

"How much farther?"

Alicja raised an arm and pointed. André took several steps forward, squinting as he scanned the precipitous cliff face, and then he saw it. A black hollow—the opening slightly shorter than the height of a tall man—appeared in the rock, its width perhaps three feet across.

"Who built that cave?" André asked, uneasy.

Alicja looked at him with a solemn expression. "No human hand. This is the dwelling place of ancient spirits."

André nodded, attempting to maintain an air of skepticism; though, in truth, he fought back a feeling of dread. The first time he had gone into battle, nearly every fiber in his body willed him to turn and run in the opposite direction. He felt the familiar twitch in his wounded thigh, that harbinger of danger—and fear. He glanced back at the slope from which they'd come, wondering what would happen if they simply turned back. Then he looked into the eyes of the woman before him, fearless and proud, and then thought of the gravely wounded man lying helpless on his back. With a deep breath, he summoned his courage and began walking toward the mouth of the cavern. A cluster of stones was arrayed in a semicircle outside the entrance. He halted, turning to his companion.

"Boundary stones," Alicja stated quietly.

"Boundary of what?"

"The realm beyond."

Looking up at André and back to the stones, her eyes betrayed fear. It was now his turn to fortify her nerves. "We've come all this way. Should we let a pile of rocks stop us?" Turning to the entrance, he recited, "Behold, I stand at the door and knock. If anyone hears my voice and opens the door, I will come in to him and eat with him, and he with me."

Then he stepped into the darkness.

CHAPTER 25

Carcourt, Normandy

Autumn 1806

"Silence!" Sophie shouted, though her voice did little to drown out the ruckus unfolding in front of her. She had ridden down the hill and passed in front of the group; for a moment it looked as if her presence was enough to quiet the crowd, but she was mistaken. A cluster of fifteen or twenty men all dressed alike in white or gray smocks and light trousers, some wearing straw hats, had gathered outside the makeshift brasserie on the edge of the creek. Some brandished farm tools as weapons. Opposing them were about a dozen similarly armed men and women posted at the entrance. The two sides were shouting insults and taunts, slowly surging forward and backward. One man from the larger crowd facing the tavern walked up to the man opposite him and spat at his feet. "Next time it'll be your boy caught up in the tree, and we'll be the ones to get him down."

"We'll get him down all right," one of his companions added. "I'll break his fall with my pitchfork."

Gaston Gavrillon, guarding the entranceway to the tavern, spread his feet wide. "No outlander scum enters this building. Shove off before we start giving you lead."

"Stove his head in!" one of the men from the larger group screamed.

"Come try it," Gavrillon growled.

The two sides were preparing to charge when a sharp crack cut through the air. One of the women guarding the tavern cried out, and several of the others ducked their heads. Sophie held a pistol in the air while smoke lingered around her. When she had most of their eyes on her she urged her horse slowly forward between the two groups.

"You all know who I am," she called out, halting the animal to form a natural barrier. "Now, before anyone needs to be dragged to jail in chains, I'd like to hear in civilized speech what this fuss is all about." Silence. On the slope behind her a flock of sheep trotted away from the sound of the gunfire, several bleating noisily. Her horse whinnied, but no one spoke. She placed her pistol in a saddlebag. "One of you is going to tell me what this commotion is about."

Gaston Gavrillon spit at his feet. One of the men beside him took a few puffs from a pipe; a woman behind them bit on her nails and gazed out to the stream.

"Madame Valiere." The leader of the outlanders stepped forward, his boots kicking up dust. Removing his cap to reveal a crop of curly blonde hair, he said, "I am called Mollac. I can explain, if no one else will."

"Very well, Monsieur Mollac," Sophie said. "Please tell me what has led to this."

"Well, madame," the man answered, "you see, a few weeks back my son was chased up a great big tree. He climbed up there for safety, as some of the other lads were throwing rocks and threatening to beat him. He was shaking from fear when I finally got him down."

"I'm aware of this story, monsieur," Sophie cut him off. "I am very sorry for this incident, and so are the people of this estate. I have received their assurances that it won't happen again."

"Thank you, madame," Mollac said. "But it is not as simple as you've been told. Your boys were there. I've seen your two lads; they're good boys. They were defending their friend, that is all."

"Please, go on, Mollac."

The Breton continued, urged on by a small shove from one of his companions. "The boy fled up into the tree because he struck one of the local boys in the nose, but he only struck the boy because that one brought a hound into our chicken coop. The animal did away with three of my chickens. It was a terrible mess, and seeing my anger, my son gave that boy a knock on the chin, is all. I'm sorry he did, but the other boy deserved it."

Murmurs and shouts erupted from both sides before Sophie was able to regain silence. "I was not aware of the fact, and I am sorry. The boy who let loose his dog will hear from me."

"That's not the end," Mollac replied. "Yesterday my friend caught the same boy, Lucas, in his barn. With his daughter."

A furious roar erupted from the outlanders, and Sophie urged her horse out of the way. She loaded another ball into her pistol and again fired a shot into the air. The two sides separated once more; Sophie used the moment to position her horse between them again. Her anger now was enough to cow some of the less-eager brawlers into taking several steps back. A welcome silence fell over the crowd.

"Since you all find yourselves unable to resolve your differences peaceably, I will do it for you. You men," she pointed to the group of locals, "go inside the mill at once and wait for me."

No one stirred.

"Now!" Sophie commanded. Lowering their heads and grumbling, the men turned and shuffled inside. One spat as he walked out of sight. "And you," Sophie said, rounding on the group of outlanders, "this is how you betray the hospitality we've shown you?"

"Madame, it weren't our fault—"

"Enough! I cannot have you brawling with my people at every minor incident. You are well-meaning, decent folk, but you have thus far caused more harm than good on this estate. I have decided we can no longer manage all of you here. We simply cannot. You, Mollac," she called. "Thank you for putting words to this foolish scene. You, monsieur, are to ride to the estate of Count de Montfort in Graimbouville—do you know where that is?"

"I'll find it, madame."

"Ride to the count and inform him that by the end of the week no less than one hundred of your number will be moving to Graimbouville. Any who go willingly will be offered my carriage for the journey; those who are compelled to leave will be departing on foot."

Sophie put the pistol away. "Now," she called out, "all of you, go back to your homes, and begin packing your belongings. You will not lose work; indeed, you may find more of it, and I will separate no man from his family. But you may not stay here. Violence on my estate will not be tolerated."

CHAPTER 26

Naples

Spring/Summer 1806

Afer a long and uncomfortable two weeks at sea, the frigate *Arnaud de Barbizan* entered the Gulf of Naples, where it weighed anchor within sight of the port. In his cramped cabin, Jean-Luc penned the finishing touches on several documents, one of which was a letter to his children, whom he now sorely missed. In the port city of Toulon, he lingered on the deck, watching the mountains grow steadily distant, feeling a growing sense of disconnection. He wondered how long he would be gone, if he would return at all. These thoughts were an abrupt change from the excitement and purpose he'd felt when he departed Paris.

He placed the senatory seal on his last document and mounted the stairs to the quarterdeck, accompanied by two administrative clerks from the Tuileries, Pierre-Henry and Maximilien, assigned to help manage his travel arrangements and care for his luggage; a luxury that he was not accustomed to but did have its advantages.

"Gentlemen," Jean-Luc said. "We now must turn to the serious business that has brought us to this city. We will all feel a certain temptation to indulge in the casual conduct of our Mediterranean partners, but we are here on state business and must act as ambassadors of our emperor. Remember Hannibal—"

"Yes, senator," said Pierre-Henry. "'Capua corrupted Hannibal,' we know."

With an approving smile Jean-Luc tucked his small notebook into his breast pocket and surveyed the cityscape before them. "I expect we will be treated with the dignity due all emissaries in a foreign land, but don't forget the people of this city fought a bloody campaign to maintain Bourbon rule; Queen Maria Carolina is Marie Antoinette's sister." The two men shed their smiles when they heard the name of their former queen. "While I don't expect we'll be given any trouble, don't stray far from the palace grounds."

It took until early that evening for the crew to finish loading their supplies so Jean-Luc and his retinue could leave the ship. The *Arnaud de Barbizan*'s captain had traveled ashore with the necessary paperwork for Jean-Luc to land, but minor customs officials at the docks had to be pleaded with, and finally shouted at, to deliver the documents to their master in the city's palace.

It was well after suppertime when Jean-Luc and his two secretaries set foot on dry land. The captain bade them farewell, informing them that their return ship would arrive in seven days. Before leaving, however, he took Jean-Luc aside and quietly informed him that he'd been instructed to linger outside the harbor for two days as a precaution.

"The Neapolitans claim to be our friends," he said to Jean-Luc, "but I've heard of what the peasants did in '99 when they took the city back from us. Cut the throats of soldiers, civilians, and ladies alike. If anything goes wrong, there are Frenchmen at Casa Laganà, a diplomatic bureau where credit and insurance are issued and notarial registration and other book-keeping of that sort is conducted. I'm told they get on well with our lot. Good luck."

Slightly disconcerted, Jean-Luc nevertheless thanked him with a smile and assured him that he would keep a wary eye. The captain was rowed back to the frigate, and Jean-Luc and his men walked across the dock, passing fishermen and their small boats along the quay.

Shadows deepened among the jetties lining the harbor, and the setting sun lingered on the horizon, casting an orange glow on the low-hanging clouds blending with the azure sky and shimmering water to create a vista worthy of a Renaissance master. Mount Vesuvius loomed in the distance, its slopes catching the last flickers of sunlight. Jean-Luc and his small retinue stood transfixed; a rare instance of words being superfluous and silence the only proper tribute.

A church bell tolled, mingling with the calls of the gulls, and soon they were greeted by a group of men dressed in livery of the city's insignia, led by one who was draped in flowing red and black robes. "Welcome to our city, messieurs," the robed man said in a thick Italian accent. "I am Cardinal Corbino. If you would please follow me, my masters have instructed me to bring you to your quarters." He turned and strode away from the wharf, leading Jean-Luc's party through several narrow side streets. These appeared empty, but, as they passed, Jean-Luc noticed men in groups of twos and threes loitering in the entrances of houses and taverns, watching as they followed the cardinal's men. They were all dressed in the same loose pants and yellow or green hats that looked disconcertingly similar to the red caps of Paris's sans-culottes during the Revolution.

The cardinal's men indicated for Jean-Luc and his party to enter a waiting carriage. As Jean-Luc climbed in, he saw a man seated on top of a building across the street. He wore a black coat and was sitting cross-legged, smoking a pipe; in one hand he held a blunderbuss, and a jezail Arab musket lay across his lap. His dark eyes never left Jean-Luc. The words "*napoleone il cane*," and "*morte al francese*" had been scribbled on a nearby wall. Jean-Luc did not need a translator to understand the message. Napoleon claimed to be ruler of the continent, but these streets were far from pacified.

After a short ride up narrow, winding streets, the carriages pulled into a large plaza, halting in front of a magnificent stone edifice. As they exited the carriages, one of the men from the cardinal's retinue passed Jean-Luc and he clasped the man by the hand. "These bags—they must not disappear, understand? No disappear, *capisci?*"

The man shrugged. "*Signore*, your baggage are take care. If you wish for them no disappear, our men can take a little bit money. *Grazie, signore, grazie.*" Jean-Luc sighed and took some coins out of his pocket. The man pressed his hands together. "*Si signore*, bags good, he come with me. *Grazie.*"

Before the man could depart, Jean-Luc reached into his breast pocket and pulled out one of the documents he had penned. He placed it firmly into the hands of the man and spoke in a hushed but firm voice. "Take this to the Casa Laganà on Via Duomo. Very important that they know I am here in the city. Jean-Luc St. Clair. Return with a signature of receipt and I will give you twenty francs, *capisci?*"

"*Si, signore*, I take for you. I bring receipt for you, no problem." The man turned on his heels and quickly disappeared.

Jean-Luc's party was led across the Piazza of the Royal Palace and into a smaller building on an adjacent street, where they were shown to their rooms. No food or drink was provided, so Jean-Luc informed his companions that they might look for some, but that they were to be ready to walk to the palace at sunrise. He set his travel bag on the stone floor and collapsed onto the straw mattress.

The following morning Jean-Luc and his party were taken on foot to the Royal Palace. Jean-Luc presented himself to Cardinal Corbino and a man in civilian clothes whom he had not yet met. The two sat in tall chairs at the end of a long table. Jean-Luc took the seat opposite.

"Welcome to Naples, Monsieur Senator," the man beside the cardinal began. "My name is Giacomo Severino. I serve as viceroy to King Ferdinand. You have already been introduced to Cardinal Corbino, so if you have no objections, I should like to proceed straight to business." Jean-Luc nodded his agreement. "Very well, then. The timing for your visit, signore, could not be more appropriate. Since your emperor's victory at Austerlitz we have rid nearly all ties with our English and Russian *contraparti*, enabling us to forge greater ties with our French friends. We have many items that we wish to discuss, and we would do so in a spirit of friendship and cooperation, leaving old hostilities and political blood-feuds in the past where they belong."

Jean-Luc indicated his agreement, and for the next several hours the three men discussed a host of issues, including the trajectory of Napoleon's career, to which Jean-Luc was happy to add an offer of renewed friendship to the Bourbon king of Naples, in exchange for his neutrality with regard to the vaunted English navy. The two Neapolitans gave every assurance that they would relay the emperor's sentiments to their sovereign but offered no guarantees.

"And, lastly," Viceroy Severino mercifully declared, "we come to the matter of conscription, for which your emperor has chided us for several years now. This idea may be more troublesome than your master realizes. For, you see, our people rarely take kindly to forced servitude, much less in service to a foreign power."

"My emperor does not wish France to be viewed simply as a foreign power," Jean-Luc replied. "Rather as a brother standing in mutual opposition to the greedy English and barbarous Russians."

"I understand your emperor's wish," Viceroy Severino replied, "but I am afraid that he does not fully understand our city or our people. The

Lazzaroni are not your ordinary subjects. If you'd spent a day down at the wharves or in the city's harder streets, you would perhaps understand more clearly what I am telling you."

Jean-Luc had seen enough the evening prior to understand his meaning.

"In addition," Cardinal Corbino cut in, "you will find that they are deeply rooted in the holy faith of their forebears. Your republican generals might find it difficult to sway conscripts from this caste."

"Even so," Jean-Luc answered evenly, "our emperor is famed for his ability to employ troops from all corners of the continent; we even have Mamelukes from Egypt in our ranks. As to the *Lazzaroni*, how do *you* manage them?" he asked.

"*Manage* them?" Cardinal Corbino replied disdainfully. "Why would we wish to manage them? In a society that has withered under the stupor of wealth and decadence, it is precisely these *lower* members of society that retain the virtues of godliness and patriotic feeling."

"I see." Jean-Luc folded his hands. "Well, I will be sure to inform my superiors of all that you have thus far informed me."

The two men looked at him dubiously but nodded in agreement.

"One final question, messieurs," Jean-Luc said, resisting the urge to check his timepiece. "Will it be possible to obtain an audience with the king and queen during my visit?"

Viceroy Severino and the cardinal exchanged a look. "That may be difficult. Our king no longer resides in the palace, but at his grounds in Reggia di Caserta. As you know, we have had hostile invasions in recent years." Jean-Luc knew full well that it had been a Republican French Army that last stormed the city. They had ultimately been thrown out by the fierce, pro-royalist resistance of the *Lazzaroni*. "Moreover," the viceroy continued, "the king and queen have departed for the country. I believe they plan to visit several inland towns and go for a bit of hunting. I'm afraid a visit does not appear likely."

"Very well," Jean-Luc answered, disappointment written on his features. "My superiors had led me to believe that I should be granted an audience at *some* point, but if that must come at a later date then I can wait. I shall see you both tomorrow."

The two men exchanged a brief glance before rising and offering Jean-Luc a bow as he took his leave.

Back at his temporary residence, Jean-Luc briefed his two assistants on the day's deliberations over supper. As he prepared to retire for the evening, Pierre-Henry explained excitedly how they had nearly been ridden over by the king's household coaches.

"Nearly killed by a king," he said, tapping Maximilien on the arm. "At least our *families* would get some compensation out of this expedition."

"I'd imagine they'd be given a royal indemnity," Maximillien replied with a grin.

"That cannot be," Jean-Luc said, his brow furrowed. "The viceroy just informed me that the king had departed to the country."

"Well, senator," Pierre-Henry said, "either the king has returned, or you've been deceived."

Jean-Luc nodded absently, puzzling over the confusion. "At any rate," he said, fighting back a yawn, "it has been a long day, and I must get some rest if I am to have my wits about me tomorrow. You two seem in no mood for sleep or quiet contemplation, so take your drink and carousing out into the streets and leave me be for the night." Both men held up hands to protest their innocence. "Oh, don't bother denying it, I can smell your breath—you reek of wine. I don't care what you get into as long as you are fit for work at dawn. Now get out, and do be quiet when you come back in. At least one of us intends to sleep tonight."

* * *

Hours later, Jean-Luc was startled awake by the sound of raised voices downstairs. He sat up in bed, disoriented and half-asleep. Pulling on his night-robe, he dashed down the stairs. If his two associates had brought their carousing back to the house, he would give them a rake over the coals. As he descended the last flight of stairs, he could hear voices in the street, shouting in Italian.

"What in heaven is—" he paused midsentence upon entering the kitchen. His assistant, Pierre-Henry, stood holding a cloth in one hand. He was looking at Maximillien, who sat on a stool beside him. One of his eyes was bruised shut, and blood was streaming from his nose.

"My apologies, Monsieur St. Clair. We were set upon by surprise."

Jean-Luc grimaced at the sight. "Who was? You and Pierre-Henry?"

Maximillien nodded, wincing as Pierre-Henry dabbed the wet cloth around his swollen eye. "The bastards had us cornered; they came from all sides. I was on the ground before I knew what was happening. They must have followed us."

"Who followed—" he paused. The voices in the street grew louder.

"I don't know, sir." Maximillien exhaled slowly. "There must have been dozens—hundreds of them out there.

Jean-Luc took a look out the nearest window but saw nothing but a row of cherry laurels. After thinking for a moment, he looked up. "Pierre-Henry, Maxime, stay here. Do not move from this table. I am going to the palace to inform them of this unprovoked attack."

Jean-Luc trudged out into the night still in his nightgown and slippers. He crossed the street and passed into the Piazza of the Royal Palace, where he halted abruptly. Before him stood hundreds of people milling about in the square. Some carried torches. Across the piazza a large crowd had clustered around a man perched atop a statue. When he was within shouting distance, he tried to make out what the man was saying, but little of the Italian made sense to him. When he heard the words, "*Si alla nostre santa fede, no ai bastardi republicani! No a Napoleone!*" Jean-Luc knew that this was not a place where it would be wise to linger. His fist raised in unison with the clamoring crowd, he carefully made his way back toward his residence.

When he arrived back at the house, his heart sank. Three men stood huddled outside the door, two of them holding clubs.

"Eh, *buonasera, signores,*" he said, slowly walking toward them.

One of the men rounded on him. "*Chi cazzo sei?*" he demanded. He was short, his neck was thick; his black mustache distinguished him from his clean-shaven comrades. *Lazzaroni.*

Jean-Luc held his hands up in deference. "I am Senator St. Clair, from France. I am a guest of Viceroy Severino and Cardinal Corbino."

"*Ehi, guarda! Lui e francese!*" The man raised his club, motioning to his comrades. "*Lui e francese.*" Jean-Luc's heart nearly leapt from his chest when the man seized his collar and dragged him into the house, where Pierre-Henry and Maxime were laid flat on their stomachs, their hands tied behind their backs. The man holding Jean-Luc's collar jerked him down to his knees. A group of men stood on all sides of the room.

"Maxime, Pierre, don't worry," Jean-Luc said. "I will speak to the palace and we will—" A rough hand cuffed him across the cheek. One of the men standing in the opposite corner crossed the room and exchanged words with the man who held Jean-Luc. The man let Jean-Luc go with a shove and stalked back outside.

The taller man responsible for his release had short black hair and blue eyes. He crouched down beside Jean-Luc. "My apologies for this rough treatment, signore, but we must take our precautions. Our people are now at war."

Jean-Luc, relieved to be able to converse with someone, laughed at the comment. "Monsieur, I don't know what you have heard, but I am an official ambassador from Emperor Napoleon. I can assure you that we are not at war."

"Signore, I am sorry to disappoint you," the man rejoined, "but you are mistaken. You are the enemies of my people—and my men you see here like nothing more than to slit your throats and take all your nice possessions. If you like to see the sun rise, you close your mouth and do as I say, yes?" Jean-Luc nodded. "Si, very good."

The man rose and called out several orders. Maxime and Pierre-Henry were brought to their feet, and Jean-Luc was led to the doorway.

"Now, signore," he said. "I am told you are big, important man. You will be taking your own accommodations at the Castel Sant'Elmo. Your friends, they not so lucky. They must coming with me, but do not worry; I take good care of them. Squalo likes prisoners alive, not dead." The man whistled through two fingers. "*Ciao*, my friend, we see you tomorrow!" He turned and departed. Jean-Luc, separated from his two assistants, was blindfolded and taken on a long walk uphill.

CHAPTER 27

Tatras Mountains, Poland

November 1806

As André shuffled forward through the darkening passageway, the sound of the wind howling outside faded to a dull hum. All he could hear were his own shuffling footsteps along the cavern's stone floor. The light spilling in from the entrance diminished abruptly, and soon he was groping his way through a tunnel that gave off a damp, earthy odor. He halted for a moment, allowing Alicja to catch up to him, straining his ears for any sound. He could hear the faint trickle of running water up ahead.

"Why did you stop?" Alicja whispered.

"I thought I heard water."

"We must not stop. She is already waiting."

She? Who is she? André thought uneasily as he moved forward. He was not comforted by the notion that someone who had chosen this cave as their dwelling place awaited them. As they continued forward with outstretched hands, André felt a vague but unmistakable change passing over him. A mysterious source of power, almost magic, seemed to inhabit this cave, as if the domain of rules and laws belonged to another world. He could not shake the feeling that some unseen force was pulling them closer.

Gradually, a dim light became visible further down the passageway. André continued a few paces until a vision stopped him dead in his tracks.

Thinking his mind was playing tricks on him, he blinked several times, turning his head to either side. The sight remained. They had stepped into a chamber wider than the tunnel. When his eyes had adjusted, aided by the faint light ahead, he stepped forward and beheld a sight he could never have imagined, even in his most vivid dreams. Depicted on the walls around them was an awe-inspiring scene that must have come from a time before history. Painted in dark colors were animal figures—horses, bison, deer— some with antlers, others with great horns. They were rendered in impressive detail and great numbers, appearing to run or walk in herds. Some of the scenes depicted crudely drawn men with bows and arrows, firing at their prey or driving them off cliffs. André suspected he was in the presence of something as ancient as it was breathtaking. *Who had crafted these paintings? What meaning had this place borne in a different age, before it had been lost to the haze of time?* Spellbound, he was shaken back to reality by a tug on his sleeve.

Alicja indicated an opening ahead at the far side the chamber, the source of the light. With a quick look back at him, she crouched and walked through the portal. Ducking low to ensure he did not bump Moreau's head against the stone, André shuffled in after her. The air inside this second chamber felt less crisp than the one through which they had just passed. Surveying the space, a room perhaps forty feet long and thirty feet wide, he was struck again with a sensation of disbelief. Scattered around the chamber was a strange collection of items: bowls and plates, bits of cloth, stones, feathers, and a number of wicker baskets overflowing with what looked to be seeds and roots. A small fire in the center gave off light, and the smell of kindling blended with spices, herbs, and spruce branches created an aroma that was not altogether unpleasant.

The figure seated on the other side of the chamber did not move. From where André and Alicja stood, it was impossible to see the stranger's eyes as their head was cast down toward the fire. All they could distinguish in the flickering light was a thickset body garbed in a robe that seemed stitched together in a patchwork of different cloths. A fleece shawl covered their head and shoulders.

As the two visitors took a few tentative steps closer, the figure raised its head, revealing not a pair of eyes but rather a fringe mask of tiny beads that dangled over the nose down to the mouth. André cleared his throat to speak, and the seated figure turned in his direction. After an interminable silence, a voice spoke.

"Why come you to the womb of nature?"

The Szeptucha had feminine inflection, but her voice echoed with a low-pitched force that sounded like a man.

At length the old woman spoke again, "What business have soldiers here?"

André chose his words carefully. "We've come in hopes of helping our friend. He is dying." He stole a glance at Alicja, who looked enraptured. Their host did not stir. After waiting another minute, André leaned forward. "Did you not hear me?"

Alicja gently placed her hand on his arm. "*Jesteśmy przyjaciółmi.* We have come in peace, Szeptucha," she said in a quiet voice. "We are in search of anything that might help our friend."

The old woman motioned for them to come closer. When they had taken several small steps forward, she motioned for them to be seated. André and Alicja obeyed. André then carefully set Marcel down on the mossy stone. Glancing around the chamber, he noticed an engraving on the wall to his left. It was not a depiction of animals or a scene of the hunt, but a coiled serpent with its raised head twisted around an egg. He recognized it as a symbol of the masters of magic, from ancient times.

"You come from the great king, but he has not sent you," the old woman intoned.

"Yes," he replied, taken aback. "We come from the army of the emperor of France. Though we come of our own will, with our own purposes."

"The chain around your neck, let me see it."

André instinctively drew a protective hand to the crucifix around his neck, a gift from Sophie. After a prompting look from Alicja he reluctantly reached under his coat and pulled it out, tossing it gently to the old woman.

She studied it in silence, running her leathery fingers over its surface, turning it about in her hands. "You seek to turn base metal into gold?"

André exhaled. "That is already gold. At least some of it."

The old Szeptucha nodded, seemingly indifferent to the value of the piece between her fingers. "There is no profit without loss, and there is no loss without gain. All things rise and fall. Tell me, soldier, what does gold count for you when measured against your friend's fate?"

André sensed her meaning and felt a sinking feeling in chest. When Sophie had given it to him her face had been full of fear for his future and hope for their reunion. It was his only tangible connection to her. He sighed regretfully.

"If you must have it, it is yours."

"Only thieves and fools barter in the currency of their own appetites," she stated impassively. "If gathering gold was my aim, I would serve two masters, and a pitiful servant I would be." She tossed the necklace onto the ground beside André.

Despite his relief, it wasn't long before he felt another swell of impatience. How much more of this cryptic, nonsensical rambling would they have to endure? He looked at Moreau as he addressed the woman: "I do not wish to hasten or distress you, but frankly, we do not have much goddamn time!" He shut his eyes, taking a moment to gather himself. "I am sorry. My friend is gravely wounded, and we have traveled a great distance. I would not—*we* would not wish to see him perish at the very moment of his possible deliverance."

The woman reached a hand up to her head and slowly removed the shawl, letting it drop to the ground. Beneath a cluster of curled gray hair was the creased face of an old woman. Her blue eyes gleamed as they met André's, appearing as two clear windows into the depths of a timeless soul. André had been raised in the presence of priests, friars, and nuns, but he had never looked into the eyes of a mystic. Though he was not aware of it, tears welled in the corners of his eyes.

"In time we will attend to your friend," she said softly.

Reaching inside one of the baskets beside her, she pulled out a large pinecone and set it on the ground beside the fire. She then removed what appeared to be a handful of seeds. These she rubbed in her hands before dropping them onto the floor in a semicircle. She proceeded to dump more of the contents from the basket into a small cup: pine needles, two smaller pinecones, a handful of herbs, a collection of roots. Lastly, she produced a small bowl and poured a clear liquid into the cup.

"Thyrsus Bacchus," she intoned in a quiet, clear voice. "Every tree, every drop of water, every grain of sand lives its own life, bound to every other thing in the universe. All is one."

She scooped the seeds from off the ground and dropped them inside the cup. "*Ve Gedulah…* Do you come seeking the light which renews hope?"

she asked, not lifting her eyes from the ground. "Or will you follow the way of the lost, cursed to the unbounded nothingness that leads to an eternity alone in the darkness?"

Without waiting for a response, she stood and walked slowly around the fire. When she was standing over Moreau, she paused. André saw a wildness in her eyes; he and Alicja both leaned forward instinctively. The Szeptucha dipped a hand into the bowl and sprinkled some of the contents over Moreau, intoning as she did so: "*Ve Geburah.*" She repeated this several times before emitting a deep, guttural sound that seemed more animal than human. One of Moreau's feet twitched, and the boot thudded on the stone floor. She blew down at the small fire that flickered faintly, causing embers to flare and pop. She inhaled deeply, letting out another moaning howl "*Cheth... Resh... Mem...*"

The old woman turned to André. "You must help me raise him."

André lifted his comrade, propping him upright against his own ribs. Moreau let out an almost imperceptible groan. The Szeptucha leaned in, not taking her eyes from his face. With another primal call she raised the cup to Moreau's lips. Tilting his head back, she poured the brew into his mouth. Once satisfied that he'd swallowed enough, she allowed him to cough and gasp for air.

She motioned for André to lay him back on the floor. Once he was prone, she whispered, "I am a son of earth and starry sky. I am parched with thirst and dying; but quickly grant me cold water from the lake of memory to drink."

Moreau remained still. André looked at Alicja, whose face betrayed a deep anxiety. The silence seemed endless.

Moreau's head began to rock from side to side.

"What is happening?" André asked in a hushed voice.

"In order to live, first he must die. He is standing on the threshold of the great void; who can tell what he will see there? Who knows when he will return, if at all?"

Slow tremors shook Moreau's body, and his back heaved violently as his waist lifted from the ground. He let out a bloodcurdling scream. His body shuddered in a fit of convulsions, and his breaths came in deep gasps as if he were choking. André, recalling stories from his childhood of men and women whose souls had been taken by demons, dashed to where his crucifix lay on the ground. Snatching it up he held it in the air over Moreau, thinking desperately of a prayer to recite. The Szeptucha put a hand on his shoulder, her calm touch soothing him from his fear.

"That cannot help him now. We must wait." Reaching into a pocket of her ragged coat she pulled out a small cluster of animal hair or fur and held them above Moreau's writhing body. She then held a strip of cloth over the fire, setting it alight from the still-smoldering embers. Holding the burning cloth just above Moreau's face, she chanted in an unknown language. The fibers burned into black smoke. André and Alicja stared, transfixed.

"What is happening to him?" André asked.

"I have offered his spirit shelter. If he trusts in it, he will see the light shining from within. There is no teacher higher than one's self, if you are willing to listen."

"Will he die?" Alicja asked, her voice trembling.

"If he wakes, he will not *cease* to be himself, but he may be beyond what he has long *believed* to be himself."

To his companions' great relief, Moreau's spasms softened until his body calmed, and he collapsed onto the ground. His gasps for breath became less and less desperate. Wiping tears from her eyes, Alicja gathered Moreau in her arms, whispering soothing words in his ear. To her amazement, he blinked several times and his eyes opened. She expected them to be wide with fear, but they displayed only a look of fatigue. She kissed his forehead, and he sat upright on his own strength, letting out a pained groan as he stretched his back and shoulders.

"Where are we?" he demanded. Confusion and disorientation were written plainly on his features. "And who is this?" he asked, eyeing the Szeptucha.

"You've been in and out of fever dreams for many days, and you're very weak," Alicja said in a soft voice. "This woman has brought you back."

Moreau rolled his stiff neck from side to side, the bones cracking audibly. He reached underneath his coat, touching the scars on his chest.

André knelt down beside him. "We can discuss your wounds and how you received them at a later hour. For now, my friend, we must bring back your strength."

Moreau held André's gaze for several seconds; André was still not sure which version of the man had returned. Would he be dealing with the reckless, fatalistic madman from their earliest days together?

The Szeptucha held out a hand, signaling for Moreau to come closer. "I cannot know what you have seen or offer you any instruction. You must draw your own conclusions. Your dreams of transformation have shown you the forces that have hunted you—beneath the glassy sea of your own self; your dormant self." He cast a stupefied look at the strange woman, whose own face remained impassive. "What you've seen is discernible only beyond the senses; that which man cannot damage, and time can never extinguish."

She turned her attention to André and Alicja.

"Three warriors have come, three warriors who balance on the wheel of life and death. A choice lies before each of you." She looked at each one of them in turn with something resembling a smile. "When the stars of the morning sing together…" she said, turning to Moreau, "nine muses in the symphony of Mnemosyne…" She then looked into André's eyes; her expression cold but unthreatening. "To which fidelity will you hold, when deference meets demand? The first stranger to whom you speak beyond this cave will bring an answer to the question that has tormented you and will not cease to, until your decision is made."

André flinched slightly. "My *decision?*"

The Szeptucha offered him the last of her enigmatic smiles before lowering her head.

"Farewell. Adonai."

CHAPTER 28

Saint Elmo Castle, Naples

Summer 1806

J ean-Luc was confined in a windowless ten-by-twelve-foot cell with nothing but a small bucket to relieve himself. Hours—perhaps days—passed with no contact from the outside, when at last the door creaked open. His host dropped a small tray of food and slammed the door shut before Jean-Luc could see anything, or anyone, outside. This process was repeated three more times; he estimated it had been nearly two days since his capture. Finally, a visitor bringing more than stale bread and water arrived. He came in the form of a pike-wielding brute. "Get on your feet" was all he said, motioning for Jean-Luc to follow him out of the cell.

Jean-Luc instinctively raised a hand to his eyes as he left the cramped space, shielding them from the blinding sun. The guard led him out into a courtyard enclosed by tall stone walls. Scanning for landmarks, Jean-Luc saw only sacks of grain or flour, and the waving flag of the Kingdom of Naples, with its distinctive Bourbon fleur-de-lis and the lions passant of England draped beneath a large crown.

"You stand here," the man ordered before turning and departing.

Jean-Luc let out a long exhale; two days prior he was a senator on a diplomatic errand; how in God's name had he come to be a prisoner of these rebels? He was shaken out of his thoughts by the appearance of several men. From the stubble on their chins and their forlorn expressions, he guessed they were prisoners as well. Perhaps two dozen of them were led out into the courtyard, where they were shoved into two lines beside Jean-Luc. A shout came from somewhere behind them and three more guards appeared from the same door. Jean-Luc recognized the taller man as the one he had spoken to prior to his arrest.

"My friends," he cried out in a thick Neapolitan accent, "you are our prisoners. I offer to you my apologies for any harsh treatment, but what shall I say? We are now in a state of conflict, and Frenchmen are the enemy." He shook his head ruefully for dramatic effect.

Jean-Luc stole a look around: the men did have the look of compatriots. He could not help but feel a humiliating shame: these men, his country-men, over whom he held all rank and responsibility, had been allowed to fall into captivity. Quickly dispelling the thought, he diverted his mind to a more hopeful subject: escape. He conjured an image of the city and how he might scale these walls and reach the port; the *Arnaud de Barbizan* could not have gone very far, if it had left at all—

"If any of you wish to be bold and try your escape," proclaimed the speaker, as if reading his thoughts, "you are welcome to try. But know that any attempt would be quite foolish; all roads have been cut by the king's troops, and they will shortly be reinforced by our British and Russian friends."

An earsplitting din erupted, distant at first, but growing ever louder until the walls around the courtyard seemed to shake. The man in charge continued, lifting a hand to his ear, "And now you hear, my friends, the sound of your ships being smashed by our guns." The ferocity of the bombardment continued for several minutes. "If your sailors have wisdom, they go by now. So, as you can see, safest choice for now is to remain here, obeying all orders. Perhaps you are freed for ransom by your Emperor *Napoleone* once he realize how hopeless your situation is."

Jean-Luc's lingering hopes sank. He knew the emperor would never pay ransom to a foreign kingdom, especially one that he had just offered peace to, who were now kidnapping his emissaries and firing on his ships. Jean-Luc swallowed hard, realizing this might be a long captivity.

The man continued with the cheerfulness of a *maestro* introducing a new opera series. "Cooperate and maybe you return home to your families. Attempt to escape and we kill you in front of your countrymen. Signores, Napoli is your new home!"

Days passed before Jean-Luc was allowed out of his cell again. He was brought up a flight of stairs to a rampart overlooking the azure waters of the bay of Naples. Two bored-looking guards flanked him. Below was a view of the courtyard where he and the other prisoners had first been marshaled; it was empty, for now. The bright morning sun shimmered off the waters of the bay, causing him to squint as he watched two far-off skiffs listing in the breeze. Such stirring natural beauty—heightened by the encroaching specter of death.

The sound of voices in apparent dispute reached his ears, and a moment later he heard footsteps approaching. They halted a few paces behind him. "I am not Medusa, French ambassador," an accented voiced called out. "You may look upon my face without turning to stone."

Jean-Luc turned to see the tall, blue-eyed leader of his captors. "Permit me to introduce myself; my name is Mario Ennio D'Ascanio."

Jean-Luc returned his offered handshake. Though wary, Jean-Luc noticed how the man's demeanor brought an attitude of affability to the cold business of kidnapping, ransom, and possibly murder. A jolly pirate.

"My men tell me that you are somebody, no? That you come on an important diplomatic mission from your emperor? Well, I suppose you can say we put you out of business." The man's grave face wavered; he soon burst out in a fit of laughter. "Ah, *dio mio*," he uttered, resting a hand on Jean-Luc's shoulder. "I am sorry to make light of your misfortune. It is not kind. Now, if you would please tell me your name then we can have a proper conversation."

"My name is Jean-Luc St. Clair, senator of the French Empire," he said, straightening his posture. "I came to your city on behalf of Napoleon and Joseph Bonaparte, to express to your king and queen our desire for peace between our peoples."

Signore D'Ascanio nodded his head. "Si, I am glad to hear you say so, for I had known all this, but I wanted to make sure you told me true and were not a lying coward." His smile remained, but his eyes probed Jean-Luc's for signs of weakness. Satisfied he was dealing with a worthy counterpart, he continued. "It is regrettable how things have turned. Your men seem to be fellows of courage who I would not desire to harm, but I leave politics for the men born in castles. I was raised in the dirty streets where a man stabs his enemy from the front."

"What do you wish of me?"

"That is simple." D'Ascanio cleared his throat and spit over the wall. "My masters are willing to offer you in exchange for our brothers kidnapped by your army."

"You offer to parole me for what, one hundred, two hundred of your fellows?"

"The number is not for me to decide, signore."

"Very well." Jean-Luc nodded. "If you wish to parole me back to my countrymen, I accept. On one condition. My two companions come with me."

Jean-Luc returned to his cell disappointed but not defeated. His conditions had been refused, but, with some diplomatic dexterity and a little luck, he might possibly convince his otherwise congenial captor to permit their release.

He was awakened that evening by the sound of raised voices, followed by footsteps running to and fro outside the door of his cell. Several minutes passed as Jean-Luc strained to hear what was happening. Finally, a faint noise came from the other side of the door. Someone, or something, was digging. He crawled over to set his ear against the door when suddenly something slipped past his feet. He flinched, thinking some rat or vermin had scurried underneath the door. His fears were quickly dispelled when he saw a small piece of parchment on the floor. He snatched the paper like a starving man at a feast. He unfolded it and held it up to read—but could not make out anything in the darkness of the cell. He cursed, tucking the parchment into his shirt, saving it in case he gained an opportunity to examine the contents. Not long after, the door to his cell swung open, and a voice demanded that he get out and into the courtyard at once.

Men carrying torches cut across the courtyard in all directions, barking out orders, the flames casting eerie shadows that crept along the ancient stone walls. Jean-Luc was soon joined by his fellow captives, and they were lined up in their accustomed formation. A man mounted the ramparts overlooking the courtyard; it was not Signore D'Ascanio. This man wore a gray smock with short sleeves, revealing muscular arms. His mustache and large, bulging eyes were visible even from a distance.

"Servants of Napoleone!" he barked out. "Signore D'Ascanio has been called to the front, to destroy your comrades before they assault our people. I am your new commandant, Anguilla. I have gathered you here to inform you that you are all in grave danger." He leaned forward, placing his stocky arms on the balustrade. "One of your comrades has escaped," he shouted, his voice rising. A murmur broke out among the prisoners; it was silenced by the report of a pistol shot from one of his men. When a tense calm was restored, Anguilla, silhouetted against the pitch-black sky, resumed his oration. "The rat killed one of our guards!" He yelled with unbridled rage. Several pike-wielding men, foot soldiers of the *Lazzaroni*, stalked through their ranks, willing any captive to make eye contact. "So what shall we do? The city shall be scoured, your comrades in the low city shall be interrogated..."

As the man rattled off a list of declarations and threats, Jean-Luc recalled the parchment in his shirt. He glanced to either side to make sure no guards were nearby; he took out the paper, slowly unfolding it. His hands trembled as he lifted it to catch overhanging torchlight. It was a short message scrawled in apparent haste.

> *P-H is in trouble. I cannot last much longer, will attempt to free you and make our escape—Maxime.*

For a minute Jean-Luc found it difficult to breathe. Pierre-Henry was in trouble? Maxime was the one who had escaped? Their captor's harangue continued, interrupting Jean-Luc's frantic thoughts.

"You men all claim the Corsican's genius for yourselves." His growling voice had now turned calm. "So, we will find out just how clever you are. My guards will now search each and every one of you for evidence of treachery."

Jean-Luc's knees almost gave out, and his heart began pounding. His mind raced before it was overtaken by a numbness that simultaneously froze his body as rigid as a statue.

"But before we begin searching," the leader bellowed, "we have an example of that which awaits those who commit treachery. Bring out the wretched filth!"

His attention turned to a corner of the courtyard, and the eyes of the captives followed. Two guards dragged a man by the arms and brought him to the front of the prisoners' formation. Jean-Luc strained to get a better look, but the prisoners standing in front obscured his view. The captive's hair and profile appeared familiar. Suddenly, a chill ran through his veins; standing a mere ten paces away was Pierre-Henry. His hair was disheveled, small cuts lined his arms and face, and his left eye was badly bruised. Jean-Luc moved to step forward when out of the corner of his eye the man called Anguilla joined them in the courtyard. At this distance he appeared shorter, but his dark eyes—cold, malignant, and utterly pitiless—more than compensated for his diminutive stature.

He circled Pierre-Henry and forced him to his knees, before stroking a thread of his hair. "Tell your comrades your crime."

Pierre-Henry lifted his head slightly. "Go to hell."

Anguilla clicked his tongue. "For one who has committed the gravest sin of all—murder," he said, with convincing incredulity, "you dare condemn me to the inferno?"

"I was not the one who killed your guard," Pierre-Henry spat.

The captor turned his head sharply to one of his men before turning back to Pierre-Henry. "You were not the one who killed Ciro?"

"No."

"You are sure?"

"Yes."

"I see," Anguilla said, holding out his palms. "But you will die anyway."

In a chaotic moment that felt like something out of a nightmare, the leader of the *Lazzaroni* held out his hand for a pistol. He lifted it to Pierre-Henry's head and fired. With a jerk, the young man slumped, and his head dropped to his chest, his torso still propped upright on his knees.

Curses and protests erupted from the captives. Anguilla unleashed a savage tirade. "*Bastardi*! You have come to our city to rape our women, enslave our children, and destroy our holy faith! We have shown you mercy, and you repaid our restraint with murder. Mercy no more! *Compagni*, search these *cani francesi*. If their pockets hold anything other than cloth, shoot them. *Coglione!*" Anguilla spat at the corpse of Pierre-Henry, then stalked out of the courtyard.

Bile rose up in Jean-Luc's throat. He could see no safe place to hide the parchment. The guard searching his row was six men away, forcing a captive to remove his clothes and turn out his pockets. Half in shock, a shadow of despair descended upon Jean-Luc. It felt as if time had ceased, and he felt his chest constrict. The weight of every failure, disappointment, and heartache he had ever endured seemed to suddenly drop down upon him. Terrible thoughts coursed through his mind like poisonous vapor, and his vision blurred. He looked up at the walls looming above him, wondering if he could clamber up and leap to a quick death.

The guard was now only two men away. His thoughts turned to his children, robbed of their mother, soon to be orphans. Overwhelmed by regret and self-loathing for the choices that had led him here, he lifted his eyes and wondered if these were to be his last moments on earth.

He sighed as his chin drooped, and he felt a brief moment of acceptance—of peace. When he lifted his chin, however, his thoughts turned to something, someone, he had not thought about in some time. An image formed in his mind's eye—one that shook his soul: the face of his love. Young Marie Germain. She was beautiful, her fierceness tempered gracefully with a mature intelligence and intuition that saw in him a man worthy of her love. Groaning aloud, Jean-Luc nearly dropped to his knees; but he managed to gather himself, refusing them permission to buckle. Marie's presence remained, and Jean-Luc imagined her giving him a reproving look, the one she wore whenever he had failed to live up to his better self, when he'd indulged in weakness or self-pity for too long.

He glanced cautiously at the *Lazzaroni* inspecting the naked man next to him, willing himself to think of anything that he might do to ensure his survival. Catching the guard's face, he felt a vague recognition, unclear at first, but then it finally struck him like a thump to the chest. The porter who had taken his bags from him at the grand palace! He took a step toward Jean-Luc. No recognition dawned on his features, despite Jean-Luc's attempt to offer a full view of his eyes and face. Jean-Luc spoke a few words of French, and the man responded with the back of his hand to Jean-Luc's face.

"*Spogliati, sbrigati!*" he barked.

Avoiding any French words, he stammered out a short phrase in Latin. "*Memento mei?*" he whispered, removing his shirt. The man did not strike him, nor did he respond. "*Latine loqueris?*" Jean-Luc persisted, removing a sock. "*Quando venit occurrit, tradidisti annotare. Adduxistis illum domum gallico.*"

The man's face changed slightly, almost reluctantly.

"*Non posse reddere tantum.*"

The man peered cautiously over his shoulder. He turned back to Jean-Luc with a wide grin. "You are very sneaky, Frenchman."

Jean-Luc sat in his cell, stunned. He'd successfully negotiated a stay of searching in lieu of promised money. A noise issuing from across the cell caused him to turn his head—a barely perceptible rap at the door. He crouched down against the thick wooden door and whispered, "Who's there?"

"Senator," a whispered voice replied, "it is me."

Jean-Luc nearly cried out. "Maxime! You're alive!" He felt a swell of profound relief. "And Pierre-Henry," he whispered, "you're aware of what happened?"

After a lengthy silence. "I know he is dead."

Jean-Luc sighed heavily. For the past few days his mind had returned to the night they were taken; he had sent them out of their lodging house because of their drinking. Perhaps if he had not sent them out, none of this would have happened. He banished the thought. "Then there is nothing we can do for him now. We must remain strong and find our way out of this bloody mess." He leaned his head against the door. "Have you learned anything of what is going on in the city?"

"The *Lazzaroni* bastards are rounding up Republicans, locking them away, torturing some, killing others. I've heard guards muttering about ships arriving in the harbor. French? English? I don't know."

"It could be our countrymen coming to save us." He thought for a moment. "Or the English arriving to assist in the uprising."

"We won't be around to find out." Maxime continued, his voice growing louder, "I've dressed myself in the smock of the man I killed; once I find the keys I will come and get you out."

Jean-Luc felt a wave of guilt hearing his companion's unsolicited confession. The young man had appeared so carefree upon the start of their journey; now he was a killer.

"You've shown courage beyond any doubt, Maxime." Jean-Luc said. "But you must leave and find refuge in the city. I will come for you—"

"You wish me to hide?" Maxime interrupted. "After I've killed one of the bastards and returned for you? Why ever would I—"

"I am a senator, Maxime, they will not—"

"What good is rank or title when locked in a prison cell?"

"Patience, Maxime. If you and I are caught breaking out of this cell, it will cause an uproar! What good is an escape that only serves to delay our deaths? These villains have made a grave mistake; they are only beginning to realize it, but when they've had time to think on it—"

"Pierre-Henry was killed!" Maxime replied heatedly.

"If the English have, in fact, arrived," Jean-Luc replied evenly, "at least they are not the *Lazzaroni*. They may be our enemies, but they're also aware of the larger game being played. Prisoner or not, I am still a senator of the French Empire. By treating me this way, the Neapolitans have invited the full wrath of Emperor Napoleon. The English might hate him, but they know enough to fear him. They will not willfully allow me to be tortured or killed." Jean-Luc cleared his throat. "Plant yourself where you can see the offices of Casa Laganà on the Via Duomo and wait for me. I believe I have someone who can smuggle me there before daybreak. Join me while the streets are still quiet. We'll wait for the English, or Russians, when they arrive. I will offer the two of us as hostages for which they may negotiate with our emperor."

Maxime made a sound that resembled laughter. "What if the *Lazzaroni* demand our heads?"

"Naples is dependent upon the Royal Navy for its very survival. My guess is that the English look down on these people as much as we do."

CHAPTER 29

Tatras Mountains, Poland

November 1806

The three travelers emerged from the mouth of the cave into a howling snowstorm, the biting cold stinging their faces. With a renewed sense of purpose, they cautiously descended the mountain.

André shook his head, thinking the strange woman offered more questions than answers. In his mind's eye he replayed the events in the cave, pondering the meaning of her cryptic message to him. "*The first stranger to whom you speak beyond this cave will bring an answer to the question that has tormented you and will not cease to, until your decision is made.*"

When at last they reached camp, they found their two troopers huddled around a fire, cold and ornery. Nevertheless, they greeted their resurrected executive officer with an embrace that nearly knocked the enfeebled man to the ground. To André's relief, Moreau was able to drink some broth and swallow a few bites of bread before they mounted their horses and began the long ride back to Posen.

On the second day of their ride, they began to encounter signs that a large army was approaching. Groups of Polish civilians, small at first but growing steadily in number as the day wore on, rode or walked past on the road. Some traveled with carriages or on mules laden with household items. Alicja asked them why they were leaving, and they replied with curt shouts of "*Uciekamy przed Wojna*," which, she explained, meant they were fleeing the fighting.

Trotting along snow-covered roads, the group saw abandoned wagons, saddles, and heaps of clothing. The flotsam of a people fleeing in panic served as a sobering reminder of what they'd soon be returning to. André urged them to move more rapidly.

On the morning of their third day they encountered the first French units; cavalrymen who were, in fact, Polish. A troop of uhlans passed them on the road, fifty or sixty horsemen bearing long pikes, the red and white Polish flag flapping from the tips. They asked why André's party was approaching from the east. Some of them eyed Alicja with curiosity and not a little covetousness. Hoping to avoid an unfortunate misunderstanding, André, through Alicja's translation, informed the uhlans that they had been sent to Warsaw to deliver an important message and were now rejoining their unit in Posen. Their leader laughed cheerfully, claiming they had left the city two days prior, heading northeast to fall in under the command of Marshal Bernadotte and help find the advance Russian patrols. André noted the zeal and enthusiasm on the young men's faces, several of whom were no older than boys. He felt an unexpected pride knowing that these men from a strange land were so eager to join the fight against their common enemy. Reading the expression on Alicja's face, he guessed that she shared the feeling.

"You like join us?" The commander called out to André as his horse turned in circles on the snowy ground.

André smiled his appreciation. "No, thank you," he cried out. "We've been ordered to return as quickly as possible."

The leader of the uhlans nodded. "Yes, understand," he called out with Alicja translating. "Our officers give us orders too, but in Poland sometimes Wawel bring tidings that even greatest general cannot hear. So, when in need, sometimes we are following our own commands."

André, confused, nodded respectfully. "Good luck!" he cried out, unsure if his voice could be heard over the wind gusts.

"Go, go!" one of the other uhlans cried as they prepared to depart. "Rosjanie and Cossack come, no good. You go!"

They thundered away into the white and green landscape to shrill trumpet blasts that caught the howling wind, producing a strange and melancholy melody that lingered long after they'd passed out of sight.

André's small party remained still for a moment, and he turned to Alicja. "What is a Wawel?"

Alicja licked her lips, which were cracked and practically bleeding from the cold. "A hill," she answered. "Near Krakow. Some say there you can hear the spirits within the earth, carried on the wind." She drove her horse forward, and they resumed their journey to rejoin the French army.

Later that evening, with the sun fading and the temperature falling rapidly, they came upon the foremost units of the French army. André decided to make camp for the night; in the morning, hopefully, they could reunite with their squadron.

That night as he lay shivering in a small tent, wrapped in all the cloth he could scrounge from the quartermaster, André resolved to tell his superiors all he had learned about Major Carnassier and his plans for seizing the hidden fortune of Hesse-Cassel. If he could convince them of what he knew, surely they would at least look into the matter. But was he too late? For all he knew, the hussar major had found his loot and was on the verge of earning a marshal's baton, or more.

***

André's party rejoined their squadron the following day, in a snowy field near the banks of the Vistula. Sergeant-major Mazzarello's relief at his commander's safe return was surpassed only by his utter surprise to see Major Moreau walking on his own two feet.

André briefed his subordinate, bypassing specific details of the Szeptucha, thinking it best to save that story for after the campaign. In turn, Mazzarello briefed André on the events of the week prior: forced marches and frigid weather. He also informed André that despite his best efforts to cover for his absence, Colonel Menard had learned of it and had voiced his displeasure to Captain Vitry with an angry reprimand.

For his part, Moreau's spirits seemed to be improving a little each day. He greeted the troopers who'd ridden out to see him in his customary way.

"It's good to be back," he told the small group clustered around him. "But don't think a few scratches have softened me. If any of you try to kiss me, I'll smash your teeth in."

Once he had relieved Captain Vitry of command and gone through the squadron's administrative reports with his sergeant-major, André rummaged through the letters that had arrived while he'd been away. The last one was from Colonel Menard and stated in no uncertain terms how displeased the brigade commander was to learn of André's extended absence. André did not relish the thought of their reunion.

CHAPTER 30

Saint Elmo Castle, Naples

Summer 1806

" **R**aise yourself, *francese*."
Jean-Luc woke to the sound of a turning key and dim light spilling through the open doorway. The figure blocking the light in the doorway was the *Lazzaroni* guard he'd bribed.

"We go quick, while they are asleep." With hurried motions the man gestured for Jean-Luc to follow him. Not wholly convinced of the man's intentions, Jean-Luc nevertheless allowed his hands to be bound before being prodded along a stone path that skirted the courtyard and passed through several dark passageways. The man's grip on his arm was strong and tight. Finally, they emerged onto a dark, empty street. By the light of the stars and an occasional lantern, they groped their way through the city, walking for a quarter of an hour before turning onto a narrow thoroughfare that seemed to stretch for miles. For the first time in what felt like ages, Jean-Luc allowed himself to think of the possibility of liberty. The man halted in front of a large door, let go of his arm, and knocked three times, waited a few seconds, then knocked twice more. A minute or so later the door swung back, and an elderly man dressed in a cap and nightgown peered out from the shadows. "*Cosa vuoi?*" he asked.

The two Italians exchanged several heated words, and, with a reluctant scoff, the old man opened the door, barking at Jean-Luc and his chaperone as they entered the house. The old man lit a candle and waved his hand, ushering them through what appeared to be an office. Jean-Luc guessed that this was the Casa Laganà diplomatic bureau. The host motioned for him to be seated in a large wooden chair while he and the guard stepped into an adjacent room.

Jean-Luc's eyes adjusted to the faint light of the candle. He noticed several books lining a nearby shelf, and, sure enough, several had French titles. He felt incredulous at how successful his spontaneous bribe of this *Lazzaroni* had turned out. The two men, who had been talking in Italian, fell silent. Jean-Luc turned around and found himself staring down the barrel of a pistol. The old man held the weapon with a steady hand and said a few words in Italian, turning a quick eye to the guard, for translation.

"He offers his apologies, monsieur," the younger guard said, "but you have come to his place of business, so he must give you his terms."

Jean-Luc felt his heart pounding in his chest. "All right," he said quietly, not wanting to startle the man holding the pistol.

"Your presence puts me in quite big danger," the guard continued translating, "so you will obey my commands—or I will say you've broken in. I only allow you to stay because I received word a week ago that if fighting were to break out, Frenchmen would seek refuge here. I was offered compensation for offering protection. I allow you to remain in my attic for a few days."

Jean-Luc nodded gratefully, breathing a long sigh of relief that his advance payment had found its destination and evidently achieved its aim. "Very well. I do not wish to put anyone's life in danger."

Satisfied that his point had been made, the older man lowered the weapon. Placing it on the table, he threw up his hands; whether in exasperation or relief, Jean-Luc could not tell. The guard then informed Jean-Luc that he was welcome to a straw mattress in the attic but was not to step outside under any circumstances. The elderly man rose and led them up three flights of stairs; Jean-Luc was shown into a cramped room with a slanted ceiling that ended just above the crown of his head. The old man nodded, spoke a few words in Italian, and left the room.

"What does he say now?" Jean-Luc asked quietly, removing his boots and climbing onto the mattress.

"He says," the guard replied, rubbing his eyes with both hands, "that you French think you are bringing us liberty, when all you bring are the wild offspring of your own wars. Your own hatred."

Jean-Luc merely nodded as the guard bid his farewell. The door closed, and Jean-Luc shut his eyes and fell quickly into a deep sleep.

After a couple of days spent writing letters to his colleagues—as well as one to the family of his murdered assistant—Jean-Luc was taken to the grand palace. He kept his promise to the *Lazzaroni* responsible for his escape, leaving the promised fifty-franc Napoleons, which his host at Casa Laganà had withdrawn using Jean-Luc's bank number at the bureau that had sheltered him. Maxime, who had made his way to the bureau the day before, accompanied him on the short walk to meet with their new captors. No longer serving in the official capacity as diplomat of the French Imperial Senate, Jean-Luc presented himself at the palace as a hostage—albeit a valuable one.

Following several hours of negotiations with the British admiral now commanding the city, Jean-Luc was instructed to prepare to travel north to French lines. He was to be released—exchanged along with two dozen of his countrymen for twice that number of the enemy's own prisoners.

The following morning Jean-Luc and Maxime found themselves at the head of a train of carriages crossing the Italian countryside, making their way to French-held territory outside Rome. As the carriage ascended the hills beyond the gates of the city, Jean-Luc did not turn back. Though he felt an enormous relief that he and his young associate were to be freed and united with their families, he nevertheless felt a shadow of intense guilt at the loss Pierre-Henry, and he found himself recalling the night of their capture repeatedly in his mind: What if he had locked the doors and instructed his young companions to stay inside? What if he had asked for an armed guard? He did not share his thoughts with Maxime, who by some miracle had escaped his own captivity and managed to find his cell, joining him in refuge a few days later. For now, the thought that the young man was returning with him was enough to keep his thoughts from descending into total gloom.

For two days they crossed the rolling hills of the Kingdom of Naples, passing magnificent olive vineyards and orchards of cypress and cherry laurel. On the third day their convoy approached the outskirts of Rome, which, in days of peace, would have inspired all of Jean-Luc's enthusiasm and curiosity. But the nagging shame and trauma, which had only grown worse as the journey wore on, stifled any sense of wonder at his first sight of the eternal city.

It was in this mood that Jean-Luc found himself awaiting the formalities of the transfer of prisoners. The tedious process took the better part of the night; English officers and their Neapolitan escorts rode ahead to meet with the deputies of Marshal Massena. Jean-Luc and his companions passed the evening on the grass, sleeping under the open stars. When the negotiations were concluded, the French prisoners were marched to a municipal building nearby, where they were welcomed by a brigadier general of the Grand Armée. Their joyous "first homecoming" was little more than a rehearsed greeting, followed by a reading of the morning's Grand Armée Bulletin, wherein his newly freed compatriots were briefed, somewhat insensitively, on all the charms of Naples, the city of their recent captivity. Most significant among the news to Jean-Luc, however, was a proclamation from the emperor regarding Joseph Napoleon:

> Napoleon, by the grace of God and the constitutions. Emperor of the French and King of Italy, to all those to whom these presents come, salutation. The interests of our people, the honour of our crown, and the tranquility of the Continent of Europe requiring that we should assure, in a stable and definite manner, the lot of the people of Naples and of Sicily, who have fallen into our power by the right of conquest, and who constitute a part of the grand empire, we declare that we recognize, as King of Naples and of Sicily, our well-beloved brother, Joseph Napoleon, Grand Elector of France. This crown will be hereditary, by order of primogeniture, in his descendants masculine, legitimate, and natural...."

Ignoring the cheerful embraces and exclamations of his compatriots, Jean-Luc stood aside, contemplating the meaning of this announcement. His mood quickly turned sour. *We were sent to Naples, delivered to the* Lazzaroni *as live bait to be saved by the emperor's valiant troops. Meanwhile, his brother will enjoy the spoils of another conquest by the placing of a foreign crown upon his head.*

His return from Rome took nearly a month, and as he inched closer to Paris the letters of relief, and even congratulations, began finding him. At long last he received a letter from Isabella, from whom he had not heard since his captivity. The tone of her letter was one of fear and grief, almost to the point of despair. He felt relieved to be returning to her, not wishing to cause her any further pain. Her letter touched upon Mathieu and Mariette, whom he anxiously longed to see and hold. He had spent countless hours after the night of Pierre-Henry's murder in candid meditation upon his own possible death, but the thought of leaving his children orphans in a mad world was unbearable. Her letter assured him that they were well and over-joyed to hear of their father's imminent return.

CHAPTER 31

Posen

November 1806

Colonel Menard sat in his tent with his elbows propped on a small wooden desk, and when André presented himself, the brigade commander let out an exaggerated exhale.

"Valiere," he said slowly, rolling his eyes before dropping them to the ground. "I truly don't know what to do with you. In the handful of straightforward missions I've given you, you've managed to get yourself ambushed, meander your way behind enemy lines, allow your executive officer to nearly get murdered, and now, I have a *captain* reporting to me that his commanding officer has disappeared for two weeks with a Polish peasant in search of a witch in the mountains!" The colonel's face flushed.

"It wasn't a fortnight, sir."

"What?" The colonel seethed.

"We were only away from our billet for four days—"

"Oh, bollocks." Colonel Menard stared at him, exasperated. "You do realize that there is a war going on?"

"I do, sir, and I understand that my recent absence would appear unwarranted, but it is because we are at war that I deemed it a necessary risk. To do whatever was in my power to save the life of my executive officer, Marcel Moreau. He is an excellent officer, sir, and one I consider indispensable for when the time comes to close with the enemy."

Colonel Menard waved dismissively. "Save it, Valiere. Your decision to abandon your squadron in the middle of a campaign is a dereliction of duty punishable by court martial. If only you had the requisite discipline to perform your duties as required, and not as you *wished*, you might have made something of yourself. Like that fellow, Carnassier, who snatched you from the ambush and saved your hides. It's a shame you did not learn a thing or two while you were under his charge."

André nearly fell over when he heard the hussar's name.

"Now we are ordered into winter quarters by the emperor, who sits in Warsaw enjoying his latest prize, and I don't know whether to send you home or return you to the enemy, as you seem to prefer their company over that of your own army."

"Sir, I'd like to reiterate my gratitude to Major Carnassier and his brave hussar troopers. Without them, we'd surely have been lost."

Colonel Menard grunted in agreement.

"As embarrassing as it is to admit, colonel, you are absolutely correct. I could only ever aspire to be the commander and soldier that he is. If only I could thank him in person. Do you know where the Seventh Hussars are camped?"

Menard eyed André with a look bordering on disdain. "Valiere, I don't mean to be unnecessarily cruel, but I believe you should have left this war to the career soldiers. You may have been an adequate junior officer during the Revolution, but those days are long gone. This empire requires a different sort of man. When this campaign has been won, perhaps it would be for the best if you returned to your farm in Normandy."

André's jaw clenched. "Sir, in that we are in perfect agreement."

Menard nodded almost sympathetically. "For the time being," he continued, "you will remain in command of the Seventeenth Dragoons, but you will not depart from the regiment without my explicit authorization. Lieutenant-Colonel, I will offer you this one final warning—do *not* get yourself into any more difficulties. I will be watching you, just as the emperor's eyes are watching me; we must not disappoint him. The Russians may be inept, but, nevertheless, we must remain vigilant."

André went to attention, saluting with feigned enthusiasm: "*Vive l'Empereur!*"

Menard offered a half-hearted salute in return. As André turned to depart the colonel called out, "Oh, and Valiere, if you wish to convey your thanks to the major by courier, Carnassier and the Seventh Hussars are camped in Mława with Marshal Ney's corps. Near the city of Soldau."

✳   ✳   ✳

"So, we find him and kill him, right, sir?" Mazzarello asked André that evening. They were joined by Moreau, the three of them huddled around a fire, holding their hands over the flames for warmth. André had been ordered to hold the squadron across the Vistula in the outskirts of Posen, to guard the city's eastern flank, where they would take up winter quarters. Every man in the squadron was eager to be out of the elements and under a roof once more, but the crowded roads and bottleneck of thousands of soldiers trying to cross a single bridge into the city meant they must bivouac in the snow for another day or two.

"It's not quite that simple," André replied, wrapping himself tighter under his cloak. "If I depart on another wild-goose chase, the colonel might kill me himself. I must stay here with the squadron."

Moreau jabbed at one of the logs in the fire with a branch.

"And if that is the case," André continued, "I will not send you or any of the men to risk their lives while I sit here in safety."

"But the Silesian man is our enemy," Mazzarello replied. "And he is working with that hussar devil. How do we stop them from getting the riches if you are stuck here?"

André exhaled a visible cloud of icy breath. "I'm thinking on it, Paolo."

The three sat brooding with only the sound of the crackling fire and a howling wind to accompany their thoughts. At last Moreau spoke.

"If Carnassier is using spies to further his ends, why don't we use our own against him?"

Mazzarello laughed aloud. "Our own spies. Should we call on the emperor and ask if we may borrow some of his agents?"

Moreau gestured to where the rest of the squadron was camped. "We have a resource, sir. One that I doubt our allies or enemies would ever suspect."

After a moment of consideration, a look of understanding dawned on André's features. He shook his head slowly. "No. Major, I won't allow it."

Moreau set the stick he'd been using to tend the fire on the ground beside him. "Colonel Valiere, her grandfather was *killed* by the man himself. She rode a hundred miles across an active theater of war of her own will; when I was passing through the door of death, she wrenched me back. If this were beyond her capacity, I would gladly oppose it. But we are out of sound options, and Carnassier must be stopped."

Mazzarello turned to André. "He makes a decent point, sir."

"I know he makes a decent point," André replied irritably, "but we have to consider the danger involved—"

"Fuck the danger involved!" Moreau snarled. Instantly conceding his insubordination, he lowered his eyes and apologized.

"I understand your reasoning, major." André sat back wearily. "But before we send a woman—one not duty-bound to our own nation—into the lion's den, I would like to consider all potential courses of action. And besides, I would like to know: Is this truly about stopping Carnassier? Or seeking revenge? You still have three 'worthy' duels left, remember?"

Mazzarello looked at both men. "What worthy duels?"

Moreau wrapped his coat tighter to his chest. "Only two remain now."

André stared at his executive officer. "What?"

Moreau stared into the fire. "When I was set upon," he said in a quiet voice, "and wounded in the village on the road to Posen, it didn't happen by chance. The evening we'd arrived, after the inn had all but cleared out, I challenged Alderic to a duel. I found a drunken infantryman to serve as my second, and we met behind the town church. It was an hour after midnight. Alderic allowed me to choose the weapon; I chose swords. We would fight to prostration, though we both knew a mortal wound to be the desired end for both parties. I wished to kill him with my own hand, to feel the life depart from his body. In the duration of a minute, perhaps less, he had slashed me along the ribs. I had pierced both his right leg and his shoulder, and he was losing strength quickly. Another cut and I would have had him. I was on the cusp of victory when I felt a staggering blow to the back of my head. I fell to the ground. I saw a gang of six or seven of Carnassier's men descending on me, knives drawn. I tried to defend myself, but after the third or fourth wound I felt the air in my lungs depart." The wind calmed, and only the hushed pop of dying embers could be heard. André and Mazzarello stared at Moreau, who threw the stick onto the meager flames. "I regret the trouble I have caused both of you in tending to me in my condition and the journey you were forced to make. I have failed you."

Mazzarello looked obligingly to André, as if ceding the response to his commanding officer. After a tense silence, André leaned forward, removing the cloths covering his face. He eyed Moreau with an icy stare.

"Major, you haven't failed the two of us. I understand the need to defend your honor, as any soldier would. But by putting your own selfish desire for vengeance before your duties as an officer and leader, you abandoned every trooper in this squadron and repaid their loyalty with weakness." He stood up, wiping a layer of snow from the sleeves of his coat. "Go to sleep, both of you. In the morning I will tell you what I have decided to do."

He stalked off into the freezing night, his boots crunching in the snow. He had not gone far when he nearly bumped into a sack set alongside another fire. He halted, taking a few seconds to warm his hands. As he stomped his feet to keep them from losing feeling, he looked up at the wintry sky, noticing the clarity of the stars. On nights like these he could not help but admire their brilliance. In a strange way, not unlike the experience of battle, he considered them a glimpse into the face of the almighty. Was there something more than this realm of flesh, blood, and dirt? Was God watching him in this very instant, sending love and protection? Or would a bullet or saber find him on the field and put an end to his earthly existence? Was man simply a heap of flesh and bone passing down the never-ending stream of life? His heart longed for home.

Suddenly, a movement to his right caused him to reach instinctively for his saber. The sack he had nearly trampled over moved, and a figure emerged from beneath a wool blanket. "You may sit if you wish."

"Alicja, is that you?" he asked, laughing away his startled nerves. "I almost…"

"It's me, lieutenant-colonel. I was almost asleep."

André sighed as he sat down beside the fire. His body ached from the days of riding. "I've just found out that Moreau was not attacked arbitrarily by Carnassier's men. He was attacked, to be sure, but only after he had wounded Alderic in a duel."

"Yes, I know," she replied quietly.

"You do?" André shook his head. "Is there any other information concerning *my* squadron that you two are hoarding you might consider worth sharing?"

Alicja laughed at André's earnest irritation. "Colonel, perhaps Marcel knew the hussar would be coming to challenge him and decided to preempt it by calling him out. After all that he's been through, I hardly think he deserves to be punished for an excess of bravery."

"Mademoiselle Jarzyna," André began, hoping to expose some fault in her logic. Finding none, he kicked the snow with his boot. "I've never dealt with anyone quite like Major Moreau before. I really don't know what to make of him."

"Truly?" she asked, holding a half-frozen hand over the fire. "Or is there something else troubling you and you are letting your anger out on him?"

André eyed her sideways: How had a Polish peasant woman come to understand so much about people? He closed his eyes with a yawn. "Well, if you can't fall asleep, go see the major, he has a task for you."

"Colonel!" she said, smacking his shoulder. "I have my dignity—"

"I'm not referring to whom you share a bed with, woman." He glanced at her, his expression serious. "I'm telling you truly, we have a mission for you. A dangerous one."

My beloved André,

When a month passed with no word from you, I feared the worst. Your latest letter has found me, however, and though I am overcome with relief to receive word, my heart breaks for your executive officer Monsieur Moreau. From your description he sounds a rather useful fellow to have beside you in a fight, and I don't want to think about you braving battle with anything less than heroes by your side. I hope he recovers his health soon and know that I pray for you and your men every night and will not cease until you arrive safely home.

I must now share with you the painful reason for writing this particular letter. Something has occurred here at Carcourt that has caused me no end of grief and distress, and while I do not wish to place additional burdens on you, I feel you must be aware of what is happening; for this is your home, and we are your family. I would hear any advice you have on the matter, and I will implement it.

You surely recall what I told you in my previous letters about the Count de Montfort, a man named Jean-Claude, and his affairs on our estate. I told you of our invitation for him to Carcourt for dinner, and I can say that I have given as true and sincere an offer of friendship that I can, but André, something has gone terribly wrong. I will not share with you all of the details of our dinner party, but ever since then he has shown a growing coldness toward me. That, of itself, is no particular cause for alarm; it is what has happened lately that truly disturbs me. Our efforts to build a tavern on the sight of the abandoned mill on the Saint-Paër stream have caused a great mess, and, after speaking with the concerned parties, I wrote the count, asking for any advice he might have to offer. He sent no reply. Strange though that might've been, I thought nothing was amiss until I received word from Monsieur Le Bon that the count would not be visiting Carcourt anymore, and that he was "indisposed." Again, I thought it a strange development but hardly anything to worry over until I was handed, once again by Guy Le Bon, ever the bearer of pleasant news, an article recently published in the Norman Gazette, *the count's newly purchased journal. The article is riddled with cruel and unfounded rumours, and I wished you to hear of it from me before any soldiers' gossip or calumny finds you at the front. The closing lines were the most damning, and try as I might I can find no reason for the man to have resorted to such base cruelty, especially in light of the friendship the people of Carcourt-sur-Seine have shown him and his associates.*

"The lady of the estate, Sophie Valiere, wife of Lieutenant-Colonel Valiere, where she has failed using seduction and licentious offers of romance, now tries to affect by force; principally, the dumping of scores of Breton and Chouan exiles, families who have seen no end to suffering in the uprisings of the Vendée, onto the estate of Count De Montfort, who has welcomed them with the limited resources at his disposal, since they've been scorned by the woman who initially posed as their savior."

I hope you understand that his words are all nonsense. The man himself offered to house and employ one hundred of these outlanders, as well as have his chamberlain assist Le Bon in tax collection duties. My only "offer" was a friendly supper with our people. Everything else originated in his own mind, which, to me now, seems slightly disturbed. Perhaps he did not bear the Revolutionary terror and exile with the fortitude of others.

To make matters worse, this morning I was informed that several Gypsies, whose families have been housed on the count's estate, have fled to Carcourt. They claim the count has accused them of the murder of one of the outlander farmers dwelling on his land. Sylvain Lavalle, chamberlain to the count, has written me a letter demanding that I return these unfortunates to De Montfort's estate for a "fair and public hearing" to determine their guilt.

Oh, André, I don't know what to do. Affairs with this count, which started so pleasantly, have truly fallen into such disrepair that I'm thinking of going to his estate in person; perhaps I can reason with him. Please, my darling, if there is anything you have heard or think might help ease tensions, do tell me. I am floundering.

With love and affection,
Sophie

CHAPTER 32

Paris, France
Summer/Autumn 1806

A cluster of letters sat on Jean-Luc's dining table, all offering the same sentiments: relief and celebration of his triumphant return, some even alluding to a "Roman Triumph" along the Champs-Élysées. He laughed sullenly, considering his hapless and unwitting role in the upheaval of that war-torn Italian city. The idea of being lauded as a hero would have been insulting, were it not so comical.

As the afternoon sun gave way to evening shadows, his long-awaited reunion with Isabella came at last. He was sitting on one of their velvet sofas when she entered the house. At first she did not notice him, nor did he move to get up, sitting quietly as she set down her purse. Removing a pair of earrings and turning her head, she caught sight of him in the drawing room and gave a shout. After their tears and embraces settled into something resembling a conversation, they sat together on the sofa.

"Oh, my poor St. Clair," she said, resting a hand on his weather-beaten coat. "The things you've missed in recent days! I hardly know where to begin, other than to say with certainty that you are sure to find the reception of a hero! When you are ready, of course."

"I saw some of the letters; it seems my return from the dead is something to be celebrated," Jean-Luc said, his tone tinged with regret.

"I should think so, my love," Isabella replied, lifting his chin. "*I* knew you would be fine, but plenty of these folk fairly fell about themselves when they heard that one of our noble senators had been seized by those brigands."

Jean-Luc spent the next quarter of an hour recounting the story of his abduction and captivity, shuddering as he recalled the image of young Pierre-Henry's body falling lifeless to the ground. He omitted that detail, hoping to spare Isabella undue distress. When he finished speaking he looked at her, hoping his account had not been too unsettling. He sensed she was unable to comprehend the severity of his circumstances and how close his brush with death had been, for she looked neither fearful nor relieved, but strangely distant. The two sat quietly for a minute.

Isabella broke the silence with a sigh. "How dreadful the world can be, darling. I'm so relieved that you're finally safe at home. Life in this city has not been all charm itself; we have no shortage of brutes in our own quarters." She brushed a hand across her lap, smoothing her dress. "Why, for all the appeal of the Saint-Germain we are still just a pebble's throw from the university quarter, and those students are worse than Turks. In your absence, I've had to find chaperones to escort me safely past those ruffians."

Jean-Luc nodded absently, still seeing the torch-lit faces of his captors and the young man he had brought to Naples but failed to bring home.

"Darling," she went on, "I don't wish to trouble you so recently returned, but you've been absent for quite some time, and there are matters that must be attended to."

Jean-Luc sat forward in his seat, as if listening for something. He turned to her. "Isabella, where are the children?"

Although they had shared a bed the evening prior, they now sat in silence. The breakfast of toasted bread, butter, sliced apple, and coffee sat undisturbed. Jean-Luc, his elbows resting on the table and his hands clasped tightly together, leaned forward in his chair, staring out the window. After several minutes Isabella could bear no more.

"Jean-Luc, it was not done with ill intent. You said yourself you weren't able to manage on your own, so I took the necessary steps—"

"You took it upon yourself to send them away without even consulting me?" he asked sharply.

"It was not *I* who marched off to Naples in pomp and splendor," she replied, raising her chin. "It was you who left the children behind."

"How dare you say that." Jean-Luc rounded on her with a ferocity that surprised even himself. "Do you think I asked to become a prisoner to those beasts? Don't *ever* accuse me of willingly abandoning my children, do you hear me?"

She took a sip of tea. "He warned me of your anger."

"What?" Jean-Luc asked incredulously. "Who warned you?"

"The minister of police," she replied, chin still raised in defiance.

Jean-Luc froze. "You've been meeting with the minister of police?"

"With you gone it was my duty to maintain relations and a posture of calm. It's not as if I invited him into our home. He came calling, and it is not my place to turn away a guest of influence in your absence."

Jean-Luc could hardly believe what he was hearing. "What did he want?"

"He did not *want* anything," Isabella answered. "He simply offered me the latest news on your condition, which I had requested from the office of Joseph Bonaparte—*he* offered *no* reply. At least the minister of police had the decency to address my inquiries."

Jean-Luc scoffed. "If he addressed your inquiries, I assure you it was not done out of decency. That man is not stirred by such sentiments."

"Well, whatever it was that compelled him to walk through the wind and rain to provide me with news of your absence, it was more than that younger, feebler brother of the emperor could bring himself to do."

His cheeks red and his eyes smoldering, Jean-Luc fought to restrain his temper. "Whatever business you had with that man—it doesn't explain why I've returned home to find my children departed without my consent."

For a moment Isabella sat silent as a statue, her eyes fixed on Jean-Luc. "I only did what I thought you would have wanted—is that so terrible of me? I was tending to the house and your children, alone. I have never had children of my own, and I wished only for their future happiness. My love, you had your duty. I do not think I deserve the complete share of blame— nor such cruelty."

Jean-Luc sighed, running a hand through his hair. After some consideration, he looked up. "I am sorry for leaving. Tell me again the name of the boarding house she's gone to."

"It's the former convent at Saint-Jacques-de-la-Baudinière," she replied with a sniffle. "It really isn't so bad; the church is quite lovely. I think she'll find her catechism quite suitable in that setting, and besides, she'll be away from the barbarian boys of the quarters nearby."

Jean-Luc stood up and began slowly pacing the room. "And she put up no fuss? She did not mind leaving her home?'

"No. I believe she was rather happy to go."

Jean-Luc looked down at her, nodding pensively as he gently placed an arm around her shoulders.

"Then I suppose my fears were misplaced. Forgive me; the experiences of the past few months seem to have unnerved me. I should be thanking you."

Isabella wiped a hand over her eyes.

"Now, what was it you were mentioning earlier? Mathieu's patron?"

She took another sip of tea. "A rather peculiar and ugly fellow from Normandy. Monsieur Sylvain. I was disinclined to admit him into our house, but he mentioned the name of the woman from whose residence he had come, Sophie Valiere—formerly de Vincennes. I recalled the name as an old friend of yours, and a woman of some reputation."

Jean-Luc brightened at the mention of Sophie Valiere. "Yes, she and her husband are dear friends."

"This Sylvain proposed a number of fanciful ideas, which he claimed originated from Sophie and a Monsieur Count de Montfort, his master. I mentioned Mathieu's admiration for the horsemen parading about town. He declared that this count was a wealthy man and would happily sponsor his application at the École Militaire. I told him it was not my decision to make. He informed me that he would be in Paris for another week and to call on him should we change our mind. Two days later I learned of your capture. I waited for word of your condition. Hearing nothing from Joseph Bonaparte, I'll admit I was unsure if I would ever see you again. So I called on Sylvain and informed him that young Mathieu would be overjoyed were he to be granted a commission. And, as so happens with young men in times of war, the robe of peace was cast aside in favor of the mantle of war, and a little over a month later Mathieu made his way to the École Militaire."

"Young men...he's only a boy." Jean-Luc forced a proud smile. "But if it was his wish, then I will not interfere."

CHAPTER 33

Saint-Germain, Paris

Autumn 1806

"Smile, darling." Isabella sipped her wine sparingly as she looked around the gathering, buoyed by the rapturous welcome they had received upon their arrival. "I understand emerging back into society takes some adjusting to, but remember, you are a senator."

They had accepted a last-minute invitation to a mansion on the Champs-Elysées to commemorate the emperor's latest construction project: a grand, triumphal arch to celebrate the heroes of the Grand Armée.

Jean-Luc shook the hand of a well-wisher. "I don't like this suit," he said, turning back to Isabella. "It is a dull gray color. I prefer blue."

Her look indicated that she did not appreciate the tone with which he spoke to her. "Senator or not," she eventually replied, "we must be wise in how we spend our money, my dear. The preparations for our new estate fell entirely on my shoulders while you were absent."

Jean-Luc ignored the comment and took another sip of wine. At that moment, a finely dressed couple appeared. The man, sporting a long brown coat and fashionably tight-fitting riding pants, was short and rather overweight. The woman beside him introduced the pair as Monsieur and Madame Levasseur, owners of the house.

Monsieur Levasseur extended his arm. "I should like to shake the hand of the hero of Naples."

Jean-Luc forced a smile. "How do you do you, monsieur?"

"I believe we speak for all true Frenchmen," the man continued, "when we extend our well-wishes to the emperor's most faithful operatives. If there is anything we can do to be of service to a hero of your stature, please do keep us in mind."

The hostess also shook hands with Jean-Luc before turning to the other guests. "Pardon, mesdames and messieurs," she called out in a piercing voice, "we are delighted to inform you that tonight we are all privileged to be in the presence of a national hero!"

Taken aback by this unexpected proclamation, Jean-Luc nevertheless turned to the crowd with a smile. Perhaps it was the wine, or the seemingly endless congratulations, but the room seemed to heave and lurch around him. Monsieur Levasseur then grabbed Jean-Luc by the hand and hoisted it in the air in a display of mutual triumph.

"Jean-Luc St. Clair," he cried, "has only just returned from the front lines of the Kingdom of Naples. True to the treachery of that country and its king and queen, Monsieur le Senator was arrested without cause and left to rot in a dungeon." The assembled guests seethed with an air of indignation. "But due to the intervention of our emperor's brother, Joseph," the host continued, "our hero has been returned to us at last. And it is but a matter of time before our Grand Armée marches triumphantly under the portals of that traitorous city."

The applause and cheering gave Jean-Luc a moment to exhale, bristling at the mention of Joseph Bonaparte, whom he considered responsible for placing him in the mess to begin with. He affected a gracious smile at Isabella as she nudged him forward. After a nod of appreciation, he lifted his hands and a hush fell over the crowd.

"Thank you, Monsieur and Madame Lavasseur, for hosting us in your lovely home. I am humbled by your kind words, but I assure you, I am no hero. I undertook my duties and found myself caught in a tangle of events far larger than any one individual; becoming, in the process, a target for the wrath of a people long resentful of our ideals of liberty, equality, and fraternity." The crowd brimmed with enthusiasm at the mention of the hallowed three words of the Revolution. "In my absence," Jean-Luc continued, "my family was left behind to manage on their own. It was only because of them that I found strength in an otherwise hopeless predicament. I could not manage without them," he said, turning to Isabella. It is to you, Marie—" he stopped short, his voice catching in his throat. It took the assembled guests a few seconds longer to catch his mistake. "Isabella Maduro," he said, quickly reshuffling his thoughts, "is the rock of my life, and it is to her that

I must give my gratitude and love." He wrapped up his speech, his blush betraying the severity of his mistake. Though still wearing a charming smile, Isabella bore her eyes into him with such intensity that he turned back to the crowd.

When he had concluded his remarks, she gracefully slid beside him, clasping his hand and smiling to the assembly. "Thank you, darling." She turned to the guests. "We have prayed for his safe return for months. Now we finally have him back. And although his speeches could rival the eloquence of Cicero, I must confess his instincts for fashion have clearly not developed as such. He insists on these drab, dull coats." The guests laughed at this jab. Her warm smile was relished by all present—save for Jean-Luc, who recognized the chill in her eyes. "Now that he is back in Paris, I wish he would try something a bit more exciting, like blue. Why, if Napoleon can capture Vienna, anything is possible; perhaps even I can turn Monsieur St. Clair into a fashionable member of society!" The crowd erupted into even more applause. "But enough about my Jean-Luc's unfortunate fashion sense. Now allow us to express our tremendous gratitude to the emperor and his brave soldiers for Senator St. Clair's deliverance. To the return of our brave Senator St. Clair, and all the heroes who serve our glorious Empire!"

She stepped aside and graciously turned the attention to Jean-Luc. "He has returned home to us, and we will not let him leave again."

Jean-Luc's mortification, though concealed behind a proud smile, twisted his insides like a cinch.

The morning following the disaster at Maison Levasseur, Isabella left the house while Jean-Luc still lay in bed. He did not have to guess the motive for her early departure; though he thought a moment of separation might benefit both their moods.

As he sat reading a note from his mountain of correspondence over breakfast, he admitted that he'd be better served doing penance with Isabella rather than sitting idly at home. He decided to pay a visit to the merchant whom Isabella had made an unofficial promise of sale for a team of horses. Though he'd initially objected to this action, another decision taken in his absence, she had convinced him that it was in their interests to own a fine team. The trader was located near Les Halles.

He turned out from the Rue du Bac and made his way along the Quai Voltaire, breathing in the fresh autumn air as it drifted off the Seine. The sun had not yet emerged from behind its blanket of clouds, but the morning was bright enough to see small puffs of mist on the river, its barges and ferries slowly winding their way as they had done for centuries. For the first time since he had returned home, Jean-Luc felt his spirits lifting. The exercise refreshed him, and after a lengthy walk he arrived at the office of the horse trader.

To his surprise, he learned that a down payment for the horses had already been paid—over five thousand francs—with more payments due over the course of the following six months. After overcoming his initial shock, he attempted to renegotiate the deal, only to learn that it had been signed and completed. Isabella's signature leaped off the page, and he flinched as if it were a coiled snake. He thanked the clerk and left the shop, his mind running through the calculations of future payments as he crossed the Pont Saint-Marcel and turned toward home. An assembly of carriages was parked along the quai, and a group of well-dressed men soon filed out from a nearby house. Jean-Luc slowed his pace to see who they were.

"Is that you, Monsieur St. Clair?" Gazing out of from one of the carriages with his customary cold stare was the minister of police, Joseph Fouché. He affected no pleasure upon seeing Jean-Luc, yet addressed him with the courtesy befitting his title. "You look well enough, senator," Fouché declared as Jean-Luc approached the carriage, "given your ordeal. So the fox found himself outwitted by the hens, then." The minister's small talk had the effect of a fencer lifting his foil, or so it seemed to Jean-Luc. The man in the carriage next to Fouché leaned back when he realized he did not recognize Jean-Luc. "In the end, one must be grateful the English arrived in time to induce some civility upon the brutes of that city."

"I suppose I was rather fortunate," Jean-Luc replied, wishing he had taken another street home.

Minister Fouché eyed Jean-Luc without blinking, offering a cold smile. "I shall not waste your valuable time, senator, other than to inform you that the senate will be meeting at the Luxembourg Palace one week from Friday. The emperor's couriers from the Prussian front will be providing us with their own accounts of the action, as well as dispatches from the emperor's own hand. There is talk of the emperor calling on his senators to join him should, rather I should say, *when* he captures Berlin." Jean-Luc was relieved the conversation had turned to something other than his own captivity. "I presumed you would enjoy the reception, given your recent acclaim,"

Fouché continued, quickly dispelling any relief. "When domestic life is unhappy, one often finds solace in the rigors of his profession."

"Domestic life," Jean-Luc replied, "in a lovely house with a lovely woman is certainly preferable to the hospitality of *Lazzaroni* cutthroats. I shall join the senate's meeting."

"That is well." Fouché indicated for the valet to shut the carriage door. "An hour before noon. Madame Maduro is certainly welcome to join us on the grounds after the session. If you wish, you may certainly bring your children along as well." Jean-Luc gritted his teeth and nodded, protocol and frustration wrestling within. "The senators will be honored to welcome home *the hero of Naples.*" Fouché tapped the roof and the driver shook the reins. "It is well deserved, St. Clair! You endured great hardship, while Joseph Bonaparte was gifted the entire kingdom merely through his happy relations." The carriage lurched forward and Fouché leaned back, disappearing from the window.

A quarter of an hour later, Jean-Luc returned home to find Isabella sitting on one of the drawing room sofas across from a man wearing the frock coat of an army officer. He was tall, sported a large black mustache, and looked to be of a similar age to Jean-Luc.

"Darling, you've returned at last," Isabella said, with an unexpectedly convivial smile. She rose and greeted Jean-Luc with a kiss. "I was beginning to wonder whether you had run away and left us again."

Jean-Luc offered a brief explanation of his morning, leaving out his encounter with the minister of police. He turned to the man seated across the room. "Good morning, monsieur."

The man stood slowly, his sword swaying at his side. He offered Jean-Luc his hand. "My apologies for this unannounced visit, Monsieur le Senator. Allow me to introduce myself. I am Francois Pettit, colonel in the chasseurs of the Imperial Guard."

Colonel Pettit's uniform was immaculately pressed and clean, and Jean-Luc found his initial discomfort at the man's presence dispelled somewhat by his soldierly bearing and high rank; perhaps he had come with news of Mathieu? He motioned for his guest to be seated.

After a servant had brought three saucers of tea, Jean-Luc began with the courtesy expected of polite society. "How may we be of service to you, colonel?"

"Monsieur," Colonel Pettit replied, "it is *I* who ought to be offering my services to *you*; the hero of Naples!" He turned toward Isabella. "Take good care of your gentleman, Madame Maduro. It is quite uncommon to find a politician brave enough to journey into the whale's belly and emerge alive and intact."

Isabella peered up slyly. "No need for flattery, colonel; he has me for that."

"I am sure you make him quite a happy man," Colonel Pettit exclaimed, leaning closer to Jean-Luc. "You are quite the envy of Paris, monsieur. My compliments indeed."

"You are too kind, monsieur." Stealing a look at Isabella he turned back to Colonel Pettit. "Have you come to offer us any word of Mathieu, my son?"

The colonel tapped his forehead. "My apologies—yes, senator. Mathieu St. Clair has been entered into the École Militaire, to be commissioned an ensign upon completion. He is to be enrolled in the school of cuirassier cavalry near the chateau of Écouen."

Jean-Luc nodded. "Will I have the chance to visit him?"

"Oh, senator, you must understand the call to duty as well as any other; now is not the time to reintroduce feelings of paternal affection—your boy must be made strong! He must learn the ways of flint and steel—to endure privations and fatigue so as to be hardened into a man!" Colonel Pettit's eyes flashed, but after seeing Jean-Luc's look of earnest disappointment he cleared his throat.

"Of course, once that is all finished, then, senator, you may see your boy."

Jean-Luc nodded, attempting a smile. "Yes, of course. The life of a soldier is no easy thing. He must be made to bear it on his own."

Jean-Luc thanked Colonel Pettit and offered his guest wine, pouring a generous glass for himself. The colonel politely declined. Bidding his hosts a good afternoon, he bowed elegantly and left. Jean-Luc rubbed his eyes and let out a sigh. As he gazed around the room, he noticed a cluster of small bottles on a table near the entryway.

"What are those?"

"Pardon?" Isabella asked, glancing in the direction Jean-Luc indicated before returning to her knitting. "Those are just some perfumes. A gift from the colonel."

Jean-Luc expected more in the way of explanation. When none came, he changed the subject. "I happened upon the minister of police today. He looked to be departing his house with several gentlemen of significance."

"Of course he was. When he's not intriguing behind closed doors, he's always to be found in the presence of someone powerful. And still," she continued, resuming her sewing, "while you were away, he *was* the only man from the government to visit me. That's more than Joseph Bonaparte could bring himself to do. While you were rotting away, he gallops off to make himself a king."

Jean-Luc's bitterness at Joseph was quickly replaced by the tremor of anxiety he felt at the idea of Minister Fouché meddling in his professional and private affairs.

"Before departing for Naples," he muttered, "I had no plan should things go wrong. Now I find a have no plan for things having gone right."

Isabella sighed. "You mustn't allow your fears to unnerve you to the point of delusion."

Perhaps she was right. Perhaps he had allowed himself to become paranoid. And yet, a part of him knew beyond any doubt that his suspicions were not merely the fanciful whims of an unsettled imagination. His ordeal in Naples had shaken and disturbed him, but it had also served to rekindle a long-dormant instinct within: sensing when danger was near—an instinct that had been honed at a steep learning curve in the days of the Revolution, when his naïve idealism had been rolled harshly back, and, in its place, a cold and clear-eyed pragmatism had crystallized.

"Jean-Luc," Isabella said, retrieving him from his ruminations, "have you heard anything I've said? What has come over you?"

He noticed the biting tone in her voice; he was too weary to allow it to affect him. "No, love. You're right." He stood up, forgetting where he intended to go, but deciding he would go all the same. "Everything will be all right."

As he turned to leave, Isabella informed him that another letter had arrived that morning, from Sophie Valiere. "I set it down on a table in the front hall."

He nodded with a smile. "I'm glad to hear it." He kissed her on the cheek, went upstairs, and fell asleep.

CHAPTER 34

Posen, Poland

November 1806

The return of their leaders and a few nights of undisturbed rest did wonders to revive the spirit of most of the troopers in the squadron. The sun returned and brought a slight rise in temperature. They passed the morning back in the city of Posen, where André would maintain a headquarters; which meant a roof over their heads, a bit of food, liquor or wine, and, above all—women. When the squadron had stabled their horses and found their billets, André assembled his leaders for a brief council of action. Moreau, Mazzarello, Captain Vitry, and a few of the other junior officers and sergeants joined them at their makeshift headquarters in an old schoolhouse.

"I will begin with an admission," André began, hoping his troopers didn't notice the return of the twitch in his cheek. "Since assuming command of this squadron, I've made my share of mistakes: I allowed us to wander into an ambush; I put my trust, however briefly, in the hands of a madman; and thus far I've failed utterly to thwart that man—who is also responsible for Major Moreau's wounds. Major Carnassier is a crooked, power-hungry hussar with designs that could affect untold numbers of people, even our families and countrymen."

After a brief silence, Captain Vitry shrugged his shoulders. "From the day we came across him, sir, we've all known Major Carnassier is a good-for-nothing shit. If you plan to go after him, I'm with you."

"Thank you," André said, turning his attention to the map spread over the table. "This is what we know: Carnassier and his squadron are after a cache of hidden riches on a scale that is hard to imagine. Friedrich Wilhelm, governor of the German state of Hesse-Cassel, has recently escaped to Denmark, but nearly the entirety of the wealth of his state has gone missing; it is believed to have been secreted away by a regent. Carnassier plans to seize it. He expects the emperor to be so grateful for its recovery that he is likely to receive a title of nobility and a marshal's baton, in addition to whatever else Napoleon grants those in his personal favor. We've all seen Carnassier's brutality, we know of his ambition; but retrieving this much wealth for the emperor would grant him the power to command armies—even nations. I will need all of your help to stop him."

Mazzarello looked around the table. "Where you lead, I'll follow, sir." A few of the other troopers murmured their agreement.

"While your confidence in my leadership is appreciated," André replied, "I am under strict orders by our regimental commander not to step foot outside the city until we have been ordered out of winter quarters. So, it will not be me who holds the key to our mission." Nodding to Moreau, André stepped slightly to the side.

Moreau stepped forward. "Right now our only connection to Carnassier is the Silesian, known simply as Conrad. He was the quiet man dressed in black and green, who traveled with Carnassier's company. As yet, none of us truly knows who he is or whom he serves. Perhaps he is his own master, but we also know he serves the enemy; according to a source known to Lieutenant-Colonel Valiere and myself, he's been known to pass with relative ease between Russian lines and our own. So, our plan is simple. *Our* agent will shadow this Conrad, and, when we've tracked him down, I will seize him. If he does not wish to come willingly, I will oblige him." Moreau waited a few moments. "We know that the Seventh Hussars are bivouacked in the vicinity of Soldau, only thirty or so miles from the town of Lobau, where the Russians have recently installed their imperial house cavalry. So, this Silesian has easy access to either camp."

"That's all fine and good," Mazzarello interjected, "but there's something you've yet to explain. The Silesian is their agent—who is ours?"

"One they will never expect," replied a woman's voice from behind the assembled soldiers. Emerging from a corner of the room partially concealed in shadows, Alicja greeted their dubious stares with a defiant smile.

"Gentlemen," André broke the silence, "the hussars know what we look like. And from my last interaction with Carnassier, they likely know we're coming. None of us know this land, its language, its people, or its culture; Alicja does. Moreover, the man Carnassier shot in Zaręba was her grandfather." Mazzarello and Vitry started in surprise.

"For the past several weeks, Alicja's presence has been an unforeseen boon; without her, Major Moreau might not be standing here right now. So, given her unique position and capabilities, should we not make use of her and put her to work against our common enemy?" After exchanging glances and a few muttered words, Mazzarello and Vitry shrugged their agreement.

"Good," said Moreau. "Now that we've agreed in principle, we will waste no time. Alicja will leave today, reaching the city of Soldau by nightfall. With any luck, some drunken trooper will direct her to Carnassier's men, and she will have sighted our quarry before they even think to be suspicious."

André nodded. "Once she has discovered the whereabouts of the Silesian, she will return to Posen. Major Moreau will then take a small party and apprehend him. Once we have him, I will personally ensure we extract everything he knows of Carnassier's plans for that treasure." André paused for a moment, allowing his words to sink in.

"And then what, sir?" Sergeant Laporte asked.

"Then, we find the horde of riches and do what is necessary to that hussar bastard."

CHAPTER 35

Paris, France
November 1806

The Friday following his encounter with Fouché found Jean-Luc arriving at the Palais du Luxembourg to a good bit of fanfare. As his carriage passed through the palace gates, he caught glimpses of a small, eager-looking crowd. His thoughts were preoccupied, however, as he indulged his last-minute doubts over the course of action he was about to take before the senate. His breast pocket held two speeches, and he had not yet decided which would be delivered.

Jean-Luc stepped out of the carriage with all the grace and grandeur befitting the elegant elites of the French Empire. Sporting the customary dark-blue coat, whose gilded collar reached up beyond his neck, a regal tricolor sash about his waist, and the ornately gilded senator's sword, he appeared before his colleagues the image of a proud statesman. His senate peers greeted him with warm handshakes, and he was ushered personally into the palais by the president of the senate, Gaspard Monge. When the glad-handing finally concluded, the senators made their way up the grand *escalier* and began filing into the chamber hall. Jean-Luc, who had become engaged in a rather deep discussion with Senator Marquis de Barthélemy concerning the virtues of the Gregorian calendar over that of the Revolutionary version, found his path blocked. Standing with two of his peers was Joseph Fouché, who wore a mask of pleasant humor. He looked almost congenial.

"Senator St Clair," the police minister said in a mild tone.

Jean-Luc bowed slightly. "Minister." He extended his arm and shook Fouché's cold hand with as much grace as he could manage. The minister's grip was gentle, yet unyielding.

"I've become accustomed to recognizing ambition, and I'll admit I admire your boldness." Fouché eyed Jean-Luc for several seconds. "Welcome home, St. Clair, though I don't suspect you will get too comfortable, given our emperor's recent entreaty." Without further explanation, Fouché offered a curt bow and passed into the hall of sessions.

When Jean-Luc entered the grand chamber, he took a moment to admire its grandeur. This was only his second time in this magnificent hall, and his gaze moved down from the domed ceiling to the seven marble statues of the great philosophers and statesmen who presided over the emperor's Conservative Senate.

President Monge mounted the dais and waited for the quiet murmur to subside. After extending the customary greetings and attending to formalities, he paused for dramatic effect. "We will commence this session with a dispatch from Napoleon I, emperor of the French." With the help of an assistant, President Monge unfurled a long parchment. In a voice that echoed across the cavernous room, he began reading: "Having made a triumphal entry into the celebrated capital of our sworn enemies, the good people of Berlin now find cause to hope for the liberation from the yoke of a nobility that has subjected them to debasement, servitude, and the pains of war. The leaders of this land, who have so pitilessly driven their people to war for their own selfish profit, will find our demands clear and unwavering. First, they are to cede all of the lands possessed between the Elbe and the Rhine, to be given to the rightful rulers of a confederation of new and peaceful German states. Second, for their crimes they are to pay an indemnity to the rightful princes of this new state, which will bring prosperity and peace to the newest allies of France…"

As sporadic applause broke out, Jean-Luc reached into his breast pocket and pulled out the speech he had resolved to give. The president concluded the proclamation and announced that Senator St. Clair was to be awarded the prestigious order of Knight of the Empire. Jean-Luc rose from his seat to rapturous applause. He walked past his colleagues and mounted the rostra beside President Monge, who placed the ceremonial medal around his neck. Jean-Luc accepted the ovation of his fellow senators with deep satisfaction, keenly aware that it came as a result of events that had nearly cost him his life. President Monge signaled for Jean-Luc to step forward and address the assembly. As he stood in front of this illustrious group of senators he glanced down at his speech, cleared his throat, and began speaking in a clear voice.

"In the years since the directory was given over to a young Corsican general, the people of France have reaped a harvest sown from the bloody fields of our Revolution. From the ashes of this great inferno arose a man of genius. Napoleon, *our* Napoleon, warrants passage to a charitable posterity not merely for his victories and capacity as a general of unrivaled talent; this man ought rightfully to be lauded for his string of accomplishments in the domain of diplomacy and civil governance. He has united a collection of warring factions into one law-abiding people, brought an end to counterfeiting and profiteering, discarded the worthless assignats and established a stable and enduring currency in their place, ratified a concordat with the Roman Church that restored religious rights, and last, but certainly not least, he has bestowed upon his people a code of law both unprecedented in scope yet true to the ideals of our Revolution. These accomplishments warrant the recognition of the senate, and the gratitude of the people."

More thunderous applause. Jean-Luc waited somewhat impatiently, lest he should lose his impetus of thought. He scanned the eyes of the approving senators, choosing not to look in the direction of Minister Fouché. At length the applause settled, and he resumed his oration.

"Truly, Napoleon Bonaparte has shown himself to be first among his peers—as consul, and now, as emperor—worthy of the laurels of Caesar Augustus. The people of France, who have endured unrivaled suffering and hardship, willfully submit themselves to this great man; submission borne of gratitude for the peace and prosperity he has delivered." The senators, swept away by these words, did not even think to clap. Jean-Luc paused for a moment, a smile on his lips. "And while we give thanks to our emperor for the many gifts bestowed upon us, we assuredly remember our history as a kingdom, wherein a timely act of clemency from a sovereign often did more to evoke the loyalty of his people than the crushing of a thousand revolts." A noticeable hush fell over the assembly; Jean-Luc allowed it to turn into a murmur before he resumed. "As such, along with the distinguished senators present in this body, Napoleon has shown that if we are to enable France to reach new heights and amass future glories, we must do this with diplomacy and reconciliation, and not violence and suppression. That is why I ask for this body to grant a pardon, with all due haste, to a list of currently held prisoners." Jean-Luc held up a parchment. "Foremost among them Monsieur Pierre-Yves Gagnon, a petty merchant from Faubourg Saint-Denis."

Those who did not recognize the name looked to their companions for explanation, and those who were acquainted with the man appeared exasperated. A senator in the front leapt to his feet and shouted, "What good will come from releasing criminals into our city? Are we not better served with these corrupt swine behind walls of stone?"

Jean-Luc smiled. "In Naples I was seized unlawfully and branded a criminal; would you be better served with me thrown behind a wall of stone?"

Many of the senators erupted into laughter; some even applauded Jean-Luc's witty rebuke.

"This nation has no place for traitors and criminals!"

Jean-Luc held open his arms. "Napoleon welcomed the return of the émigrés, once considered criminals. Do you question *his* judgment too?" Some of the senators began to whistle, shouting for the man in front to be seated and allow Senator St. Clair to finish. "If there is one indulgence the 'hero of Naples' would ask of this body, it is clemency for those who, owing to the ignorance of simple minds and even simpler motives—greed—trespassed foolishly on the leniency of our emperor. Those whom, with a stroke of a pen, might be brought back into the fold as grateful and indebted servants to our emperor. This, I believe, is the cornerstone of Napoleon's benevolence." Jean-Luc bowed slightly and made his way back to his seat. President Monge eventually managed to restore order to the hall and called for a vote on this measure.

After a few minutes of ceremonial protocol, the matter was put to a vote. To Jean-Luc's relief, and even greater surprise, his motion passed by a margin of 124-2, with twelve abstentions. Notable among those who favored the release was Minister Fouché, who had sat with his customary impassiveness throughout St. Clair's address.

The session came to a conclusion with the decision to acquiesce to Napoleon's wish for a delegation to join him in Berlin. The group of senators to make this voyage numbered near a hundred. Jean-Luc St. Clair, *L'homme de L'heur*, would be among them. The minister of police would remain in Paris.

The discharge of Monsieur Pierre-Yves Gagnon occurred that same evening. The unscrupulous merchant of Saint-Denis departed Le Temple prison into the cool autumn evening. The first face to greet him was that of Jean-Luc, who eyed the newly freed convict as he would a stray dog that had wandered into his drawing room. Gagnon, for his part, offered no friendly greeting to the man he still considered largely responsible for his imprisonment. Donning the coat that Jean-Luc had brought for him to wear until he could find more suitable attire, he ran a hand down the front to smooth out the wrinkles.

"How about you buy me a goddamn drink," Gagnon said.

A few minutes later the two men were settled in a stall at Le Prevost tavern. Monsieur Gagnon took several gulps from his second cup of wine.

"I suppose it would be a waste of my time to say you're welcome."

Gagnon licked his lips as he savored the drink. "Fuck yourself." He set the cup down and called for another.

"It's senator now, Monsieur Gagnon."

"I don't care if you're the bloody pope," Gagnon replied. "You sent me to rot in that accursed dungeon. You can go hang for all I care."

"Perhaps I deserve that; even if you were sentenced at the emperor's decree before I'd given a closing statement. At any rate, as you are currently a free man, I have something I wish to propose."

Gagnon's mouth twitched, and he blinked rapidly several times. "Propose what?"

"As I have attained the rank of senator, you can surmise that I have made certain enemies. Men whose apparatuses for spying and espionage operate on a level that I cannot match as a ceremonial public figure, let alone as a private citizen."

If Gagnon held any curiosity for this course of conversation, he did not show it. "So you've become a rich senator while I've spent the better part of a year dwelling among the rats. Forgive me if I fail to give a care for any of this tosh."

Jean-Luc bore the man's insolence patiently. After another few gulps of wine and a mouthful of bread, his patience was rewarded. "Who is this enemy that so troubles *Monsieur le Senator*?"

"Joseph Fouché," Jean-Luc answered in a hushed tone. "He has enemies among the entire Bonaparte clan; as such, Joseph Bonaparte's patronage of my own career has marked me as an enemy. I know he is watching me, and furthermore I believe he has designs for ruining me."

Gagnon dipped a chunk of bread in a small pool of wine he had spilled. "Well, monsieur, all this news has me just brimming with confidence. Why, I've leapt out of the frying pan and right into the—"

"That's enough," Jean-Luc snapped. "It wasn't I who brought charges against you; take that up with more powerful men. I *was* responsible for getting you out, and I can have you thrown back in just as easily." Gagnon grunted as Jean-Luc drew a breath to compose himself. "What's done is done. I do not wish to drag up old quarrels, and I care even less about what you think of me. But I do believe we can help each other."

Gagnon wiped his mouth with the tablecloth. "And how is that, then?"

Jean-Luc leaned forward. "This morning I sermonized to the most influential men in the empire about the virtues of clemency and mercy—it was all a load of nonsense. You are once again a free man, not due to the senate's sudden compassion, but because you have use to another, more powerful man. Given my current status, I held just enough temporary influence to get your mangy head free." Gagnon smirked. "I am being watched, and I do not doubt that the police minister has surveillance on my house, perhaps even my family."

"It's an odd thing, is it not?" Gagnon asked with a malevolent smile. "Running afoul of powerful men." He sighed wearily. "All right, *senator*, let us say I agree to help with whatever it is you're cooking up; what's in it for me to keep my head above water, as it were?"

Jean-Luc stared across the booth, weighing his next words carefully. "This is a state secret, so I trust you will not share it if you wish for me to uphold my end. In a few days I depart with the other senators for Berlin, perhaps Poland. I can offer you five hundred francs before I depart and another five hundred upon my return, if you perform the duties I ask of you." He extended a hand across the booth. "Do we have an agreement?"

Gagnon slowly licked his lips. Pulling a rough hand out from under the booth, he offered it to Jean-Luc. "Very well."

Jean-Luc arrived home late, his first thought to kiss his children goodnight. Remembering that they no longer shared his roof, he sat down in his study with a gloomy sigh. "What good is such a fine house," he asked himself, "with no children, no laughter, no warmth to make it a home?"

He directed his attention toward his work, for though it was late he was very much awake. He began reading the dispatches given to each senator from the Grand Armée in Prussia, astounded to learn of the details of Napoleon's whirlwind campaign. André Valiere was still somewhere in the field with the army. Perhaps he might have the opportunity to visit his old friend again in Berlin, if he had not been wounded or killed. His thoughts drifted from André's well-being to the man's family. He wondered how Sophie was faring alone in Normandy with an entire estate and two children to manage on her own. He suddenly recalled Isabella telling him of the letter recently arrived from Sophie, which he had forgotten to read.

He jumped up from his desk and walked across the hall, groping his way through the darkness and into the drawing room, when he bumped into something that caused a clattering sound—glass bottles. Reaching out quickly, he managed to keep them from falling, realizing they were Isabella's perfumes, gifts from Colonel Pettit. After glancing at one of the small bottles, he set it back down on the table. A strange thought occurred to him. When he reached out and touched the bottle once again, he noticed that its shape seemed unlike any of those he had seen in Isabella's boudoir. He picked it up, carrying it over to a window where the moonlight spilled in. He removed the lid and sniffed its contents; it hardly had any smell at all. He set the bottle back down and turned toward his desk but found himself paralyzed by several thoughts that seemed to hit him at once. Unable to shake the idea that was gradually forming in his mind, he looked back down at the bottles on the table before him. "Could it be?"

For several days Jean-Luc said nothing to Isabella of his discovery. On the day prior to his departure, they both passed the morning like bees, buzzing to and fro while setting their affairs in order. Isabella had anticipated that they would be attending the farewell banquet in honor of the departing senators; the pinnacle of European society would be in attendance. That afternoon, to her dismay, Jean-Luc informed her he would forego the event so he could attend Mathieu's regimental review that evening. "Darling, I cannot

miss this chance to see my son before departing for God-knows-how-long."
She bit her lip and accepted Jean-Luc's decision with a look of displeasure.

His mind still acutely affected by his time in Naples, he wanted to leave
no stone unturned in the event something should go wrong. The nagging
threat of Minister Fouché crept over him like a shadow, and he wanted to
leave his family and his home with some semblance of protection. Thus
he paid a call on his former-assistant, Maxime, who promised to check on
his daughter and son as well as ensure any letters from either of them were
sent to him with the swiftest postriders at the earliest opportunity. Though
Maxime had received a large annuity as recompense for his difficulties in
Naples, Jean-Luc offered him a generous payment for his assistance, wishing
to take no risks this time with the care of his family.

The better part of his day, however, was spent in the dwelling of Pierre-
Yves Gagnon, who had rented the top floor of a drafty garret in the Faubourg
Saint-Antoine. Jean-Luc had sent his carriage away and made his way to the
man's home on foot, careful to conceal his face as he walked quickly up the
stairs and into the merchant's sitting room. The dwelling was strewn with
wine bottles, leaflets, and half-assembled furniture, and occupied by two or
three less-than-savory-looking individuals. Jean-Luc paid no mind to the
man's lack of decorum, rushing straight into the business he'd come for. He
thrust a piece of parchment into Gagnon's hand, and from a small briefcase
he pulled out one of the vials of Isabella's perfume. He requested that the
men watching them depart. After a tense silence, Gagnon consented, shoo-
ing them from his apartment with a grunt.

"I leave for Berlin tomorrow," Jean-Luc explained once the men had
gone, "so I have no time to waste. That which I am about to show you cannot be seen by anyone, understood?" He placed the parchment on a nearby
table. Taking the perfume bottle in his hand, he removed the cap and gently
sprinkled some of the liquid onto the paper.

Gagnon yawned. "A demonstration of one of Newton's laws?"

Jean-Luc pointed a finger, and to the astonishment of his host the
parchment, which previously contained several lines of handwriting, now
began to produce another layer of text in the blank spaces between the orig-
inal lines.

"What the devil?" Gagnon exclaimed, leaning over the table.

Jean-Luc leaned back with the air of a teacher who has just gifted a
profound revelation to a stupefied student.

Gagnon squinted, turning to Jean-Luc. "Care to explain this, or should I assume it's just some manner of witchcraft?"

"Invisible ink. Used in the practice of *spy craft*. And, until now, it had been hidden from me in plain sight. More specifically, on one of my drawing room tables."

Jean-Luc, sparing the more personal details, explained that he had reason to believe that Isabella, most likely along with Colonel Pettit, was in league with Minister Fouché. To what ends, he could not say.

"If the good colonel is guilty of *liaising* with your woman..."

Jean-Luc eyed Gagnon with silent censure. "*If* it is true," he replied with a rueful frown, "then I will deal with personal matters myself. You concern yourself with what I've come here to ask of you."

"Which is?"

"First, your men apprehend this colonel and, without harm or undue violence, find out what designs he has on me and my family. Once you have confirmed the colonel's complicity, you'll have my semaphore password. You will send me the names of any other recipients of his secret correspondence. Once you've heard, inform me but do nothing; I will take the necessary actions to track down his contacts."

Gagnon nodded. "All right. Then?"

"Second, you will use this invisible ink to send me a message. Send this dictation verbatim." Jean-Luc pulled a paper out of his briefcase and set it on the table. "This has my traveling address with our cavalry escort. It will be intercepted by one of Fouché's agents in the field, and he will be put onto the wrong scent, at least for a little while." Gagnon began to read the letter out loud before Jean-Luc gently took it from his hand and placed it back on the table. "Not now. Wait until I've gone. Are we clear?"

"You can count on me, senator." Gagnon rubbed his knuckles along the seam of his coat, his face contorting in a smile that appeared somewhat less than trustworthy.

"Gagnon, I am no fool." The candor with which he spoke seemed to catch Gagnon's attention. "I am sure you've already been approached by Fouché or his people. And if I were a gambling man, I would wager that you've already taken his money. Fine. It is not my concern if you accept his bribes or guard yourself from his blackmail. He will be aware of all my movements in the east, and I do not care; in fact, all the better. I ask no personal loyalty from you; I understand a man has to tend to his survival in the way he best sees fit. However, if you wish to receive the second half of the payment I've promised you, you will assist me with what I need."

"Me, need money, senator?" Gagnon let out a hoarse laugh. "You don't see the luxurious trappings I've draped myself in?"

Jean-Luc ignored the quip. "Monsieur Gagnon, heed the words I speak. If you do anything to jeopardize the well-being or safety of my children, not even Fouché's web of spies and assassins will protect you from my vengeance. I will pursue you to the ends of the earth. Do we understand one another?"

Jean-Luc sat silently across from Isabella in the carriage as it rolled toward the École Militaire. Camille rode atop in his typical fashion; even he sensed the strained mood between them. Over the clop of the horses' hooves, Michel could be heard speaking to the young man, perhaps pointing out the collection of captured enemy banners and flags flying beneath the shimmering golden dome of Les Invalides. Jean-Luc wore a mask of normality. The feelings of guilt for leaving her again, which under normal circumstances he would have felt, were annulled by his newfound suspicions. He peered out the window, trying to savor the last Parisian sunset he would look upon for some time. The fading daylight shimmered in an orange glow. Whether it was his curiosity that got the better of him, or a desire to salvage his fraying relationship, Jean-Luc submitted to a sudden surge of reckless abandon.

"Isabella," he began, instinctively rubbing his hands together. "I am sorry that I left you alone while I was in Naples. It has been unfair of me to lay the blame for my current troubles at your feet. I owe you better, and I am sorry." He sighed, looking out the window as they approached their destination. "But to tell you plain, my greatest loyalty is to my children, whom I swore to myself I would protect above all else when my wife died. In order to do that properly, I must be truthful with you. I have heard rumors to the effect that Colonel Pettit has become improperly close with you. If these rumors are untrue, then I sincerely apologize." Isabella parted her lips in evident shock. "But I must confess," Jean-Luc continued, "last night I took a closer look at your bottles of perfume. I had a feeling that this gift was an inappropriate token of his friendship. So, I ask you directly: Is there anything you wish to tell me? Is there anything I should know about the woman who shares my bed and offers the role of stepmother to my children?"

An interminable silence followed. As if on cue, the carriage came to a halt. It sat parked in front of a large brick building with massive pillars, and the coachman opened the door. Neither of them moved. Isabella, whose face up until now had been a mask of calm, spoke, enunciating each syllable slowly, "Stepmother?"

Jean-Luc was determined to weather the verbal onslaught he knew was coming, reminding himself that in all likelihood she had been cavorting behind his back—possibly even conspiring against him.

"Well?" he asked at last. "Is there any truth to this?"

"So now you're looking through my private possessions?" Isabella scoffed loudly, her eyes narrowing in disgust. "I have given you so much; enduring that horrendous captivity with no guarantees as to my condition should the worst have happened."

Jean-Luc rubbed his eyes. "I endured the inconvenience of my captivity as well, Isabella."

"And by all accounts," Isabella replied, "you endured it with fortitude and dignity, and upon your return, you resort to baseless accusations? Well? A gift from a friend gives you cause to *pry through my belongings?*" Her eyes flashed with a vehemence to match her words, giving her an animated aspect that Jean-Luc found somehow beautiful, if not ironic. "How in God's name am I to know what is in a bottle of perfume given to me? *Cómo te atreves a acusarme de esto, pequeño cobarde?*"

"You know *nothing* of the true contents of those bottles?"

"I do not," she replied. The heat of her temper, which seconds before had coursed through her speech, was replaced by an icy chill. "I am beyond ashamed that you would think me capable of such a scheme."

Jean-Luc looked out the carriage window at the group of guests assembling at the steps of the building's façade. He was not as recognizable to the guests, who were now peering brazenly into the carriage, as he had chosen to forego his ceremonial senator's regalia for the plain dress of a civilian. He did not wish to take away any of the evening's attention from his boy. He forced a smile for the onlookers, but in his mind a struggle was being waged between what he knew and a lingering desire to believe Isabella.

"You've changed, St. Clair; sometimes I hardly think you're the man I first met. I hate to imagine what precautions you've taken against me, as you seem to imagine phantoms and enemies everywhere." She lifted her skirts and departed the carriage.

CHAPTER 36

Paris, France

November 1806

The morning of Jean-Luc's departure was spent writing a few final letters to colleagues and neighbors. When he had finished, he quietly stepped out from his house to get a little exercise before his long voyage. Turning back on to Rue de Grenelle a little while later, he was surprised to see Camille sitting on the steps in front of his door. The boy sat with his back hunched halfway down to his knees, and he rocked himself slowly back and forth. He turned his head as Jean-Luc approached, his left cheek pulling back, as though half his face were smiling.

"Hello, Camille." Jean-Luc smiled at the boy, who nodded twice in reply but did not get up. "Do you mind if I pass?"

Camille looked down the opposite end of the street. After several minutes of silence: "Letter." He looked back down between his knees.

When the boy said nothing more, Jean-Luc said, "A letter? All right. To whom?"

Camille again rocked his body back and forth before he said, "Mariette." He twitched his head to the side several times. "Letter. From. Mariette."

Jean-Luc took several steps toward the boy, who leaned nervously backwards. He held up his hands. "I will not bother you, Camille. I'm going inside the house. If you do have a letter from Mariette, I would love if you could show me. All right?"

Camille lifted his head, but his eyes remained cast down. "Mariette."

Jean-Luc, whose curiosity was turning into alarm, did not wish to frighten or unnerve the boy. He took a cautious step forward. "Very good, Camille. We all love Mariette." He took another step forward. "Now I'm going—"

"*Alone!*" The exclamation caused Jean-Luc to take a half step back. "Mariette all alone." The boy resumed his rocking.

Jean-Luc lifted his coattails and sat down on the step beside the boy. He sighed. "You've always been a good friend to Mariette," Jean-Luc said softly. "I'm sure she misses you."

With a twitch of his head, Camille reached into his coat pocket; after a few seconds of deliberation marked by several more twitches, he placed an envelope into Jean-Luc's lap and pulled his hand back slowly like one would after setting food before a wild dog.

Jean-Luc opened the paper, and a white feather fell to the ground. He picked it up, turning it in his hands for several seconds before his breath caught in his throat. After a quick glance at Camille, he gently placed the feather in a coat pocket and began reading.

> *Hello papa,*
>
> *I miss you. I will be in truble for writing this leter, but camille is kind and said he wood give it to you. i am all rihte at school, but i miss home. I wish I could com back. i am sory for what I did to make you send me away. isabela says i should try and be a better girl. she's not very nice papa. I hope i can come home and se you and mathieu soon. I love you.*
>
> *— mariette*

Jean-Luc stared down at the letter, which shook in his trembling hands. His eyes were wide, and his hair stood on end, and he did not notice when Camille stood up beside him and went inside.

✳   ✳   ✳

The first day of the journey was occupied more with the fanfare of their departure than actual traveling. Jean-Luc made the acquaintance of his new traveling assistant, Monsieur Charles Bourque, and he smiled and waved as the caravan of overladen carriages, baggage carts, and a largely ceremonial cavalry escort crept its way through the Paris streets at a snail's pace. After this long procession, the senators at last passed the Parc Monceau and departed through the Porte d'Italie, where the pace of travel picked up. Jean-Luc, periodically peeking from the carriage to admire the autumn foliage of the countryside, got to work on his correspondence. His heart ached for Mariette. He penned her a long letter expressing his love and affection, promising her he would be home as soon as possible. He sent a dispatch to Maxime, ordering him to arrange for Mariette's return from school at the earliest possible opportunity. He then penned a shorter letter to Mathieu, expressing his pride and admiration at how quickly the boy had progressed in his training. He wished him continued success in his studies and to keep a courageous heart, omitting his paternal desire for the boy to remain home and away from war for as long as possible. After this, Jean-Luc turned his attention to business. He was thankful to have received a last-minute dispatch from Monsieur de Landreville, but his enthusiasm was quickly dispelled.

> I take no delight in delivering this message, St. Clair, but to be frank I will admit that I have taken a liking to you. Your abilities as a statesman and, even worse, a lawyer, have not yet wholly taken from you your sense of faithful duty and integrity. I see it flickering brightly within your spirit. Forgive an old man for preaching, but do all that you can to keep this fire lit; for once it has gone, you will be left with nothing with which to tether yourself when the storms come. And make no mistake, sooner or later they are sure to come.

> I share with you now something my father once told me as a young man: "The devil is not so frightening because of the harm he can do to you, but because he will uncover your greatest weakness and induce you to harm yourself." Be cautious with those closest to you. It is often through them that the enemy will bring about the most severe harm.

> Travel safely and remember that a man is not truly great for the power he exercises over others, but for the suffering and

grief he eases from their lives. Where you are now going—
to the edge of the cannon's mouth—there will be suffering of
momentous proportions; perhaps it is there that you will find
the source of your greatest and most meaningful work. Vive
l'Empereur!"

—*M. de Landreville*

Jean-Luc folded the letter, oblivious as the carriage rolled along bumpy, rutted tracks. Now more than ever he regretted that his duties required him to travel so far from home.

That evening, when the group halted in the town of Coulommiers, Jean-Luc shared a brief supper with the other senators and their aides before retiring for the night, politely declining offers of liquor, cigars, and gambling.

Once alone in his room, he undressed and penned two more brief letters to his children to be sent the following morning. Once these were completed, he walked over to his personal travel trunk. Reaching around his neck, he pulled out a necklace to which was tied a small, silver key; using it, he opened the trunk and began rummaging through piles of clothes and various travel items, eventually finding what he was looking for. He uncorked the vial now in his hand and, as he had done more than once in recent days, dipped a stylus into the vial and swiped the toner across the parchment—the letter from Monsieur de Landreville. The message hidden between the lines of text revealed itself quite clearly.

Your question was justified. Your assistant is indeed on the
minister's payroll. How and where he sends his messages,
I was unable to discover. If I were to venture a guess, I
would imagine the man sends his dispatches via a gener-
al's courier or aide. If you learn which general, you might
try tracking the courier down. For the right price he may
let you intercept one of his dispatches. Two months' wages
should do.

Dieu et Le Roi

—Julien-Henri

After he had reread the letter, Jean-Luc passed several minutes thinking as he gazed into the fire. He had not been foolish enough to ignore the possibility of his assistant reporting his movements, but the confirmation did little to ease his mind. Monsieur Borque's spying might be nothing more than the relatively routine interference in the private affairs of one of Napoleon's senators. Still, he considered how he might discover which aide or courier, in an army with tens of thousands of such posts, was responsible for conveying correspondence from the army back to the minister of police. Who was the likely informant? A thought occurred to him, and he began penning a note. As he finished, he cast an instinctive look over his shoulder before dipping his quill in the second inkwell for the final touches, which would be written in invisible ink. He waited a few minutes for the ink to dry, then placed the note in an envelope addressed to Pierre-Yves Gagnon and set wax to it, stamping it with his senatorial seal.

Jean-Luc tossed a few more logs onto the hearth and stared into the flames. A cold chill blew in from the room's only window, rousing him from his thoughts. The nights were growing colder. Once the fire was burning and had brought some warmth to the room, he tossed the letter from Monsieur de Landreville into the flames. Removing his socks, he climbed under the heavy woolen blanket and settled into bed. A brief fit of coughing struck him, and when it passed, he closed his eyes. Finding sleep elusive, he passed much of the night staring up at the shadows dancing on the ceiling.

CHAPTER 37

Posen, Poland
December 1806

A t dawn on the second morning after Alicja's departure, André's regiment received an influx of replacement troopers from France. He was surprised at how young they looked. Seizing on the arrival of these new recruits as an opportunity to bolster the spirits of his half-frozen squadron, he called them to assemble in an orchard outside the city to conduct basic maneuver drills. They sat in their saddles, waiting for André to speak. Instead, he nodded to Mazzarello, who urged his horse forward.

"To those of you who have recently arrived, heed my words," Mazzarello thundered, his horse pawing the snow and snorting white billows in the frigid air. "Your former lives of comfort and ease are over. You are soldiers in the army of the French Empire, and the life of a soldier is one of suffering, privation, and hardship without end. If this is too much for you, admit it now without shame!" He rode his horse slowly before the formation, pausing to allow his words to settle in. André scanned their faces for fear or reservation and was pleased to see only defiance in their eyes. "If you stay," he continued, "you may be sure that you will face horrors worse than any nightmare. If you live to see spring—*if* you live that long—you will have earned the right to be called men. I tell you now, your first taste of battle will bring more fear than you've ever known." Mazzarello turned his horse and rode in the opposite direction. "But when you *confront* that fear and overcome it, *then* you will find that what lies behind it is the soldier you've always wished to become! We are in quarters now; have no doubt that the emperor has plans for the enemy. While we wait for action, we will prepare. Preparation! That is the key! In preparation, we distinguish ourselves from our enemies and create the conditions for victory. The soldier who masters himself in peace is the one who will master his enemy in battle. As warriors in the vanguard of the empire you exist to carry out your duties with unflinching efficiency, and any of you unable to keep pace will be hastily removed. Do you understand?"

The squadron shouted loudly, "*Vive l'Empereur!*"

"I said, do you *understand?*" the sergeant-major bellowed.

"*VIVE L'EMPEREUR!*" the squadron screamed in unison.

André nodded at the sergeant-major, satisfied at this display of spirit. "Execute the formation we discussed earlier," he said in a voice only Mazzarello could hear. "Repeat it until they can do it blindfolded. We may never need it, but someday it might save our skins."

Mazzarello saluted and called for the squadron to follow him as he cantered down a nearby hill. Kicking up thick clumps of mud and snow into the air, the squadron rode out of sight.

Turning back in the direction of the city, André noticed a rider approaching. He nudged his horse forward and trotted out to greet them.

"Lieutenant-Colonel," Moreau said, reining in his horse. "She's returned."

André opened the door to his makeshift headquarters to find Alicja standing over the map on the center table. Her face was red and windburned, but she appeared in good spirits.

"What news?" André asked, joining her at the table.

"What a pleasant greeting," she said, frowning. "It is a delight to be back with you well-mannered gentlemen. I am well after my ride, thank you." André grinned at Moreau. "*Very* well," she said, rolling her eyes. "I gained a good bit of information. I believe it is safe to declare my mission a success. I have two significant morsels of information, the first concerns that Silesian—"

"Were you able to find him?" André interjected.

"I was. Though, as I tracked him, I learned of another development that concerns every man in your squadron; indeed, the entire army."

"Where did you find him?" he asked.

"Outside of Lobau."

"Lobau?" André asked. "You followed him across enemy lines?"

"Why shouldn't I? I am a woman of this country; I go where I please."

André nodded, visibly surprised. "Yes, of course. Please continue."

"Unfortunately, I was unable to follow him into his meeting with Russian officers. The guards noticed me standing outside, one even telling me I would be allowed admittance if I were one of the officers' paramours. I thought better of being the only Polish woman in a room full of filthy Russian soldiers." She spat on the ground with contempt.

"A wise decision," Moreau said.

"I did not gain any useful information in Lobau. But as the Silesian gentleman mounted his horse to depart, something strange happened. I hailed him with a Polish greeting, and he nodded in response—but having spent weeks around both soldiers and brutes, I can tell with certainty when a man has no idea what I've said." André and Moreau looked puzzled. "You don't understand? He doesn't speak Polish."

"What does that matter?" Moreau asked.

"What does it *matter*? Well, my handsome Marcel, it means that a man referring to himself as Silesian who doesn't speak Polish is either deaf and dumb, or is not Silesian at all."

"We were already aware of that," André said, disappointment in his voice. "We still do not know whom he serves; it could be anyone."

"Colonel, if you would allow me to finish."

André held up his hands in exaggerated apology.

"I followed him to the inn where he passed the night. The next morning, in the courtyard, while hiding behind a small hedge, I was able to observe him. After looking around to make sure he was alone, he pulled out a key and unlocked a wooden box. From out of that box he pulled a bird—a pigeon. He placed a note into the small transport case secured to its leg. As he was doing this, a man came out from the stables and joined him. I did not recognize this other man, but he looked to be a civilian. At first their words were unintelligible. But then it struck me: the two spoke in a language that I did not understand, but I did recognize." André and Moreau leaned forward eagerly. "They were speaking English."

André and Moreau glanced at each other with matching looks of disbelief.

"You are *sure?*" André asked.

"They spoke several words in English, I swear of it. Then the Silesian said a word or two in Russian. It was—*Speshnyi?* Yes, that is it."

"So, this Silesian," André gave voice to his thoughts, "after meeting with Russian officers in Lobau, rides back to our lines. Before he reaches them, he stops at an inn in no-man's-land and converses with another man in English. He sends out a post-pigeon to an accomplice, perhaps his superior. He mentions—"

"*Speshnyi* is the word he used," Alicja repeated.

"Is that a city?"

"None that I've heard of," Alicja replied. "Perhaps a person? His commandant?"

Moreau shrugged his shoulders. "Whatever it is, is our plan not to catch him? I can find out when I apprehend him. It could be the name of a ship."

André looked up from the map and Alicja's eyes widened. "A ship!" she exclaimed. "What if that's it? The ship they'll use to transport the gold!"

"It very well could be," André agreed. "But as Moreau has pointed out, while we still have his location, we must act. We don't know how long he will remain in Soldau, so, major, you will leave at once." André looked down at the map once more, and Alicja loudly cleared her throat.

"Colonel Valiere, there's one thing you're forgetting to take into account."

"What is that?"

"The second development that I have not yet told you about."

André nodded. "Please continue."

"The Russians do not plan to remain in winter quarters; they are currently making preparations for an *attack.*"

"Attack?" Moreau asked incredulously. "It's the dead of winter, and they've done nothing but run from us this entire campaign."

"How did you come to learn this?" André demanded.

"In Lobau, the Russian soldiers were drunk, brawling and fornicating in alleyways. I found my way into a filthy meetinghouse where a disproportionate number seemed sober and well-dressed. Speaking a few words of Russian, I asked why they looked so gloomy. These men, perhaps officers, were wary of telling anything to a harlot. So I made my way to a table where they looked desperate for a *friend.*" André noticed Moreau fold his arms. "I asked one of these lads which house they were billeted in for the winter, telling him I'd like to come and see them. Sure enough, one of his comrades blurted out, '*Moya dorogaya*—we not leaving. Bonipart think retreat, but we have them across Vistula and back in Paris by end of winter!' He was quickly hushed by his comrades, but, colonel, I saw the cannons and the cavalry marching through the city with my own eyes."

"Did you hear anything else?" André pressed.

"Nothing. But I did see large groups of soldiers clothed for winter passing through the streets."

André took in the measure of what this woman had accomplished in a few days. "I wish I had you as a permanent member of our staff, Miss Jarzyna. You're as bold as the best of my troopers." Alicja blushed with enthusiasm. "Truly, thank you. I will inform my superiors of what you've told me, though knowing their opinion of me, it is doubtful they will heed a word of it. Major, it is time for you to depart for Soldau. If any of the Seventh Hussars gets a close look, they will surely recognize you, so I recommend waiting until nightfall before entering the city. Once you have, take pains to avoid spending undue time anywhere with large crowds: taverns, inns, or anything of that sort. The exact method for how you apprehend the man is up to you. It's just you and Sergeant Laporte, correct?"

"Yes, sir," Moreau replied.

"Very well. Good luck, and for God's sake, don't risk your life needlessly. If it proves too dangerous to get the man, then return here and we will sort it out."

"Don't fear, lieutenant-colonel," Moreau replied, slinging his musket over a shoulder. "We'll have that bastard back here before he knows what's gone wrong."

CHAPTER 38

Posen, Poland

December 1806

I t took nearly three weeks for Jean-Luc and the convoy of senators to reach the outskirts of the city where they were to conduct their first diplomatic meetings. They were weary and uncomfortable, but their fatigue seemed to dissipate as the carriages began passing ever-growing bodies of French troops marching along the road. Jean-Luc had received no response from Gagnon, but he held out hope that the man would discover Fouché's liaison in this wing of the army.

With each mile the convoy became acutely aware that they were riding into the heart of something momentous. The swelling multitude of soldiers, horses, cannons, and all manner of discarded equipment recalled to Jean-Luc's mind the approach of a great storm, like those that gusted up from the Mediterranean into the harbor of Marseille. His blood rose at the sights before him, and he noted with trepidation that a tempest was usually something one hurried away from and not toward.

André Valiere walked past the phalanx of Imperial Guards posted outside the town hall entrance—men even taller than him beneath massive bearskin caps—and up the stairs into the building, grateful to be out of the cold night air. The presence of the Imperial Guard meant that the emperor could not be far away. Once inside, a servant led him through the atrium and down a stairwell into the grand vestibule—an open gallery with a vaulted ceiling adorned with painted scenes from classical and biblical mythology. André admired the exquisite detail of the images, recognizing a few of the biblical heroes such as David, Moses, and a colossal man who appeared to be Hercules in the maze of the Minotaur. He heard footsteps entering the great hall behind him.

"For accommodations in such a place," André said, turning to greet his old comrade, "I hope they're getting their value out of you on this journey."

Jean-Luc embraced André warmly, seizing him by both shoulders. "So you've thrown yourself back into the thick of it, eh, my friend?"

"I found the peaceful farmer's life to be anything but," André said, noticing how much his friend had aged since he'd seen him last. Jean-Luc's eyes still shined with their youthful zeal, but the skin below them sagged and wrinkles extended from the corners. Specks of gray dotted his black hair. He still carried himself with his customary dignity and composure, and yet, he seemed tired, as if the years of toil and struggle had finally begun to take their toll. "And you, a senator of the empire! What have we gotten ourselves into?"

For a few peaceful moments, Lieutenant-Colonel Valiere and Senator St. Clair walked through the great hall in relaxed conversation and good humor. Jean-Luc guessed his friend had had enough troubles on the front-lines and did not mention his captivity in Naples. The conversation turned to Jean-Luc's children and his new female companion.

"Mathieu is fascinated by the army," Jean-Luc admitted with a sigh. "He's too young to be sent to the front anytime soon, thank heaven. But, as I sometimes fear for your life, my friend, I worry about him going off to war. I tremble to think of the cost in human lives this empire may exact of us. 'Only the dead have seen the end of war.'" Jean-Luc turned so André wouldn't see him wipe a tear from his eye. André rested a hand on Jean-Luc's shoulder and smiled sympathetically. "I don't want to lose my son."

For a moment André allowed his thoughts to drift to his own sons, God-willing safe and sound at home with their loving mother. Gathering himself, Jean-Luc informed André all he had heard from Sophie about Monsieur de Montfort. "A man of refined tastes and noble stock, apparently."

"Have you met this man?" André asked.

"I have not had the privilege. He wrote me a letter several weeks ago, seeking advice about a purchase on Sophie's behalf. I found it somewhat strange, but it is not my business to interfere with matters of *your* estate. I simply told him what I thought, and that was that."

André nodded. "Thank you." From time to time he would find himself worrying about his family, but he rarely dwelled on it for long. He trusted Sophie and Guy Le Bon to take care of the family and to manage the property.

"Jean-Luc, I can't express my happiness at seeing you! But I confess that the main reason I've come here tonight is to share an issue that has troubled me for some time." He looked around, ensuring that no eavesdroppers lurked. "I consider your arrival here at this exact moment a gift from providence, my friend. I would not waste your time with what I'm about to tell you if I did not believe it to be of utmost importance. A few weeks ago, my squadron fell into an ambush in the woodlands outside of Görlitz. A squadron of hussars came to our assistance. They were commanded by a major called Fabien Carnassier. Believe me when I tell you this: he is not one to be trusted. His men assaulted my executive officer, nearly killing him; but that's not the worst of it. I watched as he hanged a Polish burgher and shot the man's sister before I could intervene; the killings were completely unjustified. Afterward, he informed me that he and a small group of his comrades are aware of a great horde of riches, the entire fortune of the Hesse-Cassel estates. Apparently, it was last seen near Frankfurt, hidden somewhere out of the emperor's reach—for now."

Jean-Luc looked incredulous. "How does a major of hussars come to learn about something like this?"

"He's working with a Silesian agent who goes by the name Conrad, whom I've also met. According to Carnassier, he intercepted a dispatch from the governor to one of his wardens, a man by the name of Rothschild. Now Carnassier believes this Silesian can find the treasure and procure it for the emperor. Or Carnassier plans to lay claim to it himself; I wouldn't be surprised if that was his true purpose. And I shudder to think what a man like he would be capable of, were he to fall into possession of such resources or be rewarded by the emperor for finding such a trove. We believe the Silesian is riding ahead to Frankfurt as we speak, to secure the fortune. If something can be done to stop him, it must be done quickly."

Jean-Luc stood in silence, assessing the story in his mind.

André stared at him expectantly. "Do you doubt the truth of this?"

"Not at all," Jean-Luc replied. "My tenure in office has brought me into the orbit of certain individuals: men of high station with regular access to the emperor and other resources of their own design. One of these individuals is the minister of police, Joseph Fouché."

André drew back instinctively. There were few in France, or its army, who had not heard of the infamous minister of police. "One who lies down with dogs may get up with fleas," he muttered.

"How you aristocrats love Benjamin Franklin," Jean-Luc replied with a smile, though his eyes betrayed something closer to cunning. "Don't fear for me, my friend. I know who Fouché is and what he is capable of. The minister's network is a finely tuned instrument spanning the continent— England, as well. It is highly probable that Fouché is already aware of this major's plan and is most likely assisting in its execution."

The two men looked at each other, Jean-Luc with the air of one who has solved a riddle, André with astonishment.

Jean-Luc patted his friend on the shoulder. "I'd hoped coming to the very edge of war would give me a reprieve from politics and intrigue."

André scoffed. "The lust for power and prestige doesn't diminish as you move toward the sound of the guns. It grows stronger."

Jean-Luc nodded his agreement, thinking of his assistant and Fouché's machine of espionage. His thoughts then briefly turned to Gagnon, and he wondered if he would ever hear back from him. The semaphore lines were supposed to pass information faster than a horse; why had he not received word by now?

"André," he said, "I know you. Ever the gallant knight, you are thinking of a way to bring justice to this man responsible for the murder you witnessed."

André shook his head. "It is the deaths that I know will come were Carnassier to ever wield the power of a marshal of France."

Jean-Luc thought for a moment. "There may be a way to track down Carnassier and his men, even if they are hundreds of miles from here. There isn't a man in the empire who can stay hidden from Fouché's eyes indefinitely, much less a squadron of light horsemen; but it may still be possible to track Carnassier as he rides—"

"You think *Fouché* would help us?" André asked.

Jean-Luc smirked. "Not him; he gives with one hand and takes with several others. But someone within his network might have the necessary information. Is there anything else you can tell me of this plot?"

"Apparently the hussar colonel has been given a *special mandate* that shields him from prying eyes, inside the army and out. But my superior, shrewd colonel that he is, told me that Carnassier was last seen in Soldau. I have someone hunting for this Silesian as we speak; if we're able to find him, you'll be the first to hear of it. But if he has already left for Frankfurt, the distance is too vast. How would we ever coordinate a plan to intercept him?"

"I am a senator, André," Jean-Luc replied, his face once again assuming a cunning grin. "When I must pass crucial information quickly, or have it passed to me, there are ways of doing so."

André looked at him with a bewildered expression.

"It is getting late," Jean-Luc said, putting away his pocket watch. "I am sorry, but I am now late for a meeting. Allow me to make some inquiries. Perhaps I can find something that might help you. I'll send for you as soon as I am able."

Monsieur le Senator,

I write to you with warmest regards, from myself, as well as a gallant young colonel of the guard, Francois Pettit. Unfortunately for the colonel, a few days past he happened to have a run-in with a group of ruffians when he wandered onto the wrong street in the Saint-Antoine quarter. After he was smacked around a bit and relieved of the notes in his pockets, he became amenable to a little chat.

With a bit of gentle prompting, he revealed to his new friends that he was in fact on the payroll of Minister of Police Fouché and that Madame Isabella Maduro had been keeping the minister abreast of Senator St. Clair's movements and business investments, via Colonel Pettit.

Next, we moved on to the subject of Senator St. Clair's traveling assistant, Monsieur Charles Bourque. The rascal sends daily dispatches back to Paris; he also receives and forwards notes from the police minister to several of his chief field agents, all field-grade officers: Major Georges Bounaix, Lieutenant-Colonel Jean-Pierre Devaux, and Major Fabien Carnassier, all of whom are currently with the emperor's armies in the Prussian theater. My new friend Colonel Pettit tells me that if you were to intercept a letter from one of these men bearing both the Imperial bee and the official seal of the police minister, you will have found the dispatches in question.

The semaphore messages sent personally from the minister, which are rarely used due to the network's heavy traffic of army communications, always begin with the words N-I-E-V-R-E; the good colonel did not know the meaning of this word.

My apologies for the following disclosure, but the good colonel did confess to his "improper familiarity" with Madame Maduro—but I won't interject myself into that business of a personal nature any further.

Vive l'Empereur.

Monsieur G

CHAPTER 39

Posen, Poland

December 1806

The evening following his rendezvous with Jean-Luc, André presented himself at Colonel Menard's headquarters to report on Alicja Jarzyna's reconnaissance. The colonel had been away from the city, forcing André to wait an entire day to inform anyone of the possible enemy mobilization. He considered bypassing his direct chain of command to report the intelligence, but, given the unorthodox means by which they had acquired it and his current standing with his superior, he deemed it wiser to wait.

André saluted the sentries posted outside and ascended the steps, walking into a warm, well-lit, and impressively decorated Prussian mansion. Turning his eyes upward, he marveled at the chandelier above, finished in silver and gold with ornately sewn linen shades. Walking through the foyer and into one of the sitting rooms, he found himself surrounded by neatly dressed officers in finely embroidered blue, green, and red coats. They sipped champagne and red wine while they dined on sausages, *Vorschmack*, and a Tilsit cheese spread. Slightly fewer in number than the French officers were the ladies from nearby towns, eager to welcome the emperor's famed marshals and generals, perhaps hoping to catch a glimpse of the great man himself. Wearing high-waist, short-sleeved dresses of blue and white muslin and adorned in glistening jewels and pearls, the women seemed to relish the opportunity to display their knowledge of French language and culture.

André groaned quietly. No stranger to this world, he nevertheless found the contrast between a filthy, stinking army camp and the sights and sounds of a society fête somewhat jarring, and he preferred not to grow too comfortable while the campaign was ongoing. Scanning the room for his superior, he recognized Brigadier General Pierre Margaron, the man who gave Colonel Menard his orders, standing off to the side with some of the other officers. André doubted that the good colonel would appreciate a subordinate bypassing him in favor of speaking directly to a general, so he continued to look around the room. Strolling casually and nodding to several rather lovely ladies, André saw no sign of Menard.

Just as he was turning to depart, a voice called out his name, "Lieutenant-Colonel Valiere, I thought that was you."

André turned and saw General Margaron. He stood with an upright posture flanked by his entourage, his dark blue coat embroidered with gold trimming and epaulettes marked with two silver stars. His slightly receding hairline revealed a large forehead and a crop of wavy hair; his polite features were hardened by war. André walked across the room and presented himself. "Good evening, general," he said, with a reverential nod.

"It is. Quite a lavish party. I hope you're relishing the refreshments," he said stiffly. "Now then, where is Colonel Menard? I have a task for that rascal, and I'm afraid he's hiding after losing all his money at cards again."

André almost laughed aloud. "To be frank, general, I'm looking for him as well."

"I suppose we'll just have to wait until—"

"General!" A voice piped from across the room. André turned to see Colonel Menard striding confidently through the assembled guests.

"My apologies for the tardiness, general. I was trying to ensure our kitchen did not burn down. Allow me to compliment you and your men on your panache—you look suited to rival the best dressed of Parisian society. Valiere, is that you? I wasn't expecting you this evening."

"Colonel," André replied, thinking *sycophantic fool* a more appropriate designation, "I do not wish to disturb you, but I've come upon a bit of intelligence I believe you might need to hear."

"I'm sure it is of the utmost importance," Colonel Menard answered, trying to hide his agitation. "But, since we are in the presence of General Margaron, I believe we ought to show propriety and attend to our guests before we address operational duties. I'm sure it can wait an hour or two."

"No, that won't do," Margaron cut in. "If the matter is important enough to bring you here it must be significant. Speak, Valiere."

"Sir, I have cause to believe that the enemy is currently in preparation for a surprise attack toward our present position, from the city of Lobau."

The officers surrounding the general stood expressionless for a moment before utter disbelief showed on their faces. Colonel Menard, with a look of mortification, motioned to the general, "Sir, if you'll excuse Monsieur Valiere, I don't think—"

The general held up a hand for silence. "How did you come by this information?"

André hesitated, shifting his weight uneasily. "Sir, a Polish civilian who traveled across enemy lines informed me. This individual saw the buildup with their own eyes."

The general furrowed his brow, seeming to weigh the possibility. "This has not been corroborated by any of our scouts or reconnaissance. Who is this Polish civilian, and what cause do you have to trust him?"

André had been hoping to avoid this line of questioning. "Sir, this person has traveled alongside my squadron for several weeks now; their knowledge of the countryside and local customs has been invaluable."

The general raised an eyebrow. "Valiere, I will not approach Marshal Bernadotte with intelligence brought to me by an anonymous Polish civilian without sufficient evidence. So, I ask again: who is this person?"

"Her name is Alicja Jarzyna, she comes from the village of Zaręba in Silesia—"

"Colonel, that is enough." General Margaron lifted a hand in the air, cutting him off. "In truth, I admire your coming here and risking your reputation to convey information you believe will affect our operations. But Poles are notorious for their ability to be brought to agitation when it concerns the Russians."

André bowed his head. "Understood, sir."

"Continue to carry out your duties faithfully and efficiently, and trust that the emperor will not allow disaster to befall this army."

"Yes, sir," André said. Bowing his head formally, he took his leave. The guests in the room trained their eyes on him, yet he felt a strange sense of relief. He had done his duty, reporting to his regimental commander and to the brigadier general. What happened next would be out of his hands.

As he crossed the drawing room, he noticed a peasant standing at the front door; he wore a long, brown fur coat and a large fur cap. The figure looked utterly out of place in such a genteel gathering.

"Colonel, it's me," the man said. He held his arms out in a quasi-triumphal display of his clothing. André jerked his head back in surprise. "Sergeant Laporte? What are you doing here?"

Remembering from where the trooper had just arrived, André looked back instinctively to Margaron and Menard, who both stared at him inquisitively. He offered a deferential smile and bowed, seizing Laporte by the shoulder and ushering him out of the room and into the cold night air.

"Apologies for disturbing you with the big-wigs sir, but Major Moreau insisted I come straight to find—"

"Yes, yes, it's all right, Laporte. Your timing could not have been better; I was just leaving." Sizing up his traditional Polish winter garb, he motioned for Laporte to follow him. "I suppose you will explain your clothing at some point."

"Sir, Major Moreau thought it best to hunt our quarry without giving ourselves away. And, sir, it worked out quite well. The man is bound and waiting in your headquarters."

André smiled and clasped the man on the shoulder. "No more time to waste, let's go find out who this devil is."

The Silesian André had seen in Czocha Castle two months prior wore the same black uniform with green piping and stripes on the pants, but his outward appearance could hardly have looked more different. His reddish-brown hair was tied back in a ponytail, but it appeared unwashed and disheveled. Stubble colored his neck and chin, and his expression appeared gaunt and exhausted.

"Stand up!" Mazzarello barked, prompting the man with a grip to his collar. The Silesian complied, rising to his feet with an erect posture and an air of self-assurance. He met André's scrutinizing gaze with a look of calm politeness, as if he were a guest in the house of an unfamiliar but friendly host.

André approached his prisoner. "You were introduced to me under the name of Conrad; that was just one of several falsehoods spoken by the Major

Carnassier. So, I ask you plainly, what is your name?" The man remained silent. "You don't speak French?"

"A little French." His accent was curious.

André looked at his two comrades, then back to the Silesian. "I've been informed that English is your native tongue; at least you are conversant in it. Is this true?"

He met André's question with a look of bemused curiosity.

André turned to his two subordinates, "I don't suppose either of you speaks English."

Moreau shook his head, but Mazzarello nodded. "My father served on a merchant ship out of Ajaccio; he had dealings with the English merchants. I learned a little bit."

"Very well, do your best to translate." André motioned for the Silesian to sit down, pulling up a chair and taking a seat beside him. He spoke in a slow but firm voice, pausing to let his Sergeant-major translate. "With a word, I could send you to my commanding officer. After a nominal court-martial, you'd be found guilty as a spy and then taken on a quick ride to the scaffold. Spies are not granted death by firing squad. I need not remind you of the instrument my countrymen utilize for execution."

For several seconds the man betrayed no understanding, until, with a slight jerk of his chin, he leaned forward. "La guillotine."

André folded his hands together and placed them on the table. "I admit freely to you that I've seen that blade do its ghastly work, and I do not wish to be responsible for any more of it. So, I offer you this chance once, and only once. If you cooperate with me and tell me what I wish to know, then there is a chance that when our business is concluded, you may be granted safe passage across our lines and returned to your countrymen unharmed."

Mazzarello's translation was followed by another silence that hung thick in the air. Following a quick barrage of follow-up questions, the prisoner finally spoke. Mazzarello turned to André. "Sir, he tells me that he has no objection to cooperating with you, he simply wishes to know what it is you want from him."

Without taking his eyes off the prisoner, André spoke, "Tell him I plan to thwart the designs he has concocted with Major Carnassier for retrieving the hidden fortune that we both know to be their objective."

At the mention of Carnassier the seated man interjected. "Sir," Mazzarello translated, "he says he is not in league with that hussar butcher."

André examined the prisoner for any sign of trickery or deceit. "Ask him what he knows about the fortune; we heard last that it was en route to Hamburg," he lied.

The sergeant-major translated André's request. "Sir, he says you are mistaken. He claims the treasure is currently en route to Danzig, hidden in a train of civilian wagons."

André nodded. "The emperor expects Danzig to fall to Marshal Lefebvre any day now. What will they do if the city falls into our hands?"

"He says that if the city fell, he was to use his status as a French agent to ensure its safe passage to another secure site in allied hands, from which it can be smuggled across French lines, with his help."

"You are no French agent," Moreau interjected. "You're a devious spy who ferrets his way across enemy lines to do our enemy's bidding. Why shouldn't we kill you and go seek the treasure ourselves?"

After a lengthy translation that taxed André and Moreau's patience, the sergeant-major answered, "He says by the laws of war we *are* within our rights to hang him as a spy. But he proposes an alternative."

"Of course he does," Moreau cut in.

"He claims that he knows where the wagon train carrying the riches is to be taken and the proper words to gain access to it. He also claims that Major Carnassier departed yesterday morning to intercept the convoy and that if we wish to stop him then we would best move quickly, for it is only several days' ride from here to there, and we don't know when the enemy will begin their offensive."

"Please tell the gentleman," André answered, "that we have no need for the counsel of a captured foreign spy and that he may keep any advice to himself while we discuss his fate."

At this last exchange the seated man nodded deferentially, a slight grin on his face. André deliberated with Moreau, inquiring as to whether anything was seen or heard of Carnassier while they were acquiring their prisoner. Moreau said they had not seen him.

André turned to his captive. "You say Carnassier has left. Tell me where he departed from and where exactly he intends to arrive, and we may not send you to the guillotine just yet."

"He says that he departed with a small escort of hussars from Soldau yesterday morning. The ride from here to Soldau is perhaps a day; if we left now, we'd already be two days behind him. Though he says we have one advantage."

"And what would that be?" André asked.

"He doesn't know we're coming for him."

André narrowed his eyes at the man seated before him. "Tell me, why should I trust the word of a man who practices so duplicitous a trade? You certainly do not lack methods to mislead; how do we know you're not sending us out to the hunt with the wrong scent in our nostrils?"

The prisoner waited for the translation, considering the question with a sigh. "We are men of action," he began, pausing for Mazzarello's translation, "duty-bound through oaths of loyalty and fortified by sentiment to serve our respective nations and sovereigns. The man who you pursue is not a man of honor. He is a plunderer without regard for the laws of war, or plain Christian morality. His swift recourse to violence and consequent lack of remorse are only surpassed by his insatiable appetite for riches. Men such as this have not been chastised or reduced under Emperor Bonaparte; to the contrary, they have flourished, and their appetites have grown larger. In thwarting the plans of such a man, I am not merely serving my sovereign, but doing a service to the entire continent."

André showed no sign of agreement or disagreement, but leaned back in his seat, staring at the ceiling for several moments.

"There once was a farmer," he said, "who lived on the outer edge of one of the seven hills of ancient Rome. One morning as the man plowed his fields, he came upon something solid buried deep in the ground. After some digging, he discovered a large wooden chest. Inside, he found a great cache of silver and gold coins. As a good citizen should, he sent a note to Caesar for guidance, and some days later he received a written reply, two words: 'Use it.' The man hadn't the slightest idea what to do with such wealth, so he wrote to Caesar telling him as much. Caesar wrote back, this time with three words: 'Then abuse it.'"

The foreigner sat silently for a moment, taking in the story. At last he replied through translation, "Tell me, colonel, should you ever happen upon such a horde of wealth, would you refuse it?"

André considered the idea, his mind's eye flashing with thoughts of a grand new home in Normandy, lands and titles restored rightfully to his lineage, and the safety and comfort of his family never again in question. Then he recalled the dream he'd had: Carnassier riding through Paris, triumphant.

Would he desire the same treatment? Did he covet the same adoration? At length he said, "It is better for the gold to perish for Aristippus than Aristippus should perish for the gold."

André looked his prisoner in the eye. "Should Fabien Carnassier acquire this treasure, with or without the emperor's blessing, he could not be trusted to do anything but abuse it."

The prisoner cleared his throat. "Such riches would no doubt bring their advantages, but my thoughts are more taken with another consideration. Have you not heard of his *great plan?*"

André and his men looked at their prisoner with blank expressions.

"The man is capable of murder now," he continued. "I shudder to think what cruelty he would visit on his Polish subjects. After all, that is his final aim. Using his marshal's baton and the dukedom which he will petition the emperor for, Major Carnassier plans to 'rule in the east;' molding these Poles in the image of Revolutionary France, civilizing a barbarous people for the propagation of an ordered, prosperous, and peaceful continent—no doubt with the blessing of powerful men back in France, whom I will not name, though one might guess which intriguers in the Tuileries Palace are aware of such a plot. We all know what it would look like should a man like Carnassier ever rule over the Poles, a race he sees as lesser than his own. All that is to say, I believe the man must be stopped."

For a moment the room fell silent, each man lost in his own thoughts. "I agree with your conclusion," Mazzarello eventually said. "We have to stop the bastard."

"Of that we seem to be in agreement," the prisoner answered. "But that doesn't change the fact that this very mission has been, if not conceived, at least consented to by your emperor. If you thwart the hussar, and by extension other, more powerful men, does that not conflict with your duty as soldiers? What of the glory of your empire?"

"Damn the empire," Moreau said eagerly. "A trunk of gold would be safe enough with me."

"Well, you have his answer," André said, laughing.

"And mine too," Mazzarello muttered with a wide grin.

A moment later André turned to the prisoner, his expression serious again. "It is time for you to tell us who you are."

The man looked around the room at each of his captors, and for the first time since being captured he wore a look of unmistakable pride, even defiance. To their astonishment he spoke the following words in near-perfect French, "My name is William Hackett, and I serve his royal majesty, King George III."

✳   ✳   ✳

"I've come into the news we've been hoping for, my friend."

André had been summoned to the town hall by Jean-Luc, who wasted no time explaining the contents of Gagnon's letter, which had arrived the day prior as he was packing for his return to Paris. "That's not all. I found my curiosity far from sated, not least because this chain of intrigue was passing through my assistant."

"Did you find anything else?"

Jean-Luc replied in a hushed voice, "You told me that you'd been unable to learn anything of Carnassier's movements, due to his special mandate. Well, this morning, while attending our closing meeting, the contents of this dispatch still churning in my mind, I came across a cavalryman—Lieutenant-Colonel Jean-Pierre Devaux. He is rumored to be supplying a powerful intelligence agent with information from the front. I have reason to believe it is Joseph Fouché. It's not anything hostile to his master, Napoleon, mind you; rather the man has several mistresses when he is on campaign, and—"

"You learned of all of this this morning?"

"Mademoiselle Jarzyna informed me. In fact, she has a rather charming way about her when she wishes."

"*Alicja* is—"

"Calm yourself, André, she isn't the general's lover. She's only allowed him to believe that she is amenable to the idea. Anyhow, in order for the general's indiscretions to stay hidden, from time to time he feeds this 'powerful intelligence agent' back in Paris. I was able to gain an audience with Devaux this morning, as I've said, and I told him of a friend's abundance of gratitude to one Fabien Carnassier, a hussar major, for rescuing his squadron outside Görlitz. Hoping that through their mutual *friend* the colonel had heard of Carnassier, I asked him offhand if the major was in the city so that my friend could buy the major a drink in appreciation." Jean-Luc paused and nodded politely as a group of officials strolled past. "The general informed me that the Seventh Hussars were last seen driving hard toward

Płońsk with Marshal Soult. André, if the fortune the major seeks is moving, and you and your men are marched east to face the inevitable Russian onslaught, you may be heading in the wrong direction."

André let out a dejected sigh, craning his neck and looking up at the ornate ceiling above. "I don't see any way of stopping him even if we were to find him."

"Do you recall what I said last time we spoke?" Jean-Luc asked. "Regarding the minister of police?"

André shrugged slightly. "That he is something of a weasel and a villain?"

"That is certainly true." Jean-Luc grinned. "But a fool he is not. There isn't a word of gossip or intrigue spoken on the continent that Fouché is not capable of learning. Rumor says even King George's cooks are on his payroll. How do you think he relays so much information in a timely manner?"

He took a step closer, placing an envelope in André's hand. Its wax seal bore the Imperial crest. "It's my personal watchword for use of the semaphore lines," he whispered. "They carry a message in less than half the time it would take a galloping postrider. If you find yourself in need of communicating across any distance, use it."

André stared down at the envelope in disbelief.

"Don't look so surprised. I trust you more than any other man alive. Use it well. I am on my way back to Paris; if I find any information on Carnassier's whereabouts, I will send word immediately."

André took Jean-Luc's hand in his._ "Thank you, my friend. Farewell. For now."

"Do your duty, colonel." Jean-Luc smiled warmly. "We shall speak soon."

CHAPTER 40

Posen, Poland
December 1806

The afternoon following the discovery of the Silesian's true identity, André's squadron was ordered out of winter quarters, effective immediately. Soldiers across the city scrounged whatever winter-weather clothing they could lay hands on and began assembling in the streets and around the squares. The fate of André's prisoner had been decided: Monsieur William Hackett would travel with the squadron, under close observation, as a local attaché. Another attaché was Mademoiselle Jarzyna. To avoid trouble with Colonel Menard, André could not allow her to travel with the squadron itself; however, after all she had risked in service to him and his men, she would be permitted to travel with the baggage trains in the rear.

As André looked over a map, planning their route, Hackett informed him that should they find the semaphore telegraph unavailable to them, he had other means of dispatching intelligence.

"That is well, Monsieur Hackett," André said, looking up from the map. "I'd rather find a use for you than send you to the scaffold."

André reported to Menard's headquarters for his orders, leaving Mazzarello and a handful of troopers to watch Hackett and pack up the squadron's kit while the rest groomed and saddled the horses. The colonel, sick with fever, reported that an unexpected concentration of enemy troops had been seen marching south of Lobau.

"*Unexpected* indeed," André said under his breath.

"The Russians have brushed aside Marshal Ney's corps at Liebstadt," the colonel uttered into a cloth held up to his mouth, "and they are now marching south, thinking they might as well brush *us* aside. Well, we will thwart these plans, and in so doing prove our worth as cavalrymen to Marshal Bernadotte and, by extension, the emperor. Do not stray more than a couple miles from your adjacent squadrons and see to it that you report all vital reconnaissance to me as promptly as you can. Dismissed."

Later, André joined Moreau on the steps of their headquarters building to observe the troopers as they prepared to depart. Sensing in the man's silence an unspoken agitation, André asked if there was something he wished to say.

Moreau spoke in a quiet voice. "Sir, I request the permission to conduct the Englishman to Danzig and to intercept Carnassier before he reaches the gold."

"No," André replied flatly. "You will not go."

Gripping his riding gloves tightly, Moreau spoke with restrained vehemence. "Sir, I know in the past I should have set aside my own petty grievances and vendettas and considered the men under my command." His intensity of feeling threatened to get the better of him. Looking away from André, he continued, "I would have thought, colonel, that my loyalty to you and this squadron has been appropriately demonstrated by now. I do not wish to be consigned to the rearguard in the hour of decision."

"Major," André sighed, "it is not that you have lost my trust. I would not relegate my best soldier to insignificance over an excess of bravery, foolish though it might be. And I would not describe any of the grievances of your past as petty; I saw the Revolution and what it turned men into. I don't envy the part you were obliged to play." André looked at the men as they mounted their horses. "You're a born soldier, Marcel, and though I may not like to admit it, better than I. The troopers of this squadron would follow you anywhere. That is why it is time for you to lead them."

"Sir?"

"Carnassier is a dangerous man. I cannot expect a subordinate to be responsible for thwarting another squadron commander, one who carries a mandate from the emperor, no less. I must do it. And you must lead these men while I'm away."

With a stunned look Moreau replied, "You do me honor, sir."

"Nothing that you have not earned yourself, Marcel. But there is something else," André said, lowering his voice. "For some time I've pondered the meaning of the Szeptucha's final words in the cave, something about deference and demand. But something I had almost forgotten struck me last night as I lay awake."

Moreau's expression turned solemn, almost melancholy. "The first stranger to whom you speak beyond this cave—will bring an answer to the question that has tormented you."

"And will not cease to until your decision is made." André nodded. "Good memory. At the time you were a half-delirious invalid."

"Was it not a troop of cavalry, sir? Poles, if I'm not mistaken."

"Yes. Their commander mentioned something about Wawel, which caught my attention, but then I remembered what he said after. 'In Poland, sometimes the Wawel brings tidings that even greatest general cannot hear. When in need, sometimes we must follow our own commands'...or something to that effect." André shook his head with a grin. "I'm not sure if it would pass as sound reasoning with our brigade commander, but we are in need, and I do believe thwarting Carnassier to be a service to the greater good."

Moreau spat onto the snowy cobblestones. "Colonel Menard's a fucking idiot, sir."

"I will not argue the point," André laughed. "When we reach the city of Saalfeld, I will ride for Danzig with our double-turned agent. I don't delight in the idea of putting my life in the hands of an Englishman, nor in departing the squadron again, but *when in need we are following our own commands.*" Horsemen from other cavalry units rode past. "You still haven't told me one thing, major. William Hackett?" André said. "How in the world did you come to apprehend the man?"

The regimental bugle sounded, and the troopers of the Seventeenth Dragoons assembled on the road leading out of the city. André motioned for his squadron's standard-bearer to take his position alongside him.

Moreau put on his helmet and tightened the chinstrap. "We stalked the streets of Soldau and found him departing a coffeehouse, sir. Laporte speaks German, so I sent him to ask the bastard if he knew the way to Czocha Castle. While the bugger was speaking, I crept from behind and dealt him a blow to the head with my pistol. We bound his hands, tied the rope to my saddle, and rode our way back here."

"Well done, major," André replied with a grin. "That man may prove useful in the coming days. Let's go!"

André's dragoons rode north, keeping several miles ahead of the main body of Marshal Bernadotte's infantry corps. To the relief of the squadron, the snowfall had abated, though the wind still gusted with an icy bite. The roads were clear enough, but with temperatures so low the puddles of mud had frozen into hard, rutted tracks that resulted in an ever-growing pile of disabled carts and carriages languishing on either side of the road as the infantry marched past. André's squadron skirted the impediments with little difficulty; nevertheless, their presence drew curious and fearful looks from the local inhabitants, who knew what the presence of so many soldiers meant.

By the third day of their march, food was running low, and it would not be long before desperate soldiers began breaking into farmhouses and granaries in search of something to eat.

On the fourth day, André woke in the predawn darkness, before the gray sheen of daylight emerged over the horizon. The leafless birch branches swayed gently in the morning breeze, as life stirred in the sleeping bivouac. As he saddled his horse and ate a meager breakfast, a brilliant sunrise crept over the rolling hills, bringing more light than had been seen in days, perhaps weeks. Much of the snow had melted, and André detected the unseasonal yet strangely pleasant odor of mud and grass that seemed to reinvigorate his spirit. The peaceful solitude of morning allowed him to focus his thoughts on the task before him, bringing a renewed sense of purpose.

Once the mists had cleared, the squadron was saddled and ready to march. Several of the horses whinnied and pawed the ground nervously. Mazzarello and Laporte rode on either flank of the formation, examining the men's kits and speaking encouraging words. Rumors began to spread that one of the outlying patrols had been ambushed by Cossack horsemen, who slaughtered them to a man before disappearing into the forest.

An hour or so into their morning march, Moreau rode up alongside André. "The men are ready, sir. We await your orders."

André's face was stern as he eyed his executive officer. "It's your time to lead these men, Marcel. There isn't an officer in this army that I would rather have taking them forward."

He then rode over beside Mazzarello, speaking in a hushed voice. He briefed him on where he was going, how long he expected to take, and what to do if he should not return. The Corsican looked stupefied. "Are you *sure* about that, sir?"

"We've executed these drills countless times, Paolo. Just do as I say, and all will be well."

André turned his horse so that he faced his squadron. He nodded at Mazzarello, who let out a loud whistle. Five dragoons, his best riders, rode out and presented themselves. "You men follow me." He turned and led them toward the trees on the opposite side of the open ground where a narrow path disappeared among the large pine trees. The five riders followed his lead, their horses' hooves churning up dirt and snow as they crossed the field.

Inside the forest, they rode at a slow pace in a single file with André at the front. An eerie silence hung over the trees, broken only by the occasional calls of crows perched overhead. The troopers had brought loaded muskets and ammunition, but their kit bags had been left behind to avoid equipment rattling or reflecting the sun. André expected to be found, but on his terms. They rode for perhaps a quarter of an hour before coming upon a small brook, from which the horses drank greedily. Casting a glance in either direction, André motioned for them to cross over and continue moving. The forest thinned out on the far side of the brook, and André noticed a clearing ahead. Several seconds later one of the dragoons stood abruptly in his stirrups. "Lieutenant-Colonel, look!"

André turned in his saddle, scanning the terrain. Beyond the trees he saw an open field that rolled gently up into a small hillock. Then he saw them. Three men mounted on white horses: Cossacks. They were clad in dark fur coats and wore large hats, each man carrying a formidably long lance. Their spearheads glistened in the sun. Taking a deep breath, André climbed down from his horse, motioning for his men to do the same. Once dismounted, André tugged the reins, urging his horse forward. His dragoons exchanged nervous glances and then followed him out of the forest into the open ground.

As the melting snow squished under their boots, André fought the urge to look directly at the enemy before them. His heart beat faster, and he felt a twitch on his left cheek. He looked back at his troopers to make sure they remained steady. "You're been grumbling for weeks about seeing no action, Baudin. Are you not happy that you're finally in sight of the enemy?"

"To be frank, sir," replied the young soldier pulling up the rear, "those buggers on the hill have me fairly fucked."

André smiled. "Just follow my lead. It won't be long before they—" *Crack!*

A shot rang out, echoing across the open ground. André held his hand up, at last allowing himself to look at their waiting enemy. He had known what to expect. Nevertheless, his hair stuck on end. At least fifty Cossacks emerged on the hillock from the low-ground behind, their fur coats, hats, and long spears giving them the look of some ancient barbarian tribe. And there were, no doubt, untold more waiting behind those visible on the hill.

"Mount and follow me!" André cried out, leaping into the saddle. He turned his horse with a violent jerk and galloped toward the woods. *Crack!* More shots followed, this time so close he heard the hiss of the bullets.

André and his men crashed through the brook and into the trees behind, not daring to look back until they had put some ground between themselves and their pursuers. Once they'd reached the path taken earlier, they would be in less danger of envelopment. André had heard of the riding prowess of the Steppe Cossacks, widely recognized to be the best light cavalry in the world. "If I had Cossacks in my army," Napoleon had once claimed, "I would go through all the world with them." Rumors abounded of Cossacks firing from under their horse's belly or snatching up a coin from the ground at full gallop. André did not wish to test these abilities for himself.

Looking behind, he saw several riders galloping through the woods, alarmingly close. When he glanced to his right, his blood ran cold. He had imagined the forest on either side of the path too thick for horsemen to traverse in number, but on either side, he now saw shapes moving through the trees like phantoms—too fast to be seen as anything beyond a blur. They were almost level with André and his men. A few agonizing minutes later, André caught a glimpse up ahead of the field where his squadron was waiting. He urged his horse on faster. His five troopers, all ahead of him, now drove their steeds at a breakneck pace. Once they had all reached the open ground, André spotted his squadron. To his immense relief, he saw that they had assembled in the intended formation.

Eight long years had passed since André had marched through the sands of Egypt. His mind would often drift back to his time in Alexandria or the hospitals and streets of Cairo, but the sight that had left the most indelible impression on his memory was the magnificent and unrivaled pyramids of Giza, under the shadow of which the French Republican Army had fought a bloody battle. At the time, André couldn't have known it would go down in history, growing to almost mythic proportions in the years since. In the hour of combat, his thoughts were only of survival as the seemingly never-ending tide of Mameluke horsemen hurled themselves into the killing zone with reckless bravery. The French muskets had shot them down like turkeys and still they charged, shouting angrily in shrill voices for the French to leave the protection of the formation that shielded them from the relentless wave of charging warriors. The square.

The carnage a tightly packed and well-disciplined square of infantrymen could inflict on a vastly superior number of cavalry was a lesson André would never forget. A square offered a four-sided wall of men and bayonets to any charging mass of horsemen, nearly impenetrable if the soldiers held their nerve. In Egypt, the French had formed squares in vast numbers; today André's squadron formed two small hedgehogs, each square with slightly more than a hundred dragoons, their horses protected inside either square.

André was relieved to see that the two squares were placed diagonally apart from each other, minimizing the risk of friendly crossfire. But his thoughts were soon interrupted by musket fire from his right. At least two dozen Cossacks had emerged from the woods and now had an open view of the field. They were raking André and his riders with fire as they hurried to the safety of the squares. When he had ridden to within a hundred paces of the nearest square, André noticed one of his troopers fall to one side of the saddle, then slide off his horse. Swerving at the last second, André managed to avoid crushing the man. As he quickly dismounted, he heard the rumble of hooves to his rear: more enemy were pouring into the field. He swore, stooping low as he ran toward his fallen dragoon. The sound of musket balls hissing past his ears and smacking the snow beside him was a mere distraction now, as he felt his instincts guiding his frantic movements.

A boy was lying facedown in the snow. André gripped him by his coat and in one motion heaved him onto his own horse, but before he had managed to get himself onto the saddle, his horse bolted. Nearly falling off, André grabbed the pommel and clung for dear life. With his other arm he managed to grab the reins, twisting violently in an attempt to steer the terrified animal back toward the squares. Eventually the horse allowed itself to be guided in the right direction; all the while the Cossacks rode forward. They were so close now André could hear them shouting. Turning back, André saw a mustached man galloping perhaps forty feet behind him. In his right hand he held a long lance with its murderously sharp point leveled at André, slowly gaining on the double-burdened horse. The man bellowed a deep battle cry. André considered dropping from the horse to roll out of the way. If he was lucky, he could draw his sword before his enemy skewered him. As he was about to let go, he saw the Cossack's torso heave back with a violent jerk, and the man fell from the saddle as his horse galloped away. André turned his eyes forward and saw that he had reached the closest square. He released his one-handed grip of the pommel and fell to the ground in exhaustion. Two of his troopers grabbed hold of his coat and pulled him into the relative safety of the square.

When André had caught his breath and regained his feet, he scanned the field in front of him and caught a glimpse of the other square, where Moreau was sat on his horse, barking orders to his men. A few feet from André, Mazzarello did the same, but he cut his words short as the Cossacks, now flooding out of the forest, formed up in a line across from the two squares. Without hesitation, the group of horsemen let out a deafening cheer and spurred their horses to a gallop. Almost all had spears, with a smaller number choosing to wave swords or pistols over their heads as they charged. They outnumbered the dragoons perhaps three to one.

As the horsemen approached the squares, André's dragoons discharged a volley; most fired high but several found their mark. The enemy fired their pistols at the square, and a man near André fell into the mud, holding his stomach and groaning in pain. But none of the enemy horsemen advanced close enough to break the square, as their horses flinched and reared to avoid impaling themselves on the rows of the dragoons' bayonets.

Those who managed to get their horses within arm's length began to stab at André's men with their lances, thrusting and poking wildly with little success. One enraged Cossack rode in front of the square smacking the dragoons' bayonets with his spear, shouting in broken French, "Coward dogs! Coward *Frantsuszkiy!*" André felt a violent swell of anger every time he saw one of his men fall; his instincts urged him to step out of the square and to avenge the wounded, but that ill discipline would weaken the square and allow the enemy to break through and slaughter them. He clenched his jaw and shouted at his men to stand fast.

The squares held, but the attrition slowly began taking a toll. A growing number of wounded and dying troopers lay on the ground in the middle of the square; one let out an agonizing cry as a nervous horse trampled on his legs. André tried to estimate the number of enemy still remaining in the field, but the smoke from the rolling musket and pistol fire obscured his view. Although the ground in front of them was strewn with corpses and the snow was now stained red with blood, he knew there were more waiting.

A light breeze had begun to blow, and soon the smoke drifted past, allowing André to see the horsemen on the opposite side of the field. To his relief, and surprise, they appeared in complete disarray, and their numbers had been more depleted than he'd realized. Several of the Cossacks shouted loudly at each other. By now, André had enough experience to sense when the tide of a battle had begun to shift. Sizing up the enemy's dead and wounded, he now judged the two sides' numbers as generally even. Having just inflicted a mauling on the Cossacks, he knew their morale had been shaken. Deciding in that split second that weathering further attacks would deplete his squadron to unacceptable levels, he ran to his horse and mounted. Calling for his men to do the same, he ordered the bugler to sound the call to battle order. The troopers began shouting and shoving their way past each other in a scramble to mount and form into position. After half a minute to allow for a semblance of formation, André rode out in the front of the haphazard line and held his sword aloft. The bugler piped out the order to charge, and André spurred his horse to a canter, screaming wildly, "*VIVE L'EMPEREUR!*" Behind him the uninjured troopers of his squadron echoed his call, their horses' hooves splashing brown snow and mud high into the air. In the rear of the formation, Major Moreau rode slower than the rest, watching for dangerous gaps in the line and urging slacking troopers to keep up.

Within seconds, André and the foremost dragoons were falling upon the stunned Cossacks. Although a brave handful spurred their horses to meet the dragoons, the majority sensed the initiative swinging in favor of the French and fled quickly into the woods. A brief but bloody melee followed, in which the remaining Cossacks were dragged from their saddles and dispatched with bayonet thrusts.

Breathing heavily and half-crazed from the fight, André eventually managed to gain control of his men, many of whom wanted to plunge into the forest to pursue the fleeing Cossacks. Moreau paced his horse in front of the tree line, sword in hand, obstructing any overzealous trooper who thought about giving further chase. The troopers stared at him, their faces begrimed with sweat and powder, but none challenged his order.

CHAPTER 41

Border of Prussia-Poland

January 1807

Shortly after the fighting ended, a bone-numbing exhaustion set in, replacing the unspeakable joy and relief of surviving the battle unscathed. André penned a brief combat report to Colonel Menard while Moreau wiped his bloodless sword on the fur coat of a dead Cossack. André squinted at him.

"Just want to keep its shine, major?"

"Force of habit, I suppose." Moreau sheathed his sword and spat. "Remind me never to forgive you for turning me into a real officer. Detestable." He looked over the field scattered with dead men and horses. "So, what do we do now, sir?"

"Now I must leave, Marcel." André took a long drink from his canteen and passed it to his executive officer. "I'll be taking two experienced troopers to keep an eye on that man over there," he said, eyeing the English agent, who was sitting on a dead horse and writing into a small ledger. "I was curious what he would do if the fighting took an ominous turn."

"I'm surprised the weasel didn't try and escape," Moreau muttered, resting his musket on his forearm. "I would have."

André smiled. "That's why I had Mazzarello put him in your square. I knew you wouldn't let him get away."

Moreau grinned. "I would've happily shot the bastard."

"I know you would have," André said. Both men laughed.

"Here," André said, pulling out his pistol, "why don't I do it for you?" His hands shaking, he mimicked a pistol shot toward the Englishman. Their laughter grew even louder, and several of the troopers pillaging a dead Cossack looked at their two half-crazed officers with curious expressions.

"I need you for one last mission, my friend," André said, regaining his senses. "I need you to lead these men."

"So now we're friends, then?"

"Yes. Though you'll still salute me. I may only be gone for a matter of days, but if something happens to me, I need you to look after these troopers—our troopers. Don't trouble yourself thinking what I would want you to do; do what you feel is right, and all will be well. Now is your time."

Moreau stared at him with a blank look, but André knew that hidden beneath his stoicism was a wellspring of unspoken feeling. He wished he could better express his pride at having served alongside him.

"I'll do all I can, sir."

André maintained a look of calm, but his heart swelled with conflicted emotion. The pride he felt as he looked out over his men was matched only by his regret at having to leave them; they were marching into a fight and, if he returned, some of them might no longer be alive.

"Well," André said, wiping his face with a dirty sleeve, "it's time to check the butcher's bill." He finished scribbling into his ledger and tore out the sheet of paper.

"Mazzarello took a round."

André turned to Moreau with a look of distress. "He did?"

Moreau nodded. "A bullet to the foot."

As if on cue, the Corsican limped into their field of view. He waved away their worried looks. "You two look like old milksops that have seen a ghost. They're pinpricks—nothing."

The look on André's face did not change. "You're sure of that, Mazzarello?"

"I can still hold a sword and level a pistol; don't worry your noble head about it."

André nodded. "Is the pain manageable?"

"All pain is manageable." The old Corsican smiled grimly. "Now, enough wasted time—take care of those worse off than me."

André called out for the Englishman to join them, while Moreau, to the sergeant-major's protests, inspected the severity of his wound.

Monsieur Hackett approached with an expression of amusement. "A nasty little scrape, eh, gentlemen? I've spent some time with the czar's army, but I've never had the...em...*privilege* of seeing Don Cossacks in action. Nasty buggers, aren't they? Even so, Lieutenant-Colonel Valiere, you seemed to have made mincemeat of them."

"Shut your mouth," Moreau said, though his words lacked the biting edge they usually carried when addressing the Englishman.

Hackett nodded compliantly. "I regret the loss of any men in your command. If I can be of any use, please do not hesitate to ask."

"I intend to put you to use," André replied, "as soon as we've managed our wounded and buried our dead. In the meantime, don't walk around my troopers speaking English or conversing in Russian with our prisoners. For your safety's sake."

Hackett replied with a curt nod of understanding.

"Sergeant-major, bring our traveling wounded back to the regiment; have Laporte bring the tally to Colonel Menard. And have your own wounds dressed—don't argue with me, just do it. Major Moreau, reconnoiter the ground and set pickets anywhere you deem appropriate. Any sight of additional enemy, you let me know. You, Silesian, come with me and we'll discuss our next move. Go."

Hackett followed André, who, after saddling his horse and refilling his canteen, said, "It's time for us to leave now, Monsieur Hackett. We'll bypass the city of Saalfeld and take the road north to Danzig. I haven't the slightest idea what we'll do if Carnassier has already come into possession of the treasure horde—but if he hasn't, we may still have time to pass a message along St. Clair's semaphore to thwart the bastard." He stood for a moment with a hand resting on his horse's saddle, looking like a ship captain lost at sea with no sun or stars visible to chart a course. He placed his helmet on his head, saying to himself as much as anyone else, "It may be difficult, but we will manage. We must."

When André had leaped into the saddle and taken the reins, the Englishman cleared his throat. "Monsieur Valiere, have you forgotten that I was in league with the hussar major for several months? As far as I am aware, he does not know I no longer serve him. I have means of corresponding that bypass the standard army intelligence networks. And I know every allied agent from here to Mainz."

"Do you have means to write a message and be sure that it finds him?"

"I can write a message and be sure that it finds its destination; whether or not the good major will come upon it is another matter."

"Speak more plainly," André ordered.

"As I tried to tell you before we departed Posen, colonel, I have access to three lines of communication via post-pigeon. One that runs across the German states and goes as far as Mainz. Another that runs through Vilnius, and my last and shortest line ends in Danzig. I could quite easily send a message to the terminus there informing my true superiors that I am little more than three days' ride distant, and request that they inform me where to meet the baggage train as it travels toward the city."

"That is all well, but how can I be sure you won't lead me into a trap and have me killed?"

The Englishman held out his arms. "I am your captive. You need not trust me, but in the present circumstances, I am the only one who can lead you to what you seek before the hussar finds what we're all searching for. It is assuredly a gamble worth taking. And besides," he added, "killing the man who spared my life would be rather poor form."

"Very well then, *Conrad*," André said, his features relaxing slightly. "Though it is treasonous and I could be arrested for sending false intelligence, I will send a message along the semaphores that just may throw Carnassier off the trail, at least for a day or two. That may be enough for us to outpace him. But now the question is: How do we get this traveling cache into our hands once we've found it?"

"I've not been sent all this way to find my quarry and ask politely for it." Hackett smiled, revealing a dangerous guile that belied his hitherto friendly expression. "If we find it, it will be ours."

André turned his head, looking at a point on the horizon. "I didn't expect to have to betray my own countrymen, my own nation."

Hackett finished scribbling the final words of a message, tore the page from his notebook, snapped it shut, and placed it in his breast pocket. "One might look at it like that," he said, rolling the note and sliding it into a tiny cylinder designed for the passing of secret correspondence. "Or you might consider what will become of your empire if a man like Fabien Carnassier gains true power."

After passing temporary command to Moreau and offering a brief, regretful farewell to his troopers, André set off for Saalfeld with Hackett and two experienced troopers. Carnassier would not be stopped without a fight, and two extra muskets might prove useful.

CHAPTER 42

Strasbourg, France
December 1806

Jean-Luc's carriage crossed the Ponts Couverts Bridge and entered Strasbourg in the early evening. More than two weeks had passed since he had bid farewell to André in Posen. As he passed onto French soil, he felt his heart yearning for the sight of his children, while at the same time his mind was preoccupied with thoughts of the war in the east.

Jean-Luc settled into his room at a boardinghouse overlooking Waffenplatz Square. With a discreet look, he ushered a guest inside without offering a formal greeting. He closed the door quietly behind him and locked it. Maxime, his erstwhile assistant, surveyed his master's furnishings enviously until Jean-Luc offered his hand.

"It is good to see you, young man," Jean-Luc said, sounding weary but sincere. "Thank you for making the journey."

Maxime returned the handshake heartily. "After the journey *you've* made? I consider a little jaunt through country lanes to the Rhine a fine distraction. It is *you* who's had to bear living in a frozen backwater."

Something in his words gave Jean-Luc pause. "Be that as it may," he replied, his tone somber, "there is still much work to do." He motioned for Maxime to clear plates and silverware from the table in the middle of the room. He then grabbed one of his travel bags and set it down, pulling out papers and several inkwells and quills. They each pulled up a chair and sat down. Jean-Luc put on a pair of reading glasses and held up one of the papers.

"About a week ago, while passing through Nuremberg—" a fit of coughing forced him to pause and catch his breath. "Excuse me," he continued, waving away a cup of water Maxime held out. "About a week ago as our convoy halted in Nuremberg, I came upon a man whom I had been searching for a long time, though at that moment I didn't know it. He was a cavalry sergeant, perhaps twenty years of age, and I thought I had seen him somewhere before. I thought for a moment, then recalled that I had come across this fellow in the Polish hinterlands perhaps two weeks prior, and now, coincidentally we found ourselves together several hundred miles west of any fighting. I would have dismissed the matter, had I not noticed him entering my assistant, Charles Bourque's room—don't look at me like that, Maxime, he's my *traveling* assistant. I plan on putting *you* back to work in earnest as soon as we return to Paris."

Maxime scoffed at the accusation, but his demeanor indicated relief.

"Anyway," Jean-Luc continued, "I saw this man enter Bourque's chamber, so I went downstairs and waited for him in the street. He emerged a short while later carrying several documents. I held out my arm as he passed, and upon recognizing me he doffed his cap and smiled—an uncomfortable smile that we both knew to be false. I informed him that I knew of Bourque's indiscretions and that I would not interfere; but for a bonus of one hundred francs, he might let me look at the latest dispatches my assistant Bourque was passing to the front. One hundred and fifty francs later, I found a letter bearing the Imperial bee, as well as the official seal of the police minister. 'Reseal it with the stamp that I know you carry,' I said with false confidence, hoping this was, in fact, possible. He made no objection, so I tore open the letter. It was from Joseph Fouché to Major Fabien Carnassier of the Seventh Hussars. I committed to memory the important parts: 'Has left Frankfurt,' 'inform me via telegraph when you depart for Danzig,' *Speshnyi* docked in port on North Sea,' 'my password is N-I-E-V-E-8-9.'" Jean-Luc coughed again into a handkerchief and accepted a sip of water.

"Major Fabien Carnassier?" asked Maxime.

"I'll appraise you of the specifics another time," Jean-Luc assured him. He took a drink, then continued. "The missive did *not* mention any agent accompanying Major Carnassier, so I demanded of this cavalryman if he knew of anyone who might be helping the major. He replied that the major worked under his own mandate and that no one accompanied him. I asked about local informants or agents—but the young soldier was adamant. I mentioned the name Conrad, a man whom my friend serving at the front, Lieutenant-Colonel Valiere, has met personally, to see if the man's features betrayed any recognition; alas, they did not." Jean-Luc sighed as he leaned back in his chair. "But the information gleaned from this letter might yet prove invaluable, for we now know—before Major Carnassier—that the fortune he is hunting has been moved, and we know that he will be en route to Danzig. I offered the man another three hundred francs to keep the contents of our conversation private. So," Jean-Luc said, removing his glasses, "through a bit of luck and, dare I admit, a sharp eye on my part, Lieutenant-Colonel Valiere might have a fighting chance of finding the treasure before Major Carnassier."

Maxime shook his head. "Senator, while I don't fully understand what you are talking about, I can see you have been busy."

Jean-Luc nodded in reluctant agreement. "Though it is all likely to land me in deep waters. By now, Fouché is certain to have learned that I've met with Colonel Valiere, and that we were old acquaintances during the Revolution. I was his defense counsel against the tribunal."

"With respect, senator, what does that matter?"

"Have you not heard what, more precisely who, is set on stopping Carnassier and, therefore, Fouché?"

Maxime smiled dolefully. "Lieutenant-Colonel Valiere."

"Precisely so," Jean-Luc said through a cough. "The police minister can scarcely hide his disdain for me now, when he hears about this." Jean-Luc sighed. "Anyhow, as I've already gotten you into one mess that we were lucky to escape, I would understand if you wish to stay as far away from this as possible."

Maxime tilted his head. "To be truthful, monsieur, while just the *name* Fouché gives me pause, I nevertheless find this whole game more exciting than the drudgery they've given me at the Tuileries." He grinned eagerly. "Where do we begin?"

"Very good, Maxime!" Jean-Luc spoke with a vigor he had not shown in quite some time, and he started pacing the room. "We will begin by doing everything we can to help my friend Valiere mislead Carnassier and foil Fouché's scheme for finding this fortune. What I've intercepted is merely the tip of the iceberg; he is bound to be playing at other games." He took a moment to gather himself.

"Now, tell me. What news of home? Is my family well?"

His subordinate lowered his eyes to the floor. "Senator St. Clair," he said quietly, "it was not my wish to spoil your return, but I regret to inform you that I don't believe all is well." Maxime went on to explain how he'd passed along Jean-Luc's letters to Isabella, but it had now been several weeks since she permitted anyone into the house. The servants had received all subsequent letters without admitting him. "I stopped by the house on my way here," he explained. "The servants informed me that Isabella was gone and had not been seen for days. She had left them with no instruction and had taken many of her possessions with her to wherever it was she had gone."

Jean-Luc forced a smile. "Thank you, Maxime. We'll just have to sort it out when I return home. I suppose I should be grateful that I have at least *one* partner I can trust."

With that he bade farewell to his young assistant and soon after fell into a deep, fitful sleep.

CHAPTER 43

Paris

January 1807

Five days after his brief stay in Strasbourg, Jean-Luc was back in Paris. He returned from a five-hundred-mile trip to an empty house, despite having left instructions for Mariette to be brought home from school. Isabella, too, was nowhere to be found. Profoundly agitated, he would not be able to rest until he knew Mariette was on her way home.

The following morning he set off in plain clothes to visit Monsieur Gagnon in Saint-Antoine. The wine merchant received him with a gruff "Good morning" and a handshake before ushering him into his home. The interior was considerably cleaner than the last time Jean-Luc had visited, with documents and ledgers scattered throughout the sitting room, but little evidence of excessive drink and debauchery.

"Could it be," Jean-Luc asked as he took a seat across from his host, "that in my absence you have managed to turn yourself back into a professional and organized man?"

"Hardly, senator," Gagnon grumbled. "I've only refocused my depravity from drink toward more *engaging* pursuits."

"I don't care to know the details of all you've been doing, so I will come directly to the point. Please tell me the latest news you've had of Minister Fouché and his agents in the east. There are developments of which I've learned during my travels that I must begin to make out more clearly."

Gagnon launched into an account of his doings: bribing government officials, supporting local families struggling to pay rent, meeting with the police minister's network of informants, seizing Colonel Pettit and racking him for information. At this last revelation, Jean-Luc sat up in his chair.

"Well? Have you any updates from him?"

"That colonel might look a fine, dashing soldier on *parade*," Gagnon replied with scorn. "But the fellow fairly shit himself when he saw us in masks, brandishing pikes. We brought him out to a copse in Montmartre and threatened to remove his balls if he failed to cooperate."

"Jesus—" Jean-Luc's eyes dropped to the floor.

"Oh, don't fret your lawyer's head about it. The big dandy weren't in no *real* trouble. We were just having a bit of fun with the chap who shagged your woman mons—er, senator."

Jean-Luc passed a hand over his face. "Gagnon, I don't know whether I want to punch you or embrace you. Though I suppose the colonel deserved it. It doesn't matter. I'm not here to sort *that*. Just tell me what information he offered concerning Fouché and his agents in Poland."

Gagnon divulged his latest intelligence, most of which Jean-Luc already knew, but then the merchant mentioned something new.

"According to our good colonel," Gagnon explained, "this hussar major should come upon this treasure horde that everyone seems to be seeking within a fortnight at most. And, from one who's done a bit of smuggling in his time, I'll confess that the plan for him to intercept it from the Prussians as it is transferred to a Russian ship is a peach. The major is to pose as an émigré aristocrat or some such, no friend to the emperor at any rate, and safeguard it as it is passed through our lines at Danzig."

Jean-Luc stared at Gagnon, doubt written plain on his features. "Let me understand you. Major Carnassier plans to masquerade as an aristocrat émigré and steal the horde from under their noses? How would that fool the Prussians or English?"

"Oh, senator, you're missing the best part." Gagnon was practically trembling with excitement. "The very man who's arranged all of this from his own web of diplomatic channels? Minister Fouché! Isn't he a rascal to admire?" Jean-Luc, though not sharing Gagnon's enthusiasm, nevertheless admitted that the idea was plausible. Gagnon licked his lips. "This Carnassier fellow may be the dog hounding out the riches, but it's Fouché managing the affair from the shadows. He's convinced his contacts in the enemy camp that there's a big-wig émigré living in East Prussia who wishes to thwart Napoleon, and he can help them sneak the wagons through our siege lines at Danzig. They're supposed to rendezvous somewhere outside the city; where was it? Ordensburg. That's the place they'll be fetching it to be put in the possession of this aristo."

"And you heard this from Colonel Pettit directly?"

Gagnon nodded. "Pettit, his lips well-loose as he shook from fright, started jabbering about the two rats keeping the riches for themselves. He said something about leaving a little gold behind for the English, so it ain't so obvious. Fouché and that hussar bastard have their own designs for its use."

"Ordensburg." Jean-Luc slapped a thigh. "Well, Gagnon, I asked you to be my eyes while I was away, and you've given me an extra pair—as well as ears, nose, and your own big mouth. I can hardly believe I'm saying this, but thank you, my friend."

Gagnon chafed at the gratitude. "It weren't no real trouble. Seeing that idiot colonel squirm reminded me of the good old days before Bonaparte mucked everything up with his *law* and *order*."

Jean-Luc didn't know whether he felt revulsion or relief. Nevertheless, he tapped the wine merchant on the back and took up his coat. "Monsieur Gagnon, your help thus far has proved invaluable," he said as he opened the door. "Now I have a conspiracy to thwart."

When he returned to his house, he found an envelope lying just inside the front door.

He picked it up and tore it open:

My Dear Jean-Luc,

Your absence has compelled me to take the management of your senatory estate into my own hands. I shall be in Sainte-Maure for the foreseeable future. I do not have any expectations of you joining me, as I understand that you have your duties to attend to.

Since you did not approve of my decision to initiate Mariette in catechism studies, I have taken her with me. If you wish to speak with her, I will gladly pass along any message you might have, provided it serves to aid in her current development of manners and erudition. Mathieu has taken his education and development boldly in hand. I would see your daughter begin to do the same.

—Isabella

Jean-Luc took the news like a punch to his stomach. He folded the note and pressed it to his lips with a kiss. A fit of coughing forced him to sit. His inhalations came in short gasps, and several minutes passed before his breath calmed. He thought perhaps it was time to see a doctor, but too many other pressing matters occupied his mind, and he dismissed the thought. He then wrote a brief response to Isabella, declaring in no uncertain terms that Mariette was to come home at once. *Mariette is coming home, or I will go retrieve her.*

Early that evening, Jean-Luc summoned Maxime to his house and shared all that he had learned from Gagnon.

"Now I must ask something of you, Maxime," Jean-Luc said. He examined his assistant, observing how much he had changed since Naples. He had been a lad then; now he looked every bit a poised and capable young man. "If you refuse, I will not think any less of you, for this is no small undertaking."

"How can I be of service, senator?"

"I have just today come to learn of information that I do not trust to pass safely along the semaphores, not with Fouché's agents spread along the route. It must be delivered posthaste by someone I can trust. You must bring it to the Grand Armée headquarters directly in Berlin. If you deliver it there, I trust it will find Major André Valiere of the Seventeenth Dragoons."

Maxime reached for his wine glass and proceeded to pour the contents down his throat. With a hearty exhale, he wiped his lips with his sleeve.

"Very well, senator. When do I depart?"

Though his thoughts were preoccupied with his family, Jean-Luc still managed to attend a banquet hosted by several of his senate colleagues at a restaurant in the châtelet. As he walked into the gathering in a private room and saw the men who had made the journey with him to Poland, he felt a genuine outpouring of camaraderie. After so many days traveling and boarding in close proximity, they had come to learn much of each other, and the experience served to form a bond that could not easily be broken, or so he believed. As he made his way around the table to greet the senators, he noticed something strange. The salutations of the senators who had stayed behind had never before seemed so universally friendly.

The meal progressed from hors d'oeuvres to the main course of roast beef, mutton, lentils, white beans, and an abundance of Bordeaux and Burgundy wines. Jean-Luc was enjoying the company of the man seated next to him, Senator Louis-Nicholas Lemercier, one who had traveled with him to Berlin and then on to Poland. As the laughter and conversation rose in pitch, Senator Lemercier rose to his feet, raising a hand for silence. After a good deal of shouting and whistling, the tumult died down and the senator began speaking.

"Esteemed gentlemen and senators of the French Empire," Lemercier said in a loud, somewhat slurred voice. "And especially to our truant friends who avoided the journey to the east, passing a leisurely autumn in the salons and gaming houses of Paris, warm in bed with their mistresses."

A fit of laughter and knee-slapping ensued.

"Allow me to be the first to extend a happy and grateful greeting from our leader, our general, our very own genius—Napoleon Bonaparte the first, emperor of the French."

At this the entire room roared with approval. Jean-Luc, whether from the wine or the mood of his compatriots, joined heartily in the exclamations.

"It has hardly been a week since we *intrepid* members have returned; alas, we must return to a life of ease in the company of our wives and children, sleeping in our own beds and not passing our days in an endless march across frozen dirt and snow-covered fields."

Jean-Luc glanced around the room; the smiles on some of his colleagues' faces had faded at this description of their time in the hinterlands. He envisioned this overfed new breed of aristocrats marching with André and his soldiers. *Educated men talk while strong men bleed and die*, he thought.

"Now, gentlemen," Senator Lemercier said, "you'll be delighted to hear that two more of our esteemed and powerful friends have come home. Senators Talleyrand and Fouché have today returned from absences, and they have called for an impromptu meeting of our body tomorrow." A grumble rolled over the room, with some of the senators throwing their napkins at Monsieur Lemercier in mock protest. "So," Lemercier continued, raising his arms to shield himself from the barrage of cloth. "We must resume our work tomorrow; do not drink yourselves blind." With that Lemercier raised his glass, and the assembled senators took long gulps of wine. Jean-Luc sipped from his own, but the mention of Fouché had brought him back to sobriety.

My Dear Friend André,

It is my sincerest wish that this letter finds you and your brave compatriots safe and well. Surely you and your men endure daily privations and miseries to a degree that we civilians can hardly imagine. If it is any small consolation, know that you march on behalf of a proud and grateful nation, who hold their army and their emperor in such high esteem that it's hardly an exaggeration to compare you to the heroes of antiquity.

But let me come to the point; you should know that I've learned of two important developments in the case of your man Carnassier and his designs. First, a source in the army— whose name and rank I will not risk being revealed—informs me that Major Carnassier has learned of the location of the hidden fortune of Hesse-Cassel. It is no longer in Frankfurt. We believe it is currently being transported in a carriage train traveling north. We do not know by whom, only that they must be allied to the Prussians. We suspect our enemies wish to convey it to one of the cities in northern Prussia that has not yet fallen to us, perhaps Danzig, so that it may be shipped across the North Sea. If that happens, it will then be in the hands of the Russians or the English, which will be disastrous for our Empire. However, if it should fall into the hands of this Carnassier fellow, that may be worse in the long term as by now I have every reason to believe that Carnassier and the police minister are working with common purpose.

This brings me to the second bit of news. From this same source I have learned that there is no Silesian agent called Conrad in service to the minister or the emperor, not in your sector of the war, at least. I've been considering what this could mean; the first possibility, this being rather unlikely, is that your man Carnassier has taken it upon himself to hire the services of this Conrad for his own purposes, and none of Fouché's agents or informants have heard of him.

The second possibility is that Conrad is not who he says he is. Perhaps Carnassier is hiding his identity to cover his tracks and remain autonomous, or it's even possible that the man has kept his own identity secret and is working with his own designs. Without knowing his real name and place of origin, who knows what game he might be playing at?

I earnestly regret that in disclosing all of this information I have burdened you beyond your current troubles, but, my friend, you are the only man I know who possesses both the means and the honor to be trusted to act on this information with no designs above patriotic duty and regard for your fellow countrymen. If I may be of service in the coming weeks, please do not hesitate to contact me. I will reply with all possible haste. Godspeed.

Vive l'Empereur.
Senator St. Clair

CHAPTER 44

Luxembourg Palace, Paris

January 1806

J ean-Luc walked alone into the palais and mounted the grand staircase, keeping a watchful eye out for Minister Fouché. Upon entering the great chamber, he noticed several of his colleagues from the evening prior, who, despite looking the worse for wear, still managed to carry themselves with the dignity of Napoleon's senators. And yet, Jean-Luc noticed that most of them barely looked at him—and the ones who did offered only passing glances and cold expressions.

The session began with the customary roll call and formalities of State, followed by the reading of a lengthy bulletin from Napoleon. The dispatch, though couched in confident language and heroic imagery, conveyed that the latest campaign was far from decided. After the reading, President Gaspard Monge called on several of the senators who had traveled east to mount the podium and offer their conclusions on the diplomatic work conducted with the Poles and Prussians. The speakers' conclusions came across as noncommittal, but they asserted that the emperor's overwhelming victories at Jena and Auerstedt had changed the paradigm of power in Eastern Europe and expressed confidence that their diplomatic efforts would ultimately bear fruit.

Hours passed with debates ranging from how to raise money for the construction of new monuments and bridges to an argument over the feasibility of oil being supplied for a new network of streetlights in the city. Jean-Luc noticed several of his colleagues dozing in their seats. After a brief interlude for tobacco and coffee, the discussions resumed. Jean-Luc was staring down at the hands on his pocket watch, willing them to move faster, when he heard something that caused the hair on the back of his neck to stand.

"And for the sake of continuity," exclaimed the senator speaking from the rostrum, "Senator Talleyrand has requested that the following senators join him for a follow-on journey. He does not wish for the progress that has been made to be lost, and the Prussian and Polish envoys have expressed a desire to resume discussions with men of good faith and with whom they have developed a professional rapport." The senator then proceeded to call out the names of members who had just returned; Jean-Luc's heart sank when he heard his own. "We are perfectly aware," the senator continued, "that this decision comes at a great personal inconvenience, but let us not forget that we are a nation at war, and while this summons arrives via Senator Talleyrand, it originates from the emperor himself. If our soldiers can brave the frosts and bitter winds of Poland and East Prussia on our behalf, who are we to sit idly?"

A half-hearted cheer arose, mainly from those whose names had not been called or those who had just awoken and missed most of the address. Jean-Luc searched the room, hoping to find a like-minded ally who might speak against this proposal, but no one disturbed the silence that lingered in the great hall. All he could think of was how long it had been since he had seen his daughter. He jumped to his feet.

"Monsieur le President, I cannot agree to this." Every head in the room turned toward him. Some of his colleagues, who had spoken to him so kindly the evening prior, now looked at him with disdain. He could hear a murmur growing, but he did not care. "Monsieur le President, I cannot go back."

He took a deep breath and prepared to explain his position, ready to meet any challenge leveled against him, when he saw that hardly any of the senators were paying him any attention. He glanced across the hall to where a clamor seemed to be originating. A moment later he saw the source of the commotion—the arrival of two men in ornate uniforms. Foreign Minister Charles-Maurice de Talleyrand entered the hall, resplendent in a fleece coat of crimson, with the silver star of the Legion of Honor on his left breast. Behind him walked Police Minister Fouché. They took their time walking through the first row of senators, Minister Talleyrand's bonhomie on full display as he shook hands and patted the shoulders of his lesser-ranking colleagues. Fouché's face remained impassive, himself offering a brief bow or nod in greeting to his fellow senators. He shook the hand of the man next to him and sat down beside Minister Talleyrand.

President Monge waited for the clamor to fade before calling for order. He turned in Jean-Luc's direction: "Senator St. Clair, I believe you held the floor. Do you wish to repeat your previous statement objecting to our emperor's latest request?" Monge motioned to the two newly arrived ministers.

Minister Talleyrand turned in his seat, frowning at Jean-Luc.

"Monsieur President and esteemed ministers," he began, his voice catching. The appearance of Fouché had unsettled something within him. He began again, "Messieurs, I was stating my regret that I do not consider myself able to attend the latest mission to Prussia. It is not my wish to fall short of my duties to the empire, but I have personal matters that regrettably force me to remain close at home for the present moment."

In the front row, Minister Talleyrand smirked. "I am sure there are several hundred thousand of your countrymen who would prefer to be attending to personal matters at home. Unfortunately, they find themselves inconvenienced at war, doing their duty." The senators broke out in laughter—all save Minister Fouché, who remained aloof.

Jean-Luc nodded his understanding. "I do not doubt it, minister," he replied. "I have just returned from the Prussian theater myself, and I have seen firsthand the sacrifices our brave soldiers are making. But while I gladly offer my time and energy in service to the nation, a father with a deceased wife nevertheless has responsibilities that he cannot readily forego."

A handful of the senators murmured their assent; Minister Talleyrand did not say anything. A heavyset man seated a few rows down from Jean-Luc rose to his feet.

"Where do our greatest duties lie," the senator boomed, "if not to the emperor? Why, would you refuse this order to his face, were he to walk into this chamber now?"

At that very moment a man walked into the great hall, causing the senators' heads to turn almost in unison. Jean-Luc's pulse quickened and he feared the worst, but soon he could see that the new arrival was, in fact, just an errand boy. The lad paced quickly along the front row of the assembly, and the senators turned their attention back to Jean-Luc, who noticed the youth stoop in front of Minister Fouché and hand him a note before turning and walking out the way he'd come.

"Well?" The senator challenged Jean-Luc. "Would you place your own interests over that of your sovereign?"

Jean-Luc, who had until now felt somewhat embarrassed, felt his face flush with anger. He turned his attention from Fouché toward this truculent colleague.

"The same empire that sent me as an unwitting *ambassador* to a kingdom roiling with rebellion, to be captured and forced to watch as my compatriots were slaughtered in front of me? An empire," he persisted, heedless of the tumult his words were causing, "that has time and again exacted the price of service and unquestioned loyalty without returning it in kind?"

Minister Fouché turned slightly in his seat. "Your financial compensation," he said calmly, "and hectares of land in your senatory estate say otherwise, senator."

Jean-Luc, too agitated to reply, said nothing. But the heavyset senator in the adjacent row had not finished.

"Ingrate!" he cried. "Have you not heard, monsieur, that *gratitude* is not only the greatest virtue, but the parent of all others?"

"I am of the understanding, senator, that the man you quote was a fervent republican," Jean-Luc shot back. "Cicero gave his life defending the senate *against* his nation's tyrant." This was a step too far, and Jean-Luc knew it.

"Do you call Napoleon a *tyrant*?" the heavyset senator roared.

"I would sooner call you a fool," Jean-Luc replied, his quip gaining him a few seconds to think while his colleagues' laughter filled the hall.

For a moment, a general murmur echoed throughout the chamber. Jean-Luc, his temper brought down to a manageable level, waited for the harangue he knew was coming. But it was not a thunderous voice of censure that broke the silence. Throughout his exchange with the fat senator, Jean-Luc had kept one eye on the minister of police, as the timing of the note that had just been delivered seemed curious. He felt a sudden dread as he watched the police minister quietly confer with Talleyrand. Jean-Luc watched Fouché hand the note to the foreign minister, who rose to his feet and walked to the speaker's podium. The senators' side conversations died down.

Minister Talleyrand pulled out a pair of reading glasses and lifted the note for all to see. "I put forth to the body of the Imperial Senate of the French Empire a letter originating from an unknown party, undersigned by a concerned and patriotic citizen of the French nation." He then read aloud:

To the president and honored members of the Conservative Senate, I deliver this message with trembling hands and a heavy heart, as I have come to know the individual in question reasonably well in recent days, and I took him to be a man of reputation above reproach. It is thus with great sadness that I must submit to a higher loyalty—my conscience and my country. I proffer the following information to the Senate for their consideration and final judgment.

Jean-Luc St. Clair has been charged with possessing documents, seized lawfully from his senatory estate on the morning of November 24, 1806, under the authority of the minister of police, pertaining to a conspiracy of treason directed at Emperor Napoleon. A collection of correspondence, a portion of which was allegedly written by Senator St. Clair himself, has been found which incriminates a group of no less than six individuals, all known and formerly convicted of crimes against the state. The parties in question have all been summoned to the estate of Senator St. Clair at Sainte-Maure for the purpose of discussing grievances shared by all members of the aforementioned conspiracy against his Imperial and Royal Majesty Napoleon Bonaparte.

The list of conspirators is to be found in the adjoining document, with a legal summary of each party. A common point of reference of all aforementioned suspects is the previous or former membership to the Society of the Jacobins.

All of the identified conspirators have a record of imprisonment, with one suspect recently returned to France from the penal settlement of Cayenne in the West Indies, otherwise known as "the dry guillotine." Needless to say, this assembly comprises a collection of known traitors and conspirators who have all been convicted and pose a threat to the well-being of the empire. If Senator St. Clair is found innocent of any crime, then God forgive me for disclosing false information and bringing accusations against a good man. If circumstances are to be found otherwise, then the safety of His Royal Majesty Napoleon and, thereby, the fate of our empire, rests on a decision of swift judgment.

I leave any further actions or decisions in the capable hands of the Senate and Imperial administration.

Vive l'Empereur.
—A concerned and patriotic citizen

Jean-Luc fell into his seat like a sack of potatoes. As the charges being read became more and more incriminatory his face went blank; he hardly noticed the final phrases due to a throbbing hum in his ears. His vision blurred, and the embarrassment he'd felt was replaced by a feeling of detachment that revealed itself in a twisted smirk that seemed to alarm those sitting next to him. He gazed up at the ornate ceiling far above, his vision swayed and contorted until it felt as though he were drifting upward toward it. The chamber had fallen silent. Many, so distressed by what had been disclosed, did not have the heart to look at Jean-Luc. Not that Jean-Luc noticed. He appeared as one drunk; he moved as if to speak, but whatever point he wished to make died on his lips.

Minister Talleyrand exchanged glances with Minister Fouché. "So, it would thus appear," Talleyrand proclaimed with an exaggerated sigh, "that our steadfast Republican, he who decries the tyranny of the very man who bestowed upon him the rank of senator, stands accused of being a conspiring, rabble-rousing anarchist. An anarchist who has made overtures to our mortal enemy, the English!"

Whistles and cries of indignation filled the hall—a scene worthy of the National Convention. Jean-Luc recognized the sound of a mob baying for bloody vengeance. He had contended with the dreaded Revolutionary Tribunal, that body known as the antechamber to the guillotine. Only this time it was howling its lethal accusations at him.

CHAPTER 45

Saalfeld, Border of
Prussia-Poland
January 1807

The afternoon sun vanished behind the clouds, darkening the horizon at an early hour. Gray shadows cast by the trees stretched across the white fields like phantoms slinking from a primeval forest. In the copse where André and Hackett had halted, icy droplets of water fell from the trees. One pinged softly off André's helmet, while Monsieur Hackett used a sleeve to wipe one that fell onto the parchment he was examining. The two troopers who accompanied them sat shivering on their horses a few feet away. When he had finished reading the contents of the dispatch, Monsieur Hackett lifted his eyes to meet André's anticipatory stare.

"Well?" André asked.

The Englishman's nose and cheeks were a bright red and his lips quivered as the evening freeze set in. "It appears, colonel," he said, rolling up the parchment with stiff fingers, "that our man has not yet reached the traveling cache of riches. As far as my contacts are aware, he is currently in the Polish-speaking town of Jonkowo. Carnassier has halted his mad dash to demand payment from the town elders in exchange for the Grand Armée's *protection* from marauding Russian heathens. Goodness, your man has some contempt for the Poles, eh?"

"He is not my man," André replied, snapping his small spyglass shut. "But yes, he seems to hold some particular hatred for them."

"A wonderful ambassador for your emperor."

"He isn't ambassador of anything. The man serves his own whims: greed, cruelty, hatred—all the cardinal virtues."

André surveyed the hills before them; they were receding from view in the failing light. Just visible was a semaphore tower across the valley. He calculated something in his mind and turned to the Englishman. "There are three semaphore towers left between us and the one outside Danzig. We must send the dispatch now." He called one of his troopers over and handed the man an envelope. Issuing a few words of instruction, he pointed to a cluster of trees farther down the valley. The trooper nodded and galloped off. "Let's hope Jean-Luc's password works and they send the damned message," André said. He peered through his spyglass for several minutes. Nothing. He turned to Monsieur Hackett. "What else was in the dispatch?"

Before Hackett could reply, André said with a shout, "Look, there! Ha, ha!" Just barely visible in the waning daylight was the semaphore tower perched on a small hillock. The insect-like arms of the telegraph were contorting in awkward, laborious movements. "Thank you, Jean-Luc," André whispered, handing the spyglass to his English companion.

"It is quite an extraordinary invention, your telegraph," Hackett mused, lowering the spyglass and passing it back to André. "Now, considering our business here is finished, shall we be on the move?"

André clutched the reins in his hands. "First tell me what else was in the message."

"*Wir fahren nach Ordensburg*," Hackett said, in near-perfect German. "Colonel, we are going to Ordensburg Castle."

The contents of André's message sent along the telegraph threw several of the minor outposts along the Danzig road into a state of chaos. He had known his false report from Senator Jean-Luc St. Clair would startle the French patrols in the immediate vicinity, but seeing their reaction up close created a new uneasiness: there was no turning back from their current course. If Hackett enjoyed seeing confusion sown among his sworn enemies, he kept his pleasure constrained out of respect to his captor.

Their small company had passed a miserable night around the warmth of a tenuous fire and had risen before sunrise. As they rode at a hurried pace north in the direction of Danzig, a large troop of lancers thundered past them without slowing down. The two troopers riding in the rear seemed to sense that something was amiss. "Do they know something we don't, sir?" Corporal Leveque called forward.

André trotted his horse through the tracks left behind by the lancers. "They've just learned a force of Imperial Russian household cavalry has emerged east of here near the town of Preussisch-Holland."

"They have?" the trooper called back, sounding nervous.

"It's not true," André called back, "but they think it is."

When they halted to water and feed their horses, André explained to his two troopers, under threat of confinement should they reveal what they were hearing, that he had sent the report of enemy approaching from the north and the east, to throw the roads into confusion. Carnassier, André hoped, would be slowed and possibly sent to face the enemy, while they continued west toward Danzig. He withheld their ultimate aim, should one of them be captured and coerced under duress or torture.

To avoid being pulled into action by an overzealous officer riding the opposite direction, André decided they should move off the main road. Hackett, who was reasonably familiar with the terrain, offered no objection, and they resumed their ride, aiming to take a quieter path at the first opportunity. They had not gone far when a pistol shot echoed across the snowy fields, forcing them to turn in their saddles. A lone rider was approaching at full gallop. He was perhaps a kilometer distant when André recognized the man as one of his own. They halted on the side of the road and waited for Private Baudin to catch up. Several moments later, Baudin reined his horse in alongside them. He saluted André.

"Good thing you found us when you did," André informed him, "we were about to leave the main road."

Private Baudin tapped his exhausted horse's neck as sweat dampened its gray coat. "There's only one main road from Mohrungen to Danzig, sir," he said. "A troop of lancers just passed on the road; I asked if they had seen four riders hurrying north. Sure enough, they had, so I set out at a gallop and let out a shot when I sighted you."

"Well done," André commended him. "Now, what is it that caused you to gallop all the way from—"

"Mohrungen, sir," Private Baudin nodded. "The enemy has taken nearly all the roads leading into the city, so we was ordered to screen the ones still open; Marshal Bernadotte himself rode with our squadron for a bit. He left us to go into the city, so it's just our squadron, a legion of polish lancers and…the Seventh Hussars, sir."

André took a moment to process this latest development. A flock of crows burst out noisily from a nearby tree, squawking as they beat their wings and flew out of sight in the late morning sun.

"Did you see their leader?" André asked. "Carnassier, was he there with them?"

"None of us saw the major, sir. Looked like the hussars was following their captain."

"Alderic," André said. Moreau was not likely to relish his presence so nearby.

"The men was talking about Major Moreau's duels, sir," Private Baudin went on, "how he's got only two left; maybe he'll have a chance to kill that Alderic bastard then."

Or, André mused, *perhaps Moreau will let his grievances die, putting the care of his men over his own desire for revenge.* The idea seemed doubtful. "That's not your or any of your comrades' business. But time is pressing; have you ridden all this way just to inform me of this?"

"No, sir. I've come to bring you this." Baudin reached into a knapsack hung from his saddle. "This came from the emperor's own headquarters; they say it's from a senator, but that's officer business over my own head."

He pulled out a note and handed it to André, who tore the envelope open and read through it quickly. When he had finished, he folded the note and put it into a breast pocket. "Thank you, Baudin. Were you given any further messages?"

The trooper shook his head. "Just instruction from Major Moreau to deliver the letter to you at fastest possible speed, sir."

"Very good," André replied. "I thank you for coming all this way. Major Moreau will need every man he has, so now you must return as quickly as you've come."

"Sir." Baudin saluted his commander and turned without another word, galloping back in the direction from which he'd come.

André's horse fidgeted, and he reached down to pat its neck. "Monsieur Hackett," André called out, turning to the Englishman who sat patiently atop his horse on the other side of the road. "I've just been informed that your allies, a column of fleeing Prussian notables, are currently traveling north, escorting a dignitary of some importance. A French nobleman, Monsieur le Count de Chambrun, is due to arrive at Ordernsburg Castle sometime within the next two days." André patted his breast pocket. "This aristocrat is fleeing Napoleon's unholy onslaught and seeks safe passage through French lines to Danzig, and a ship to safety."

Hackett smiled. "Your police minister is a clever bugger. Well," he said, turning to look along the road leading north, "I wonder if any genteel French aristocrats have come this way?"

"I thought we were all supposed to be dead." André jerked the reins and spurred his horse forward. "Let's go."

CHAPTER 46

Paris, France
January 1806

Following the public reading of the anonymous letter, Jean-Luc was looked upon as if he were the carrier of a deadly contagion; his calamitous fortune seen as something to hide from rather than assault. He had left the chamber without publicly answering the accusations and returned home. A brave colleague visited later that evening, suggesting it would be wise to remain in his house until the senate had decided what to do with him. Jean-Luc did not object. He simply nodded and sat motionless on his sofa until the following morning.

A day passed with no word from the administration; then another. After nearly a week of unofficial house arrest, during which time he did not receive a single visitor, Jean-Luc at last received a note delivered by one of the servants, who informed him it had arrived unceremoniously via the servant quarters. He set it down on a stand in the hall and did not read it until he had summoned enough courage the following day. It served to wake him from his stupor:

> *Due to a pending investigation of the crimes of conspiracy to commit treason against the state, Jean-Luc St. Clair, formerly member of the Conservative Imperial Senate, is hereby revoked of all rank, titles, honors, and properties bestowed upon him by his Imperial and Royal Majesty Napoleon Bonaparte, Emperor of the French, effective 7 January 1807.*

Upon the verdict of final judgment by Emperor Bonaparte in consultation with his council of state, Monsieur St. Clair will be informed of his status as a citizen at liberty to hold property and pass freely within the boundaries of the French Empire. The citizen in question will not be permitted passage to lands or domains outside of the empire, and any travel within the boundaries of France are to be reported to the minister of police and the interior.

Undersigned,
Minister of Police and the
Interior Joseph Fouché

Jean-Luc turned the letter about, examining it as if it were the pistol to be used for his execution. He felt a strange fascination that this piece of nondescript parchment had just rendered his entire life's work null and void. He set the letter down and laughed—a bitter, morbid laugh. He turned, startled to see the servant who had delivered the note enter the drawing room. She informed him she'd come to check in on the master of the house. Jean-Luc thanked her, telling her he could manage on his own. Before dismissing her, Jean-Luc cleared his throat.

"Why was this letter brought to the servants' entrance and not to the front door?" he asked.

"Begging pardon, monsieur," she replied, "but it was under the orders of the lady of the house for all correspondence to be brought and taken via our domestics' entrance. I do apologize, senator."

The lady of the house. "It's all right," Jean-Luc replied, distractedly. "I am no longer a senator." As painful as it was to his pride, saying this aloud brought an odd feeling of relief. He no longer held any duty or obligation to the nation or the empire. *I don't know what I am*, he thought. "No longer a senator," he muttered. "Released from service; released from obligation and responsibility. An old man tottering into dotage, crawling back into infancy; the grave his bed in place of the cradle." This realization stung him. He looked up at the young lady, who wore an expression of grief, as if his sorrow were her own. "I'm sorry," he said. "You do not need to hear the dirges of a weary old man."

The woman smiled. "You're not *old*, monsieur. You've just had a bit of bad luck, is all. All will be set right in the end. I'm sure of it."

Moved by these words of encouragement, he looked away so she would not see his sadness. "Well," he said, summoning enough will to rise to his feet, "I suppose I will step out for a walk. No use in sitting here wallowing in gloomy thoughts. Thank you, Alice. You may go home. I can manage the rest of the day myself."

As he stood dressing in his bedroom, he heard a knock at the door. A few moments later, Alice entered, pausing at the door as if standing on a steep ledge. "My apologies for disturbing you, monsieur," she said, "but there is something I should tell you."

"Yes?" Jean-Luc replied as he finished tying his cravat.

"I suppose I should inform you that you have a fair bit of correspondence. Some written by your hand and some intended for you. I'm not supposed to be telling you this; we were instructed by the lady of the house that all letters were to be given to her. But, as I've been the only one 'round the house for nearly a fortnight now…"

Jean-Luc stopped adjusting his cravat and looked at Alice. "What did you say?"

She lowered her eyes. "I am sorry, monsieur. It wasn't my place. I've gone and…"

"Enough." Jean-Luc interrupted her. "What did you just say about the correspondence?"

Alice folded her hands together as she raised her eyes. "We were told to deliver all your correspondence to the lady of the house."

"I heard all that. Why—no, never mind why." He took a step toward Alice, grasping her hand in his. "What has been done to this correspondence that has not been delivered?"

Alice's eyes were now wide with fear. "She took it with her. I believe she took it, along with your daughter, and went to your estate in Sainte-Maure."

Jean-Luc's eyes narrowed. "Is there any still in this house?"

She fumbled with her apron and pulled out a small stack of envelopes. "These are those come since the lady left, monsieur."

Jean-Luc snatched the letters from her hand, rifling through to see the address on each. "Isabella," he said, the color draining from his face, "what have you done?"

* * *

A servant opened the door to Monsieur de Landreville's house, and Jean-Luc rushed in without declaring himself. He walked up the five flights of stairs and rushed past the marble busts and exotic plants into the drawing room.

"Julien-Henri?" he cried out, his voice echoing down the empty halls. "Monsieur de Landreville?" He looked around the room and felt the same sensation as when he had returned to his own residence after his long journey. It felt deserted. "Julien—" he called out again.

"He's not at home."

Jean-Luc swung around and saw a familiar face peering at him from behind a doorway. Lucille Laurent took several steps into the room. Jean-Luc tried to remember the last time he had seen her, suddenly recalling that it had been months ago, at his farewell party. That evening she had been wearing a formal dress. Now she was again wearing the plain dress of a caretaker. Despite his current lamentable circumstances, he nodded and smiled. "I was not aware. Pardon my intrusion."

"Is there something I may help you with, monsieur?" Lucille replied, setting a small bundle of linens on a table.

"I've come to ask something of your master. Will he be home anytime soon?"

For a few seconds Lucille said nothing, her gaze appearing distant. "Unfortunately, monsieur has fallen ill and has checked himself into the Hôtel-Dieu until he has sufficiently convalesced."

A mournful silence passed, and Jean-Luc scrambled to think of what he should do next. His mind brought no answers. "I am very sorry to hear that."

"Forgive my impertinence, monsieur," Lucille began, "but you look troubled."

Lucille motioned for him to be seated, but he politely declined. He cast a glance around the room. The Persian carpets in purple and red, the marble busts and portraits lining the walls, the grand piano: it all served as a sad reminder of what might have been. "I've just come to thank Monsieur de Landreville for all that he's done for me." Jean-Luc then told her of the letter incriminating him. "I am on my way to my former senatory to ensure that no further damage is done."

"I am very sorry, monsieur. It sounds as if you've become a casualty in a web of events beyond your control." The two of them stood in thoughtful silence for a moment, then: "While I wouldn't presume to tell you how to handle your business, is it not *your* property? Can you not do with it what you wish?"

"No, Lucille. They've taken everything."

"*Everything*," she said, with a hint of derision. "They have taken your title and the majority of your possessions—very sad. But what of the other things in your life, monsieur? What do you still have? You have your children. They need you now as much as ever. We'd be happy to look after your daughter here while you conclude your business."

"You would do that?" Jean-Luc asked.

"The marquis would do it," Lucille replied without hesitation. "I am caretaker in his stead—therefore, it is my duty. Go and confront that woman."

Another moment of silence fell on the room as Jean-Luc stared at a painting on the wall.

"Perhaps in another life she might have made a good wife, had I been able, or willing, to be a good husband."

"I don't see why you must shoulder the blame entirely, St. Clair."

Jean-Luc lifted his eyes to meet hers. "What do you mean?"

Lucille sighed as she squinted at him. "From the little I know of that woman, she may have no understanding of her own nature, but she does seem to understand others well enough. Perhaps when she met you, she became enamored by you, and yet knew in the end you would never truly love her, and that someday you would see the real her—and leave. That may be why she never fully gave herself to you; she feared that one day you would be gone, and wrecking you before you could leave her was the only thing she could do to convince herself that it was all your fault."

Jean-Luc took this all in, thinking to find some fault in her logic, but finally he admitted that there was truth in her words. He let out a tired sigh. "You may be right, mademoiselle, about all of it; but it's over now, so I suppose there's no use dwelling on it. However, I would like to apologize for how she treated you the night of the party. I was so caught up in my own appearance that I didn't think to come to your defense."

"I am a grown woman, monsieur; I need no one for my defense."

"All the same," Jean-Luc replied with a sad look, "at the time I found myself agreeing with you and everything you said—I still do. I must apologize for how you were treated."

"I accept your apology."

Jean-Luc put his gloves on and turned to leave. As he snatched his hat from under an arm he hesitated, he turned and looked at Lucille.

"Shouldn't you be going, senator?"

He placed his top hat on his head, "I am no longer a senator."

"Well *Monsieur* St. Clair," she replied, "I have not known you very long, but I do know that no man was ever great because of the title given to him. One ought to be judged by that part of himself that he gives to others. Senator or not, you can still do that."

Jean-Luc shook his head. "When I first met you, if you'll pardon my admission, I took you for an irritable housemaid."

Lucille picked up the bundle of linens. "I took you for a pompous fool." She offered him a rare smile.

Jean-Luc felt his spirits lift unexpectedly. He clasped his hands in front of him. "To faulty first impressions," he said, returning her smile.

Lucille rolled her eyes and nodded at the door. "Go retrieve your daughter, St. Clair."

He resolved to waste no more time. Upon returning home, he packed a light suitcase with a change of clothes and a small bundle of documents. He departed the following morning. Like his other amenities of luxury, his carriage and team had been confiscated by the government, so he hired a private team for the week. Two days later, he reached the countryside just outside the medieval city of Troyes, roughly ninety miles southeast of Paris. Jean-Luc recognized the land that bordered his property. The carriage passed alongside a railed fence and drove through a large stone gate onto the private drive and soon the chateau came into view. Having been to the property only once before, Jean-Luc fought to suppress an immense feeling of regret. They followed a winding path that passed beneath large oaks and around well-trimmed hedges. A handful of farmers and laborers looked up at him from the stables and outbuildings. Jean-Luc's selfish feelings of regret now turned into guilt; what new master would install himself here and lord over the lives of these humble folk whom he was unlikely to ever see again? Rounding a circular path, the carriage pulled to a halt. Jean-Luc climbed down and looked up at the chateau, which stood in stark contrast to the bleak winter landscape. It was an elegant, three-storied baroque house with a slanting roof of gray tile and a façade of yellow-painted stone. He climbed three steps and walked into the vestibule where a footman greeted him. The man had the trace of a foreign accent, perhaps Italian or Spanish. Although short, the man possessed broad shoulders and a square jaw, and carried himself with the bearing of a guard or soldier. He inspected Jean-Luc's appearance.

"I haven't come to pilfer the place—just retrieve my daughter," Jean-Luc said as the man eyed him with a suspicious glance. With one last appraising look, he turned and led Jean-Luc forward into the grand salon. In a far corner stood Isabella flanked by servants on either side. She wore a claret-colored dress beneath a black shawl that covered her shoulders. She was dictating a list of items to be packed away.

"The wash towels are to be placed in my second trunk," she said, her voice imperious, "along with the goose down and yellow tablecloths, and they will all travel in my carriage. In the *third* trunk, the brass serving trays will be packed with the candelabra from my chambers, along with the pewter mugs and primary silverware. The China tea set is to travel in the fourth trunk, and that will be all that goes with me. If there is no *delay*, the rest can follow behind with Matías, understood?" The servant taking down the orders replied in the affirmative while the other peered at Jean-Luc, drawing Isabella's attention. When her eyes met Jean-Luc's, she lifted her chin slightly. "Hello, St. Clair," she said evenly. "I wasn't expecting you until tomorrow."

"My regrets for any confusion," Jean-Luc said, removing his top hat. "But the time I have to visit my estate is rapidly drawing to a close." He cradled his hat in his hands and cast a glance around the room. It was largely empty save for the furniture, which was covered in white linen. "I see you've wasted little time in removing what you could."

"The senate served you with orders to vacate," she said, "along with requests for the title deed, building lease, scrip, and mortgage documents. I have ensured that they were completed and returned. I am retrieving the few possessions they have *not* relinquished to take them back to Paris so that they are not stolen. I do not think I deserve rebuke for it."

"No," Jean-Luc said wearily. "I have not come to castigate you for that."

Isabella stared at him. "You've come for your daughter?"

"Yes."

OWEN PATAKI

"Very well," she replied, motioning for the two attending servants to leave them. "She is next door in the antechamber, occupying herself with Camille."

Jean-Luc was hardly able to believe that after these many months he would finally have his daughter back safely in his care. He looked toward the doorway Isabella indicated. "How is she?" he asked, his pulse quickening.

Isabella held her hands out. "I imagine it is quite difficult for a child to manage so abrupt a change. How is anyone supposed to feel in times like this?"

"You appear to be doing well enough," he answered.

"Perhaps. Though it pains me to say it, I've seen you in better condition."

Jean-Luc laughed bitterly. "What on earth might've given you that impression?"

"The lines on your face and pouches under your eyes tell much of the story."

"Perhaps you might be good enough to fill in the details of the rest," he replied.

She ran a hand down her dress. "I haven't been entirely forthright with you."

"I'd come to a similar conclusion."

Isabella blinked slowly. "Are you aware that your daughter has an affinity for animals? You might prefer to blame me for your absence in your children's lives, but at the very least I took an interest in their pursuits. As her father, you might receive more gratitude should you do the same."

Jean-Luc looked at her with a face of stone. "It is rather difficult," he said at last, his voice disdainful but nevertheless under control, "to encourage the interests of a child who has been sent away without the consultation of her only surviving parent—circumstances orchestrated without my wish or consent. I have ridden here to retrieve her."

"You wished for her to be brought back home," Isabella replied flatly. "With you on the other end of the continent, where else would you have had me bring her?"

Jean-Luc waved away the question. "She is coming home. I no longer have professional duties to distract me from being the father I should be."

Isabella gave him a scornful look. "Let's not pretend that your ambitions have been thwarted by a sense of paternal duty, St. Clair. This latest thrashing you've suffered has likely only stoked that fire."

Jean-Luc checked himself from responding with anger, a feat that strained his self-control. He ran a hand through his hair, heedless of the satisfaction that he sensed she felt at this outward display of agitation. "Are you responsible for it, Isabella?" He motioned a hand around the empty room. "For all of this?" She moved her lips to speak, but he interrupted. "Why?" he asked, staring keenly into her eyes in an attempt to glean something of her thoughts. "It's too late now for me to salvage my career or reputation, but for the life of me I cannot understand why you would do such a thing?"

Mariette's voice could be heard from the adjoining room, cutting through the icy silence. Jean-Luc's features remained dour as he awaited a response.

"I understand this is a difficult time for you, Jean-Luc. I don't pretend to know how this will all turn out, but I always considered you to be an upright man. Blaming others for the inevitable misfortunes that follow your grandiose political ambitions is beneath you."

"There is nothing inevitable about what has happened to me," Jean-Luc seethed. "Rumors of your infidelity have spread like wildfire throughout Paris, the stack of letters you kept me from receiving—what did I do to deserve such betrayal from you?" He hoped to see guilt or remorse, but she stared back at him without emotion. Her silence was too much for the frustration he held within. "And the fact that Fouché conducted this ruinous orchestra—of that I have no doubt. What I wish to know, Isabella Maduro, is why you so willingly played to his tune? Why would you help facilitate my downfall? Was it greed? Envy? You tell me!"

His anger could no longer be restrained behind a mask of calm, and his last sentence came out in a shout that caused the footman to hurry into the room. He was quickly dismissed by the lady of the house.

"You have settled on your own conclusions," she said, "what purpose is there in asking me? I was hardly the only individual in Paris who saw your pending misfortunes, St. Clair. You offered yourself into the service of ravenous men, men who topple nations with one hand and build empires with the other; you had no idea who you were entangling yourself with, or perhaps you didn't want to know. I tried to manage, or at least restrain, your ambitions, yet you continued on your course without regard for anyone around you. In truth, though you'll despise me for saying as much, it was all selfish. But, if you must hear the uncomfortable truth, here it is—St. Clair, you are a very good man, but your flaws are as glaring as the Mediterranean sun. You adopt an air of humility, but in the depths of your heart you are as vainglorious as any preening general or marshal. You affect not to wish for praise or celebration…because deep down you covet it."

As he listened his cheeks reddened and his eyes blazed. He looked at her with the crazed smile of a drunkard. "You speak the truth," he admitted, his hands squeezing the rim of his hat so hard it bent upwards. "But no truth is absolute, and there is more to anyone than their triumphs and defeats. Take your own actions: heaping praise on me while plotting my ruin."

"Don't be absurd," Isabella retorted. "You know I celebrated your triumphs as if they were my own."

"And when triumph turned into defeat, you ran at the first opportunity," Jean-Luc scoffed. "Taking all I had built, while my world crashes down around me."

Isabella glared coldly at Jean-Luc. "In the last ten months you've spent perhaps two weeks at home, and you speak to me of running?"

"Do not continue to use misplaced guilt as a weapon against me. I traveled abroad, against my deepest wishes, at the *orders* of my emperor. *You?* You conspired with the minister of police to accuse me of treason."

At this accusation Isabella threw up her arms in exaggerated defiance. "How dare you?" Her eyes smoldered with long-dormant rage. "You accuse me of—"

"Oh, be quiet!" Jean-Luc snapped. Pulling a document out of the breast pocket of his coat, he lifted it and began reading, "*A collection of correspondence, a portion of which was allegedly written by Senator St. Clair himself, has been found which incriminates a group of no less than six individuals, all known and formerly convicted of crimes against the state. The parties in question have all been summoned to the estate of Senator St. Clair at Saint-Maure, for the purpose of discussing grievances shared by all members of the aforementioned conspiracy against his Imperial and Royal Majesty Napoleon Bonaparte.*"

He waved the paper at Isabella.

"You're so quick to blame me," Isabella retorted, "what a brave man you are to pin all of your failure and frustration on a woman! It was *you* who entered into league with Joseph Bonaparte, it was *you* who walked into the office of the police minister, and it was *you* to whom that creature directed his machinations."

"Do you think I wished to make the minister of police into my enemy? Joseph Bonaparte chose me as a friend, or at least led me to believe I—"

Jean-Luc's words caught in his throat; he coughed for several seconds, feeling a wave of dizziness pass over him. He drew a breath and continued, his voice calm, "I did not choose any of this."

"Well, it has chosen you," Isabella said, with no sympathy. "And it turns out that your little friend Lucille Laurent is not the person you wish her to be."

"What?" he asked. "What are you talking about?"

Isabella turned away from him, her eyes fixed on the wall before her. "I have heard of your visits to that woman."

"Visits to that woman?" he asked, incredulous. "I was referred to her master by *Fouché*, for a case that was resolved months ago."

Isabella would not turn to face him. "You accuse me of intriguing with the minister of police—well, you may deny you've had improper liaisons with that trollop, but perhaps you should be made aware that it is *she* who informs to him."

Jean-Luc frowned. For several seconds he considered the thought, at last shaking his head. "I don't believe you." He could hear the doubt in his own voice and knew she noticed.

"Doubt me if you wish," she replied. "But few of us remain the same person to all people. We all wear the guises life demands of us."

Jean-Luc shook his head wearily, turning his eyes back to her. "I'm through with your guiles, Isabella, and I pray that soon I will be through with you."

They looked at one another, perhaps for the last time. As he looked into her vindictive eyes, Jean-Luc could not deny that, despite his anger and hurt, he felt empathy for her.

"Goodbye, Isabella."

Pushing through the double doors, Jean-Luc stepped into the adjoining room, where he saw Camille seated on a plush sofa. Sitting next to him in a dress of blue and white stripes was his daughter. She turned her eyes from the jar of insects she had been examining and looked up at him; he had to choke back a cry. After a moment of tense silence, Camille gently placed the jar on the sofa and folded his hands. Mariette looked at Jean-Luc before slowly standing. The little girl ran into her father's arms with tears on her face. Jean-Luc tried stammering a few words of comfort to the sobbing girl, but his words caught in his throat. Even Camille, who had been looking at Jean-Luc with a cold stare, allowed his lips to part in an uncharacteristic display of emotion.

"I'm sorry, my darling," Jean-Luc said, tears running down his face. "I'm so, so sorry."

Mariette, her face burrowed into her father's coat, said nothing. For several minutes they embraced, and then Camille quietly stood up and walked several paces away, allowing them their heartfelt reunion in peace. When they had wiped the tears from their faces, Jean-Luc looked over at the boy, signaling a hand that it was all right to return. He shook his head, and it was Mariette who walked over to the confused boy and offered him a long embrace, which seemed to soothe his discomfort. Together, father and daughter walked into the main hall. Jean-Luc bid farewell to the servants, apologizing to Camille for Marie's abrupt departure. With a smile, Jean-Luc took Mariette's hand and the two walked out the front door.

CHAPTER 47

Ordensburg Castle, Northern Prussia

January 1807

I t was on a cold, cloudy morning that the man known as Monsieur Louis d'Aubert, Count de Chambrun, passed with his retinue under the looming portcullis of the fortress of Ordensburg. Originally named the Castle of the Teutonic Order of Marienburg, it was a massive compound built in the Medieval Gothic style with pointed, red-tiled roofs and long brick walls marked by stout towers and turrets. The Knights of the Teutonic Order of Holy Mary in Jerusalem had built it as a buffer against the pagan Prussians, and not unlike the wars of Napoleon, the Poles found themselves wedged in the blood-soaked borderland straddling east and west. Making their way over cobblestones and into the castle's courtyard, the horsemen rode past half a dozen carriages, whose wheels and axles received the mud and small stones churned up by the entourage. The riders accompanying the count turned their attention toward a cluster of people emerging from a small door on the far end of the courtyard. A dozen friars and sisters walked slowly with their heads bowed, behind a priest—a tall, thin man with a balding head that served as a natural tonsure.

"Welcome," he called out in German. "I am Bishop Friedrich, senior pastor of this community. We are happy to receive all visitors who come in peace." He bowed his head humbly.

The count, wearing a blue coat with a fur collar, long black boots, and clean white breeches, sat atop an impressive white mare. The animal's saddle was draped with a leopard-skin shabraque. The count shifted his weight as one of his attendants translated the bishop's words into French. Through his servant, the count replied that he was happy to have arrived after so long a journey, and he offered thanks in advance for the bishop's hospitality. He then dismounted from his horse, prompting his attendants to do the same, and dropped to a knee in front of the bishop.

"We give thanks, father," the count's translator spoke, "for offering weary travelers shelter in our time of need. All those who oppose Napoleon are united, bound by the blood of their struggle and their faith in God and his church."

The bishop blessed the count and gently lifted his chin, urging him to stand. The count then bowed once more before following Bishop Friedrich as he led the visitors across the courtyard. The nuns, friars, and armed guards of the count followed at a distance. Their boots squished in the brown snow as they walked, and the bishop grasped his visitor by his sleeve, steering him around a large puddle. "You are welcome here," he said in a low voice, "but it is our understanding that Napoleon's soldiers are only a few miles away."

"It will be a short visit, father," the count replied, his spurs clinking as he walked along the soggy footpath.

The bishop ushered the count and his party through a long hallway ribbed with pointed arches along the ceiling and checkered red-and-white tiles on the floor. They passed through a small chapel and entered into the "Knights Hall," where during the Middle Ages Knights of the Teutonic Order would meet in torchlight to sing hymns of praise and draw up plans for war against their enemies in Prussia and Poland. The bishop then guided them down a stone stairwell that opened into a large chamber that served as the castle's cellar and storeroom.

The air felt cool and damp, and the flames from several torches suspended at intervals along the walls augmented the pale light that entered through the narrow windows in the corners of the room. Gothic arches made of brick crisscrossed the ceiling, converging just over the visitors' heads. The flickering torchlight was enough to illuminate the room; nevertheless, everyone present sensed that they stood in a solemn space largely undisturbed by the ravages of time. One by one, as their eyes adjusted, they gaped at the sight before them; visible in this eerie glow were several dozen large oak casks along either side of the hall, stacked one on top of another, taller than the height of a man. The count, moved by the sight, took a few steps toward the closest barrel and turned to the bishop as if to say, "May I?" The bishop nodded.

"It is said, father," the count said as he approached the nearest barrel, "that war claims the lives of those most filled with life. And yet, as one ennobled, I cannot reasonably deny that at the same time it raises the fortunes of others to new heights. Look at me, a count born to a house elevated by the king centuries ago, forced to flee like a rat from the hold of a ship. Fleeing from Bonaparte, a man sprung from base stock, hardly above that of Corsican bandits; the very man who now rules an empire greater than that of the Caesars." He turned quickly, eyeing the bishop. "These unpredictable twists of fate that only ever come from the wellsprings of violence—war and revolution—they are part of the divine plan, are they not? Surely as a man of God you cannot deny the truth of this?"

"I cannot answer for the Lord's divine plan," the bishop replied. "But I pray that if war finds us, here in a house of peace, it will come swiftly and depart just the same."

The count crouched down on his haunches, running a hand across the oak of the barrel in front of him. A clatter of footsteps was heard, and a moment later several of the count's men entered the room carrying hammers, bars, and other tools. The count stood and nodded to his men. He made one turn around the room, surveying the barrels. "You would not be troubled," he asked, turning back to the bishop, "if we opened some of your barrels?"

"It would be ungracious for a host providing shelter to refuse his guests his wine," the bishop answered.

"Thank you," the count replied, motioning to his followers.

"However, it would be equally ungracious of me, monsieur," Bishop Friedrich continued, "if I failed to share a piece of information, which I find rather curious."

"And pray, what information is that?"

"Well, monsieur. You wear the attire and speak with the etiquette of a French count. But I confess I find this strange, as a man arrived at our gates yesterday afternoon claiming that he was a French count, also called Chambrun." The count raised his head slightly, lifting a hand for his men to cease their work. "So, I can only surmise that one of you is who he says he is, and the other is an impostor."

The count threw back his shoulders, letting his fur coat fall to the floor. He wore the uniform of a cavalryman, a curved saber hung at his side.

"Very well, priest," the man said in a cold voice. "I am no count. There, you have *my* confession." If the bishop felt surprise at the man's martial attire, he betrayed no sign. "But I tell you that whether by force or consent, I am leaving with the contents of these barrels."

"If you treasure what is inside so much," the bishop answered, "then it is yours."

With that, the man who no longer claimed to be Louis d'Aubert, Count de Chambrun, signaled to one of his companions to break open the nearest barrel. The man heaved back and began hammering at the chime that enclosed the top of the barrel. When the steel hoops had been removed, the panels abruptly fell away and, like a bursting dam, the contents of the barrel spilled out onto the cold cement floor. The red cascade caused everyone in the room to step back several paces; everyone except Bishop Friedrich and the cavalryman, who peered down at the wine flowing around his boots with a bemused expression.

"Tell me, bishop," the man said, the wine splashing beneath his boots as he stepped slowly toward his host. "Why is there wine in this barrel when I was made to believe that something far more valuable lay within?"

The two men faced each other while the others inched backwards to the walls. The wine settled around the two men's feet in a crimson pool that flickered as it caught reflections from the torches on the walls.

"I do not know to what you refer, Monsieur le Count."

"No?" the cavalryman asked, resting a hand on the hilt of his saber. "I find that difficult to believe, bishop."

"No, monsieur," the bishop replied evenly. "A representative from Königsberg paid a visit to our parish just over a week ago, informing us that an émigré count and his retinue would be traveling north toward Danzig to avoid Napoleon's troops. We were instructed to welcome the party and provide shelter if needed. The train of carriages that you have seen waiting outside in the courtyard arrived two days ago, along with these barrels. We were informed that this was a gift for aiding an ally of the Kingdom of Prussia in a time of war. We welcomed the gift gladly, though we did not ask for it."

The count eyed the bishop with a cold expression. "You have not inspected the content of these barrels?'

"We presumed wine barrels contained wine, monsieur," the bishop replied.

The cavalryman stood motionless for several moments before emitting a burst of shrill laughter. He turned to his companions, some of whom returned his smile with confused smiles of their own. Behind the bishop the friars and monks whose faces were visible exchanged frightened looks, though a few of the monks kept their faces concealed beneath their hoods.

"Very well, bishop," the cavalryman said at last, "we do apologize for robbing you of so great a quantity of wine." He motioned for his men to begin the task of opening the rest of the barrels. "But surely you understand that, as a matter of national security, we shall inspect these barrels, and then we will go and have a look at the carriages in the courtyard."

"Inspect them for what?" the bishop asked.

"For something more valuable than wine," an unfamiliar voice called out. The friars and nuns turned abruptly around to see a man standing on the stairwell. His torso was concealed in shadow. Only his boots were visible. He took several slow steps and emerged into the flickering crimson light. "We've been waiting for you, major." André's boots splashed as he took several steps toward Carnassier, cocking a pistol in his right hand. "True to form, you arrive with style and élan, but I'm afraid you will not find what you've come for."

"Ah, it is you, Valiere!" Carnassier cried out in genuine surprise. "I was wondering when I might see you again."

"Yes, major," André replied, leveling his pistol. "I've come to stop you."

Carnassier replied with a shrug, his pelisse dangling from his shoulder. "I must have left quite an impression to still occupy your thoughts, colonel. Do you dream of me at night, too?"

André's two troopers entered the room with bayonets fixed to their muskets. They were followed by a handful of men from the local village, who carried pistols or fire pokers. They trained their weapons on the major and his men.

"I see you've brought your brave troopers with you. Please lads, show mercy." Carnassier held his hands in mock surrender. "Are you here at the behest of your executive officer? He was so angry to hear my subordinate planned to have his way with that pretty little Polish girl. Alderic is likely tossing her in the hay right now, that scoundrel." André kept his eyes on Carnassier. "Nothing to say? Very well, if you're becoming nervous, then I'll take control of this little situation."

"My executive officer," André said, "can handle his business."

"The thing is, colonel," Carnassier said, ignoring André, "I haven't come all this way to be stopped. Not by you, not by this bishop. But, before any blood is spilt, I will give you one chance to lower your weapons and depart."

"We've already trained our muskets on your men outside; any move against me or my men and they will die."

Carnassier hesitated and, for a moment, André thought his bluff might succeed, but then Carnassier smiled. "This war has changed you, Valiere. When I first set eyes upon you and your men, I felt as one who has chanced upon a drowning child, arms flailing, head barely above water." Carnassier put a hand to his throat and made a choking sound. "Ha ha. Oh, but now? Ah, Valiere, I'll admit you've finally learned how to at least *act* the part of a soldier."

André did his best not to betray any irritation. "Stall if you like, major; it won't make a difference."

"Stalling? No, my friend. I'd call this a moment of amusement between old friends fated to become tragic enemies. And it will be the last, for you and I both know you have no one waiting on the walls for my men. In fact, if I were you, I'd be wondering if I haven't sent *my* men in to secure the grounds before I arrived to prevent any such mischief, especially given the *treasure* we're both after. Oh, Valiere, one might've hoped you had learned to stop wandering into ambushes."

Carnassier turned to André's men, who were aiming their muskets on Carnassier's hussars. "We're all countrymen here, lads," he called out in a friendly voice, motioning for the men to lower their arms. "Why not come to an agreement that we all find suitable? Should a few hundred thousand pounds go missing from so great a haul, who would be any the wiser?"

"I took you for one to be above pleading and bribing, major." André reached down with his left hand and unsheathed his sword. "Why not settle this as men? I will gladly walk ten paces with you by sword or pistol."

Carnassier held out both arms in a gesture of supplication. "There will be no duel today."

"Very well," André said. "But we all know you are no count—tell the bishop who you really are."

Carnassier's eyes narrowed. He motioned for his men to lower their tools, which they clutched with twitching fingers. "No violence today," he shouted, his voice tinged with a hint of growing frustration.

"Tell us what your true purpose is here, major."

"Take that up with this one here," Carnassier said, nodding toward the bishop. André turned his eyes away, and that was all it took. Carnassier sprang at the bishop with a quickness that startled even André, shoving him to the ground. André leveled his pistol but checked himself as Carnassier crashed into the crowd of frightened monks and nuns. André lost his mark in the mass of shouting and shuffling bodies before seeing a glint of drawn steel. As the group of bystanders dispersed on their hands and knees, André noticed one of the sisters, her hands trembling at her sides and terror visible in her wide eyes. Standing behind her was Carnassier, his saber held across her throat.

"You see what fear you've brought to these innocent folk, Valiere?"

"Shut up," André growled.

Carnassier tugged the habit from the elderly sister, revealing a messy crop of tangled brown hair. Her eyes bulged wide in terror, and tears streamed down her cheeks. One of the monks slipped away up the stairs behind André.

"I warned you that this war would turn you into something different, Valiere," Carnassier hissed. "A different war for different soldiers. Your kind is out of place here." He shuffled back, dragging the woman with him.

"It's all right, sister," André said in a low voice.

The woman sobbed loudly, and Carnassier tugged at her hair. "Shut up." He took several short steps back, his boots shuffling on the cement as he stepped away from the spilled wine. He glanced at one of his men. "What are you waiting for, you cowards? Kill him!"

After a brief moment of hesitation, the hussars raised their tools and bellowed angrily. They took no more than two or three steps before several shots rang out, filling the room with a smoky mist that lingered for a few seconds before dissipating across the cellar. One of the men who had not been hit charged André but was impaled in his ribs by the bayonet of one of André's troopers. André leapt past the dying hussar and ran after Major Carnassier, who had vanished in the smoke.

André climbed the stairs at the opposite end of the cellar, gaining three or four steps with each bound. He held his sword over his head, ready for the major to spring out at him. One of his men trailed a few paces behind, bayonet at the ready. The other trooper was escorting the civilians to safety.

When he reached the top of the stairs he paused, glancing in either direction. He continued ahead cautiously, motioning for his trooper to watch behind them as they moved along the hall to the left. They passed several doors, all locked, and continued down the narrow corridor until they arrived at an arched doorway that led out to the courtyard. André looked out and saw nothing amiss, so he ordered his trooper to check down the hall that led right while he continued slowly along the corridor. After several paces, he heard muffled shouts only a few feet away behind a large door. André opened the door and peered inside. Huddled together in a corner was a group of frightened friars and sisters. Carnassier stood with his pistol trained on them.

"After I've burned down those carriages, I'll burn this castle; would you prefer that?"

André swung the door open with no more pretext of stealth, aiming his pistol at Carnassier. "Let them go, major," he said, shuffling slowly into the room. "This is between us. These people have done nothing."

"Nothing?" Carnassier lowered his pistol nonchalantly. "They harbor the known enemies of our emperor, of France, smuggling a fortune through our lines using treachery and deceit, and you say they've done *nothing?*"

"They're only doing what their masters have instructed."

"As am I," Carnassier replied with a hint of grievance.

"These people do not deserve this cruelty."

"Lieutenant-Colonel Valiere, *bringer of light to the children of men,*" Carnassier declared in a mocking tone. He turned his pistol back on the group. "You say I am cruel because I pursue my own designs without the burdens of shame or remorse. Did the man we call emperor feel remorse when he slaughtered royalists to advance his own ambitions? Should he apologize to the generals he defeats or the nations he conquers? Would they not conquer him if they were able? What is life but a primordial struggle for survival in an indifferent world?"

"Is that what you tell yourself, Carnassier?" André replied. "To justify working for Fouché *and* Napoleon, as if you'd be able to play one against the other once you've captured the fortune?" André laughed, exasperated. "Did you truly think you could find so great a haul and keep it a secret? Perhaps your aims *are* as mad as they appear."

"Who are you to condemn me?" Carnassier cried in a savage voice. The hostages, already cowed, crouched lower to the ground. "Tell me, righteous Lieutenant-Colonel Valiere, you sprung from noble stock, raised from birth to believe the world belongs to you—are you so different?"

André's face remained impassive as he exhaled wearily. "Years from now," he replied, "if I survive this war, I will see the faces of my children and my wife. I will see the lives that I've helped grow and be happy. That will be sufficient. You will always be hunting for a fortune beyond your reach—that you can never reach—left to die alone with nothing and no one but your own insatiable desires. Yes, you and I are quite different."

Carnassier glared at him. After a moment of consideration, he grinned, his eyes squinting. "Valiere, you really are a simpleton. You truly think I've come all this way on some romantic *treasure hunt*?" André kept a tight grip on his pistol, stealing a look to either side of him in case the major had some last trick to play. Carnassier laughed. "I will be *rewarded* with a marshal's baton, with dukedoms and lands, here in the east. The Grand Duchy of Warsaw will be my fiefdom, and everyone therein will fall under my command. Until these Poles have emerged from their backward superstitions, they will not be worthy of nationhood. Frankly, it is absurd to think otherwise. Napoleon is fooling himself if he thinks he can bestow upon a child what ought be exercised by a man. Liberty and equality are laudable ideals, in theory, but only where liberty has fertile soil and where equality is possible. Poles? Russians? Equals to Frenchmen? Tell me: Is a mule the equal of a stallion just because one claims it so?"

"You talk of war raising the fortunes of some, major," André said, his voice adopting a tone he might use when speaking to one of his sons. "But your pride has taken hold of you, and, sure as anything, it will devour you. I don't hate you, but a small part of me does pity you."

Carnassier swung his pistol at André. "Take your pity to the grave then, coward." A shot rang out. Before André had time to pull the trigger, Carnassier's body jerked violently, then slumped to the floor. One of the monks, his face concealed by his cowl, approached the body. He reached down and poked the ribs to confirm that Carnassier was dead. Picking up the major's pistol the man said with a sigh, "The fortune was not meant for you, old boy." He then pulled back his hood and turned to André, holding out the pistol. "A war trophy, colonel?"

André, still half-dazed by the jarring turn of events, shook his head. "No, Monsieur Hackett. It is yours."

CHAPTER 48

Saint-Germain, Paris

January 1807

After their return to Paris, the weeks passed in quiet tranquility for Jean-Luc and Mariette. Their days were spent strolling along the Seine, feeding the fish in the ponds at the public gardens, and watching dancers and marionettes. Every so often a passerby would recognize Jean-Luc and call out, "The hero of Naples!" and Mariette would squeeze his hand, old enough now to appreciate her father's level of erstwhile success. But Jean-Luc could never fully dispel a secret suspicion that it was said in mockery. He bought her a parakeet and a pair of kittens, one of which wandered out the front door of their house one morning and never returned. Nevertheless, Jean-Luc's efforts at sharing and encouraging her interests, especially her fascination with animals, seemed to be paying off. As far as he could tell, the little girl was happy.

Mariette often asked about Mathieu, and Jean-Luc would tell her that he had left to be a soldier for Napoleon. Her older brother's martial pursuits seemed of little interest to her, and she would scowl whenever she saw a procession of horsemen or national guard troops march past. One cold morning as they walked through the Tuileries garden, Mariette again asked, "Where is Mathieu, Papa?"

"He's gone to be a soldier," Jean-Luc replied patiently, as they strolled along a row of lime trees. His cough had continued intermittently, and he

held a gloved hand to his throat as he wheezed into it. He tried to recall how
the park looked when the flowers were in bloom and the trees were flush
with green leaves and shiny red apples, but his memory failed him; all he
could see were gnarled branches reaching up toward the dreary winter sky.

"So, he's brave?"

"Yes, I suppose he is."

She turned her head away, looking at a group of boys as they chased
each other around carrying toy muskets under their arms. "Then he'll die
like the rest of them."

Jean-Luc said nothing for a moment, his heels crunching a pile of leaves.
He smiled down at her. "No," he said with as much resolution as he could
manage. "He'll be all right."

When they returned home, Jean-Luc noticed that a long-awaited letter
had arrived. He helped Mariette out of her winter coat and started a small
fire, sitting down on one of the remaining sofas. He had come to accept that
in all likelihood their days in the house were numbered, so he'd sold most
of the furniture to his neighbors or given it to his servants, who rarely came
to the house anymore. Before he opened the letter, he gazed at the unmistakable crest of Joseph Bonaparte, now king of Naples. For a moment he
allowed himself to hope that the letter might contain some miraculous news
for him. The letter did, in fact, begin with news that reassured him significantly, but, as he read further, his face sagged, and eventually he stopped
reading altogether, letting the paper fall to the floor.

Monsieur St. Clair,

*I write to you in a troubled mood as I have received no reply,
apart from your most recent brief inquiry, to any of the previous letters I've sent you. I hope you are managing yourself
as well can be hoped for, given your difficult circumstances.
As per your request several weeks ago, I have spoken with
Napoleon and owing to his present engagements in Poland
he has granted me complete discretion as to the removal of
the restrictions imposed upon you by the minister of police.
As of today, you are officially permitted to pass freely within
the boundaries of France and the lands within the empire,
with no restrictions or conditions upon your liberty or status*

as a free citizen. So you need not fear imprisonment or worry about your family.

Unfortunately, I have received confirmation from the senate that the revocation of your rank, titles, and honors remains, and that any possessions or properties bestowed by the emperor have passed permanently back into possession of the government. I am sorry, my friend.

As to your second question, I've had a rather difficult time obtaining the information you requested, but after a thorough search, circumventing the network of the police minister, which greatly narrowed the field, I have learned of several details concerning the former Marquis de Landreville and his household. First, the man is in fact deathly ill, and his doctors are not sure how much time he has left. But to your specific inquiry, I have learned of a rather convoluted network involving the former marquis, Fouché, and the agents the police minister utilizes within the social circles of the Saint-Germain. As the story goes, there is a young woman—in fact the very same to whom you had alluded in your previous letter—who is alleged to be an informant to the police minister from within the marquis's household. The evidence indicates that she provides information to Fouché directly regarding the "aristocratic mood" of the Saint-Germain quarter. As to what particular kind of information she has conveyed I have so far been unable to ascertain, but to all appearances she is a woman who shows one face to her master and another to her employer. So, if you have cause for any further engagements at the residence of the marquis, I would advise you to avoid any potentially incriminating conversation in the presence of this double-dealing woman.

If I come into any further details, I will be sure to keep you informed, as those of us who have come to know you all agree that you have been dealt a rather unforgiving hand, and you are not the treasonous criminal some have painted you to be.

*If I can offer any further assistance, I will do all that distance,
duty, and my brother allow me to do.*

*Your friend,
J. Bonaparte
Vive l'Empereur.*

For several minutes Jean-Luc sat still, staring into the flickering fire.
He had felt considerable relief knowing that he would not be arrested or
separated from his family, but that relief was quickly dashed, as Jean-Luc
had allowed himself to hope, irrespective of his professional circumstances,
that Lucille Laurent might one day become a friend to him, perhaps someday more. This latest information had snatched that one ray of hope from
him. The thought of Lucille Laurent, so direct and unyielding, informing
to a scheming man like Fouché struck Jean-Luc a blow to the gut. With a
grimace, he picked up the letter and threw it into the flames, yet another
misfortune to add to his string of disappointments. After the paper had
blackened, burned, and vanished up the chimney in a coil of smoke, he
walked to the pantry and took out a bottle of wine and quickly drank its
contents. Half an hour or so later, he repeated the act and eventually fell into
a sleep on the sofa in his evening clothes.

$$\ast \quad \ast \quad \ast$$

A week later, Jean-Luc was startled by several muffled knocks at the front
door. A few minutes earlier he had given his consent for his daughter to play
with some of the children next door, and now he wondered if they might
have gotten into trouble. He wiped his face, threw on a shirt without but-
toning it, and trudged downstairs. When he opened the door, he saw standing in front of him someone he could not have expected, and, in spite of his
low spirits and ragged appearance, he smiled warmly. The visitor stepped
inside, and Jean-Luc led them into the drawing room.

"Well, it is quite a lovely house," Sophie said diplomatically.

Jean-Luc had hardly noticed the unpleasant odor until that moment,
and his face tightened in an apologetic expression. Strewn about the floor
and on tabletops was the evidence of his domestic disrepair: bottles, cups
and saucers, breadcrumbs, dirty handkerchiefs, unwashed clothes. With his

servants no longer employed, the ground floor had taken on a smell; one that mingled with the smoke from the fireplace and wafted throughout the rest of the house. Sophie glanced politely at the paintings on the walls and out the windows, avoiding the wreckage on the floors and tables, but, from the look on her face, Jean-Luc sensed that he had allowed his neglect to go too far.

His offered her a seat on a sofa across from him. She wore a dark-gray riding cloak around her shoulders, beneath it a gray sweater and white riding pants. "I am sorry, Sophie. Truly, I can't hide my embarrassment. If I had known you were coming I—"

"It's quite all right. I came unannounced," she interjected. "Besides, I oversee an estate and have two boys of my own. It's nothing I haven't seen before."

Jean-Luc smiled, no less embarrassed but appreciative of her courtesy. "Well, thank you. The house now suffers from want of a woman's touch." He cast his eyes around the room with a sigh. Sophie smiled graciously but remained silent, allowing him to choose which direction he wished to take the conversation. "It once belonged to a nobleman from Tours," he resumed. "A lord who was a cousin to the Duke of Orleans. The day I purchased it, I marveled at the remarkable turn of fate that allowed a lawyer from humble stock to take ownership of such a place. But now it looks as though it will soon pass on to another. Perhaps a nobleman; changing hands from a republican revolutionary who was unable to retain it, returning once again to the noble class for which it had originally been built." Jean-Luc looked at Sophie with a sad smile. "A house whose destiny mirrors that of its country, hm?"

"Do you have plans to sell it?"

"Do I plan to sell it?" Jean-Luc glanced around the room. "No. Well, I have no current buyers offering, but the way things are going they won't have need to offer."

"I'm not sure I understand you; what has happened?"

Jean-Luc would have laughed if a fit of coughing hadn't struck first. Sophie found her way to the kitchen and returned with a glass of water. Jean-Luc nodded his thanks and took several long gulps. "Thank you," he said, out of breath. He finished the water and set the glass down. "It's this damned grippe; I've had it ever since traveling east. It is quite cold in Poland, as you might imagine."

"You were in Poland?" Sophie asked, her concern evident. "I had no idea you'd made such a voyage. Was this duty with the senate?"

"Yes, yes," Jean-Luc replied with a wave of the hand. "We went to discuss the treaties being signed, to assist the locals in drafting something of a constitution. Mostly formalities and diplomatic ho-hum. But I did come across a certain lieutenant-colonel of dragoons."

"You saw André?" Sophie's eyes widened and she leaned forward. "How is he? Is he all right?"

Jean-Luc nodded. "He is fine. He appeared reasonably well-fed and in good spirits with his band of loyal horsemen following him and obeying his every command. Though before we said our farewell, he did inform me of a certain difficulty involving a rival officer and his men."

Sophie did not speak for several seconds, and Jean-Luc gave her a careful look before continuing. "I will not trouble you with all of the details, but—"

"You *must*. Jean-Luc, you must tell me everything." She took a moment to gather herself. "I'm sorry, I don't mean to make demands of you. Clearly you've been dealing with difficult circumstances that I know nothing about. I just miss my husband and worry for his safety."

Jean-Luc folded his hands together, his brow furrowing as he collected his thoughts. He told her of André's unexpected entanglement with Major Carnassier, explaining how he had intercepted the correspondence from Minister Fouché to Carnassier by bribing the courier, and how he had conveyed what he knew to André by semaphore about the Hesse-Cassel fortune being moved to Danzig.

"And that was the last word I sent to André," Jean-Luc concluded. "If indeed he received the message."

After taking it all in, Sophie sighed. "That is André," she admitted. "Plunging in to help others even at great danger to himself. As if war weren't dangerous enough." She sat back in her seat and covered her face with a hand. "Oh, André, why can't you keep your nose out of trouble?"

Jean-Luc placed a reassuring hand on her shoulder. "I understand your concern, Sophie," he said. "I assure you that the men serving alongside your husband are as brave as any I've ever seen, and I have no doubt that they are capable of handling themselves—whatever the danger. If André can survive a march across Egypt, he can manage his business in Prussia and Poland."

Sophie lifted her head, returning Jean-Luc's strained smile. "Thank you," she said, wiping a tear with her sleeve. "It helps me more than I can say to know that you have seen him and he is well. Forgive me for my weakness."

Jean-Luc brushed aside her apology. He went to the kitchen and brought out a tray of tea with a meager breakfast for the two of them. For several minutes they talked of their children and the difficulties they both shared in raising them on their own. After they finished the meal, the conversation returned to their present circumstances. Sophie listened with unconcealed astonishment as Jean-Luc informed her of his recent fall from political favor, as well as his troubles with Isabella.

"Is it an irrational fear," Jean-Luc mused, "to think that she detested my children as rivals for my own affection? So she tried to remove, or at least lessen, their role in our lives?" Sophie appeared uncomfortable at this line of questioning, but Jean-Luc rose to his feet and, after a minor fit of coughing, continued speaking, his voice taking on the tone he might use before a jury or body of his senate peers. "I never set out to hurt her," he exclaimed, "or anyone. We try to do well by others, and we hurt ourselves. So we try to do well for ourselves, and we harm those we care about most. At times, I've felt as if life is just some parlor game designed to thwart and obstruct you; the obstacles change, but never cease to appear—as if the entire world conspired against happiness. One's existence nothing but a meaningless object to be harried and chased into submission, so the game can begin again with some-one else in the unhappy role of fox fleeing for the amusement of the hunter." He sat back down, his mind racing as he forced himself to catch his breath, which came in quick bursts. He looked at Sophie, who eyed him with deep concern. His energy spent, he dropped his eyes to the floor. "I'm sorry," he said. When his breath had calmed, he rubbed a hand through his hair. "I am sorry to lay all of my troubles at your feet, but I see little in myself of which to be proud. My career has been scuttled by vengeful enemies, my family has been torn apart by a vengeful woman, and now everything I've worked for seems to be lying in ruins. Perhaps it is all finished."

At this last remark Sophie cast a sharp glance at her friend. "Jean-Luc St. Clair," she said in a pointed voice, the same one she used on her children when they misbehaved. "I see rather plainly that you are unhappy, and for that I am sorry. But I must confess to you that I do not approve of your end-less self-reproach. Frankly, I find it pitiable." Jean-Luc's eyebrows raised, but he did not interrupt her. "For God knows what reason you blame yourself for things beyond your control. You see life only in terms of what you have failed to accomplish, or still have yet to do, all the while ignoring or dismissing all that you *have* accomplished: a rise marked by perseverance against terrible odds, a second career marked by fortune and fame. Most importantly, you've provided a life for your family with possibilities unthinkable to you when you were their age. And you've done it all practically on your own. If you could manage to appreciate the good in your life and see what you mean to those who love you, you might find real happiness again."

Jean-Luc heard the truth in her words, but even as his mind worked to see the potential for something to hold to, something to work for, his thoughts turned back to the image at the root of his pain and he shook his head. "I was married to the woman of my dreams," he said. "And she died. I tried to move on, Sophie, I truly did…" His voice trailed off, and he lifted his hands in the air.

"During the Revolution," Sophie replied, "when you and your family offered me shelter, I enjoyed our talks tremendously. Listening to you and Marie speaking and sharing your passion for politics was always an enjoyable way of passing the time. I felt I could learn something, and your enthusiasm was shared by all in your presence. But life has a way of changing us, and perhaps it is my unfair perspective, knowing all that you've endured these years, but I can't help notice that the earnest and humble enthusiasm with which you used to converse, even in debate, has been replaced by a selfish cynicism. And it makes me sad." Jean-Luc looked up and, to his distress, saw tears in Sophie's eyes. "Jean-Luc, I've come all this way to tell you something. Your friends are in trouble; *I* am in trouble, and I need your help."

She informed him of de Montfort's machinations, about the slanderous article and the count's latest hostility toward her. "And now," she explained in a trembling voice, "I've learned that this villainous count has sent a pair of Gypsies to spy on me, only they've been accused of murdering one of the poor outlanders that I sent to the count's estate. My steward believes that the count's chamberlain paid them to attack the outlander men, only they took it too far and killed one of them by accident, and now they've fled to my land. Monsieur Le Bon, my steward, always seems to know more than I about transpiring events; I really don't know if I can continue to place my trust in him. Anyway, I don't know what to make of any of it. It's all become a terrible mess."

Her head drooped, and Jean-Luc stared at her. After a long silence, he cleared his throat. "You don't deserve any of these troubles; I am sorry,

Sophie, I truly am. But look around…I've lost everything, and I'm barely holding myself together as is." Tears welled in his eyes. "There is nothing I can do to help you."

The pain on Sophie's face was evident. She bit her lip, nodding stoically as she stood to her feet. "Many years ago," she said after she had wrapped her riding cloak about her, "when I had everything taken from me and fled in fear from my uncle and his pack of fanatics, you and your family took me in. You saved my life. Your *true* friends, André and I, will always support you; not like others, who are happy to exploit your success and then drag you down when they fear it will take you from them." Her thoughts drifted back many years; the Revolution had pushed everything and everyone she knew to the edge of a terrifying abyss, and yet, somehow, they had survived. "I once heard it said," she continued, "that in times of crisis a strong man sees a trial to be met and overcome, while a weak man sees only inevitable defeat. I once knew you to be a strong man, Jean-Luc. I pray you remember that before it is too late."

CHAPTER 49

Ordensburg Castle, Northern Prussia

January 1807

André stared vacantly at a frozen puddle nearby as the falling snow-flakes piled on its surface. Beside him stood Bishop Friedrich, who had done all he could to quell the panic caused by Carnassier's assault on the parish. Still, some of the brothers and sisters eyed the visitors with a suspicion that was only heightened by the distant rumble of cannons.

Hackett had removed his monk's cloak and once again wore the black and green of his Silesian uniform as he conferred with André. "It appears that the only cargo these wagons are taking north to Danzig are flour, barley, salted meats, a barrel of herring, and a half-dozen barrels of ale."

André kicked a clump of snow. The day before he had played the part of French nobleman, le Count de Chambrun, with all of the grace and pomposity of his noble birthright, going as far as mouthing a few phrases in Latin cursing Napoleon. Under this pretext they'd convinced the bishop that Carnassier was a dangerous rogue who sought the content of the barrels for himself. The day's events had convinced the bishop unequivocally that Carnassier was, in fact, the violent man they had claimed him to be, but Andrè and his men had also given the bishop clear cause to second-guess their intentions. Their current appearance indicated that their small group was *not* the entourage of a highborn émigré fleeing Napoleon's armies. Furthermore, their lack of concern at the sound of French guns hinted that they were not truly fleeing to Danzig, nor did they show any interest in the gifted barrels of wine, several of which they had opened at random.

Bishop Friedrich conversed in German with Hackett, who did his best to answer the clergyman's questions. "Well," Hackett said at last, "he claims to know nothing of this fortune at all."

André had a decision to make: he could return to his men—who were either engaged or soon-to-be engaged with the enemy—or he could spend more time scouring the castle grounds and the nearby villages looking for the fortune. "Do you believe him?" André asked, examining Hackett for any hint of duplicity.

Hackett finished scribbling into his leather notebook and snapped it shut. "I do."

André groaned. "And these drivers," he motioned toward the wagons, "who are they to deliver their cargo to once they reach French lines?"

"They say that's up to the count," Hackett answered. "Whose instructions they were to follow upon their arrival here."

"If I were a clever officer like most of my peers," André smiled ruefully, "I could make good money selling the contents of those damned wagons to the hungry inhabitants of the nearby villages." He impatiently put his gloves on. "You're absolutely sure there's nothing else in those wagons?"

"Lieutenant-Colonel, I watched your men inspect each one. If there was a German prince's fortune within, it's likely they would have seen it."

"Damn." André cast a glance at their host, a few feet away. "And what does he have to say of the matter?"

"He knows you are no count."

In the distance, a low rumble of thunder echoed, followed by another. Hackett looked up at the bleak, gray sky. The clouds hung low, and in the distance a layer of darkness rolled in, threatening the waning afternoon light.

"That's no storm," said André.

"It's the Russian army," Hackett concurred.

"*Your* allies," André said. He glanced up as if the sky held the answer to his predicament. "I have to help Marcel."

André's two troopers, who had emerged from the scuffle in the basement with new pistols and a few coins the richer, appeared from the stables leading their horses. André instructed Hackett to inform the bishop of their true identities and apologize for their deceit. The bishop was unmoved, simply responding in German, "If you would please depart quickly as recompense for our troubles, then we might enjoy our newly increased store of wine in peace." André shook the man's hand, and the four men then led their horses from the courtyard. André cast a regretful look at the carriages as he passed by, all too aware of how close they had come to a fortune they would likely never chance upon again. At the entrance to the bridge jutting out in front of the castle, they halted.

"As much as I regret leaving without finding our mark, we must," André said, wrapping a cloth around his neck as protection from the half-frozen rain that now pelted down. "Will you be safe riding north without us, Hackett?"

Hackett coughed. "I've come all this way with my head still attached. I can manage my way past your siege lines to the ship that is waiting."

"That is waiting to take you back to your countrymen?"

"Indeed."

Deep rumbles sounded off the eastern horizon. André checked the time and estimated that they could reach the location of the fighting by nightfall. A clatter arose from the castle. The horsemen peered behind them and saw the first wagons from the train rumbling out the castle gate at a slow pace. One of André's troopers chuckled. "They might reach Danzig by summer, sir."

André sighed. "I wonder what became of the real convoy?"

Hackett eyed him with an almost sympathetic look. "The fortune of Hesse-Cassel is gone now," he said. "Your soldiers need you, colonel. Tend to your duties knowing that you stopped a madman and the powerful master he served."

André held his hand out. "I suppose I should say thank-you, Conrad."

William Hackett took André's hand in his with a smile. "Another officer would have had me hanged as a spy. Thank *you*, Valiere." Hackett took the reins in his hands, and his horse started forward. He nodded farewell to André's soldiers and led his horse onto the bridge. As he rode across, he called back, "Perhaps fate will see our paths cross again, Valiere. *Au revoir!*"

André and his two troopers galloped at a blistering pace, following the Nogat River and crossing north of the marshy waters of Lake Drużno. Nearly all inhabitants of the nearby villages remained shuttered behind closed doors, wary of the distant cannon fire. André's party reached the outskirts of the city of Mohrungen as the sun sank below the horizon.

Along the ride, André did his best to dispel his disappointment, yet his inability to account for how the treasure had disappeared nagged at him. He contented himself with the fact that they had stopped Carnassier and likely saved the bishop and his acolytes. As they drew nearer to the front lines, his attention returned to the task ahead. He slowed their pace to a trot as mounted sentries emerged from both sides of the road, calling out the challenge. Thankfully, the password had not changed during their brief absence. The sentries permitted them to pass through the outer pickets, warning André that each mile they rode east they'd be moving closer to a large body of enemy troops who were marching on Mohrungen in the tens of thousands.

A few minutes later, they emerged from a small copse of trees into open ground of fields and orchards. The cannon fire no longer bellowed in a distant, sonorous rumble; it now resounded starkly across the dimly lit meadows. From the direction of the loudest firing an orange glow loomed ominously, brightening the clouds that drifted over the battlefield. André brought them to a halt in a pasture where the moonlight provided a bit of visibility. A body of troops was forming up on the far side of a running brook. André exchanged a few words with an infantry colonel who was mustering his men. He asked where the nearest regiment of dragoons might be found. The colonel indicated a patch of high ground two or three miles distant, informing André that large bodies of cavalry had been seen on the ridge preparing for an assault.

"Do not hang about on the way there," the colonel shouted in a hoarse voice over the roar of the cannons. "To reach the heights, you'll have to pass open ground within range of the enemies' guns. Either avoid it or ride through it, but do not linger or you'll be blasted to pieces."

The rain had dampened the snow-covered fields, causing the men and horses to slog through ankle-deep mud. André calculated the risk of reaching the high ground, which should, ideally, offer a better view of where they were and what was happening. The distance they had to cross was lit by pale moonlight, augmented by the incessant flashes from a nearby friendly artillery battery. Like lightning during a summer storm, the field would come under bright illumination for a second or two, revealing streams of soldiers marching forward like ants. All around them, horses bucked and pawed the muddy ground in nervous agitation, and André felt the urge of a soldier to begin moving—somewhere, anywhere. In these tense moments before combat, the blood coursed in time to the sound of drums and the booming concussion of cannons; it took an extraordinary self-restraint for one to remain still in the midst of such a deafening tumult. André's troopers shared his impulse for action. He took a deep breath to steady himself, noticing that his cheek was not twitching.

"All right," he shouted over the rumble. "Nothing we haven't seen before. We're riding for that crest you see there. Stay in file behind me, no bunching up, or we might as well stop and wave at the enemy. When we reach the high ground, I will locate Major Moreau and our lads; if we find enemy, you are not to panic but follow my lead. If I go down, you are to ride for the rear until you're able to find our regiment. Tell Major Moreau or Sergeant-major Mazzarello what happened at Ordensburg. Understood?" The troopers' eyes were wide with fear, but they nodded eagerly. "All right," André said. "Let's go."

André goaded his horse slowly forward, splashing through a large puddle. Sensing the impending danger, the animal instinctively increased its pace to a canter, which André checked forcefully with his reins. If any of their horses panicked and bolted in the direction of the enemy, they might all be doomed. Holding the nervous animal to a trot, André led them over a small ditch and continued to their right. French cannon fire whistled over their heads. André stole a quick glance behind him, checking that his men were following with sufficient space between each horse. Something on the ground drew André's eye: an arm lying with its palm half-buried in mud. For an instant, the cuffs on the wrist of the dead man's uniform caught the flash from a distant explosion, flickering like coins reflecting the sun's rays. André shivered and wrenched his eyes forward. A loud crash ripped the ground several meters in front of him, spraying mud and water into the air. The cannonball flew past and his horse balked, bucking and stomping. André patted its neck, driving it forward with as calm a voice as he could manage.

Several moments passed before another loud shot tore past, and André ducked down in his saddle. Feeling slightly embarrassed, he rose back up, ignoring the next ball that bounced ahead of him with terrifying speed into a cluster of trees with a loud crash. The high ground was now only a few hundred meters away, discernible by the glare of the cannons firing from both directions. In this flashing light, a grim sight came into view; dead and mangled bodies lay all around them, and André heard the screams and wails of the wounded and dying men moving in the mud, some calling out for aid as the horsemen passed. The smoke drifting across the field blended with the churned-up earth to create a foul, sulfuric-smelling odor made worse by the smell of decaying flesh. André tried to steer his horse around the wounded, but in some places the bodies were piled on top of each other or strewn in rows six and seven deep—cut down in marching formation.

The cannon fire continued, unrelenting, like some raging beast unleashing its power on the small, helpless mortals trying in vain to conquer it. As he rode past one wounded man, André heard the soldier cry out in a horrible voice, "God help me! Please, give me a pistol!" André swerved his horse around the man just as he heard the loud thud of a cannonball smashing into the ground behind him, spraying mud in all directions. As he picked up the pace, he heard the whining and hissing of the enemy's shots landing closer. He stole a look to his left and saw a formation of soldiers two hundred meters ahead, presumably friendly, discharge a burst of crackling musket fire. To André, the midst of battle always felt like trying to steer a small ship through a hurricane; each pummeling wave indifferent to the one before it, rushing in a ceaseless and almighty fury.

His horse took off at a gallop, and he did nothing to check its speed, cursing under his breath as shots tore up the ground around him. Eschewing the pride he had felt just moments before, he ducked his head and called out a prayer for survival. Just then, somehow the fury came to an abrupt end—at least it felt that way to André. His horse, drenched in sweat, slowed to a trot. They had reached relative safety at the base of the high ground, which shielded them from the incoming enemy cannon fire. Out of range for the time being, he glanced in either direction for any nearer threats, noticing how extraordinarily heightened his senses had become. He looked behind him. By some miracle, his two troopers had made it through the barrage and were reining in alongside him. They looked equally amazed to be alive.

"All right, lads," he said, the calmness in his voice belying his pounding heart. "Well done; we've made it this far. That high ground is where we're going. We'll scout the terrain to see if our men are nearby. If we become separated, make your way to the rear behind whatever concealment is available. But under no circumstances are you to go back the way we came, understood?"

Both men nodded, and André turned and slowly led the way up the incline. He still heard the occasional ricocheting cannonball, but they seemed to be thudding into the elevated ground ahead or flying far over their heads. When they reached level ground, they noticed several dead cavalrymen, none of whom wore the uniform of dragoons. The ground was littered with equipment and cartridge pouches, with a few dead horses among the wreckage, but there was no sign of any living cavalry, friend or foe. André rode forward cautiously, aware that the enemy could be hidden among the trees, which had been torn apart by the artillery barrage. He called out the password and waited, his icy breath visible in the smoke-filled glow of the battlefield. "Help me," a faint voice called out. André held still, his ears cocked, his hands gripping the reins tightly, ready to fight or retreat. "Please, someone help me." Concerned it could be a trick to lure them forward, André shouted out the challenge. Several seconds passed before the hoarse voice returned the password.

"Where are you?" André asked.

"Here." The voice came from a nearby patch of undergrowth. André dismounted and soon came upon one of his men—Private Baudin.

"Germain! Léveque!" he yelled to his troopers. "Get over here!" He dropped down to a knee, pulling out his canteen. "It's all right, Baudin," he said. "We're here to take care of you." He poured out a few drops of water, and Baudin nodded appreciatively. André grimaced when he looked at the man's right leg: it was little more than a mangled, blood-soaked stump. The relief he felt at finding one of his own had been dashed; a wound this ghastly would likely be fatal. André took off his coat and placed it gently around the disfigured flesh and bone. "You're all right, trooper."

Baudin smiled when his comrades rode up and dismounted. He greeted them, but their shock was too great to return his smile. He cried out in agony as they pulled him upright and leaned him against a tree. André watched as his two troopers crouched on either side of their comrade, offering quiet words of encouragement. The sight moved André so much that he feared he might weep. Baudin lost consciousness, and his chest rose and fell in short bursts. André crouched down beside him and, within seconds, he had fallen asleep on his haunches. He woke with a start, his eyes darting in all directions. One of his troopers placed a hand on his shoulder to steady him. He rose to his feet, stiff and aching, too exhausted to feel embarrassed.

Minutes later, Private Baudin's eyes opened. "We weren't sure if you'd make it back," he whispered.

"We're here now. Where is the rest of the squadron?"

Wincing as he turned his neck, the wounded soldier indicated the low ground on the far side of the hill. "We last attacked that way."

André looked out over the battlefield, but the countryside lay shrouded in darkness. The cannon fire had ceased. "And Major Moreau?"

Baudin let out a throaty cough. "He saved them," he said, his breaths coming in raspy fits.

"Where is he?"

"I don't know, sir."

André let the young trooper rest; he considered what ought to be done next—should he try to locate the rest of his squadron, some of whom were likely lying wounded out in the blood-soaked fields? Or should they move Baudin to the rear in hopes of finding a field surgeon? He stole another look at Baudin, assessing his chances of survival. As horrible as the injury appeared, André could not abandon him to a slow death alone in this thicket. He ordered his two troopers to ride to the rear in search of anything that might help transport Baudin from the field. They were to search for a surgeon and, if possible, find out the location of the rest of the squadron, if they were still alive. André would remain with his wounded trooper.

Without his coat, André shivered violently from the cold. He huddled beside Baudin, the two having at least each other for warmth. For maybe an hour or two André drifted in and out of sleep. As the faintest hint of dawn began to emerge in the eastern sky, he stood up, half-frozen, blowing on his hands and stomping his feet for warmth. When he looked back down, he saw that the color had left the young man's face, and his eyes appeared glassy and expressionless. Still, he motioned a hand for André to come closer. André crouched down beside him.

"Sir," Baudin said quietly. "I will be finished soon. But I wish—"

"No," André disagreed feebly. "You're going to be all right."

"I wish to be the one to tell you what has happened. It would make me proud."

André nodded. At the very least he could honor the last wish of a dying young man.

Private Baudin inhaled deeply, fortifying himself to speak. "We came upon the town this morning," he began, "passing in front of Marshal

Bernadotte with the other squadrons of the regiment, two squadrons of hussars riding to our left. We were told the enemy held every road north of the city, and we were ordered to delay them as long as we could. The first Russian horsemen, the imperial guards, arrived late in the morning. Major Moreau hid us within the city, waiting until they were less than a league from our position before springing us out onto the open ground on either side of their column. Our sudden appearance must have convinced them that our numbers were greater than they were, for they took to their heels after our initial charge." Baudin coughed hoarsely, wincing from the pain. He drew a deep breath and exhaled slowly. "By midafternoon, more of their cavalry had come, and as they formed a line to match ours, we feigned an attack but retreated as they began their charge. We wheeled quickly and in good order, riding for cover here on the high ground. The enemy broke ranks to pursue us, and that's when our cannons opened up, pouring grape-shot into the unsuspecting buggers at close range. Any enemy who survived the slaughter fled in panic. But Moreau wasn't finished, sir. Seeing their cavalry retreat and the enemy infantry advancing without protection from horse or artillery, we charged in a wedge formation. It did not take much to break their lines, and so we plunged in among the foot soldiers and shattered their lines, sending even their generals fleeing. It was in this moment, sir," Baudin looked up at André, as if to ensure he was still listening, "it was then that the hussars emerged from the trees, half a league to our left. They were led by that mad bastard, the one from the castle in Silesia."

"Alderic," André said in a flat voice.

Baudin nodded. "They formed into a loose line formation, so we formed across from them in our own line, and Alderic came out to greet us. He called for Major Moreau to meet him. We all knew what was coming next. Alderic raised his sword in challenge, and Major Moreau rode to challenge him. They clashed and matched blades in a frenzy, neither able to unseat the other. But Major Moreau struck first. He cut the hussar's arm at the wrist, forcing him to change sword hands. The devil was just as quick with his left hand, and he matched all of Moreau's skill with his own."

"His eleventh duel," André said softly. His pulse had quickened as he listened to Baudin, who appeared to be losing strength. He gave him another sip of water from his canteen.

"By now the ground was stained red by the slain enemy, which lay in great numbers on the very spot the two were fighting. They crossed swords for perhaps another minute, the hussars calling out insults from their line, we from ours. It looked as if Major Moreau lost hold of his stirrups, and he was thrown from his horse. Before he could regain his saddle, Alderic jumped off his horse, slamming a boot into Moreau's belly. Our major then lost grip of his sword, and that's when it happened." Private Baudin closed his eyes, and André's head dropped between his shoulders. He shook his head. "Poor Marcel, if only he could've kept to his own business—"

Baudin stirred. "You think that's the end of it? Hardly, sir."

André leaned forward hopefully. "Go on then, trooper."

"With Major Moreau's sword in his hand, Captain Alderic made a right show. He kicked him once, twice again, and we all figured the major to be done for. Alderic raised both swords over his head, and the hussars went wild. Sergeant-major Mazzarello and Laporte had to hold some of us back at gunpoint. *That* was when it happened; Moreau lay still on the ground, and Alderic stepped forward for the kill. Then, as swift as anything I've ever seen, one of them dead Cossacks, who clearly weren't dead, clambered to his feet and, with a swift thrust, plunged a large knife into Alderic's throat, carving him dead before he touched the ground. The hussars fired on him, some dashing forward and plunging their sabers into the poor devil. In the scuffle, Major Moreau regained his feet and mounted his horse. As we threatened to plunge in against the hussars, our own countrymen, the enemy's artillery picked up. Only this time it was not the vanguard; we could see the main body of their troops mustering a league distant. A pistol shot rang out, and Major Moreau rode between our two forces, calling for silence. It was then that we saw it—we all saw it." Baudin gave an exhausted sigh, and André feared he might expire then and there. "Across the riverbank we saw a dreadful scene unfolding, sir. Fleeing, or trying to flee, were the people of the town. The poor folk were trapped between the river and the oncoming enemy army with only a narrow bridge available to cross. From where we looked, there weren't no way they would all make it across. Terrified shouts and screams rose up as enemy horsemen appeared, looking down on the townspeople. Major Moreau sent a runner to Colonel Menard, and we waited, readying ourselves if we should be called back into the action. Our runner returned with the colonel's message—that we had done an exemplary job of delaying the enemy and that we were to make an ordered retreat to cover the infantry as they marched back to the safety of the road behind us. But then what we had all feared happened: the Russian guns were brought up to the nearest hill, and from a range close enough to aim each shot they began to pour their deadly rounds down into the town—aiming for the bridge, but their shots began falling within the town itself. We could hear their screams and shouts as they began running wildly in all directions to escape the cannon shot." Baudin wiped his nose with a sleeve, his lips blue and quivering. He did not have long now. Closing his eyes, he continued, "Moreau called out to the hussars. If they wished to avenge their leader and keep their honor, they would follow him. They would follow us. Seeing the destruction that the enemy's guns were inflicting on the town, many of them thought better of the offer and rode away. But perhaps two dozen or so stayed. We gave a shout in honor of our leader, Major Moreau, and to our surprise the hussars cried out as loudly as we. Then we did all that was left of us to do. We formed by troop, the hussars counting as their own, and we rode around the city and charged at the enemy cavalry. They were in greater numbers, much greater than our own, and this time they did not flee. It was a terrible melee, sir—even you might have found it difficult. But Moreau would not quit the field. He sent some of us down to the city to guard the fleeing townsfolk, while he led the rest to hold off the enemy cavalry."

The sky had brightened into a blue glow, and a crow squawked in the trees above. The sound of hoofbeats approaching caused André to rise to his feet and unsheathe his saber. Several moments later, the two troopers reappeared with a third rider. The man rode a large black gelding with a small sled harnessed to it.

André breathed a sigh of relief. "See Baudin? A surgeon; just hang on a little longer."

Private Baudin smiled, but André could see the resignation in his eyes. The surgeon rode up alongside André and set a small wooden chest on the muddy ground. Lifting André's coat from the leg, the surgeon quickly set to work with a pair of scissors, removing any cloth stuck to the wound. As he inspected the mangled bone and tissue, the surgeon asked Baudin a few questions. The trooper flinched once or twice but did not cry out. After he'd answered the surgeon's questions, he continued his account.

"Then Miss Jarzyna joined us. I don't think Major Moreau saw her. Some of us tried to remove her from the fighting, but she wouldn't hear of it. She was brave as any trooper, but a charge of heavy cavalry and a saber hilt knocked her to the ground. We thought her dead. To my amazement I saw her get up; unable to regain her horse, she made her way down to the bridge. The fire had slackened, and Miss Jarzyna began shouting directions, organizing the frenzy. She spoke in Polish, so I suppose they was Polish folk—perhaps why the enemy were so keen to get at them."

The surgeon looked down at Baudin reprovingly. "Soldier, be still and don't speak so much."

"Hush up, doctor, I've a damned stump for a leg. I'll say what must be said, and you'll carry on working til it's regrown or I'm dead."

The surgeon continued his work without further interruption.

"She stayed with us, sir," Baudin said. "She could not be persuaded or ordered to leave. She carried off the wounded and brought water and ammunition to us. I've heard of men leaving the battlefield to wait out the worst of it in the rear under pretext of carrying wounded or gathering ammunition; not Miss Jarzyna. But when Major Moreau went missing, she left to find him. We haven't heard of her since."

"Baudin," André managed, stifling the emotions he was feeling, "is Major Moreau dead?"

Baudin's eyes widened, and the surgeon shot André an unsettling look. Baudin leaned his head back. "I don't know. I pray he is not."

A few moments later it was over, and the tears of his two young comrades were too much for André to bear, so he kept his gaze on the young trooper's face. His eyes were calm, almost peaceful—yet utterly vacant. André wiped a hand to close them, and for a moment all present sat in the silence of their own thoughts.

"We must go." Turning to the surgeon, André offered his hand in gratitude. "My thanks, monsieur. More of my wounded may yet be out there, and we must do what we can to help them." They left Baudin's body and returned to their horses.

CHAPTER 50

Saint-Germain, Paris

January 1807

The day after Sophie's visit dawned with cloudy skies and a light drizzle, which grew into a heavy storm by early afternoon. Jean-Luc had maintained the fire that warmed the house, but he could see their pile of wood was slowly dwindling. He had distracted himself from dwelling on the previous day's conversation by reading stories to Mariette, whose attention seemed to wander as much as his. As the fire consumed more of the wood, Jean-Luc made up his mind to go get more. Whether this was a necessary precaution or just a pretext to get out of the house, he decided that he would run the quick errand, informing his daughter that he would be back within the hour.

He locked the door behind him and set out east toward Rue des Boucheries, where he knew of a shop that sold kindling. His coat and top hat shielded him from the worst of the cold rain, which had slackened a little, but he walked at a quick pace nonetheless. Half an hour later, he paid the vendor two francs for as much wood as he could fit in a straw sack. He lifted it over his shoulder and set out for home.

Despite his lingering cough, Jean-Luc felt invigorated as he walked through the muddy streets. Perhaps it was the much-needed physical exertion; he decided to take a detour and walk up the hill toward the Panthéon, its looming black dome seeming to beckon him in the distance. Climbing the hill leading into the Latin Quarter caused his out-of-condition heart to race. At last he reached the great edifice, and he allowed himself a rest, setting the sack down and purchasing a cup of hot tea in a nearby tavern.

When he stepped outside, he noticed the rain had picked up again. He found the road he'd planned to take obstructed by a cart whose rear wheel had fallen off; a gaggle of men and women eager to lend their wheelwright expertise crowded on either side of the street. Jean-Luc turned to take an alternate route. By now his cough had returned and he felt eager to be home, so he picked up his pace. He passed a row of tall garrets that seemed to lean out over the streets, surprised at the sight of children walking up and down the open stairwells, ignoring the cold rain that smattered their ragged and inadequate clothing.

As he walked, the streets appeared more and more dilapidated and the people poorer, and Jean-Luc was reminded of how many in this city made do with a meager living, only to return home to a cramped hovel of a dwelling. A small boy dressed in a felt cap and overlarge patched coat approached him, offering half a sous for the firewood in his sack. When Jean-Luc declined the offer, the boy made a face and kicked muddy water at him before running off. Jean-Luc realized that he had gotten himself turned around and looked up at the nearest buildings for a street name. Seeing none, he continued downhill. At the bottom of the incline he still found no indication of where he was. The driving rain added to his disorientation, and he grew concerned that he had left his daughter alone too long.

The shuttered houses showed no local merchant or laborer to whom Jean-Luc could ask directions, so, with another glance around, he set off in the direction he felt most appropriate. He traversed several blocks and, as he crossed over a plank of wood that had mercifully been placed over a large puddle, his heart suddenly hammered in his chest. Barreling towards him, perhaps thirty feet away, was a horse-drawn cab. Jean-Luc dove to the side of the road just in time to avoid being crushed. The large black horse passed close enough for Jean-Luc to see the steamy breath blowing from its flared nostrils, and the hooves slammed down inches from his face. For a few seconds he held his breath as he pressed himself against the nearest building. The wheels rolled passed, spinning up water as the carriage continued on its way, the careless driver oblivious to the near-fatal disaster.

Too shocked to pick himself up, Jean-Luc sat up against the wall for several minutes, his heart racing. After he had calmed himself a little, he looked down and saw the kindling strewn all around him, most of it float-ing in the puddle like small boats. The splash from the carriage had soaked his coat and pants, and he did not bother to lift his boots, which rested half-submerged in the brown water. A few more minutes passed, and his nervous excitement gradually subsided, bringing his thoughts back to his miserable condition. He peered down again at his scattered firewood and soaked boots, and a terrible feeling welled up inside him. Suppressed rage mingled with the melancholy that he had carried within for so long, and he looked up at the sky only for his eyes to fill with the torrential rain.

Jean-Luc let out a scream that shook his entire body; a scream that came from some primal place within. He lifted his face up to the sky again, heed-less of the downpour, and yelled until his lungs were spent. He gasped for breath, and when he had no more rage to vent, he let his head slink down, his chin dropping to his chest with a groan of despair.

Jean-Luc St. Clair sat stewing in his dark thoughts, too miserable to fall asleep, too defeated to lift himself up. At last, with great effort, he lifted his head. He blinked several times to clear his vision, and a strange feeling came over him as he glanced at the garret across the street. As he gazed at the half-dilapidated building, a vague thought entered his mind. He looked to his right, then to his left, and the dawning realization began to take shape. The stairwell outside the garret to his right turned back and forth up four levels before reaching the top floor—and he recognized it. He had been on this street before; even more, this shabby, drab cluster of houses had once been his home.

He looked to either side again and saw it as clear as if the skies were a bright blue and the summer sun was shining. His old house, the garret where he, Marie, and Mathieu had once lived. Where his beloved wife had died giving birth to Mariette. A wave of feeling passed over him, and mem-ories came flooding back. He felt too exhausted to weep, and the rain would have washed away any tears that fell, but the sight of his old home made him forget his current misery, and he wished only that his family could be with him here and now.

A flash of movement to his right pulled him out of his reverie. He wiped a hand across his brow, noticing another movement. He turned his body, lifting his boots out of the puddle. He looked toward a corner of the street where one of the garrets jutted up unevenly against the adjacent building, leaving an open space between. In this alcove, shadowed by the overhanging stairwell, Jean-Luc noticed a small, mangy dog. It was crouched with its weight on its front paws, its hind legs in the air as it pulled at something with all its might. Jean-Luc pulled his hat out of the puddle and shook it several times before placing it on his soaked head. Wiping a strand of soggy hair from his face he stood to his feet, slowly stooping down to gather his pieces of sodden firewood and placing them back in the straw sack. But as he did this, he kept his eyes on the shadowed alcove, trying to see what the dog was fighting so tenaciously to possess. When he'd managed to place the last piece of kindling back into the sack, he threw it over his shoulder. He was soaked to the bone and ready to get back home. But as he turned to depart, he heard a sound that stopped him cold. He took several more steps forward and heard the sound again, this time sure that it came from someone involved in some terrible struggle or in pain. His boots splashed as he picked up the pace and the dog must have heard him, for it released whatever it was that it had been tugging on and scurried away from Jean-Luc as he approached. Jean-Luc peered down into the alcove and saw a sight that froze his heart. Huddled under a filthy heap of rags and cloth apparently meant to block out the rain were two young children. Two street urchins, a little girl and a younger boy. Clearly homeless, they sat gnawing on what looked like a bone or piece of carcass. Jean-Luc saw the girl hand the larger piece to the boy, and the sight stirred in Jean-Luc a pity so profound that he stood with his mouth agape and a lump forming in his throat. That this young girl had struggled so tirelessly with that growling dog, matching its wild and feral ferocity with a stubbornness of her own—and succeeded in the struggle—only to pass down the scrap to the boy, presumably her younger brother.

For the first time in ages Jean-Luc held not a single thought of himself or his present circumstances. He no longer noticed the rain pelting down on his head, the mud splattered on his pants, or the water in his boots. In this moment, he would not have noticed the emperor himself riding past, so focused were his thoughts on this pitiful sight before him.

It took several minutes of gentle persuading, but eventually Jean-Luc managed to convince the young girl he was not a threat, and she lifted her trembling fingers to his outstretched hand. Discarding the filthy bone she had won in her struggle, Jean-Luc helped the two urchins to their feet and escorted them to a nearby tavern, where he seated them next to a fire and bought them each a bowl of hot soup. The sight of these filthy children attracted the attention of the handful of surly-looking regulars, but Jean-Luc assured the innkeeper that they wouldn't be staying long. He paid an errand boy to fetch the gendarmes, and a quarter of an hour later two soldiers arrived.

Jean-Luc explained the circumstances and offered them five francs to escort the children to the closest hospital. When they had been fed and their ragged clothing somewhat dried, Jean-Luc explained to them that the soldiers would take them to a place where they would be sheltered from the rain. Slipping the sergeant an extra franc and giving the man his address, Jean-Luc requested that he come and inform him after the children had been safely deposited at the hospital. Before he departed, Jean-Luc asked the girl for their names so that he might come and check on them. She looked at him with wide eyes.

"I am Sistine," she said in a soft voice. "And my brother is Beaudoin. Our mother is gone."

"Well, Sistine," Jean-Luc said, "I will look for your mother, but you and Beaudoin no longer have to worry. I will make sure you are taken care of. All right?"

Sistine nodded, and Jean-Luc reminded the sergeant once more to come and inform him when they had arrived at the hospital. He then set off home. The rain had slackened to a mild shower. As he trudged through the sopping streets, a pitter-patter of footsteps followed stealthily behind. A mangy dog with a hard-won bone between his teeth skulked along behind Jean-Luc as he made his way back to the Saint-Germain quarter.

Once home, Jean-Luc threw off his sodden clothes and apologized to Mariette for taking so long, explaining what had happened. He then went upstairs and settled into a hot bath. Later that evening the gendarme sergeant kept his promise, informing Jean-Luc that the two orphans had been installed at the Hôtel Dieu. That night he fell into a restful sleep for the first time in ages.

The following morning, Jean-Luc peered out the window and noticed a stray dog lying out in front of his doorstep. He managed to chase the animal down the street, only for it to reappear on his doorstep a little while later. Jean-Luc repeated the effort twice more, but the animal could not be induced to stay away. When he left his house on an errand later that morning, the dog following him down the street.

"Follow me if you must, you mangy mutt," Jean-Luc said, grinning as he looked back at the stubborn animal. He left Rue Grenelle and turned toward the river. "I don't have time to care for you, but I know someone who might."

Jean-Luc was welcomed into Pierre-Yves Gagnon's garret with a curt chuckle, as the wine smuggler no longer felt obliged to put on airs.

"So," Gagnon said as he handed Jean-Luc a cup of tea, "Monsieur le Senator is now simply monsieur. How the mighty have fallen, hm?"

Jean-Luc winced as he took a sip of tea and burned his tongue; at least, that seemed like an adequate pretext for his involuntary reaction. "Yes, Gagnon, your wishes have come true at last. You no longer have need to address me as your superior."

Gagnon rubbed his hands together with apparent relish. "I've seen worse things happen to better men, so I suppose we all must take our lumps in due course. Now, what brings you to my house on this fine winter's day?"

Jean-Luc, relieved that the conversation had shifted from his personal misfortunes, eyed the other man with a skeptical squint. "I have a rather significant favor to ask of you. Now, wait—" Jean-Luc cut off Gagnon before he could protest, "—this has nothing to do with my position or the police minister; you need not worry about any political repercussions. This is simply a matter of honor, a virtue I know you place high on your list of personal prerogatives. It involves leaving the city to pursue a course of action that involves a little danger." Gagnon appeared unmoved. "I didn't think that would convince you," Jean-Luc admitted. "So I'll weigh your appetite for enterprise and offer you a week's wages for the trouble."

Gagnon shrugged, rubbing his nose. "I make a decent enough living now, monsieur."

"Gagnon, you've gone from smuggling wine to running gambling and whoring houses."

"I didn't say it was an honest living."

Jean-Luc folded his hands together. After a moment, it was Gagnon who broke the silence. "Let's set one thing straight," he said. "Even if there is *sufficient* coin for my troubles, I will not be serving you in any capacity as a subordinate. Is that plain enough?"

"You owe me no service or deference. But if you help me, you'll be able to rest easy in the knowledge that you've offered help to a friend in a time of great need."

The two men looked at each other in silence. "And yes," Jean-Luc said at last, "I'll pay you what you deserve when we've done the damned business."

Gagnon laughed quietly. "You know I take payment from that bastard Fouché. As he has eyes in the darkest corners of the empire, I'd sooner cooperate than run afoul of the palace." A tense moment passed. "But, truth be told, I don't care much for the bastard. He has his network—we've our own. If the price is agreeable to me and my lads, then perhaps this little adventure might be a worthwhile excursion after all. Where will we be going?"

"Normandy."

Gagnon's ears twitched. "*Normandy?*"

"Yes," Jean-Luc said with a cunning look. "But I am glad you mentioned your lads, as they are the very reason I've come to you."

Gagnon raised his eyebrow in a puzzled expression.

"There is a *nobleman* out in that province," Jean-Luc explained, "who is attempting to rally up a band of displaced Bretons and Chouans to remove a soldier's wife from her ancestral lands. This woman is a dear friend of mine, and she fears that if someone does not come to her aid, this nobleman will seize the land with violence, displacing the families who have tilled the soil for generations. This nobleman claims to desire law and order—and he particularly despises smuggling above all other corruptions." Jean-Luc could not have said whether this last statement was true, but he added it for good measure anyway.

"Sounds like a right prick," Gagnon grunted. "When do we depart?"

"At first light the day after tomorrow. Round up your men and see to it that they remain sober and behave within the boundaries of the law until we arrive at our destination. When we get there, they should have ample opportunity to lend their…less-than-savory talents toward a just and worthy cause."

Gagnon nodded, the wheels of his mind turning. "I'll tell them there will be wine and women."

Jean-Luc put on his top hat. "Tell them whatever you must to get them to come along." He placed a hand on the merchant's shoulder. "Do not let me down on this."

Gagnon clasped Jean-Luc's hand in his, then removed the other from his shoulder. "If this *nobleman* and his fellows are as dodgy as you claim them to be, then we'll have a proper caper on our hands, monsieur."

"Good," Jean-Luc said, opening the door. "One last thing. There's a mangy-looking mutt sitting outside your door. It followed me all the way from Saint-Marcel. I think you and he would make a fine pair. I will see you tomorrow!"

CHAPTER 51

Mohrungen, Prussia

January 1807

Riding to the top of the hill, the three dragoons looked down into the valley where the fiercest fighting had taken place. The carnage was not as bad as André had imagined, given the fury of the previous night's cannonade. Nevertheless, strewn across the muddy fields were blue and green coats, many of them their countrymen, casualties of a battle so far from home, fighting to defend a town whose name they would never learn. André led his men through the fields, soon coming upon an area where the sight of dead and maimed horses revealed where cavalry had fought. Slain hussars intermingled with Cossacks in a scene of muddled horror. Anguished groans and cries from the wounded and dying could be heard from all directions.

At last they came upon the green coats of dragoons, discovering that which they'd feared to see but knew was coming—the sight of their fallen comrades. As they slowly walked their horses among the dead, they set about identifying the men they had once called brothers. His two troopers called out the names of the fallen to André, who recorded them in his ledger. One by one he passed men whose faces once bore the vibrancy of youth and promise of life, but who now lay in the muck among their fallen comrades. André did his best to bear the scene with dignity, but the weight became too much when he came upon the body of his old friend—Paolo Mazzarello, who lay twisted and bloated beside his dead horse. André choked back a cry as he climbed down from his horse and gently lifted the body, cradling the brave Corsican in his arms as he sobbed. Mazzarello appeared to have been shot by no less than a dozen small rounds of canister shot. Germain and Léveque stood several paces off, weeping for their fallen sergeant-major.

After André hauled his friend's body onto his horse, he surveyed the cadaverous scene in bewildered despair. Had his two troopers not been present he might have gone mad, but his sense of duty held his mind together like a frayed cord, its strands ripped and tattered but still clinging with rugged obstinacy.

They had counted nineteen slain comrades, and they accounted for a dozen wounded. Those able to walk were helped from the field. Upon arriving at the nearest French encampment, a few dozen of their comrades who had survived the battle unharmed greeted their commander and comrades with respectful nods, too exhausted for anything more. Thirty more of their squadron lay wounded in nearby tents. André visited the men one by one. The remaining number were still missing, Moreau among them.

Lying unconscious among a group of local civilians wounded or killed was Alicja Jarzyna. She was flanked by several of the surviving dragoons, and even a few of Carnassier's hussars, who all knelt reverently beside her injured body. She looked small and frail next to the soldiers all around her. The surgeon tending to her demanded that the cavalrymen move back so he could work.

"She was an angel sent to us, sir," one of André's troopers said.

"She went down to the villagers, sir," said one of the hussars. "Spoke to them in their own tongue. Kept them calm as they crossed the bridge, showing them where to run when they'd made it across. We were driven back by the enemy; their cannons picked up again, but most of the locals had gone over the bridge. I saw with my own eyes—this lass was one of the last to leave. Their canister shot found her as she made the crossing."

A feeling of guilt struck André like a hammer to the chest. His heart ached to the point of breaking. For the first time in several days he allowed his thoughts to turn to his wife and sons, whom he longed for more than anything. To keep his mind from dwelling on the battlefield and its grisly aftermath, he willed his attention to remain with them, thinking of nothing and no one else.

In the early evening after eating a small supper, André made another visit to the wounded. Two more had passed; Alicja Jarzyna one of them. Beside her shrouded body several of the troopers wept, while others were unable to bring themselves to say goodbye. Her loss was felt by all present; even soldiers from other units seemed to sense to the loss of this Polish girl so beloved by the dragoons and hussars gathered around her body.

"We rode into her village bringing violence and death, and here she lies, having given everything," André said, wiping away a tear. "She gave without asking anything in return, because she loved him, and she learned to love us…. It has been said that light goes where it is most needed, conveying love regardless of what any of us may think of its messenger. All we can do now is honor her memory. She was an angel in a cauldron of death. May God keep her and welcome her home."

CHAPTER 52

Tuileries Garden, Paris

January 1807

The following morning as Jean-Luc and Mariette ate breakfast, he weighed the dangers of bringing her to Carcourt, ultimately deciding that leaving her behind was the only sensible conclusion, especially as he would be riding in the company of rough men prepared to do violence with even rougher men. He was thinking of whom he might trust with her care when she spoke.

"Papa, I have something to tell you, and please don't be angry with me."

"Nothing you could say would make me angry, my love."

"Are you sure?" Her pluck appeared to rise somewhat.

"Of course," Jean-Luc said, though he felt a slowly growing unease.

"Isabella told me to never ever tell a lie. When I did, she would be cross with me. So, I want to tell you Camille has snuck away from her. He's been visiting me in our garden."

Jean-Luc took a deep breath. "Sweetheart, is Camille *really* here? In our garden?"

Mariette nodded enthusiastically. "I've been bringing him some of my supper so he won't go hungry. I'm sorry, Papa." She began to cry, and Jean-Luc, though his mind had begun to race, laid a hand on hers to calm her.

"It's all right, Mariette. I'm not angry, I promise. Camille is a smart boy." He smiled and cleared his throat, looking toward the garden. "Shall we let him inside?"

"He's not here now. He only comes in the evening. He gave me something last night that he took from her."

Jean-Luc squinted at Marie. "What did he give you, love?"

"He said it proves she's a mean lady." Mariette rose from the table and walked upstairs. Jean-Luc considered whether he should call the authorities. She returned with an envelope. "Camille said his real name is Camillo, and that Isabella is the *real* liar."

Jean-Luc opened the envelope and began reading the letter within.

Cardinal,

As you've inquired about the boy on several occasions, and now that I no longer have need of keeping up family pretext, I will confess to you that there is more to the Maduro family's story than you have been led to believe...

When he had finished reading, Jean-Luc set the letter down on his plate. He sat with his hands arched together in a steeple and his elbows resting on the table. When he had assembled his thoughts into something of an ordered cluster, he rose and hurried upstairs to his bedroom. He emerged again, wearing his coat, riding gloves, and top hat, and holding a thick envelope.

"Mariette, my darling, you and your friend Camille have just done a very good thing in telling me the truth. I don't think I've been happier in years." He took a knee and hugged her, and she returned his affection fully for the first time since she had come home. "In fact," Jean-Luc said as he stood, "the letter young Monsieur Camille, or, should I say, *Camillo,* delivered has given me quite an idea. I must take care of something I should have done weeks ago. After that I will be departing to Normandy to visit Aunt Sophie."

Sophie stared up at her father. "May I come, too?"

"My darling, if I could bring you with me, of course I would. Sophie has asked for my help. But as soon as we've taken care of her problem, I will send for you to come and join me. I promise you, Mariette. Does that sound all right?"

"All right, Papa."

Exhaling in relief, Jean-Luc kissed a hand and placed it on her forehead.

"But please be quick when you help Miss Sophie, Papa. I would like to visit her soon."

An hour later, after a visit to the national banking house, Jean-Luc found himself standing at the high black gate outside the Tuileries Palace. At one time he had commanded entry with a wave of the hand; now he stood alongside several children. He made his way west along the river until he reached an entrance where the guards were letting in sightseers hoping to catch a glimpse of a famous personage. Jean-Luc pressed himself in among a small throng and passed the sentries. Once inside the courtyard, he walked briskly along the gravel pathway that led to the grand staircase, the entrance he'd used to visit Joseph Bonaparte. As he approached the second entrance, he reached into his coat and took to hand the thing he hoped might sway an indolent guard to admit him into the palace. With an affected air of authority, Jean-Luc set down the letter he had received from Joseph, ensuring the Imperial seal was visible, at the guard's desk, "I have come to meet with an aide to his highness Joseph Bonaparte, king of Naples. The emperor's brother has instructed me to come collect several items that he no longer has need of."

"And who are you, monsieur?" The guard said, without looking at the envelope.

Jean-Luc reached into his pocket and handed the man his expired senate identification papers. "I am Jean-Luc St. Clair. Formerly Senator St. Clair. I have been ordered to present myself at Monsieur Bonaparte's offices to—"

"Yes, yes," the guard interrupted, handing back Jean-Luc's papers." I have beside me a list of expected visitors into the palace residence today." The man ran a finger down the list of a dozen names. "Unfortunately, monsieur, you are not on it." He set the roster down and picked up the letter.

Worried now that the man was about to call his bluff, Jean-Luc snatched the paper out of the guard's hands. "Soldier, you are speaking to a former senator who has come at the *personal* invitation of the king of Naples."

Jean-Luc displayed the letter with the signature visible. "I have all the documentation required, and yet *you* seem to think it wise to bar me from satisfying his request. You are interfering with an important matter of state. The minister of police shall hear of this. I see your rank is lieutenant. What is your name?"

The young lieutenant appeared discomfited, and both men felt the eyes of those in the courtyard turning to them. With a sigh of contempt, Jean-Luc turned his back on the soldier and shouted, "The police minister will hear of this, I tell you!" He then set off toward the main entrance. Before he had gone ten paces, the lieutenant had leapt from his desk. Pleading for calm, the man held out an arm, gesturing for Jean-Luc to return. Jean-Luc feigned a great effort at composing himself. "If *you* don't believe me, lieutenant, there is a man employed here, and *he* might vouch for my identity. Monsieur Meneval—the personal assistant to His Majesty Napoleon. I believe he is still on duty in the palace?"

"Meneval?" the lieutenant said uneasily, glancing at a group of curious onlookers who were now gathering behind Jean-Luc.

"Yes, Meneval," Jean-Luc said imperiously. "Go find him so I can tell him why you've refused me admittance—"

"No, no," the guard said, exasperated. "Monsieur, I have heard of you, and if you do in fact have business with his highness the king of Naples..." He reached out and grabbed the envelope, examining the seal. When he was satisfied that it was authentic, he handed it back. "If it is to retrieve a few items, I will allow you to pass. But do not be long, monsieur. I am under strict orders."

The soldier waved him through, and Jean-Luc entered the building and made his way up the grand staircase. A few minutes later he was standing outside a familiar office. The secretary in the antechamber asked him who he was and what his business was with the police minister; this time Jean-Luc had no need for deception. *The one advantage to being utterly ruined,* Jean-Luc thought, *is that there is nothing left to fear losing.* He admitted the feeling was rather liberating.

For the first time since he had met the man, Jean-Luc felt not a hint of discomfort in his presence. As he walked into the room, Fouché filed several parchments into an envelope and folded his hands over them. Jean-Luc grimaced in a mask of stoic suffering and cleared his throat.

"I do not wish to waste your time, minister, and I have not come here to settle old scores or voice any displeasure at my disastrous circumstances. I am departing my life in Paris, tail between my legs, as it were. I've come only to ask after an old friend who seems to be in his last days."

Fouché's eyes drooped slightly into his customary squint. "You wish to know of de Landreville's condition? He is dying. The surgeons believe it is cholera. More than that I cannot tell you."

Jean-Luc eyed Fouché with a rueful grin. "I doubt you have uttered those words truthfully many times in your life, minister." Fouché's lips curled into a bemused smile. "Nevertheless, I believe you. The old man held to his truant, aristocratic ways. Eating, drinking, hardly working—except to enlarge his estate. What do the Berbers say? Male lions rarely do the business of hunting. Imagine old de Landreville keeping himself active enough to maintain a strong constitution! Still, there was something endearing about the old man."

Fouché stole a look at his stopwatch. "You haven't slipped your way into my office to reminisce on the habits of a dying aristocrat, St. Clair. Speak plainly or take your leave."

"You are quite right, monsieur," Jean-Luc said with a shrug. "I am having difficulties finding friends these days, for reasons apparent enough. But I do not hold any one person responsible. I effected my own ruin, and it is something I must live with. It is—well, imagine my disappointment when I discovered that Monsieur de Landreville was divulging the intimate details of our private discussions." Fouché stirred in his seat, and his eyebrows lifted in a sly expression. "By now I've learned something of your talents, minister. I dare say it was foolish of me to have spoken so candidly and so often in the house of a well-known personage without expecting my slips of the tongue to pass beyond his walls. Eh, but I will lament his departure all the same." Jean-Luc's show of regret was tinged with an uneasiness that played its effect on Fouché perfectly.

"We will all lament his passing." Fouché folded his hands together. "And perhaps I was wrong about you. Perhaps you are motivated by greed, as any other man."

Jean-Luc achieved an expression of indignation. "Monsieur, I have no idea what you're talking about."

"Well," Fouché replied, "as helpful as the old marquis has been to us here, there are others in the Saint-Germain who have ears, St. Clair."

Jean-Luc's pulse quickened, but his face remained passive. "I'm sure there are. What has that to do with me? I have nothing to hide."

Fouché looked at him with a malevolent smile. "Not from me, that is true. But from your woman? You have never kept any secrets from her?"

Jean-Luc eyed Fouché with a piercing look, then scoffed. "What could I possibly have to hide from her?"

"Your secrets are your secrets, monsieur. We both know of them; there's hardly reason to conduct a review. But, one that *did* catch my eye: your allowance from the marquis. One hundred francs per month, to keep him informed of the senate's doings?" Fouché could not conceal his smirk now. "I trust that your friendship was genuine. But nothing fastens the bonds of loyalty like the adhesive of a stipend. Or is that something you don't care to admit to yourself?'

Jean-Luc's surprise was genuine, so he did not have to pretend; in the same moment, a wave of relief passed over him. He willed himself into a show of growing humiliation with a quick glance to either side of him. "You liar!" He gripped the arms of his chair until his knuckles turned white. "What need would I have of that man's money? He would never level such a slanderous accusation against me unless—" He contorted his face and appeared to be putting the pieces of a puzzle together. "Unless. It wasn't he who told you." Fouché reclined in his chair and crossed one leg over the other. He held his hands apart for a second, suggesting Jean-Luc was close to solving the riddle. "Could it have been that governess woman? *Laurent?* Did she tell you that?"

Fouché could not conceal his pleasure, which did not come forth in an expression of amusement or laughter. Rather, his face seemed to gleam with a wicked enjoyment, and his intelligent, probing eyes betrayed the turning of the gears of his mind. He had played a game and won. And now, he savored in its ultimate expression—the look of rage and distress on a man he had outwitted.

"But as you are a ruined man, and de Landreville's residence will no longer serve as the den of...*activity*...it had in more dangerous years, I will do you the mercy of sharing with you a little secret. It is true—Lucille Laurent has been in my employment since the first days of her working in that house. I don't know what will become of her now that her master is on his way out, but I'm sure a girl of her cunning will find enterprise elsewhere."

Jean-Luc glared at Fouché, his body practically shaking with anger. But within his own mind he was grinning joyfully, hardly able to contain his surprise at what the minister was revealing to him.

"She did not take up the business out of any friendship to me or disloyalty to her master; on the contrary, she began the work as a *service* to her master."

"What do you mean?"

Fouché appeared to hesitate, but Jean-Luc's anger seemed sufficient to induce him to continue. "It was some years back, during the Consulate. An event transpired that left the Marquis de Landreville in rather hot water. He had returned from Revolutionary exile in Austria, around the time Mademoiselle Laurent was taken in, and he was approached by a party of conspirators. Among them were names unknown at the time but that have since achieved notorious stature. Generals Pichegru, Saint-Victor, Limoëlan, and Georges Cadoudal were all said to have been in correspondence with Marquis de Landreville. You are aware these are all men who were executed for attempting to assassinate Napoleon." Jean-Luc was unaware that the marquis had been involved in this plot, but, recalling the private conversations they had had together, he began to admit that it was possible. "Some say," Fouché continued, "that Georges even passed a night under the old man's roof when he was a fugitive in this city. Of that, who can be sure? What is sure is that the marquis never received punishment for whatever part he might have played in the plot. Furthermore, his name was never even offered to the First Consul."

"You knew."

"Of course I knew," Fouché said casually. "What good is a police minister who watches his master nearly blown to bits and doesn't reach the bottom of the matter? Be that as it may, my belief was that the marquis was not an *enthusiastic* plotter. My suspicions were corroborated when I spoke with Mademoiselle Laurent, who, short of confessing her master's guilt, assured me he had no love for the Bourbons; that he had returned to Bonaparte's France willingly, desiring nothing more than passing the remainder of his years in peace. I believed her, but he was still a conspirator, and conspirators who plot against Napoleon do not escape justice. I offered Mademoiselle Laurent her master's freedom, and my assurance that I would profess his innocence to Napoleon, if she were to work for me. The Saint-Germain quarter is, after all, a hotbed of royalist conspirators."

Jean-Luc absorbed this revelation, grasping the terrifying power that the minister of police held over so many citizens like Lucille Laurent, men and women with no choice but to inform on their neighbors in order to keep their own necks.

"So now you see," Fouché said after a lengthy silence. "I have sworn to keep the marquis's secret to myself, and, in return, Mademoiselle Laurent keeps me abreast of the nobles who come and go in the Saint-Germain—and any conspirators are dealt with."

Jean-Luc looked at Fouché with a growing frustration that was no longer contrived. "Like you dealt my career a false accusation of the same?"

Fouché dismissed the statement with a barely perceptible smirk. "Your own folly led to your ruin. You chose Madame Maduro, you could not keep her content, so she betrayed you."

As much as this last revelation stung Jean-Luc, it was a small reassurance to hear the truth, or at least some form of it, spoken aloud. Furthermore, Jean-Luc's pain at the thought of Lucille's betrayal had all but subsided, as he now understood her motive for informing to the minister. Jean-Luc almost chuckled at Fouché's accusation of greed; he had never once taken money from de Landreville, and he was sure that Lucille had made that up to mislead the police minister into misunderstanding Jean-Luc's motives.

"Well," he said at last, resignation softening his voice, "I am defeated. But I ask you out of curiosity: as you're surely aware by now that I know Isabella is not who she says she is, tell me this…where on earth is she going?"

Fouché's keen eyes probed Jean-Luc. "I would not be very effective if I shared my colleagues' secrets with no advantage to be gained."

"I suppose good riddance, then." Jean-Luc rapped his knuckles on the desk. "It's not as if she'll need my company anymore. I am poor once again." He placed his top hat on his head and stood up.

Fouché eyed him with a look of detached amusement. "Good day, monsieur. Good luck to you in all of your future ventures."

Jean-Luc nodded. "And to you as well, monsieur. I do not envy the responsibilities you've taken on in such faithful service to your master."

For a moment it looked like Fouché would not take the bait. "Very well, St. Clair." He pulled a piece of paper from his briefcase and began scribbling on it. "I will not detain you. But do be sure to let us know how you are faring from time to time; we wouldn't wish to lose sight of you."

Jean-Luc removed his hat and he played with it in his hands. "I may be somewhat harder to find, no longer having the public reputation I once had. But private employment does have its advantages, no? Why, we both know the frustration of subordinating ourselves to men we believe ourselves to be more capable than. It must be difficult, with your talents and ambition, to know the world will only ever see you in the shadow of another man. Quite a long shadow at that."

Fouché looked up at Jean-Luc, his face contorting; whether it was a grimace or a smile, Jean-Luc couldn't be sure. He bowed his head slightly and walked out of the room, down the stairs, and departed the Tuileries Palace for the last time.

CHAPTER 53

Carcourt, Normandy

February 1807

Jean-Luc, Gagnon, and his four hired guns rode onto the grounds of Carcourt on a late afternoon as the sun was setting behind the distant woodlands. Wrapped head to toe in scarves and fur, the riders reined in in the front yard of the house, their horses' breath billowing out in large clouds that drifted across the yard. They remained in their saddles for a moment, gazing at the beautiful stone chateau sprawled out before them. Though his teeth were clattering, in his mind Jean-Luc was comparing the architectural style of his former mansion and the one before him. His ruminations were interrupted by Gagnon's men, one of whom farted, the other lamenting the state of his bum after the three-day journey.

"None of your bollocks in front of the lady or I'll have your arse for my boot, clear?" Gagnon barked. The men nodded. "Excellent." He unwrapped one of the scarves around his neck and dismounted, his limbs stiff and aching, and motioned for the men to follow him inside.

After tying off their horses, the men removed their hats and shuffled their way into the chateau's front hall, each taking in the old house's charm with wide eyes and open mouths. When one reached to touch a small vase, Gagnon slapped his hand away and gave him a threatening look. A tall, wiry man entered from a side doorway and bowed to Jean-Luc, asking in a sober voice who he was and what business he had on the estate. Jean-Luc introduced himself, briefly explaining that he had come at Sophie's urgent request and that the men behind him had come to offer assistance to the Valiere family.

Guy Le Bon surveyed the assembled guests. After he had made a quick appraisal, he responded to Gagnon's crooked smile with a forced one of his own. "Charming," he said, looking reprovingly at Jean-Luc. "The lady is out visiting some of the families of the estate, but I have been instructed to welcome any visitors until she returns." He took another look at the gruff men before him, whose boots by now had deposited a good amount of snow and mud onto the pristine floor, before turning back to Jean-Luc. "Follow me; I will show you to the dining room, where you may set down your luggage. If you are hungry, I can inquire as to what is on hand from the stores in the pantry."

"As long as you've got wine, friend, we'll make do," Gagnon said, eyeing Le Bon with an expression of matching disdain. The two men glared at each other for a moment before Jean-Luc took a step between them. Le Bon turned and led them into the dining room.

"Thank you," Jean-Luc said, turning to Gagnon and his companions, gesturing for them to set down their luggage. "We'll wait here until Madame Valiere returns."

"I'll go see about the wine," Le Bon replied, wrinkling his nose. "Though there's plenty of ale and cider out beside the hog pen."

He left the room, closing the door behind him.

Two hours later as the group was finishing dinner, Jean-Luc leaned over to ask Gagnon where one of his men had gone. Before Gagnon could reply, the dining room door crashed open and the missing man, Simon, burst in and hurried over to Gagnon. He whispered urgently into his ear. Nodding slowly, Gagnon turned to Jean-Luc with a mischievous smile.

"Monsieur St. Clair, it appears we've a bit of news." He stood and clasped Simon on the shoulder.

"We were followed on the road from Paris, monsieur," Simon said, his chest puffed out. "Tracked if you will. But no harm done; we've found the rascal. He was prowling about the grounds near the road."

Springing from their seats, the men hurried out of the room and into the front hall. A figure sat slumped on a chaise in the drawing room, his hands bound by a thin cord of rope. His head was covered in a black hood, revealing a meager frame dressed in a black riding coat and brown trousers. One of Gagnon's men demanded the captive's name and followed his request with a smack to the head. Removing the hood and raising his hand, he asked again. Jean-Luc recognized the prisoner's face and rushed forward.

"No! Don't, please!" he shouted, swinging his body between the two. Jean-Luc turned to the group and held his hands out for calm. "There's no need for any violence. I know this boy." Camille's eyes darted around the room like a cornered animal. "Let's have his hands untied." When Camille had calmed down enough to speak, Jean-Luc crouched down beside him. "Camille, my boy, what on earth are you doing here?"

Camille moved his lips to speak but caught himself; instead he meekly lowered his eyes to the floor. Jean-Luc, along with his five rough companions, turned toward the figure now standing in the hallway.

"Does anyone care to explain what I'm seeing?" asked Sophie Valiere.

Sophie ushered Jean-Luc, Gagnon, Simon, and Camille into the study. A few minutes later, Pierre and Philippe Burnouf joined them, sitting themselves discreetly in one corner, wary of this band of swaggering newcomers from Paris. Sophie related the events of the previous few days; the men in the room hardly dared to look at her, while Gagnon offered more than one attempt at a flirtatious smile.

"What I'm still wondering," Gagnon interjected, poking a finger toward Camille, "is what the devil is this bugger doing here? Begging pardon, madame and monsieur."

Sophie turned to Jean-Luc. "Yes, is this a travel companion, St. Clair?"

"I am wondering myself," Jean-Luc said. "Camille, my lad, what brought you all the way from Paris? And all alone, in this weather?"

Camille glanced at Jean-Luc before mumbling something.

"Oi, what's that?" Simon asked gruffly. "Speak up, friend, we can't hear you."

"Mariette," Camille managed. "Mariette is afraid."

"What do you mean she's afraid?" Jean-Luc demanded.

"Mariette's afraid," he repeated.

"You already said that, mate," Simon barked, "now what—"

"No," Camille interrupted in a raised voice. "Mariette is afraid." He looked at Jean-Luc. "For you. Mariette wanted help. She wanted—I help you. So I come."

Jean-Luc exhaled slowly and rubbed a hand over his face. "Camille, I thank you for being such a good friend to my daughter, but this is hardly the best—"

"Mathieu," Camille said, turning his head to the side. "Mariette send. Mariette send me. Mariette send Mathieu. We help. We help you."

The following day Camille was sent in a carriage back to Paris, with strict orders to return to Mariette and tell her everything was all right. Thereafter, he was to send Mathieu a message telling *him* things were fine, and that he was under no circumstances to join his father in a provincial property dispute.

For the better part of a week, they waited. Sophie seemed genuinely grateful to have a few additional friends on her side, as the number of farmers and villagers pledging their support to defend Carcourt seemed to be dwindling by the day. Conversely, if the rumors coming from the nearby taverns and villages were to be believed, the number of locals as well as outlanders supporting Count de Montfort was growing. There were reports that the count sent men into Le Havre, offering free land and cash to idle dregs and criminals in exchange for a day's work with a pike or a pistol.

Sophie sent Philippe Burnouf to de Montfort's estate with a message that she desired to speak as equals and that she was willing to discuss his grievances in order to find a peaceful resolution. The day came and went with no response.

Several of the families loyal to the Valieres arrived at the house, seeking shelter until the danger had subsided. Stores of food, firewood, water, and essential provisions were stockpiled in the cellar of the main house; cattle and sheep that could be herded by Monsieur Abadain and his family were brought to the barns near the house—though they all expected that if the count's men came, they would steal or slaughter any livestock.

Meanwhile, Sophie spent the afternoon acquainting Jean-Luc, Gagnon, and his men to the grounds. She showed them the apple orchard to the south, the small ponds in the forest to the west behind the house, and they rode north along the road that skirted the snow-frosted wheat fields and grazing pastures. As they looked out over the fields, Jean-Luc pointed to a stretch of high ground half a mile away.

"I'm no military expert," he said through chattering teeth, "but if I were de Montfort, that's where I'd come from."

Gagnon was peering through a small spyglass he had purchased from one of the veteran farmers. "This bloody spyglass is shit," he grumbled.

"You're wrong about that," a voice came from behind them. They turned in their saddles to see Monsieur Le Bon. He sat in the saddle swathed in multiple fur coats and a large, fur hunting hat.

"You think this old piece of glass is worth twelve sous?" Gagnon said defensively. "Have a look yourself."

Le Bon looked at the wine smuggler and rolled his eyes. "I was referring to that hillock you pointed out, senator." Le Bon loosened his grip on the reins and rode forward.

"The lands north of those woods are riddled with marshy bogs and streams that flow downhill to the tributaries of the Seine. If de Montfort leads a party of mercenaries through that mire in the dead of winter, then he's as foolish as he looks; to say nothing of the early warning we'd have of them taking the road south through wide-open country. *And* as we've all come to know, some of these fellows are Chouans—battle-hardened rebels who have a lifetime of experience fighting in hedgerows, drainage dikes, and ditches. Even de Montfort isn't pompous enough to wholly ignore their advice. They will approach from the western woods." He pointed a gloved hand to the left where the land sloped into the ancient Silveison forest. "Moving along the trails and avoiding any main roads, under cover of darkness."

"He speaks the truth," Sophie said, her eyes set on the horizon. "Though I suspect sharing these observations is not the sole reason you've ridden out to meet us, monsieur?"

"Well, madame," he answered drily, "I haven't garbed myself like a Cossack to check on this one's faulty spyglass. I've come with news."

"Ever the bearer of good news," Sophie said. "Well—out with it."

"Philippe has returned. Monsieur Le Count demands that the property be vacated by tomorrow evening, or he will be forced to march on Carcourt."

Jean-Luc saw Sophie's shoulders slump slightly. "Well, then," she said, pausing so her voice wouldn't catch in her throat. "We must prepare."

"Gagnon," Jean-Luc said. "I hope your men know what they're doing."

Gagnon shut the spyglass with a snap and shoved it into a coat pocket. "Me too."

Sophie's horse began pawing the ground. "All of you. Back to the house; let's go!"

Jean-Luc nodded, laying a gloved hand on Sophie's before turning his horse with a jerk. The rest of the men followed. Before departing, Sophie looked out across the orchard as the fading winter sun cut between two trees in a shaft of orange light. A gentle breeze nipped at her nose, but she barely noticed, so moved was she by the calm beauty of this place, her home; a calm that seemed only to precede a coming storm. She felt a lump forming in her throat, unable to shake the feeling of guilt that this had all happened on her watch. She shivered. *Where are you, André?*

CHAPTER 54

Carcourt, Normandy

February 1807

L ate the following morning, one of the servants, believing de Montfort and his men had come at last, ran into the house, shouting frantically.

"Calm yourself, lad," Gagnon said. "Those men aren't here to harm you, so stop that pitiful squealing."

Help had finally arrived. A party of horsemen turned from the road onto the driveway leading to the chateau. Jean-Luc rushed out into the cold morning air followed by Sophie, wrapping a shawl around her shoulders. Jean-Luc estimated their number at a dozen. He hid his disappointment and offered Sophie an encouraging smile when a voice he had not heard in many months called out to him. Among the mounted men who'd ridden in from the outlying farms and villages was one who looked completely different. A cavalry trooper sat on a large chestnut gelding, his tall helmet shining, its horsetail plume swaying from side to side. A large, polished breastplate covered his chest and a long saber dangled from his left hip.

"Father," Mathieu called, raising his right arm in a salute.

"Mathieu," Jean-Luc answered, his right arm lifting in return. His breath came in labored bursts, while competing feelings of anger, frustration, and joy threatened to overwhelm him. "I told Camille to order you to stay home." Mathieu dismounted with practiced dexterity, and Jean-Luc pulled him into a full embrace, ignoring the freezing breastplate. Mathieu let out an embarrassed groan. When Jean-Luc finally let go, he grasped his son by both shoulders, taking one more look at his young soldier. "You never did listen to me, Mathieu."

Sophie walked through the snow to join them. "My goodness," she exclaimed, "is this the same Mathieu that would sit on my lap as I read him stories before bed?" Mathieu blushed, tilting his shoulder slightly in an awkward movement that belied his martial appearance.

"I tried reading romantic stories to you," Sophie said, her eyes beaming, "but all you had a mind for were the heroes and great warriors of the classics. Let's get you inside where you can warm yourself and eat."

That afternoon, Sophie called a meeting with representatives from the remaining families on the estate. She wanted to hear any last concerns they had, as well as acquaint them with the men from Paris who'd come to help. They gathered in the drawing room, where Sophie and Jean-Luc stood side-by-side facing the small assembly. They were joined by Monsieur Burnouf, his son Philippe, Pierre Abadain and perhaps two dozen of the farmers and outlanders from across the estate. Jean-Luc introduced himself, then Gagnon and his group of "security guards," after which one of the farmers' wives stood up.

"With all due respect, messieurs et madame," she called out, "we've about thirty men—some say that the count has nearly a hundred. What use is it if we are outnumbered beyond hope?"

Jean-Luc waited patiently for tempers to settle before answering. "It's not as many as I'd hoped for," he admitted, ignoring the angry look given him by Gagnon and a few of his men. "But it is many, many more than the count is expecting. Our numbers will make him reconsider his notion of simply walking in and seizing the property."

"But what about our homes?" the woman shot back. "Defending a mansion of stone is well enough, but who'll be protecting our property?"

"He does not have one hundred men," Sophie said. She turned to Monsieur Burnouf. "How many did you say he's likely to have gathered?"

"He's gotten most of the farmers from Bouville and Saint-Paër. I've heard he's cobbled fifty from the streets of Havre, a handful from among the Gypsy camp. So, I'd put his numbers at over eighty. At the least."

"Eighty men," Sophie said, mustering as much confidence as she could, "most of whom are not familiar with these lands, against thirty determined defenders who they don't know are here."

After quietly conferring with Burnouf and Gagnon, she declared that given Gagnon's knowledge of urban obstruction, his group would oversee the barricading of the main roads leading to the house. They would use felled trees and furniture from the house; Sophie forbade them from taking anything from the farmer's cottages or barns. Sophie then addressed the issue of the outlanders—Chouans. "These men are not farmers who carry muskets; they're hardened from fighting the republicans. They're some of the most-battle hardened men and women on the continent."

"It is true." One man, in his early thirties and wearing the plain clothes of a farmer, rose to his feet.

Burnouf cast a sharp look at the man. "I thought you were once one of the Chouans."

"I *am* a Chouan," the man responded, glaring back at him. He motioned to a handful of rustic-looking men and women beside him. "Many of us are. My name is Mollac. When my brother and sisters arrived in this province, Madame Valiere was the first, the *only*, to welcome us here. She said we could farm in peace if we paid our duties and respected the folk dwelling here. That is all a man leaving war can ask."

"What about the others?" Sophie asked, her tone almost pleading. "We've done no harm to them. I am grateful that you are standing with us, but haven't many of your fellows sided with de Montfort?"

"Our people are desperate," the man said with a shrug. "You offered them the best welcome you could, Madame Valiere, but the count promised them more."

"That count is a liar," one of the women in the crowd hissed. A loud murmur of agreement erupted.

"Yes," the Chouan said, nodding. "But in times of starvation and war, most people turn to the one who promises them relief. Here they were offered the chance to settle and farm amongst the prior inhabitants—taking what was left available to them. Monsieur de Montfort offered them a great deal more besides."

"What do you mean?" Sophie asked, holding her hands out for silence from the others.

"He has offered to petition the government to ennoble those who serve him loyally, and he has promised to gift the chateau we now sit in to those who fight for him. Free farmland is to be provided from the land confiscated from those loyal to you, madame."

"Where would he get the legal authority for any of that?" Jean-Luc demanded. "Or the money?"

Mollac shrugged and looked at Sophie with an apologetic expression.

"I know something of his finances, madame," Burnouf broke in. "All the taxes that, with no disrespect meant, you allowed him or his men to collect to pass into the general sum? The count has been storing them away for himself."

"That's impossible," Pierre Abadain cried, leaping to his feet. "I rode with the count's man, Sylvain or Sancho, whatever his bloody name is. I saw the duties collected, and they were all properly collected and tended to by—"

Monsieur Abadain sat back down, a look of understanding unfolding on his features. "We gave the dues to Guy Le Bon."

"I know all this," Sophie said, her face flushed. "We had an agreement that Sylvain and Le Bon would oversee the collections together. Pierre, how do you know de Montfort has been taking the duties for himself?"

"I'm sorry, madame. It happened only an hour ago—I was unable to find you before this meeting. I was in the cellar unloading the last crates of barley. Guy was closing the safe he uses for the estate's deposits. He seemed startled when he saw me enter, exclaiming that I had no business interrupting him. He then spent half a minute lecturing me, as is his way with the farmers. Anyhow, he scribbled something on a note and folded it into his breast pocket, then left in a huff. So surprised was I that I just stood there to collect my thoughts, when something out of place caught my eye. The safe. I looked closer at it and saw that it had been left ajar. Guy must have had something troubling on his mind or written in that document that he…"

"Pierre," Sophie interrupted quietly, "please come to the point."

"Yes, madame," Burnouf said. "I took a moment to look inside the safe. Now, I don't like prying about other people's business, especially as it pertains to their money matters, but I noticed a small note on top of the papers. It bore the signature of the count. I examined it and bless me if I hadn't uncovered the treachery that's been stinking about this place. Here, madame; I should have offered this to you before. I'm sorry."

Sophie took the note from Burnouf and quickly read its contents; whatever it contained was enough to make Sophie's face pale. An uneasy quiet passed over the crowd.

"Where is he?" she asked, looking around the room. "Where is Le Bon?"

That moment the door burst open and Philippe Burnouf stood in the entrance, his breath coming in short heaves. Pierre cried out to his son, "What is it, Philippe? Eh?"

Philippe straightened his posture, casting a quick glance around the assembled people, all of whom had turned their eyes on him. He turned to Sophie.

"Madame," he said, "I bring news."

Sophie stepped into the hall and immediately flinched, as she saw her two boys walking into the house. Upon seeing her they looked down and then to the other, as if searching for a way to share the blame.

"What have you two been doing?" Fear kept her voice low and her features taut. The scene of domestic drama, playing out in front of over a dozen witnesses, might have been comical were it not occurring in such a fearful moment.

"Beg pardon, madame," Philippe Burnouf said, "but the boys was with me. I didn't invite them on my reconnaissance, but nor do I think I could have shaken the little buggers. Anyhow, they showed me something, rather *someone*, I'd not thought about as yet."

"What?" she asked tersely.

Philippe looked at his father, perhaps for encouragement. "I found that little devil Lucas down by the creek leading out of the western woods. Under questioning, he said he'd been sent ahead to scout and report back to Sylvain if he saw anything indicating our, em, resistance. He then told me the group was on its way, that they would be coming via the west track through the cover of the ponds and woods. They will be arriving right around nightfall."

Sophie exhaled slowly, lifting her chin. "Christophe, Remy," she said, looking down at her boys with a grave face, "when this is all over, we will discuss you running off when I told you to stay in the house. In the meantime, Philippe, I thought I might rap you on the head for encouraging my boys' foolish behavior, but I can see something good has come of it— something *very* good. Now, you two boys are to begin helping settle these families downstairs or into the kitchen, away from the windows. Don't look at me like that; you've put yourselves in enough danger, associating with that Lucas, that you're lucky you had Philippe to bring you back. Go, help Monsieur Abadain wherever he needs you. Philippe come with me. St. Clair, Monsieur Gagnon, also with me, if you please."

As the sun fell, Sophie, Jean-Luc, and Monsieur Burnouf stood in the yard behind the house, gazing down the hill that led to the forest. Jean-Luc stole a look at Sophie who, though stoically silent, stared with apparent dismay. On three sides of the manor house blazes of light could be seen as the torches emerged from the small thickets and glades, halting just before the open ground that gently sloped up to the house. Visible in the fading winter light were distant trails of smoke, marking the cottages and houses that had been set ablaze by the approaching throng. Their cries and shouts were audible now, and flashes from the torches on metal surfaces indicated that they had not come unarmed.

"Are they carrying muskets?" Jean-Luc asked.

"I would guess most are armed with pikes or other such instruments," Burnouf replied. "Pitchforks, reaping hooks, whatever they got their thieving hands on."

Sophie had been silently counting the number of houses on fire. "Whatever they carry, they will not set foot in this house without a fight."

Her companions looked at her with concern. Her face constricted with anger, her teeth grinding visibly as she looked out over the distant crowd, which now seethed beneath the distant copse of trees.

"Don't fear, Madame Valiere," Burnouf said in a voice that belied his trembling hands. "We won't let them bring you to any harm."

"Pierre, I'm no longer afraid." Sophie shook her head. "That charlatan of a count will have to kill me to take our land."

"What did the note from de Montfort contain?" Jean-Luc asked.

"Le Bon, the old weasel, has been receiving *his own* payments from this pot of stolen duties in exchange for arranging my peaceful departure from the estate, which he was either unable or unwilling to accomplish. De Montfort scolded him for failing and promised to withhold his cut of the funds until I was *removed*." The men stood in stunned silence. "Monsieur Gagnon—" Sophie said in an icy voice, "I hope his men are killers."

They made their way to the front of the house where a cluster of armed farmers and villagers stood on the lawn; two dozen in all. Their presence gave Sophie some strength, but their numbers were pitifully small compared to the approaching horde on the far side of the manor. After Sophie had ensured the children and the older women had gone inside to the relative safety of the house, she called for the assembled villagers to gather round. Some were young boys, no more than twelve or thirteen years, others elderly farmers who had thought their fighting days behind them.

Jean-Luc scanned the movement across the field. "I see no one out front," he reported, "mounted or otherwise."

Sophie nodded. "I suppose the time for parlaying has passed."

"We'll teach them a hard lesson, Madame Valiere," Burnouf promised.

"Yes, we shall," Sophie said, her eyes smoldering. She turned her attention to the cluster of volunteers. "I don't know if I have the right words for you," she called out, her voice carrying the hoarseness of the previous days' exhaustion. "I am no Joan of Arc. All I can say to you in this moment is that I am sorry. I am sorry that I've allowed your families to be put in danger; sorry I have been unable to provide for your safety. Sorry that I could not stop that coward de Montfort from goading his supporters into taking up arms against you. I'm sorry that our own people, those who've dwelled on this land for longer than I've been alive, like Monsieur Guy Le Bon, have chosen to desert us in our hour of need. But I say this to you now—I swear on my life and the lives of everyone I love, I will never, *ever* yield to the rapacious designs of Jean-Claude Etienne-Marie Devereux, Count de Montfort. Tonight we will defend our land to the last, and that pampered child who deigns to call himself a man will have to drag his pristine robes and sealskin boots over my dead body before he steals the land of my people!"

A roar of defiance swept over the small assembly, resonating across the frosty fields and into the woods; the primordial courage of a humble people prepared to give their lives in defense of their homes.

Sophie gave the managing of the defense over to Burnouf and Gagnon. Jean-Luc followed her into the house, where Mathieu and Philippe Burnouf were stacking powder and ammunition and loading the few muskets on hand. Jean-Luc took a pistol from his son and picked up an old dueling sword taken from André's collection of prized artifacts. He walked over to an open window facing the backyard and peered out, his frosty breath the only thing visible beyond the curtains that fluttered gently in the cold winter breeze.

Monsieur Mollac and a handful of his Chouans, dressed in gray and brown and wearing hats with large goose feathers protruding from them, were walking out the front hall. He tipped his cap as he strode by Sophie and out into the yard, he and his men hardly making a sound as they disappeared into the cold winter night.

After several minutes, Jean-Luc turned his head, thinking he heard the cry of an owl. Another replied, and he felt a strange sense of security knowing that at least some of these strange woodsmen, veterans of a ferocious civil war, were on their side.

Sophie held a musket across her lap as she took a seat on the main stairwell. She had ensured that her boys were safely in the cellar with the other children and their mothers, most of whom held buckets of water in the likely event that a fire broke out in the house. She took a deep breath, knowing that the hour for violence had finally come.

Jean-Luc drummed his fingers on his pistol, stealing a look into the adjacent drawing room where Mathieu stood in his full cuirassier uniform beside Gagnon and two of his men. The two Parisian ruffians appeared as if eager to begin a game of dice. One of Gagnon's men held his gaze on Mathieu's war regalia, perhaps wondering the amount he could fetch for the equipment. Gagnon offered Mathieu a reassuring pat on the shoulder, though Jean-Luc noticed the older man swallow hard as he peered out a window. Mathieu stared ahead with a steely gaze; his breastplate, though too large for a boy of barely fifteen, shone in the candlelight and the sword at his side and large helmet gave him the appearance of a real soldier. Although anxious, Jean-Luc could not deny the fatherly pride he felt in that moment. His thoughts were interrupted by the hooting of the owls, which had taken up again. This time several calls came out in rapid succession, and for a tense moment Jean-Luc held his breath.

Several musket shots exploded in the yard, and Jean-Luc—once recovered from the initial shock—slowly extended his face from behind the shutter to see what was happening. Flashes of red and yellow illuminated the fields like lightning during a summer storm. A brief silence was followed by calls and shouts from men in the yard perhaps fifty meters away. More shots rang out, this time rolling in succession and coming from farther away. In the flashes of light Jean-Luc could distinguish little, seeing only plumes of smoke drifting across the snowy ground. As his nerves adjusted to the jolt of opening combat, he began to notice in the distance long, creeping shadows stealing across the fields like phantoms. A few more muskets fired from the nearby trees, though these were becoming more sporadic. All the while the creeping shadows drew nearer, and the muskets firing in a continuous thunder drowned out the pops from the nearby Chouans. Suddenly, the firing from just outside the house ceased altogether, and Jean-Luc peered outside to try and see what was happening.

Sophie left the staircase and joined the onlookers at the windows in the drawing room. Apart from the flashes from the muzzles of far-off muskets she could distinguish little. She reminded herself that the evening promised to be a long and drawn-out affair. Judging by the ferocity of this opening salvo, she decided that the Chouans had successfully ambushed their attackers; though, as each moment passed, she felt more and more fearful for their safety. The musket fire coming from farther away was not slackening. Just as she was preparing to check on her boys, the front door slammed open. Mollac, his face sweaty and smeared black from musket smoke, rushed in, followed by four of his comrades.

"Bandages and water!" he shouted, climbing over Gagnon's makeshift barricade. The last Chouan inside was propping up a young man around his shoulder. He had been shot square in the chest, and, as he coughed, blood splattered from his mouth. Sophie looked away so she wouldn't be sick.

"Bandages and water!" Mollac bellowed again, shoving Gagnon out of his way. The wounded youth moaned as they carried him into the kitchen, where one of the farmers wives waited with a makeshift triage table—but the boy was dead before they managed to clean his wound.

Mathieu, as shaken as everyone else at this dreadful sight, was the first to regain his senses. He rounded on those still standing in the hall. "What were you expecting, a fight without blood? Return to your positions or we'll all share the same fate."

Gagnon shoved a small bureau against the front door, after which he piled chairs and other pieces of furniture until they reached above his head.

Jean-Luc returned to his window and looked out. Nothing. "Why have they stopped advancing?" he asked. From behind him he heard Mollac addressing Sophie.

"There are many, madame," the Breton Chouan said, wiping his begrimed face with a cloth. "In truth, I did not expect to see so many. But we have made them pay dearly. We waited until they crept right in front of us and fired true. I hit two or three at least."

"Thank you," Sophie said, still reeling from the ferocity of the fight. She looked back toward the kitchen. "You're wounded—"

"Forget about him," Mollac said, spitting out the nearest window. "He knew the dangers. Just keep your men calm and we may yet survive; though these men have come prepared."

"Why are they not attacking?" Sophie asked. "If there are so many, why have they halted?"

Mollac took a swig of water from a champagne glass. "We gave them a start. But they *will* attack again. Do you have men guarding the roof?"

Sophie nodded. "Yes. Philippe and some of the others have gone up."

"Good, then we may—"

Mollac was cut off by the sound of a sharp whistle outside. "What is that?" Sophie asked as she ran toward the window. The whistle sounded again, and everyone in the room raised their weapons. A voice carried from outside, at first barely audible, but as they listened, it became clearer, at least to Sophie.

"It's him." Sophie grimaced. "It's de Montfort."

An ominous silence pervaded the grounds as the voice became clear to those in the front hall and its adjacent rooms. "We do not wish you or your people any more harm, Madame Valiere," de Montfort cried from the back lawn. "I do not trust that I won't be fired upon if I come any closer. But if you swear not to shoot, I have someone here who wishes to speak with you."

Sophie exchanged a look with Jean-Luc. "That bastard," she said, cocking the pistol in her hand. "I'll shoot him myself." She raised the pistol toward the window, but Jean-Luc grabbed her arm before she fired.

"Sophie," he said quietly, "I know you hate the man. But think for a moment. Think of your family. Perhaps we can delay them or convince them that they cannot win."

Sophie exhaled, her face void of expression. "Send him in," she called out in a clear voice. "We will not shoot an unarmed man. There is still honor in *this* house even if you have none in yours!"

The defenders kept alert at the windows in case of foul play. Pierre Burnouf waved to one of the dining room windows, and Guy Le Bon climbed through and into the front entranceway. He stopped in the hall and faced the group of angry onlookers, some of whom had to be pulled by

Jean-Luc and Mathieu back to their posts. Le Bon returned their wrathful stares with impassivity, as if he had come to see to the necessary work of tax collection. His cheeks and nose were red, almost frost-bitten, but he seemed oddly comfortable for a man straddling the two sides of a feud.

"Madame Valiere," he said, bowing his head respectfully.

Sophie seethed and Jean-Luc thought he might need to step between them, but her frown lifted into a sinister smile, and she looked down at her pistol. "Monsieur Le Bon," she said, curtsying formally. "You have come to my house at the head of a host of criminals and cutthroats. You have aligned yourself with a coward, and a thief. You have put my life in danger, and by extension endangered the lives of my children. I will give you one sentence—*one* sentence—before I have Monsieur Gagnon and his men take you upstairs and cut you to pieces. If you think I am not serious, then you clearly, in over six years of sharing my home, have not come to know me. So, monsieur, speak, or you will die."

Le Bon slowly unwrapped his scarf. When he had finished, he craned his neck to either side and reached into a coat pocket. Removing a small brown ledger, he took a few steps towards Sophie, which caused every man in the room to take a step toward him. He relented, putting his hands up in front of him.

"Very well," he said drily, "if I may not show you what is in this account book, then perhaps I might be allowed to tell you of its contents?"

Sophie nodded. "Go on."

"Madame, I have as much loyalty to the man leading the rabble outside as these men here have to the queen of England. I *was* sent to deliver a message. And, as you've likely guessed, it is the same bleating about the count's rightful inheritance being taken from him, of all the assistance offered, of how he gave you every opportunity to align with him and so on and so forth. Alas, madame, that is not why I've come here."

"I don't fucking care why you've come here," Sophie answered. "I don't care if you are here to apologize, or to grovel, or to profess your undying devotion to me. Do you know why, *Guy*? I'll tell you—this very day Pierre Burnouf found the document you so foolishly forgot to lock in the cellar safe. He also read of the agreement you had, that you were not to be paid for until you had seen me gone from my own house."

Le Bon lowered his eyes to the floor with a sigh. Raising them slowly, he lifted the ledger in his right hand, offering it to Sophie. "Madame, I don't know precisely what Pierre told you, or what he *believes* he saw me doing. But I assure you he is not entirely versed in the facts of the matter."

"In case you haven't noticed," Jean-Luc broke in, "there are men here that have come to kill. If you would, please, get on with it."

Le Bon straightened his posture. "As *I* was saying, madame, Monsieur Burnouf, loyal servant though he is, is not acquainted with the facts of which I will now avail you." Le Bon then offered a detailed but concise tale of how he, throughout de Montfort's executing of his schemes, had been keeping the receipts of all transactions, as well as forging duplicates of the ledger Sylvain "Sancho" Lavalle used to manage the stolen funds. It was a copy of one of these pages that Pierre Burnouf must have witnessed him depositing in the safe in the cellar; the payments were indeed for him, but his aim was not personal profit but rather documenting proof of the count's illegal activity. "Therefore, it is my hope that you may find faith in my actions," Le Bon concluded quietly, "if not my words, madame. I give to you an exact facsimile of the ledger of Sylvain Lavalle. You may use it as evidence in a court of law, or as a guide to start your own investigations, if that be your pleasure. But I wish to deceive you no longer, my lady."

"My pleasure would be to see those two halfwit bandits hung from the gallows." Sophie's eyes met Le Bon's. "However, your service, I believe, gives hope to us all that we are not entirely abandoned by our neighbors." She stepped forward, taking the ledger in her hands and offering Le Bon a warm embrace. "I'm sorry I doubted you, Guy." She released him and looked down at the ledger, but before she had opened the first page, Le Bon's head snapped back with a violent jerk and his body went limp and crashed to the floor.

"Guy!" Sophie screamed, kneeling down at his side. "Can you hear me?"

Le Bon blinked slowly and looked up at her. "I am going now, madame."

"No," Sophie cried out, placing her hands on either side of his face. "Oh, Guy, I'm so sorry. All this time I thought—I had misunderstood your—"

"Yes, madame," Le Bon interrupted, his glazed eyes looking up at hers. "I know it was of my doing. You need not apologize."

Sophie was oblivious to the ferocious gunfire now rattling on both sides of the house. "Is there anything I can do? Can you move?"

"I am going. I die blissfully knowing I no longer hold your hatred. For I..." his voice trailed off. "Sophie," Le Bon whispered, his eyes almost closed. "Do not be afraid. André is—"

Guy Le Bon let out a sigh that was imperceptible in the tumult raging all around them, but Sophie heard it and knew it had been his final breath. She cradled his head in her arms.

A musket ball smashed the wall a few feet away, bringing her back to the urgency of the moment. The noise of the fighting made it difficult to gauge the danger and decide where to offer help, if they were to prevent the house being overrun. Her thoughts were interrupted by the tall figure of Monsieur Mollac standing over her. She reached up to his outstretched hand and rose to her feet. Two of Gagnon's men lay on the ground, one shot through the shoulder, another dead.

"Be careful, madame," Mollac said, his calm voice belying his grim appearance. "Their bullets are beginning to find their mark. The count has many, but I will see if I can make it a bit fewer."

Sophie turned her head slowly. "What do you mean?" She felt the detachment in her voice, as if she were somehow outside her own thoughts.

"This is not our fight." Mollac slung his musket across his arms, waving his Chouan comrades over to him. "Nor is it theirs." He jerked his head out to the yard.

With that, he walked over to the window and put two fingers in his mouth. A moment later three shrill whistles rang out, followed by three longer ones; the same owl call as before. The musket fire outside did not cease, but it slackened a little.

Mollac craned his neck out the window, careless of the enemy's rounds. "Brothers!" he shouted out in a booming voice. "It is Mollac. The man you follow has lied to you! He will not give you what he's promised. I've just heard from a man who's explained the truth. Go to the tavern and I will explain more, but do not die for this coward." Mollac turned to Sophie; "Farewell for now, madame," he said. "I do not think any *Chouan* will bother you any more tonight."

He motioned to his comrades and walked out the front door as if he were leaving a formal soiree that no longer held his interest. A few moments later, the owl call came from outside the entrance. Several answering calls came from all around the house, some unnervingly close to the windows. A sharp whistle sounded, and then footsteps could be heard crunching through the snow.

"What? What is this? Where are you going?" de Montfort's voice cried out. "You vermin. You ungrateful swine. Come back or I'll have you guillotined in the market square!"

One or two additional calls echoed across the snowy fields before a long silence fell.

"Ha," Gagnon cackled, loading a musket in his lap as he peeked out the nearest window. "Sounds like your lads are leaving!" A musket ball smashed the windowpane next to his head, and he cursed as splinters and shards of glass sprayed across the room.

"Your hired guns are abandoning you, Montfort," Jean-Luc called out. "Leave now before it's too late."

"What does it matter?" yelled de Montfort, his voice rising in rage. The defenders could now see that he was mounted on a horse, his profile visible as he led it across the field. "So a few woodland peasants have fled like dogs. Cowards! It means nothing. I have your grounds surrounded, and my hundred outnumber your dwindling stock of farm boys. How long do you think you can last, *madame?*"

Sophie had made her way to a window in the drawing room. "You have failed, count," she shouted, keeping her face hidden behind the wall. "May God have mercy on you when my husband hears of what you've done here to his family. To his children."

"Your *husband?*" the count cried in a mocking voice. "The man that has left you alone to manage the land that he should be overseeing? While he whores his way through the Prussian hinterlands with a frozen prick? You think he will affect any of this?" De Montfort's laughter echoed across the half-frozen fields. "I have more fear of that heartsick little ferret Le Bon than I do of your absent husband."

"Your *hired man,* Guy Le Bon," Sophie called, "told me with his dying breath how he deceived you. You thought you were paying for his loyalty; the man kept a record of your every payment and swindle. I have it here in my hands. You'll have to kill me if you wish to retrieve it, you sniveling coward."

A tense silence followed as de Montfort, presumably wrestling with how to proceed, held back his remaining men. "You whoresons inside there," he seethed. "Have you no shame? By the gods, you risk your lives for a *woman?* For this Lorelei witch? A whore who betrayed her husband while he was away fighting for his nation, offering to spread her legs for me?"

No one inside the house moved, save for Mathieu, who was quietly reloading his pistol. "Go home, you bastard," Pierre Burnouf shouted, wincing and holding his flank where a wound had soaked his shirt in blood.

"A curse on this wretched house!"

Sophie crawled over to Burnouf and began gently dabbing his wound with a wet cloth. Even though his face showed no sign of fear or pain, his loss of blood now told on his vitality. He did not protest against her gentle touch. "Philippe is still upstairs?" She whispered.

Burnouf nodded. "He will not leave his post, my lady."

From all sides of the house a murmur arose. It seemed to grow louder by the second. Sophie looked at Burnouf with fear in her eyes.

"Here they come," Mathieu said, aiming a pistol out the nearest window. "Find cover if you can." He fired a shot. Before the smoke had cleared it was answered with a deafening eruption. He placed a hand over his head and dropped down against the wall. Bullets tore through windowpanes and curtains, some smashing into the painting just above Sophie's head. Jean-Luc, fearing for her life, grabbed Le Bon's body and tried to shield Sophie with it. She pushed him away.

Cries and shouts raged just outside the front door, which shook with a loud clatter. A few more strikes was all it took, and the door burst from its hinges and down onto the makeshift barricade. A man with a reddened face stumbled through the opening and climbed over the pile of fallen furniture. Gagnon crept up to the man and rammed a pike through his chest. The man flailed his arms, his eyes bulged, a spasm shook his body, and he fell forward with a groan.

"Close it back up!" Jean-Luc shouted, rising to his feet. "We have to close it—"

"No," Mathieu jumped in front of him, wrapping his arms around his father. The two struggled briefly before Mathieu spun his father and shoved him safely back behind one of the passageways.

"What are you doing?" Jean-Luc shouted at his son. "We can't let them inside."

"Father, be quiet!" Mathieu lowered his sword to his side, turning his head to the side. "Listen."

Sophie looked up at the two of them with a combination of terror and the crazed courage of battle. "What are you *doing*? *Mathieu*?"

"Listen," Mathieu hissed, turning to the door.

"Hear what, you bloody madman?" Gagnon demanded.

"Don't go near the door!" Jean-Luc cried after his son, who took several strides toward the front door. "Mathieu, *please* don't go out there."

Mathieu stood still in the doorway for a moment before turning slowly around. "Don't you hear it?"

The sound slowly became audible to everyone. A few shouts echoed outside from the direction of de Montfort's men, but it was not the shouting that caused Sophie, Jean-Luc, and everyone else in the hallway to walk slowly toward the entranceway. They took short steps like small children creeping downstairs, hoping not to be noticed by their parents. A distinct rumble grew in their air, and what had moments earlier been dread now turned to a desperate hope. A horse whinnied in the dark, and then another. A voice cried out, and another answered him. Now the hoofbeats could be heard clearly, and a figure appeared from the darkness, his face indistinguishable but his uniform unmistakable. A cavalryman. A dragoon. He turned his head and shouted something to his rear before raising something in his hand. He set it to his mouth, and the shrill call of a bugle rang out in the cold night air; from the darkness, a loud cry responded as dozens of horsemen rode slowly into view, walking their horses forward in a long line that stretched the span of the yard. Another bugle called out, and one rider rode forward at a canter. Mathieu dashed out of the doorway and into the yard. This time Jean-Luc did not try to stop him.

CHAPTER 55

Carcourt, Normandy

February 1807

André looked at his burning house with a vacant expression, but his flaring nostrils betrayed the rage smoldering in his chest. He turned to his left and nodded to the rider beside him. Without a word, the man turned his horse and rode off along the road from which they'd just come. André turned his eyes forward again and lifted his right arm. "Take any who surrender," he bellowed, baring his teeth. "Give steel to any who resist. *Vive l'Empereur!*"

As the dragoons rode onto the front lawn, they spread out, one troop to the right side of the house, the other to the left, the last riding behind both in a reserve. A man wearing the uniform of a cuirassier ran out from the house, waving his hands. The troopers on either side of André drew their pistols, but André held up his arm to hold fire. The man approached at a dead sprint.

"Lieutenant-Colonel, wait."

"Who are you?" André shouted, unsheathing his saber in a clear challenge.

"Lieutenant-Colonel Valiere," the man repeated, though, judging by his voice, he was hardly older than a boy. "It is me."

"Who?" André demanded, impatient, as his horsemen rode past him on either side.

"It is Ensign St. Clair," the young man repeated. "Mathieu St. Clair. I am with Madame Sophie and my father. You've saved us."

"Mathieu St. Clair?" André called back, astonished. He took a closer look, and, in spite of his hot-blooded temper, he let out a laugh. He looked up ahead at the house, candlelight flickered from within while plumes of smoke wafted across the yard. "Find a mount," André cried, signaling his riders to bring a spare horse. "And give the order."

A few moments later, Mathieu mounted and rode to the front of the long line. He raised his saber and shouted, "Squadron forward, present sabers on my order."

The horsemen spurred their mounts forward and, in a matter of seconds, were bearing down the hill in back of the house. Scattered throughout the field were thirty or forty men stampeding across the slippery ground in a confused mob, slipping and falling, abandoning their torches and weapons. A few reached the safety of the woods, but most were still stumbling across the fields when the horsemen caught up with them.

"Present sabers," Mathieu called out over the rumbling hooves. The troopers unsheathed their swords in near-perfect unison, the steel glinting from the light of the torches and flames from the house. "*Vive l'Empereur!*"

The dragoons echoed his cry in unison, descending on the fleeing enemy in a precise line formation. As they picked up speed, some scattered pistol and musket fire came from the woods, though almost all of de Montfort's men threw up their hands in surrender, many crying out for mercy. The handful that swung with their pikes or dared to fire on the horsemen were dispatched with saber thrusts.

The battle did not last five minutes, and to some of André's less experienced troopers, it seemed almost frustrating to have ridden so hard only to see their foes surrender at first sight. But to André, the one-sided nature of the fight and a lack of serious casualties to his men came as a great relief.

He rode to the front of the house, hardly noticing the black marks along the side of the chateau where torchbearers had tried to smoke out their prey. He did not even see that the thick oak beside the front door had been smashed to pieces. Three dead bodies strewn out among the lilies and roses of his garden, to say nothing of the damage done by dozens of hooves, barely caught his attention. He gave no orders for the treatment of the prisoners or for his own casualties, which were negligible, because in that moment he saw only one thing: Sophie.

He removed his helmet as he walked through the entrance of the house and felt the embrace of his wife—the entire world outside fading to nothing. They held each other for several minutes, and time seemed to stop. Sophie buried her face in André's chest, and he clung to her with an immovable grip.

The other defenders of the house—Gagnon and his men, Pierre Abadain and Jean-Luc—looked at the two with an exhausted relief. In fact, not one word was said in that chaotic reunion, and taking their cues from André and Sophie Valiere, the brave men and women who had so stubbornly defended a house that was not even theirs began embracing each other.

When André and Sophie at last allowed themselves to let go, they stared at each other, neither able to believe that their reunion had come at last. After exchanging a few words of affectionate greeting, Sophie turned back toward her comrades, embracing them each in turn.

Though moved beyond words at the sight of his home and his people, André had managed to keep his officer's bearing. But at the sight of his children, his two boys running into the hall with tears on their faces, he fell to the floor. He pulled them close as they threw their weight onto him, wrapping their arms around his neck and shoulders. He didn't care that his troopers saw his tears; he had come home, and his family was safe.

CHAPTER 56

Outside Rouen, Normandy

February, 1807

A few miles to the south, a lone rider galloped along the road to Rouen, passing through dark hollows and open fields concealed behind shrouds of fog. The drumming of the horse's hooves interrupted the silence of the winter night, and after some miles, the exhausted animal had begun to snort and buck, but the Count de Montfort forced it on, unwilling to halt before he'd passed through this dark countryside. He stole a look back and saw no pursuers on the road. He had fled unharmed from the disaster unfolding at Carcourt, and now allowed himself to hope of making a genuine escape. A smile passed over his features, and the frozen winter air that gnawed at his cheeks now seemed slightly less irritable.

True, he thought, the night had not turned out as he had hoped, but perhaps there would be a ship bound for the West Indies leaving the next day. Even better, he might be able to charter a ship himself and sail for the English blockade lurking a few miles offshore. He could make his way to England and push the memory of Carcourt and Sophie Valiere—that sweet yet beguiling devil of a woman—out of his mind forever.

"Curse this dreary country. A nation at war with itself and utterly unworthy of peace and prosperity."

He would wait, patiently obtaining the favor of English society to regain his fortune. He'd then return to France at the *proper* time—when Napoleon was defeated and deposed. All he need do was wait for that inevitable defeat, and he would then return with the victorious allies, perhaps at the head of Bourbon volunteers or as an officer in the English army.

He smiled again, looking up at the gnarled and twisted branches of the ancient oak and yew trees as he galloped beneath them. *I will return when they have killed each other off once again.*

Something in the frigid night air caused him to shudder, and he slowed his horse to a trot. He turned his head to the side, listening. Nothing. He turned and glanced back again, but saw nothing. Satisfied that it had only been his imagination, he kicked his horse on once again. A crow called out from somewhere in the forest, and the count wrapped his furs tighter around him so that they covered the bottom of his face. As he rounded a broad bend, he felt a sudden shiver crawl up his spine—in the middle of the road a few paces ahead sat a solitary rider dressed in a dark brown coat and wearing a tricorn hat. De Montfort's mouth opened slightly, and he sat up straight in the saddle, reminding himself to be calm. He was simply returning to his home in Rouen from business in Le Havre. He had done nothing wrong.

Relieved at least to see that the man appeared to be a civilian and not a soldier, de Montfort raised his hand in greeting. The rider did not respond, but sat motionless on his horse, his gaze following the count as he approached. De Montfort could see the man's eyes but little else, as he wore a mask of black cloth that covered his features up to his nose. De Montfort shuddered once again but offered a warm smile.

A moment of silence ensued as the two came face to face. So close to his escape, de Montfort felt no compunction to introduce himself; but seeing as how this mysterious figure seemed disinclined to do the same, he cleared his throat.

"Good evening, friend," the count said in as calm a voice as he could manage. "May I pass along on my route, or shall I ask you your name first?" The masked figure lifted his right arm, signaling that it was all right to pass. But it was not his right arm that caught the count's attention, causing him to gasp slightly. It was the left—or rather, the lack of a left arm from the elbow down—that startled him. "Have you had an unfortunate accident? That appears to be a rather serious injury."

The rider slowly arched his back, raising his posture. "Where are you going, monsieur?" he asked in a quiet voice.

"Me?" de Montfort asked, raising a hand to his chest. "Well, I'm not sure I see how that is the business of a man who does not wish to introduce himself, but very well. I am riding for Rouen, where I have business."

The rider laid his right hand on the pommel of his saddle. "What business calls you to Rouen at such an hour?"

De Montfort frowned; impatience beginning to creep into his disposition. He took another look behind him before urging his horse closer to the man. "My business is just that—my business. Though I might ask you the same question."

The man across from him exhaled, reaching up and removing his tricorn. His hair was dark, and a large scar across the man's scalp had replaced the hair on part of his head. The sight of this grisly wound only added to Montfort's growing unease. The man ran a hand through his hair, the parts that remained, and replaced his hat. "Are you armed, monsieur?"

"Am I—what?" de Montfort blurted.

The rider urged his horse forward, halting a few feet from de Montfort. "I asked if you carry arms."

De Montfort smiled nervously. "I don't see—" he looked to his left and right before turning back to the man before him. "You're awfully bold—for one that conceals half his face."

"If you do not carry arms," the man replied in a cold voice, ignoring the count's comment, "then it is in your best interest to say as much now."

"What do you mean, my best interest?" the count demanded. "If you must ask impertinent questions, then yes, I have a pistol in my saddlebag— for emergencies—and as you can see very well with your own eyes, I have this sword."

A muffled sound came from the man hidden behind the mask, laughter, but utterly unpleasant. He pulled up the mask, revealing his face. De Montfort shuddered.

"You do not know me, monsieur," the man said, covering his face once again, "but I know who you are." With his good arm he reached to his waist and slowly unsheathed a long saber. "I've ridden nearly a thousand miles across snow and ice, through enemy territory, through grand cities and huntsman's cottages, over frozen rivers and blood-soaked battlefields. I've come all this way and now fate has decided that on this night, along this insignificant stretch of road, I should happen upon you." The man reached out his arm, his saber point resting several inches from de Montfort's throat. "Do you know why this has come to pass?"

De Montfort stared down at the blade, his mouth moving but no words coming out. After an unnerving silence, the unknown horseman lowered the blade.

"Get off your horse." The man swung a leg around and nimbly dismounted his own. He took a few steps and looked at the count. "Did you not hear me? I said, dismount."

The count glanced behind him, considering doubling back the way he'd come. "This is highly irregular," he protested.

"You have two options, Count de Montfort—"

"How do you know my name?"

"You have two options," the man repeated. "You may turn around and ride toward the estate of André and Sophie Valiere, or you may take your chances dueling a crippled man with one arm."

Count de Montfort's face sagged, and he sized up the man in front of him once more. "And if I refuse?"

"Then I will not allow you to pass," the other man replied. "And you will be taken back to Carcourt—the place from which you are now fleeing, having failed in your attempts to seize it from its rightful owners. Get down off your horse; this is your last warning."

De Montfort swallowed hard, ultimately deciding to take his chances dueling with a cripple, where at least he had a one-arm advantage, rather than attempting to outpace him on horseback. If he managed to wound the man, he might buy himself a few precious seconds to remount and gain a head start. He dismounted slowly, removing his large fur coat once he had tied up his horse. He draped it over his saddle and reached for his pistol, tucking it into a coat pocket.

"As a man of honor, I must accept your challenge, ill-mannered though it may be." He turned to his adversary and unsheathed his sword. "Have you dueled much, monsieur?"

The man opposite lifted his saber. "One might say so."

The count assumed a fighting stance, raising his rapier, which was longer yet much thinner than the other man's sword. "*En garde.*"

The man facing him crossed one foot over the other. The count, himself no stranger to the customs of dueling, stepped to match his footwork. He then lunged in a feint before pulling back. The other man did not flinch. The count took several lateral steps. "I see you have experienced footwork—"

Before he had finished speaking the other man lunged and slapped his rapier aside, pressing his saber point against the count's throat. A feeling of terror passed through de Montfort, and he could smell the other man's breath in his face.

"Not fast enough, count."

The man pressed the saber's pommel to the count's forehead and shoved him backwards, sending him sliding and almost falling into the slush. When he regained his footing, he grimaced, aware of the impropriety of the man's behavior.

"How dare you?" he cried. He thrust forward, quicker this time, and the other man's blade whistled through the air as he swung in defense. Count de Montfort stepped back with a look of satisfaction, lowering his blade.

But then the masked man shot forward with startling speed, shoving the count's parry aside and smashing an elbow into his stomach. As the count heaved over, breathless, the man once again raised his blade to de Montfort's throat, his face contorted into a grimace. As he wheezed to try and get air back into his lungs, de Montfort sensed, correctly, that the man holding the blade was deciding whether or not to kill him.

"This is your best?" the man growled, shoving de Montfort's head backwards once again. "You are unworthy of a duel."

Count de Montfort, finally catching his breath, gave his assailant a look of hatred. His nostrils flared and the vein across his forehead bulged as his cheeks turned crimson. With a guttural scream he ran toward his challenger, who had turned his back. Raising his rapier above his head he swung down with all the force he could summon—but it was not enough. The masked man ducked his head slightly and held out his boot, catching the count's foot and sending him face-first into the mud. For a moment, the count lay still, his face covered brown with dirt and pebbles that stuck to his cheeks. He heard footsteps approaching behind him and held his breath. A hand reached down to the back of his neck, pulling him over onto his back. He closed his eyes, but no blow landed.

He opened one eye and looked up. "Who in God's name are you?" he cried out in a whimper, the other man's face now only inches away.

The man reached up and removed the cloth. He looked to be about thirty years of age, his face marred by scars that gave his otherwise handsome features a fairly disturbing appearance. "My name is Marcel Moreau, and I've come to bring revenge to the man who threatened the family of my friend, André Valiere. But you, good count, are not worthy of killing."

Moreau grabbed the count's collar with his remaining hand and head-butted him in the face so hard that he fell into the muddy snow, unconscious. He would not wake until he'd been brought back to Carcourt, where he would be held in the cellar until his formal arrest two days later.

EPILOGUE

Carcourt, Normandy
Summer 1807

A few months after the attack of de Montfort and his men had receded from immediate memory and the process of rebuilding had begun, André and Sophie invited their "guardians and protectors" for a weekend in the Normandy countryside. The restoration of the house and its interior was largely completed, and the rebuilding of barns and cottages that had been put to the torch was underway.

André and Sophie had turned their efforts toward the legal charges they would bring against Count de Montfort, who languished in a prison in Le Havre, awaiting his full sentence to be pronounced. In total, thirty-seven of the men captured by André's dragoons had followed their leader into a jail cell, though most would be considered for bail after a minimum two-year sentence had been served.

Pierre Burnouf had succumbed to his injuries, and his son Philippe had mourned the loss of his father in pained but stoic quiet. Major Moreau, recovered from his own wounds and staying at Carcourt for the time being, did much to keep the boy active and in good spirits, taking him riding or hunting whenever he was not helping with the construction of the new houses.

Moreau had been discharged from the army, with full pension, following the gruesome injuries he suffered at the battle of Mohrungen. The squadron's casualties sustained that day were so severe that they spent the remainder of the campaign convalescing outside the siege of Danzig, recovering from wounds and guarding supplies. Moreau's fortuitous arrival with André at Carcourt the night of the attack was of his own free will as he, along with the other dragoons, opted to spend their first days of leave joining their commander in his fight to reclaim his home.

Among the other guests visiting Carcourt were Jean-Luc and his new belle—Lucille Laurent.

Mademoiselle Laurent had been instructed by the Marquis de Landreville to allow the St. Clair family to dwell in his home until they managed to get back on their feet. At first Jean-Luc declined the generous offer, unwilling to impose himself on the property of a departed friend, but his house had been put on the market and the property was soon snatched up. Lucille's insistence became too much for Jean-Luc to decline. Before long they had become lovers dwelling under the same roof, enjoying a happiness that neither had known in years.

"Alas, yes, it is true," Jean-Luc said with an embarrassed smile as they finished breakfast one morning. "That was my most recent, and likely final, meeting with the emperor."

"So," André said over a cup of coffee, "the Grand Armée marched into Paris, and after all the service you've given the empire—Napoleon said that?"

Lucille placed an arm around Jean-Luc's shoulder, evidently amused at his misfortune. "That was his thanks for the 'hero of Naples.'"

"It was just my luck," Jean-Luc admitted, grinning sheepishly, "that Minister Fouché was riding alongside Napoleon. Thank God Joseph recognized me—otherwise I think I might have been arrested. But as they rode past on the Champs-Élysées, I saw the police minister whisper something into the emperor's ear. The emperor turned and offered me a scornful look—oh, I'll never forget it. He then leaned forward and said to Fouché in a voice loud enough for all nearby to hear, 'Such men as *that* deserve no place in the presence of lions such as *these*'—pointing at the tall men of his Imperial Guard marching in glory behind him. A moment later he was gone—my final meeting with Napoleon." He threw up his hands and bowed slightly.

"Good riddance," Lucille scoffed.

Sophie nodded her agreement. "Any man who confides in Fouché and rejects our 'hero of Naples' cannot possibly be a true genius." She stood and walked over to Jean-Luc, wrapping him in a consoling embrace that felt somehow congratulatory.

Moreau leaned forward. "But one last question, if you please, senator," he said. "What of the woman who ran away with the fortune from your estates? Where did this Madame Maduro make off to?"

Jean-Luc smiled ruefully, his hand still holding Lucille's. "Well," he sighed, "Isabella never told me where she would go. But after she left Paris, my brave young friend Camille seemed to behave more—like himself—perhaps no longer feeling controlled by his mother…*that* was his true relation to Isabella." A loud gasp emanated from the table, all except Lucille. "Camille, or should I say *Camillo*, had seized several letters before she made her departure. With Lucille's professional assistance, we were able to confirm that the letters were intended for the police minister—the *cardinal*—and they revealed most of the boy's history. Apparently from a young age he suffered bouts of dizziness; he would suddenly lose his vision and stumble. One day, when they still lived in Spain, Camille walked out into the street in front of a carriage; like there was no one else on the road. The horses were reined in, but not in time. The boy was struck—and in the aftermath, Isabella, who had been abandoned by her family for her outspoken republican views, had the carriage driver put behind bars, at an expensive price. The driver was a cousin or some such relation to the mayor, and this mayor demanded payment from Isabella for his relation to be locked away. It was in the aftermath of these events that she decided to make her move to Paris. Well, that is a hidden part of her story, but the worst part was the confession."

"Confession?" Sophie asked.

Jean-Luc took a sip of tea. "In a letter sent after she'd arrived in Paris, this also addressed to Fouché, she admitted to something quite disturbing. The real reason the carriage driver's prison term was bought at such a high price was that, according to his testimony, the woman escorting Camille, Isabella—she saw the boy walk out into the street and made no move to stop him. True, she reacted with horror upon seeing the incident, but if her word to Fouché is to be believed, she grew tired of fighting against the inevitable. Now, in her defense, I never saw her so much as raise her voice to the boy, and I do believe her affection was genuine; but part of me believes her guilt at allowing, or at least not preventing, such a terrible injury weighed on her so deeply that her love and devotion to him was the penance for her horrific negligence."

Everyone at the table received this news with a look of shock. It was Lucille who finally broke the silence. "I knew the woman was a devil the first I laid eyes on her. A part of me wanted to warn you." She looked at Jean-Luc. "But I was not sure about you either—at first. Arriving from your meeting with Fouché with an air of self-importance, as if your business with the canal superseded every other matter. You seemed genuinely happy with her, and I did not think it my place to interfere in a personal matter."

André smirked at his friend. "You might have saved a lot of trouble if you had."

Jean-Luc shrugged, no stranger to these ruminations himself. "What's done is done. But to answer your question about Isabella's whereabouts, major, I can say only this—while I may no longer hold the professional affections of Napoleon, and never quite *had* the affections of Fouché, at the very least I maintain rather good relations with Monsieur Joseph Bonaparte. We correspond from time to time, and on rare occasions he'll admit me to the Tuileries for a conversation; not *everyone* in the administration is convinced my word is scandalous. Anyhow, he's informed me that the affairs of Naples no longer carry much interest for him, and that he's taken to learning Spanish. After considering this not-so-cryptic news, I petitioned him for a bit of personal assistance. Namely, seeking out a certain woman from Catalonia, known to be desirous of an estate in Minorca—this knowledge coming from Camillo, who showed me the books she purchased that describe the place. So, I have word that should Joseph find himself on the Iberian Peninsula in the near future, he might send agents to investigate."

Everyone exchanged smiles, Sophie looking more astonished than the others. "Well, St. Clair," she said, "you've come quite a long way since I visited in Paris; lost to the depths of despair, bottles and plates strewn about like some pirate ship."

Jean-Luc pursed his lips. "Yes, many things have changed. For all of us. And for the better at last."

As they cleared their plates, one of the farm boys entered, followed by a certain wine smuggler from Saint-Denis. Pierre-Yves Gagnon had accepted Jean-Luc's offer to return to Carcourt; ostensibly to see the improvements made to the house and grounds, but Jean-Luc surmised that the old smuggler's roguish instincts remained and he had come to snatch another look at Madame Sophie Valiere.

Gagnon bowed to the ladies present and handed André a note. After thanking Gagnon and the boy for delivering it, André cleared his throat and read it aloud:

Lieutenant-Colonel Valiere,

Some months ago, I told you the fortune of Hesse-Kassel was out of reach, and that you would be better served tending to your duty to your soldiers and your family. I am happy to learn that you have followed my advice. Now that the cares and toils of war have eased a little, I shall offer you one final bit of advice: Come tomorrow, wait until eventide, and then bring two or three able-bodied men to the inlet between Honfleur and Pennedepie. You will notice a skiff arriving. Do not worry about tricks; you will find no danger as long as the boatman finds none.

Once again, I offer my thanks for your sparing my life when the laws of warfare decreed mine was finished. I believe you made the right choice, however, and if you doubt it, then perhaps wait until tomorrow before drawing any conclusion. We would be honored to have you visit us here on our island, but we understand that to be difficult given the current circumstances; rest assured, we will do everything in our power to bring a swift and decisive end to it.

Profiter du cadeau, et au-revoir mon ami.
—Monsieur William Hackett

The following evening as the sun fell beyond the western shoreline, André halted his cart overlooking the inlet indicated in Hackett's letter. Beside him sat Jean-Luc, and trailing behind on horseback were Marcel and Gagnon.

Moreau had said little on the ride out, and André eyed him as they looked out over the gentle dunes and rolling waves, understanding that the sea held a terrible beauty in the man's memory. André felt that his former executive officer's struggles and triumphs had somehow become his own. This moment was a triumph, and André smiled at his friend, hoping he had found a measure of peace after a lifetime of scars.

"Well," Gagnon broke the silence, "will we have to get our boots wet, or will this English rascal come to us?"

André didn't respond, as he had his own questions as to what they might expect. He did not believe, after all their trouble, that Hackett would be luring them into a trap, but the wily Englishman did have a cunning side. Even as a prisoner apparently bound for the scaffold, Hackett had maintained a level of composure and ease that André still found incredible, as if he were a player with the advantage of knowing which cards the others had been dealt.

"Perhaps," André said, "he, or they, will come to us."

As they waited, André and Jean-Luc exchanged the news they had not discussed at breakfast; chiefly, what occupation Jean-Luc would take up now that he was no longer a senator, nor a penniless outlaw.

Jean-Luc looked down at the sleepy coastal village of Honfleur in the distance. "I could return to the profession of law, but, truth be told, that no longer holds much interest for me."

André nodded as he watched Marcel and Gagnon throw knives at a nearby tree. Gagnon was complaining that Marcel had cheated in his last throw.

"What holds your interest, then?" André asked.

"Since I was young, I thought that if I could attain some measure of influence then I might use it to help others, to serve others." He threw a pebble down the hill and watched it disappear out of view. "But once I'd achieved that power it threw me into confusion. I began to fear losing that influence I'd worked so hard to attain. I grew more concerned with power than the things that had inspired me to begin with. So, I think I will do what I should have done a long time ago. I will serve others and not myself. Lucille supports my plans to open an orphanage, possibly in the marquis's mansion. Or elsewhere, if it grows."

"That one there," André said quietly, nodding toward Moreau, "charged the enemies' cannons six times, refusing to retreat. He charged the guns after being wounded, as if begging for death to take him. I guess death didn't want him. He was taken by the enemy; wounded beyond saving, so they must have thought. They left him behind when they retreated back north. He wandered through the snow for almost a week until he regained our lines." André shook his head.

"I'm slightly frightened by him," Jean-Luc admitted, smiling at André. "But I can see the love you and your men have for him. He has earned the right to live a full life. When I return to my life in Paris, if I can find a way to raise the funds, I will also do what I can to open a house for wounded veterans. Provide them with some honest work; God knows we have enough of them."

"And more still to come," André said, patting his friend on the shoulder. "Despite the many ups and downs the years have thrown your way, you're still the stubborn, industrious, bothersome, do-good lawyer that I met in a Paris office many years ago."

"I'll take that over the 'hero of Naples.'"

An hour after darkness had fallen, a gentle rolling could be heard along the road. André had pulled his cart to the side of the road, and the four men sat up, watching for who or what might be approaching. A wagon pulled by a stocky draft horse rolled into view. The animal labored as it made its way up from the inlet, rolling to a halt when it reached their cart. The driver, an old man with a large beard and wearing a felt cap, asked, "Monsieur Valiere?"

"I am he." André climbed down from the wagon and approached the stranger. "With whom do I have the honor of speaking?"

The man removed his cap and dropped the reins. He lumbered his way off the wagon and bowed to the four men. "Messieurs, I am called Jacques. I am the caretaker of the lighthouse situated on the other side of those dunes you see. I also have a ferry to transfer folks across the Crique to Le Havre."

"It is nice to meet you, Jaqcues," André replied. "I am joined by my companions, all of whom share my curiosity as to what we've come out here to find."

The old man rubbed his bald pate. He took a pipe out of his coat pocket, lit it, and said, "I share your curiosity, then." He took several puffs. "All I know is, my employer delivered this wagon to me last night. He told me it came as a gift from one of his acquaintances; who that might be, I did not inquire. I was instructed to bring it to this place after nightfall, to be delivered to an André Valiere."

André looked at the wagon, circling it once to determine if there was anything special about it. Moreau and Gagnon opened the back flap and rummaged through the contents within.

"Well, major," Gagnon called out, his head popping through the canvas, "there's three large wine barrels in here. Enough to get us all blinkered."

"This was a gift from him?" Jean-Luc asked. "The English gentleman?"

André nodded, eyeing the driver carefully. But the old man just quietly smoked his pipe as they took turns examining it. At last André exhaled, motioning for Moreau and Gagnon to climb down.

"Well, monsieur, I thank you for taking the trouble to deposit this gift with us." He handed the man several bills and shook his hand, still searching for any indication that he knew more than he let on. Satisfied that the man was simply performing his duties, André shook his hand and sent him on his way.

"It seems strange," Jean-Luc said, echoing André's thoughts, "to go through all that trouble just to bring you a gift of wine."

Moreau, who had lit a pipe of his own, walked over. "Hackett was always an odd bird. He likely still feels grateful for not losing his head."

André nodded. "I hope he's still grateful. We let him return to his countrymen while we returned to war. They probably located the horde of riches days after we parted ways."

Jean-Luc shook his head. "Better he than Carnassier."

Inside the wagon, Gagnon tapped at one of the floorboards beneath the barrels. "Holy mother of Christ in heaven," he shouted.

André exchanged a look with Jean-Luc. A moment later Gagnon's face reappeared through the flap.

"Eh, Monsieur Valiere, Monsieur St. Clair, you're going to want to take a look at this."

"What is it?" Jean-Luc asked.

"St. Clair," Gagnon sounded almost frantic, "just shut up and come look."

With a collective shrug André, Jean-Luc, and Marcel assented, climbing into the carriage one by one. When they were all clustered under the canvas, Gagnon looked at each one as if he'd seen a ghost. "Well, what is it?" Moreau demanded. "What has gone wrong now?"

Gagnon had shoved one of the barrels into a corner, so a plank of wood lay visible. As if he were staring at a feast, he looked at the plank. "Gentlemen," he began, "do you know what that is?"

"It looks like a piece of wood," Moreau offered.

Gagnon looked up, eyes wide. "Monsieur St. Clair, you're aware of my alternative occupations, are you not?"

"Apart from gaming houses, brothels, street thuggery, and smuggling? I hope I haven't missed any."

Gagnon waved his hand. "The last one—"

"What are you getting at monsieur?" André demanded.

Gagnon's features loosened, and he leaned back slowly with a self-satisfied air. "You, gentlemen, are sitting on the contents of something you can hardly fathom. But," he reached down and, after tapping the wooden plank several times at each corner, he said, "have a look at your *gift*, Monsieur Valiere."

He grabbed the plank and tugged ever so slightly—it slid off with hardly any resistance. Beneath it was a small trunk—filled to the brim. The three men watching him let out a collective gasp, and for nearly a minute they stared in complete silence.

With that they turned back in the direction of André's home, leading the cart and its unexpected contents along the quiet country road.

AUTHOR'S NOTE

This is a fictional story set in the midst of a tumultuous and epic period of world history, the War of the Fourth Coalition (1806–1807). I sought to portray historical persons, places, and events as accurately as possible. The full effects this broader conflict, known as the Napoleonic Wars, had on the people of Europe was profound, and it would not conclude until Napoleon's final downfall in 1815.

One of the many significant legacies of this era involves the illustrious Rothschild fortune. The underlying circumstances of this family and the beginning of its fortune described in the book are real, in that Prince Regent Wilhelm of Hesse-Cassel did entrust Mayer Amschel Rothschild with state finances and tax collection duties, as well as facilitating payments for the deployment of Hessian mercenaries to America during our revolution. The particulars of this fortune's fate during Napoleon's conquests are where the history begins to blend into myth.

Mayer Amschel was responsible for moving Prince Wilhelm's fortune to safety in England. While in London, his son Nathan facilitated considerable loans from Wilhelm's wealth, which he had access to through his father back in Frankfurt, to King George III for use against Revolutionary France and, later, Napoleon's France. The majority of this fortune reached London; however, it was likely in the forms of bills of exchange and promissory notes, etc. So, although Prince Wilhelm likely smuggled a good amount of valuable goods and personal effects from his kingdom during Napoleon's invasion, there is no proof that his vast fortune was ever secreted away in wine casks from Frankfurt to the North Sea. However, Mayer Rothschild would go on to smuggle goods past Napoleon's blockades on behalf of Prince Wilhelm, so you were more likely to find a hidden fortune being snuck *into* Prussia rather than trying to escape it.

Another element of the plot inspired by actual history is the presence of the "outlanders" on Andre and Sophie's fictional estate of Carcourt. In the book, these refugees and combatant "choauns" come from Brittany and the Vendée, which was the location of a brutal civil war that pitted royalists supporting King Louis XVI and who opposed mass conscription, against the republicans, who supported the revolutionary government. It continued intermittently from 1793 until Napoleon's second abdication. Marcel Moreau tells Andre of Generals watching over his marching "infernal columns" after committing atrocities against men, women, and children. This is based in truth. The "drowning of Nantes" saw the mass executions of the families of Vendéean rebels, and some histories speak of over four hundred thousand dead in this region as a result. The outlanders are based on the refugees who fled this terrible conflict.

In some cases, I've referred to certain locations found in modern-day Poland, Posen, or Tatras Mountains, for example, as part of Poland. Technically, the country did not exist in 1806, as it would still have been under Prussian rule. In 1807, the region that largely comprises modern-day Poland would come to be known as the Duchy of Warsaw, the official name of the Polish state, which lasted only a short time until Napoleon's first defeat in 1814. The people living in this region spoke Polish and fought tenaciously alongside Napoleon's troops for the creation of a Polish state. To avoid confusion, I refer to the country simply as Poland.

Alicja Jarzyna was loosely inspired by Maria Walewska, the Polish noblewoman who presented herself before Napoleon and became his mistress while he campaigned in Poland and Prussia. Whatever charms she brought to bear must have worked, as the Duchy of Warsaw was formed several months later as part of the Treaty of Tilsit signed between Napoleon and Tsar Alexander I of Russia.

The battle that Andre comes upon in chapter 49 is based on the Battle of Mohrungen, between the Russians and a French corps commanded by Marshal Bernadotte in January of 1807. This battle saw large groups of Russian cavalry pitted against French cavalry, among whom were hussars and dragoons.

Finally, eighteenth-century Naples was inhabited by the group called the Lazzaroni. In all likelihood, they spoke Neopolitan at the time, not Italian. I took this liberty for simplicity's sake and to avoid confusion. The Lazzaroni were not a specific group or faction, but rather, a collection of manual laborers, servants, and street toughs who professed a strong Catholic faith and fierce loyalty to King Ferdinand I. The Lazzaroni did not fight particularly well against the organized troops of Napoleon's armies, but they were fierce defenders of their city. If an overconfident imperial French senator ever found himself captured by them, he could have expected the same violent treatment, if not worse, than what Jean-Luc St. Clair experienced.

ACKNOWLEDGMENTS

I have to express my sincere thanks to the many people who supported this book, whether directly or indirectly. Family, friends and former colleagues who expressed curiosity in the story, offered advice or anyone who gave a supporting word—you all contributed more than you know.

To my exceptional literary agent Lacy Lynch, thank you for your tireless work on behalf of this book, as well as your patience and support throughout. At times it was a winding road, but I'm proud of the finished product. To the entire team at Dupree Miller & Associates, especially Dabney Rice, Austin Miller and Ali Kominsky, thank you for the many hours of work on behalf of this book.

My editor Jacob Hoye, even though this was the first project we'd ever worked on together (hopefully not last), we developed a quick rapport and it always felt like we shared the same vision. Thanks for being a helpful sounding board and always offering informed advice.

Allison McCabe, your notes and advice were very helpful in getting the manuscript ready to be put it in front of publishers. I appreciate your direct and insightful advice.

Allison Pataki, without your belief and willingness to co-author, this story and these characters would never have been brought to life. I owe this all to you for taking a chance on *Where the Light Falls*. Hopefully, you enjoy the latest installment in this story.

Anthony Ziccardi and the team at Post Hill Press, thank you for keeping the faith at a time when the publishing world, as well as everything else, was thrown upside down during the pandemic. To Kate Monahan, Devon Brown, Jessica Vandergriff and the entire Permuted Press team, thank you.

Curtis Hays, thank you for your assistance with the website and your patience with my occasional delinquency.

Thank you to the folks at Dial Press and Penguin Random House for bringing *Where the Light Falls* to readers around the world.

Steven Pressfield, since I first read *Gates of Fire*, I've been inspired by your work. An endorsement from you means the world to me. Thank you.

Dr. Verena Drake from the Hotchkiss School, this story began while watching Danton in your course *Anatomy of Revolution*, spring of 2006. Thank you for the inspiration.

Jonathan Champagne, thanks for tolerating me splitting my time between Filmmaking and literary pursuits. Hopefully, someday the two can come together.

Charles Scowsill, we've both had Poland on the mind for a while now. Hope you enjoy this one.

Kerry Berg, I know I told you the name Lopacki would make it into this book. Unfortunately, I couldn't work it into the narrative, but now that I've just typed it, technically it made it in! I can't thank you enough for the support as I slogged through the writing. Your patience was occasionally pushed to the limit, but you never gave up on me. Appreciate you KB.

To Dad, Mom, Emily, Teddy, Alli, and the rest of the ever-growing Pataki family, your support and encouragement means everything. Thank you for putting up with my book writing process. I love you all.

There are many, many others I should be thanking but I can't list everyone by name. If you've ever listened to me wax poetic about the French Revolution or Napoleonic era over a pint, you know who you are. Thank you all.

ABOUT THE AUTHOR

Owen Pataki graduated from Cornell University in 2010 with a degree in history. In 2011, Owen joined the Army, and in 2014 was deployed to Afghanistan, serving with the 10th Mountain Division. Following his military service, he attended the Met Film School in London. His first novel, *Where the Light Falls*, was published in 2017. He now lives in New York, where he is working as a screenwriter and filmmaker.